HEAT OF THE MOMENT

Olga Bicos

ZEBRA BOOKS
KENSINGTON PUBLISHING CORP.

http://www.zebrabooks.com

ZEBRA BOOKS are published by

Kensington Publishing Corp.
850 Third Avenue
New York, NY 10022

All Kensington titles, imprints and distributed lines are available at special quantity discounts for bulk purchases for sales promotion, premiums, fund-raising, educational or institutional use.

Special book excerpts or customized printings can also be created to fit specific needs. For details, write or phone the office of the Kensington Special Sales Manager: Kensington Publishing Corp., 850 Third Avenue, New York, NY 10022. Attn. Special Sales Department. Phone: 1-800-221-2647.

Zebra and the Z logo Reg. U.S. Pat. & TM Off.

First Printing: July 2001
10 9 8 7 6 5 4 3 2 1

Printed in the United States of America

To my sun, moon, and stars:
Andrew, Leila, and Jonathan.

And to the ladies who always answered the phone:
Barbara Benedict, Jillian Hunter, and Stella
Cameron. Thank you, guys. I couldn't
have done it without you.

Finally, a special thank-you to the Big
Kahuna, RJR, and his lovely wife, Lynn.
Merci *for this one, too, guys!*

Crash Down

ONE

Alec Porter believed in second chances. That a man could reinvent himself, could make mistakes—maybe even big ones—and still wear the white hat. Hell, give Hollywood an hour and even the Grinch turns into Father Christmas.

Strapped into the Marchetti trainer—the plane hurtling like a bullet targeting Mother Earth—he was thinking a second chance would be sweet right now.

He cranked up the throttle, the control stick shaking wildly in his hands. "Don't screw the pooch, Porter. Not today." It had been ages since he'd faced death. Judging by his heart rate, he was out of practice.

Alec rammed the stick into his lap, trying to stop the ground from spinning. The Marchetti fought him every step, trapped in a corkscrew dive. *Right the wings, guy. Walk away from this one.* Strapped to the floor of the plane, the computer he'd rigged to mimic a jet's sophisticated control system shimmied in place. *No way I can reach the abort switch.* He'd been putting the new software through its paces, pushing the system he'd designed. Now red lit up the control board like the Fourth of July, a test pilot's nightmare, telling him he was dangerously close to kissing his ass good-bye. *Got to reach the abort switch.*

The siren blasted, *too late . . . too late!* Alec flicked the toggle switch, ignoring the light show. *Push comes to shove . . . I pull a rabbit out of the hat.* He'd done it before; he just needed to focus.

Oh, yeah, a second chance would be real fine. And he knew just how he'd use it. If he got lucky—if he made it down. He'd find Sydney . . . and he'd tell her the truth.

Sydney's face popped into his head in a flashbulb image. Alec shook it off, making a go at leveling the wings. *Keep focused.* On a maneuver like this, G-forces could cut off oxygen, making everything go screwy. *Cowboy this baby back to the ground, then worry about Syd.*

But she came back just the same, making the sky and earth disappear so that the little voice inside his head screaming *Careful!* went dead. Only Sydney remained, a sweet seductress, lining up his bad-boy sins for judgment.

He'd always thought Syd was different. The one he couldn't hurt.

I'm not the bad guy anymore, Syd. Trust me.

He smiled, remembering, seeing himself take that last fatal step as he coaxed her into the hot hotel room in Buenos Aires and eased her between the sheets. *Just a taste.* The next morning he woke to the soap opera of Sydney giving him shit, because they'd done the deed. She'd been pissed enough to walk out and never look back. Months later, it was Alec who dragged his ass halfway around the world to come here and find her. Start over. Convince her. *I'm not the bad guy anymore.* Looking for that second chance.

Now, with the blood rushing from his brain, he focused to find the sky and earth crushed together, the ground dangerously close. *Now or never . . . Cut power—hit opposite rudder.* But the view from the cockpit still looked like the inside of a kaleidoscope, making him wonder if he'd ever get his shot at making it right between them. Because at that moment, remembering Buenos Aires, Alec Porter realized he was doing that life-flashing-before-your-eyes thing . . . which pretty much clued him in.

He was cooked. He was toast.

Just before he blacked out, Alec jammed the stick back to his stomach. "Ouch," he said, "this ought to leave a mark."

Petroula Reck had always thought her mother a silly woman. By the time she was fifty-five, she'd had four plastic surgeries, one for each husband. She'd invested heavily in a psychic hot line . . . she believed in aliens. And she'd named her daughters Aphrodite, Carmela, and Petroula.

Carla Reck chose the names for their meaning: Aphrodite for beauty, Carmela for sweetness, and Petroula, meaning, "rock," for strength. All of which had been fine with Dad. Why not? There was no Russell Reck Jr. to follow in his revered footsteps. No need to intervene, to imagine what it would be like for his daughter to stammer "Petroula" from the front of the classroom as others tittered.

Petroula frowned, clutching the papers from legal as she navigated the hallowed halls of the Children's Art Center. *That was then—this is now. Daddy's a different man. Forgive and forget.*

Carla had wanted her girls to feel special. She'd thought the names would build character—and she was right. At least in Petroula's case.

Rocky, as she'd come to be called, liked to wear tight suits and short skirts. She had blond hair to her waist and legs that went on forever. A lot of people stared when she walked by . . . men and women. Which was basically the point. Attitude plus.

Plenty stared now as she ate up the corridor in her Prada heels, wondering what loser fetch job her stepmother would come up with next. Woof-woof. Not that Rocky had a choice. On Daddy's instructions, she'd come here to make nice-nice with Sydney, the stepmonster from hell. Which she totally didn't get.

The thing was, her father was in jail precisely through the Mata Hari tactics of his much-younger ex. On a night that could have done a Grisham novel proud, Sydney had turned her back on a wife's sacred trust, gathered up Daddy's private papers, and given the FBI a jingle. Her lies on the witness stand had twisted their lives into a surreal circus of bail hearings and search warrants, making it possible for Rocky to see her father only through a Plexiglas barrier, speaking into a phone.

"You're kidding, right? It's a joke? Dad, I can't work for Sydney's in-house counsel. She put you here. She practically slammed the door and threw away the key—"

"If something happens to me . . . if I don't get out of here, baby. Who's going to look out for you? Hmmm?"

"Me. I'm twenty-three—"

"Rocky, hon. You just started law school. If I can't beat these charges, it's gone. All of it. Every penny."

"Gone to her—"

"Which is precisely why she'll help you. Whatever mistakes Sydney may have made, she is not a bad woman. She always loved you girls. But your mother. Rocky, we both know . . ."

Aphrodite, Carmela, Petroula. A silly woman.

To please her father, Rocky had come to work at the art center established by her stepmother and her main squeeze, Jackson Bosse, a whiz kid known for big shoulders and an even bigger bank account. Right around the time Jack developed his search engine for the Internet, the name Yahoo! still brought to mind a chocolate drink. Only for Daddy would Rocky have agreed to help Sydney with building permits and zoning laws for her precious children's art gallery.

She always loved you girls, no matter what you think. Yeah, right. That's why Rocky was stuck playing Sydney's gofer. Why Sydney watched her, eagle-eyed and wary, waiting for Rocky to take one misstep.

Just ahead, a group of schoolkids stood, hanging on their guide's every word. Rocky smiled as she wiggled her fingers in greeting. *First-graders,* she guessed. Like Madison, Aphrodite's youngest.

The children circled a painting in earth tones depicting the conception of the twin gods from the *Popul Vuh,* the Quiché Mayan book of creation. The artist was one of Rocky's favorites, Carlos Terres, a well-known Mexican painter and sculptor. In muted swirls of color, Terres told the story of the mother goddess making her choice to defy her father . . . and its consequences: banishment.

Sometimes Rocky felt a little like the woman in the

painting, caught between the wishes of her father and her own heart.

Moving past the gallery to the main offices, she swerved to avoid the creepy guard at the front entrance even as he turned and waved. Rocky glanced away. *Weirdo.* She told herself to focus on the meeting ahead. She'd been working for the stepmonster all summer, and still she couldn't get her head around her new role as inspired protégée. Sydney only made things worse, acting as if she actually cared about Rocky. As if, after everything that had happened, they could be friends.

As far as Rocky was concerned, she didn't give a shit how Sydney treated her. The stepmonster had stolen Daddy from his family, then blithely set out to destroy him. Divorce wasn't enough for Sydney. She had to wipe all evidence of Russell Reck off the face of the earth. Now Rocky was supposed to shift all her anger into reverse and cozy up to the stepmonster? Play the supportive daughter to a woman not much older than herself? *No way . . .*

Unbelievably, there had been a silver lining to her father's arrest. For the first time, he'd finally noticed Rocky. Up until then it was almost as if he'd divorced her mother, his first wife, and never looked back. Her sisters, Aphrodite and Carmela, had gone on to marry rich, selfish men, following in Mother's size-six footsteps. But not Rocky. She hadn't fallen for the woman-of-society thing. Last year she'd entered law school . . . at first with this crazy idea that maybe she could help Dad. Now, starting her second year in the fall, she and Daddy had become really close. Rocky figured she owed Sydney for that at least.

Which was why she shouldn't freak standing outside

Sydney's door as the guy fielding calls at reception checked her out. She caught his fresh smile in her direction and gave a tight grin. *Like that's ever happening,* she thought. He was another one of her stepmother's artist wanna-bes. Sydney, little Miss Save-the-world-through-art. From what Rocky could see, the kid might have started shaving last year.

Hearing "come in," she slipped inside, crushing her resentment when she saw her stepmother's sunny smile. Sydney looked her usual alert self. No sleepless nights for her. With Dad in the clink, life had become easy-breezy for the stepmonster. A redhead, Sydney looked super in a pantsuit a soft watercolor blue, the season's calming hue. Elegant but understated. Sydney, the Cover Girl commercial.

She was having a meeting with her partner, Jackson Bosse, the follow-up act after her divorce. He'd come up behind Sydney, all solicitous, dressed in Hugo Boss and Gen-X eyeglasses with funky yellow-tinted lenses. His blond hair slicked back, he flashed what had to be a laser-enhanced smile.

Maybe he's gay, Rocky thought, feeling a little mean. She could imagine them in bed. *Do you want to be on top, honey? Would you like me to squeeze your breasts? Right or left, sweetie?* Always asking permission, like at the office.

Or maybe they weren't even sleeping together? *Waiting for the big day.* She smiled, getting a kick out of the thought. That would be just like Snow White and her Prince Charming. Keeping it 100% pure like some fairy tale.

At the moment, both ignored Rocky as they pored over a set of blueprints spread out on the desk. Typical. And annoying.

Rocky dropped the pages she carried, covering the blueprints. "Legal needs these, stat," she said.

Sydney didn't even look up. She tidied the pages and leaned forward, saying only, "Thanks."

Worse yet, she sounded as if she meant it.

Rocky crossed her arms, giving a slant to her mouth and hips that said this was a trivial misuse of her time. Of course, the stepmonster didn't catch on. Instead, she flipped through the pages, reading at the speed of light.

"Legal is always in a hurry." Sydney signed the bottom of each page before moving to the next.

"Yeah. Everyone's in a hurry these days. Maybe we should all buy stock in ulcer medication."

Rocky hated when she got chatty with her stepmother. Like she needed to talk it up with Sydney? She hated even more how lame she'd sounded. As if law school hadn't taught her to be careful with words. She glanced at Jack, the six-foot-three wonder, so slick, he could grace the pages of *GQ*.

Catching her eye, he grinned.

Rocky looked away. *This job sucks.* Here she was, ready to enter her second year at the prestigious Berkeley School of Law, and she was spending her summer attending to Queen Sydney and her gentleman-in-waiting.

On the desk, the phone rang, the sound a little startling in the quiet of the office. Both Rocky and Jack looked up, watching Sydney, waiting for her to pick up.

But the stepmonster didn't make a move. She sat, staring at the phone, letting the silence stretch into what had to be a senior moment. Only the phone's whining broke the quiet. Seeing Sydney's frozen expression, Jack frowned.

She looks scared, Rocky thought. Which was just plain weird . . .

Acting on instinct, Rocky grabbed the receiver. Because the stepmonster wasn't her boss in any real sense, she answered, "Sydney's Psycho Pizza. Today's special is a delicious combination of anchovies and marshmallows. Two for one."

The voice on the other end made Rocky smile despite the disapproval coming in loud and clear from Jackson's baby blues.

"Sydney Reck? Why, certainly. She's sitting right here." She kept her eyes squarely on her stepmother, avoiding the heat of censure pumping from Jack. Holding out the phone, she said, "It's for you, Mrs. Reck."

Her stepmother came out of her stupor, taking the phone. Rocky only deepened her smile. These days, nobody called Sydney by the name Reck. The fact was, Sydney had changed her name back to Shanks the day she filed for divorce.

Sydney snapped off her clip-on earring and spoke into the receiver. "Sydney here."

Rocky couldn't understand the words coming through the phone, but she witnessed their effect. Sydney sat forward as if an electric current had just shot through her.

"Of course," she answered, opening the bottom desk drawer. She pulled out her Kate Spade clutch. With the phone cradled between her shoulder and chin, she pawed through the jumble inside and dug out her car keys. Rocky watched as the keys slipped through Sydney's fingers, falling with a jingle to the carpet. Rocky could see Sydney's hands shaking as she reached for the keys, picking them up.

"I understand. I'll be there in fifteen minutes."

Sydney was halfway out of her seat by the time she hung up. "It's Alec," she said, not looking at anyone in particular. "There's been an accident. He's at Hoag Hospital."

In a nanosecond, she was out the door. Back at her desk, Jack waited, choking on her dust.

The guy didn't even move. He looked all frozen up, staring at the door through his yellow-tinted glasses. The look on his face . . . man, oh, man. Rocky hated it, to see that much pain.

She pressed her lips against the jibe that came all too naturally—*Get a clue, guy. It's not you she wants.*

"Gee. That was weird," she said, her tone all innocent. "I hope everything's okay."

Jack turned, realizing he must look like an idiot standing there as his fiancée ran to another man's bedside. He shuffled through the papers on the desk, making busy.

"I'll take these back to legal." His words came out all tight. "Why don't you go on and get some lunch."

"You bet," she said, Miss Johnny-on-the-spot. She walked out beside him.

Only, stepping into the hallway, she rubbed up against him accidentally. She watched as he jumped a foot back, acting as if she'd burned him.

Oh, yeah. Gay. So gay.

"See ya." She wiggled her fingers as he walked away.

Dad said to be there for Sydney. To make amends. He was sorry for what had happened between them— he'd ignored Sydney to the point that she'd believed those horrible things about him . . . that he was a murderer and a fraud.

But Rocky saw another side to the woman. One that had just smacked Jack Bosse in the face.

Sydney never showed any kind of emotion unless it was for her precious museum kids. And Alec. Alec Porter, who had broken her heart.

"I feel your pain," she told Jack's retreating back.

Humming to herself, Rocky Reck walked down the hall. She figured it was a true thing what people said. Misery did love company.

TWO

Sydney Shanks learned a long time ago never to let down her guard. Life lesson number one: Just when you think you have your ducks in a row, the puzzle pieces ready to complete the picture—get married, settle down to the family you've dreamed about—Alec Porter crashes back into your life.

Kablooee. The pieces scatter. The picture doesn't make sense. And she'd be rushing, petal to the metal, to a hospital, hoping there's just enough left of him to give Alec a piece of her mind.

The voice on the phone had asked for Sydney Reck, which clued her in from the get-go. There was only one person who wouldn't let her forget the past. One man who could make her heart race like this . . . for whom it was always about life and death.

She had told the nurse on the phone she'd get to the hospital in fifteen minutes. She made it in ten.

His face stood out against the pillow, shockingly white. He'd lost weight, which somehow only added angles to his already striking contours. He could have been an actor, he was that good-looking . . . maybe he had been. Alec had always been sketchy about the past.

At a guess, he'd been working too hard. Funny, how she hadn't noticed before, this new worn look. She'd been too busy with the museum . . . and Jack. Making certain she thought as little as possible about Alec. She'd needed to keep her eyes on those puzzle pieces—financing the museum on a shoestring budget, planning her future with a man who loved her enough to raise a family together. She hadn't wanted to look too deeply into Alec's eyes and disappear there, forgetting life lesson number one.

Now watching him, he frightened her just a little. He didn't look like Alec at all. He appeared almost too vulnerable. The stitching across his forehead— the hollows beneath his cheeks. *He'll have a new scar.*

"Oh, Alec," she whispered.

Like no other man, Alec Porter could make her feel like a teenager. All hormones. A bad boy able to lure young girls still buying into the fairy tale of Prince Charming on a white horse. But Sydney knew you couldn't take the beast and make him a man. She'd been through all that before. With Russell.

Which, of course, did not stop her from dying just a little as she held her coffee cup in her hands, wired on caffeine and concern. A few times, he seemed to wake, opening his eyes before slipping back into his dreams. Five hours out of surgery, she heard him groan as he turned his head on his pillow to face her.

"Hey." She leaned in close, careful not to nudge

the IV in the back of his hand when she reached to touch him. "How do you feel?"

He closed his eyes, looking incredibly pale. David in marble. "Like someone put me through a meat grinder, then tried to pat me back together for a Happy Meal." He smiled, his slow, sexy grin only mildly changed by a split lip. A dull light in his eyes, he asked, "Did you have your way with me, Syd?"

"At least five times."

"Shit." He let his head roll back, staring at the ceiling. "I knew I was dreaming, 'cause I counted seven."

"Maybe I lost count."

"Now I know you're lying. No way you'd forget." He raised his hand to his head, massaging his temples with thumb and forefinger. "So what's the damage?"

"A few cracked ribs. A broken collarbone. Roger said you did a heck of a job controlling the crash. Oh, and they took a piece of the control panel out of your shoulder. Minor surgery, I'm told. You'll have a nifty scar—"

"I meant to the plane. What's the damage to the Marchetti?"

The last six months, Alec, a test pilot and computer whiz, had been developing a new software program for commercial aviation. Something that would revolutionize air travel and put him square into the black on "the great balance sheet called life." His words. He had spent every last penny on that plane. Now the Marchetti was so much scrap metal.

Roger, who helped out during test flights, had dragged an unconscious Alec from the smoldering wreck. He'd managed to get him to safety just before the fuel tank ignited into a Schwarzenegger wall of flames. Roger had filled Sydney in before he left the hospital. Alec had lost everything.

"You walked away from this one, Alec. That has to be good enough."

Alec cursed under his breath. "Some guys have all the luck."

Which, in Alec's case, had never been good.

"On the bright side," she said, knowing his disappointment, trying to dissipate his frustration. "At least you didn't pull a Gloria Estefan—"

"Leave me alone, Syd. Let me wallow."

"She can probably set off the metal detector at the airport with the titanium in her back, and she only crashed in a bus."

"Badum bum. You slay me, Syd. Really, I'd laugh if it didn't hurt to fucking breathe."

"An interesting way to split an infinitive. A favorite of yours, as I recall . . . ah. And finally," she said, "a smile. Hey. It's going to be okay."

"Oh, it's going to be all kinds of okay. After my creditors clean me out, I can ask for a job maybe washing down some of the hangars at night for Roger. He's a peach. Shit, I'll have enough to replace the million I doled out for the Marchetti and equipment in, say . . . never?"

But he was smiling as he said it. Leave it to Alec to shrug off even this mess.

"What?" she asked, intrigued by his bright new look.

"I had you worried," he said, all boyish and charming. "You raced down here." On her wrist, his finger traced interesting circles, the kind that hadn't come her way since she'd left him a year ago. "Not much sleep either. Oh, yeah. I had you good."

"And all it took was a little surgery."

"If I'd only known."

She hadn't noticed how tight she was holding his hand, the one carefully locked in place with pillows to protect the injuries to his shoulder and collarbone. Maybe it was the shock of seeing him alive . . . or just his seductive old self cranked to full wattage. He made her wary, enough that she took a step back.

Alec sighed, getting the message. "Does Braindead know you're here?"

"If you're referring to Jack. Yes, of course."

"That's right, the old ball-and-chain-to-be knows all." Again the grin. "I bet he's all kinds of worried."

"What? That I'll hop into the hospital bed, shove aside your bedpan, and have my way with you? Don't compliment yourself, Alec. You look like hell."

"Not even a sympathy lay?" And when she shot him a look, he added, "Whoa. Did you lose your sense of humor along with your good taste when you hooked up with Jerkface?"

"And to think I once believed you were funny. His name is Jack. You remember. The man I'm going to marry?"

"Still going through with that?" The mood in the room became charged by his smile. "I mean, it could be a big mistake, you know?" This time Alec reached for her hand. He locked his fingers around hers. "You may have a few options you might not have considered."

Alec had a face that could tell you things if he let himself. Just then he was coming in loud and clear despite the light tone. *Don't leave me, Syd. Not now. Not when I'm down.*

But that was Alec. One minute you think you're safe. Then whammo. You let your guard down.

She snatched her hand back, jumping to her feet. "No, no, no, no." She inched away as if she could put distance between herself and the trap he'd set. She came up against the console behind her and held up her hands as if warding him off. "I am not going to let you screw this up. Remember me? Once married to a megalomaniac now awaiting trial for murder? I have learned my lesson, Alec, and I have worked very hard for normal. I deserve normal."

"Maybe I'm just asking for a little time. I mean, if you really love the guy—if it's right—what's the rush?"

She shook her head. "We've danced this dance before. I am not the one who said no."

"Syd, when I was up there, about to become one with the landscape, I had this ... vision. My whole fucking life flashed before my eyes, and I got hooked up on Buenos Aires. How good it felt to be with you."

For a moment, she couldn't catch her breath. *That he could still do this to her.* "I have a shockingly different recollection," she said.

She remembered drinking too much tequila, and Alec, who never drank, stone-cold sober. The foggy recollection that followed involved a confession of her undying love while falling into his arms for a night of unbelievable sex ... only to wake up and find Alec dressed and out of bed, strangely quiet. Even fighting a hangover, she'd clung to her fragile hopes of love everlasting and, embarrassingly, proposed marriage. Five minutes later she was on the phone, making an airline reservation for one.

"Give it a chance," he coaxed. "Give *me* a chance."

"Okay," she said, sitting down, her arms crossed tightly over her chest. *Take a breath, girl. Get control.* "Let's play pretend. You like that game, don't you? Let's pretend that you do love me. Madly. Deeply. You have faced death and seen the light and hallelujah, it's me you want. So, let's set the date, shall we? Because that's what I'm signing on for, Alec. The whole enchilada. Marriage, children. My biological clock says it's now or never, and lucky me, I found the man of my dreams. What do you think? Hmmm? How's December? Lots of greenery, the bridesmaids wear red, and, as I'm talking here, I figure the only reason you're not turning white with fear is that you're a quart low from surgery."

"You want wedding bells, Syd? Because that worked out so well for you before?"

She smiled, knowing all along they would end up here. "And at last I have my answer."

"Jesus, I hope not." He sighed, allowing his head to fall back on the pillow. "Why is it always like this with us? Weapons drawn."

"Because we have history, Alec. The kind you don't forget."

Nothing could wipe away the roller-coaster ride they'd come through these last years. Alec had walked into her life, an enigma. And on many levels he remained just as mysterious. At times, he appeared equal parts superhero and villain, rescuing her from the monster she married—while making her wonder if he weren't just as good at playing the bad guy.

Only on one point had he been surprisingly clear. He wasn't sticking around for the long haul.

She told him, "I guess I'm not as good at pretend as you."

"Oh, yeah. Pretend." He grimaced, inching up the pile of pillows behind him. "I just asked you to leave the Jerk King for me because I have nothing better to do than to make an ass of myself. Okay. Forget it. I'm just a screwup and you don't want any part of it. I get it. English is my first language." He scrubbed his face with his hand and sucked in a breath. "Quick change of subject. Gifts. As in I brought you one. I told Roger to put it in the top drawer over there."

She thought about taking on that statement—*I'm just a screw-up*—really she did . . . but she stood and walked away instead, searching through the drawer, remembering how good he was at manipulating her.

Eighteen months ago she'd gone to South America in search of museum-quality artifacts, her way of jump-starting a career she'd let languish for too many years thanks to Russell's sleight of hand. She'd asked Alec along as her bodyguard, pronouncing herself immune to his charm. Her very words when she'd offered him the job: *It might be good for you, Alec. To be with a woman who doesn't find you the least attractive. It might build character.*

And there was Alec, tooling around South America at her side, searching for treasure like some beautiful Indiana Jones. Always so full of life. Chain lightning in your hands . . . until you woke up and realized your time was up. Game over.

I don't find you the least attractive, Alec. She'd even believed it when she said it.

Inside the drawer she found his gift wrapped in red silk. She unwound the silk so that a small piece of jade no bigger than a silver dollar slipped into her hand. She stared hard, a little stunned. "Alec," she whispered. "It's beautiful."

She held the stone up to the light with the practiced hand of a master jeweler. *Definitely Mayan,* she calculated. Possibly from the classic period.

The brilliant green of the jade had always been a color prized by the Mayan—the color of corn leaves, the plant of life. This particular piece had been carefully wrought to depict the hero twins from the *Popul Vuh,* the sacred book of the Maya. The carving showed their ascension into Xibalba, where they shone as the sun and the moon, the Four Hundred Boys, previously slain gods, the stars among them.

She turned the piece in her hand, entranced. This always happened when she made a new discovery. The questions came. Was this part of a larger piece? Possibly a necklace? And with her questions grew the desire to search further, to find out more.

She came to stand at his bedside, holding the piece up to the dim light overhead. "It's incredible, Alec. I do believe your best find ever."

"Mmm," he said, his tone noncommittal.

"Where did you get it?"

"Come on, Syd. You know the rules."

It was a game they played. He would bring her back these pieces and it was up to her to authenticate each. To find out how Alec had gotten his hands on a particular treasure . . . and whether or not it was his to keep. Legalities were never his strong point.

"It's a present, not a bomb," he told her, seeing her face.

Sydney wrapped the slim stone in its cloth and tucked it inside her purse. "I'll get back to you, as always."

He grabbed her arm, not letting her walk past. "What is it? What just happened here?"

She didn't know what to say. Her feelings for him seemed too complicated. It would be such an easy thing to believe that Alec *could* change—only he kept reminding her how simply he could walk in and out of her life.

Behind her, she heard the door open. Sydney turned, thankful for the interruption.

But the man standing at the door brought on a full cartoon double take. She knew she was tired. She hadn't slept all night. Still, that didn't explain the sight before her. Nor did blinking make him go away.

He wore his hair a bit long, just brushing his shoulders. Black, with just a hint of gray starting at the temples. She clocked him in around forty, with familiar intense brown eyes and handsome face.

In every way, he looked like an older version of the man in the hospital bed. Slimmer, perhaps. He hadn't earned the build of someone who'd spent fifteen years in the military. And there was a softness to his face. The man in the doorway wouldn't need to live his life looking over his shoulder.

"I'm sorry. I . . . I could come back later." He threw a thumb back, hesitating. "I didn't check in at the nurses' station." He laughed, and it sounded exactly like Alec. "I was afraid they'd throw me out."

Gaining confidence, he stepped into the room, smiling. Alec was a different story. All suspicion.

Sydney stepped aside as the stranger passed her. He came to a stop at Alec's bedside, holding out his hand, which Alec ignored, being typically rude.

"Who the hell are you?" he asked.

"My name is Travis. Travis Bentley." He glanced around the room, found a chair. He looked like he might need it as he sat down. She could see his hands were shaking.

"You don't know me, but I thought—actually, I was hoping that might change. Look, this was going to be different. It's just that—when I found out about the accident, I got here as fast as I could. I wasn't thinking. And, well. I'm here now . . . okay, I'm babbling." Catching her look, he ran his fingers through his hair to steady them . . . a gesture she'd seen Alec execute a hundred times. "I just had to come."

The similarities. His face, his laugh . . . the eyes that didn't have a right to be anywhere but on Alec's face.

Sydney knew Alec was adopted. His life read a bit like a Dickens novel. He'd grown up in foster homes, eventually landing in a state-run facility, a last resort for the unwanted. She'd come to believe his early childhood trauma was the reason home and hearth could ignite a raging case of the runaways in Alec. She knew his father had been abusive. Any real sense of family had come later in life, from his adoptive brother and sister. And now they, too, were estranged.

She stared dumbstruck. *Oh, my Lord.* The scenario before her showed every sign of becoming combustible.

"I think we share a few things," Alec's lookalike told him. He leaned forward, resting his elbows on his knees, the gesture all Alec. "I know I look familiar, because"—again the laugh—"you sure look familiar to me. Like staring in a mirror, actually." His voice dropped. "Bentley. Tell me that name doesn't ring a bell?"

But Alec didn't answer. He watched with the same closed expression, not giving an inch.

"Daisey Bentley?" he asked. "Alec, I think—I know you've figured it out. Daisey Bentley was your mother. I shouldn't have raced down here like an idiot. I should have called. But I was afraid . . . afraid I was too late."

The man looked away, actually appearing to choke up. When he could speak again, he said simply, "Alec, I'm your brother."

THREE

If there was one thing Alec was sure of in this life—
he didn't have a brother.

He was adopted, yes. But not in the traditional
sense. Alec's adoption occurred when he was fourteen, his one lucky break, when a real hero had taken
him under wing and made Alec part of something
special, a family. *Good old Conor.* Only Alec spent the
next two decades making him regret it. Like Alec
couldn't accept anything good in his life. He had to
screw it up.*

But the early years, the ones before the foster homes
and state-run institutions, the years before Conor—
those he'd spent with Ed and Daisey, the good-time
folks who were his very messed-up parents. They eventually killed each other with drugs . . . but not before
they did a nice little number on Alec.

*See *Perfect Timing*, Zebra Books, August, 1998

"I don't have a fucking brother," he told the guy. But he was staring at his own face on another man. "Yeah. I know." The guy pulled his chair closer. "It's a shocker." He tugged out his wallet, one of those sporty numbers made of nylon and Velcro . . . went along nicely with the sport jacket Alec wouldn't get caught dead wearing.

The guy handed over a business card with all the pertinent information. Travis Bentley. Journalist extraordinaire.

Alec stared at the card, listening to the guy tell his story. How they had this grandmother, a Holy Roller who had raised Travis after driving Daisey from the house with her preaching. Grams never heard from her again, her lost child.

In deference to the grandmother who raised him, old Travis had waited until she croaked last year before hiring a private investigator to track down his real parents, one Daisey and Ed Porter. He was too late for Ed and Daisey, who had found nirvana at the end of a needle long ago. Ed, the easy way—a bad trip. Daisey took a little rougher road. AIDS.

The guy stood. "I know this is tough. And, honestly, I didn't mean to lose it with you just a minute ago. Not much sleep lately, I'm afraid." The way he smiled . . . it was weird. Like watching a movie of himself in bad wardrobe. "Why don't you give me a call when you're up to it?" Then, at the door, like he couldn't leave without getting in that last word, he said, "It's important. To both of us, I think."

Alec heard the door close. He frowned, staring at the card.

Just a minute ago he'd been confessing his undying love to Sydney, grabbing with both hands for that second chance. Now she was looking at him as if she felt sorry for him.

He crushed the card and tossed it at the garbage can. He'd used his good hand, but the pain of moving shot through his body; it made him sweat. The card rimmed the trash, then bounced inside. *Three points and the crowd roars.*

"Do you think that was such a good idea?" she asked.

"Best I've had all day."

"Doesn't it get tiring, Alec? Running away?"

"You tell me. Last time I checked, you took the exit, stage left." Then, because he knew what was building up inside him, he told her, "Get the hell out of here, Syd. You said it yourself. You don't like pretend."

Rather than argue, Sydney went to the trashcan and pulled out the little ball of a card. Walking back to his side, she pocketed the card.

"Just in case," she said.

She kissed him on the forehead. It had been a while since she'd touched him like that. Almost a year. That's when she'd gone off and found a brave new life. Without him as it turned out, in the arms of another man.

It felt good, that kiss . . . and it felt like shit.

From the door she told him, "I'll be back with some of your things."

She had a key to his apartment. He'd handed it to her like the key to his heart when he'd first popped into town. *Come back to me. . . .* There'd been a few nights when he'd stayed up, making believe he could hear her turning the key in the door. But she'd never used it.

He could see she planned to fuss over him. He'd told Syd a few of his sad secrets long ago, and knowing her, she'd try to make this right. But old Jughead Jack Bosse didn't need to worry. Not anymore.

He'd totaled the Marchetti. Some asshole just claimed he was his brother ... but this guy was a regular Joe, with a job. Probably a wife and kids. For him everything would be normal. He wasn't the great fuckup Alec Porter had become, a man who couldn't even have a relationship with a woman he loved—and not just for the obvious reasons, the ones Sydney leaned on so hard. Commitment. Family.

Alec still had his secrets. The big bad kind he prayed to God Sydney would never find out.

Alec pushed the button calling for the nurse. It took her a freaking age to answer.

"I need some meds," he barked into the intercom.

The nurse who eventually showed up explained how, checking the schedule on the white board, it wasn't time for another shot.

"I'm fucking dying here," he told her. "Call the doctor, get it okayed. Get me something, dammit."

Another hour later, he could feel he'd drenched the bed in sweat. He'd never wanted to puke so bad. When he finally managed to swallow down the pill she brought, he lay back, drifting off.

His last thoughts were about second chances. Someone had stolen his ... had stepped right into his hospital room and told him that he'd already lived it. *Sorry buddy. Move on.*

Because for Alec Porter, there were no second chances.

She would not feel sorry for Alec. She would not allow herself to be that naive.

Don't be an idiot, she told herself, jamming his key into the lock. The man was the Energizer bunny, for goodness sake. Look up *survivor* in the dictionary and you-know-who would be smiling right back at you.

A year ago he'd gotten it in his fool head to make her fall in love, and damn him if he hadn't had at her until he'd charmed her into it. The fact was, Sydney was putty in Alec's hands. If she needed more proof, she could replay the last five months. Just when she'd finally reached the count of three and snapped her fingers awake—trying to make a life for herself without him—who should show up on her doorstep to start all over again?

No, sir. She would not *hurt* for Alec Porter.

Maneuvering around his incredibly clean apartment, she tried not to notice the sad little counters devoid of the debris cluttering an ordinary life. Tried not to dwell on the fact that he'd never lived in one place long enough to earn decent clutter. Except for a few toys from McDonald's Happy Meals decorating the windowsill over the kitchen sink, the only thing Alec kept for company were books—volumes and volumes—mostly nonfiction . . . and his endless array of computer software and giga-gadgets.

She dropped her purse on the couch and brushed her bangs out of her face, trying to figure out where to start. *The bedroom. Maybe find something decent for him to wear at the hospital.* His room could double as a meat locker, it was so cold.

Ten minutes later she was still foraging through his closet. All she needed to do was focus on the task at hand, she told herself. Find a robe, take it to Alec at the hospital—

She stopped. "A robe?"

She started to laugh, loud and clear. "A robe." She tried to imagine in what parallel universe Alec Porter would own a robe.

Trying to keep it together, she squirreled past his coveted T-shirt collection, many with interesting messages like "Adjust Attitude" and "Pilots Love Their Joysticks." Jock pilot jibe. Grabbing a pair of drawstring pants, she searched on. Soon enough, socks and underwear landed next to the pants on the bed. In the third drawer down, she found the photographs.

Sydney slipped to the floor, sitting back against the bed as she examined his buried treasure. He'd hidden them under a pile of undershirts like a guilty indulgence. She could see by their well-worn look that he handled the photographs often.

She ran her finger along an edge. "Oh, Alec."

The first few photographs showed landscapes. A beach. A marketplace. Mountains covered in jungle green. Each was postcard perfect. She realized they must represent some foreign locale where Alec had memories. She frowned, because she'd never thought of him as the sentimental type.

She stopped when she came across a photograph of herself. She was wearing cutoffs, her red hair in braids, making her look ridiculously young. She remembered posing for Alec's Pentax in front of the Temple of the Sun at Palenque, a Mayan ruin in the

Yucatan made famous for its depiction of a "space traveler" engraved onto a stone sarcophagus. It had been a magical day, one of many they had spent together during their time searching for their pre-Columbian treasures.

That night they'd found a beautiful resort hidden deep in the jungle. With its individual cabanas and lagoon pool, it was a honeymooner's dream. Off season in the sweltering summer of the tropics, it had been theirs alone.

She'd been waiting in front of the sliding glass door of her room, watching Alec smoke outside on the porch across the way. He'd taken off his shirt and stood barefoot in his jeans. Adonis in moonlight. She'd been listening to the orchestra of insects and frogs, wanting so badly to step outside and join him . . . knowing she shouldn't. A week later in Buenos Aires, she hadn't hesitated.

Sydney flipped to the next photo, pushing the memory aside. Front and center in the photograph, a boy, maybe nine, beamed a smile as he balanced two babies marooned on his lap. Each face was a mess of cake and ice cream, the kids waving their spoons like weapons. On the back, in a woman's handwriting: *The twins' first birthday.*

Geena's kids, she thought. Alec's niece and two nephews.

She wondered if the photographs represented all that he had lost. If he had hidden the images away in this drawer, believing that the photographs were the closest he'd come to everything he'd once loved?

The final photo showed a much younger Alec standing with his arms around a girl and a man. All three wore pilot jumpsuits. *Geena and Conor*. His adoptive family.

Sydney knew Conor had been this big hero in Alec's life. A man he had tried to emulate . . . only to betray him. Horribly. In true Alec fashion, he'd been sketchy on the details, saying only that he deserved whatever Conor dished up. In the end, the punishment had been hard to take. Banishment from his clan.

She didn't doubt Alec had earned his exile. Oh, he could be all the things he'd claimed: troubleshooter, computer whiz—test pilot, and secret agent man. But there was also a dark side.

She shuffled the rest of the photographs, watching the images slip past like a flipbook. The fact was, Alec hadn't swept into her life a knight in shining armor, ready to whisk her away from a life of abuse at the hands of her murderous husband, Russell Reck. In typical Alec fashion, he'd sneaked inside by ruse.

She remembered the day perfectly. She'd been a mess, mourning the end of her mirage of a marriage. The doorbell had rung and despite mascara bleeding down her cheeks, she'd opened it, hoping to find one of Russell's cronies, wanting to embarrass him. Russell's perfect Trophy Wife in full rebellion. Instead, when she'd opened the door, she'd found Alec wearing a coverall uniform pinned with a photo ID, flashing forms in triplicate—a disguise. And all along, he'd had his own agenda.

I'm from your security company, Mrs. Reck. You called about a glitch in the new system?

A trick to get inside Russell's house.

Sydney frowned, gently replacing the photographs in the drawer. Those had been unhappy times. For both of them. Which was why she would always accept

Alec, warts and all. She'd made too many mistakes herself to judge him.

Alec's apartment had a balcony off the bedroom, and Sydney made her way there. She opened the sliding glass door, taking in the late morning view: vacationers sunning on the long stretch of sand, surfers in wetsuits bobbing on the waves. She smiled. Leave it to Alec to find this impossible and beautiful place.

She closed her eyes, feeling the sun on her face. Oh, yes, she believed in second chances. And no matter what Alec had done, in the end he'd helped her put Russell behind bars. For that she owed him her allegiance.

Inside, the phone ringing on the nightstand yanked her from her thoughts. Sydney turned, staring back inside through the glass door. For an instant, the clear blue sky overhead vanished. She forgot to breathe, remembering the phone call in her office and how she'd reacted then. Afraid. *Just like this morning, when the hospital called . . .*

Her attorney had phoned two nights ago. About Russell. *Sydney? I'm afraid I have bad news.*

She'd been waiting for him to call back ever since, jumping out of her skin every time the phone rang.

Sydney stepped back inside, telling herself no one but Alec knew she was here. Still, her pulse clocked into panic mode as she shut the sliding glass door. After a minute she heard the answering machine click on, then Alec's voice. "Pick up, Syd. I know you're there."

She closed her eyes, relieved.

"Syd?"

She hopped on the bed and picked up, speaking into the receiver. "Yes, Alec. I'm here."

"My incredible powers of deduction at work again. Did I ever tell you I have an extremely high IQ?"

"You might have mentioned it."

"I figured I should check to make sure you swing by Steve's Charbroiler, get me that pastrami that, FYI, is long overdue."

"Eight hours out of surgery and you're cleared for a pound of pastrami? Whatever happened to Jell-O and clear liquids?"

"Looks like they're holding off on that stuff on account of how I accidentally knocked it over on the guy trying to serve it to me. Twice. Hey, do you think Jell-O stains?"

"So I should come and risk your bad temper again?" she said, smiling to herself, reminding him of their scene at the hospital.

"And bring the pastrami. God, Sydney. Finally, someone for you to fuss over."

There was silence on the other line. Then a sigh. "Drifting off again, baby. Come back to me."

The way he said it, he could have meant so many things.

FOUR

Jackson Bosse knew how to get what he wanted in life. He had more than his fair share of smarts. He wasn't afraid of hard work—he knew how to focus. *Keep your eye on the ball.* A technique that so far had made him a winner.

His junior year at Stanford, he'd dropped out to make his first million, a goal he'd accomplished before he reached the legal drinking age, establishing Zzip.com, one of the first super engines to navigate the World Wide Web. From there it was an easy ride to have the resources and time to give back to the community.

He was used to working hard, making a plan, and sticking to it.

Only, these days he was more likely to find himself sitting at this damn desk, staring into space. Waiting.

He tossed his pen and reached for the phone, then spun his chair away to glare at the wall behind him. He wouldn't call her. Wouldn't check up on her.

"I won't give Porter the satisfaction." This, spoken out loud, like a pledge.

He had to get his mind off his stupid suspicions. Forget how, these days, Sydney seemed too distant. Women had their moods, right? And things had gotten complicated lately, with Russell making a play to get the charges against him dropped. After everything Sydney had gone through to put that murdering bastard behind bars, that alone had to mess with her head. Then, out of the blue, Porter shows up, back from his adventures in the great beyond, confusing everything. Sydney was probably going nuts.

Problem was, Sydney hadn't exactly leaned on Jack for help. She hadn't said much of anything these last weeks. Which was major. He and Sydney didn't share a bed, a decision that to this day left him on shaky ground. A meeting of the minds was pretty much all they had going. If Porter could screw with that . . .

"Do not go there, buddy," he said, shaking it off. He picked up the pages on his desk, focusing. He and Sydney had a meeting at the city planner's later. He wanted to give the papers a good looking-over in case Sydney didn't get the chance.

Flipping to the next page, he told himself to be patient. It didn't make sense not to trust Sydney. Hell, she'd told him the whole sordid tale about how Porter had gone from bodyguard to lover. So what if they'd gotten physical one drunken night? Porter blew it big time. And Sydney was a smart girl. She knew what she wanted—marriage and a family—neither of which she was getting from Porter.

He glanced back at the blueprints rolled up in a tube on the desk. Right there before him was the one reason Porter's flyboy tactics couldn't touch what he

and Sydney had together. Their Dream. The art center, their vision for the future.

The knot in his chest eased. *You can trust Sydney.*

Okay, so maybe lately he'd been getting the feeling
she had a bad case of cold feet. But hell, Sydney had
been married before. Twice. Both had been complete
disasters, which was why he'd agreed to take things
slow with the sex. Give her time. Of course, she'd
have second thoughts about another trip down the
aisle. But he'd taken care of her doubts before and
he'd get through them again.

The fact was, Sydney was made to have a family.
Why should she punish herself because of some bad
luck in the past? Life was a gamble . . . marriage in
particular. And when she hadn't believed in herself
enough to allow their happiness, Jack had changed
tactics. Why punish him? A man who loved her more
than life itself? He wanted those babies as much as
Sydney did.

Maybe even more . . .

Okay, so his proposal had come off more like an
ambush than an offer of marriage, dropping on one
knee in a crowded restaurant, holding out the robin's-
egg-blue Tiffany box and grinning from ear to ear
when the place burst into applause. Yeah, he'd seen
the fear in her eyes—he knew she was on the rebound
from Porter. But why should any of that matter if in
the end Jack could make her happy? *I won't let her
down.*

He could give her the family she longed for. He
could help her make her dream a reality: the art
center, a place where kids could see museum-quality
work—a painting by Picasso or a Mayan artifact—
then try their hand at something similar in the gallery

studios. Hell, the minute he'd seen Sydney Shanks, he'd known she was the woman for him.

He smiled, leaning back in his chair, remembering the across-a-crowded-room moment. *Like a fairy tale.* He'd been attending a fund-raiser downtown, thinking he'd call it an early night, maybe check in at work to see how that problem with the linkup to their online bookstore was coming along. Then Sydney stepped inside the gallery, eclipsing every thought.

She'd been wearing this dress. Little spaghetti straps. Red, like her hair. It had tiny stones sewn into the material so that it sparkled when she moved. She'd been a walking, breathing work of art. And she'd blown him away.

He'd asked for an introduction right then. The rest came easy. He made his plan. Followed through. Six months later they were engaged to be married.

Only, lately—since Porter had shown up—Jack had been thinking: Screw the Princess Di wedding. Push for Vegas.

Staring at the phone, he thought he just might pass it by Sydney. She was thirty-eight. It wasn't like she had a lot of time to play around. And he wasn't getting any younger. His dad had been in his twenties when he'd first become a father. Jack was 34, established. Kids would be nice.

But then there was Porter to think about. Jack had never run from a fight in his life. He didn't want Porter thinking he'd raced Sydney down the aisle because he was afraid.

Which is exactly why he'd be doing it.

He could just picture the flyboy laid up in the hospital, needy as hell. How that might affect Sydney.

"I wouldn't put it past the bastard to crash the plane on purpose." To get Sydney back.

And here was Jack, sitting in his chair. Waiting.

Oh, yeah. He trusted Sydney. . . .

"I just don't trust Porter."

He grabbed the phone and punched in Sydney's number. He'd try her at home first.

He was up to six rings with no answer when the door opened—no knock. It wasn't Sydney who stepped into the room.

"Wow. Didn't mean to disappoint," Rocky said.

Sydney's stepdaughter stood before him in all her glory. She wore her blond-bombshell hair swept off her neck in a butterfly clip, the carefree style making a man wonder if she looked that good in bed. Her clingy pantsuit had a python print to it. The color complemented her blue eyes, a sort of sea green. She was tall enough, but the heels she wore set off her slim ankles.

Jack hung up, as if she'd caught him at something. The kid could always do that to him. Unnerving as hell.

She came around and hitched her hip onto the corner of his desk. The shoes looked like stiletto slippers, making him wonder how the girl could manage without breaking her ankle. One shoe dangled from her foot.

She gave him a pout. "Is Sydney missing in action again?"

"And that would be your business because . . . ?"

"Oh, Jack. Was that supposed to hurt my feelings?"

He wondered why Sydney put up with the kid. How she could separate her feelings for the girl's father and be there for the little hell-raiser he'd spawned.

She'd actually been happy to give Rocky a job for the summer . . . while Jack hated it. Hated the whole idea of how the kid used Sydney. Talk about biting the hand that feeds you. Rocky Reck had a chip on her shoulder the size of his Ford Expedition. She treated everyone around her like shit, especially Sydney.

And the kid was sexy. And she knew it.

Attitude and sex appeal—what a frigging pain in the ass.

"So, what's up?" she asked. "Is Miss Do-good still at the bedside of the ailing? Or is that *in* the bed of the ailing?"

"Here." He tossed her the pages he'd been reading, ignoring the jibe. "You look like you need something to do. Why don't you see that Phil gets a look at these."

"Thanks." She slid down the desk like a cat stretching, leaning on her elbow so that her cleavage remained at convenient eye level. "Speaking of not too busy . . . you're hanging around a lot these days. Don't they miss you at Get-a-clue.com?" A wicked smile followed the jab. "Or does the place run itself now?"

"Something like that."

With her tiny pearl teeth, she nibbled off the gloss from her bottom lip. He wondered if she practiced that move in the mirror. *How to Turn on a Guy 101.*

She inched closer to give his tie a tug. "Nice." She let the tie slip through her fingers. "I thought only gay guys had this much style—"

He grabbed her hand. The slow grin he gave wasn't meant to be inviting. "Don't work it so hard, honey. Just some advice."

She presssed forward against his hand so that his fingers practically dipped into her cleavage.

"Gee, Jack ..." She glanced down at his pants, where you could see exactly how she affected him. She scrunched up her nose, giving a cute little smirk. "I didn't mean to make you ... uncomfortable."

She stood, taking her time, putting on a show. He watched her walk out, papers in hand. She was always doing that, using any excuse to touch him. Coming on to him. Like he was an idiot and couldn't figure out what she was up to. She wanted to hurt Sydney. Bad.

The thing was, there was also a sadness to the kid. Like she had something to prove. Well, when your father is the mogul fallen from on high, that was a legacy. And divorce was the sort of thing that really messed kids up. He and Sydney, they would never get divorced.

On the table, the phone piped up at long last. He nabbed it before the second ring.

"Sydney?"

He listened as she explained how she had to be with Alec today. Could Jack cover the meeting with the city planner? She couldn't go into the details, but something had come up. She would explain tonight.

"So he's going to be okay?" Like the bastard couldn't do him a favor and lose all functions from the waist down?

"I'm sorry to cancel on you, Jack. It's just that ... he really needs me right now."

Jack hung up, thinking that was typical. Florence Nightingale Sydney to the rescue. But Alec Porter didn't bring up any warm and fuzzy feeling for Jack.

Not with the sound of Sydney's voice saying it all. *Sorry . . . he needs me.*

Jack closed his eyes. He'd always known how to get what he wanted in life. *Keep your eye on the ball.* That's why he'd pushed so hard to talk Sydney into marriage—why he'd left his team running things at Zzip.com while he cooled his heels at the museum, waiting for Sydney to show. He thought he could love her enough for the both of them.

Only, if that was true, then why did that jet jockey feel like such a noose around his neck?

Sorry . . . he needs me.

Jack swept his arm across the desk, sending the tube with the blueprints to the floor. "I need you, Sydney. I need you."

The first time Rocky visited her father in jail, the whole thing had been a bust.

After waiting in line, filling out a form with Daddy's name and booking number, she'd been informed by the prison personnel in the booth that her sister, Carmela, had come just that morning. Her father was allowed one visit a day. Two visits a week. She was out of luck.

The second time, she'd come earlier. She'd stood in line outside, making certain she'd be first to see him. Sitting in the lobby on the cement bench, she'd waited for her turn to ride the elevator to the fifth floor. She found her father waiting in one of the booths lining the hall. An inch-thick piece of Plexiglas kept them apart.

He had one hand cuffed to the stool where he sat. The other held the phone he used to speak to her.

Looking at him in the prison garb, the pit in her stomach had grown into a full-sized tree. He'd spent the last year and a half awaiting trial, incarcerated courtesy of Sydney. At each hearing, her stepmother had taken the trouble to fly in from wherever on earth she happened to be. She had cried on the witness stand about every wrong done her. *Hold the applause, please, and hand her the Oscar.* Afterward, the judge always denied bail.

Waiting in line, Rocky tried to put aside her resentment, sick to death of the churning in her stomach. Compared to this, law school felt like Club Med. A place where she could get away. She couldn't wait for the semester to start.

She focused on the visit ahead. Like a pro, she filled out her form and stowed her purse in one of the lockers lining the wall. She flashed her driver's license to the guard in the booth, getting ready to wait on one of the cement benches for her father's name to be called.

She glanced at the clock. Almost eleven. *They'll call him soon.*

Alongside her waited the working-class poor. Here in Los Angeles, Spanish seemed the language of the prisons. Very few rich people ended up here. She thought about that sometimes, if she could somehow make a difference once she passed the bar. It didn't seem right that money should always tip the scales.

Not that it had helped her father. She closed her eyes. *Another day in the life of. . . .*

She'd come to think of these times as her challenge of faith. With the quiet surrounding her, the whispered stories from the benches sounded like segments of a soap opera.

He asked me to put the house up for bail, but I told him not this time . . . the judge gave him forty years . . . the lawyer said if he didn't take the deal they offered, he could get life. . . .

Sitting there, listening to their stories, she would find herself wondering about her father. The charges against him: defrauding the government out of a couple of billion . . . even murdering his partner. Fearing deep inside that he might be capable of that.

Which only pissed her off. That Sydney could make her doubt her own father. Henry Shanks had been Sydney's first husband—Daddy's best friend and partner. A man Sydney claimed Daddy had allowed to die in a plane sabotaged by his aerospace company. She'd made up some lame story about how she and Daddy had some stupid affair. But suddenly, her Catholic guilt kicks in and she's going to confess all and go back to hubby. So Daddy has Henry killed. For Sydney, the hottie. A woman Daddy would kill to keep.

As if he'd want Sydney that badly. The more Rocky thought about it, the more she realized her father's only problem had been bad taste in women.

Relationships were the pits. Love could strip you down to your worst. Just look at her mother and the super-stud parade, how ridiculous it had gotten over the years as Carla aged and her love interests hadn't. And Jack. Pathetically waiting for Sydney to break his heart.

The voice over the intercom brought her to her feet. She'd been so deep in thought that at first she didn't realize what was different.

They'd called her father's name over the intercom.

Just her father's. Not the dozen or so other prisoners who normally shared the half-hour visit.

People were watching her, the pattern of their stay there broken. Rocky made her way to the metal detector, ignoring the stares. The permit she'd filled out earlier waited on the counter, just like at every other visit. Only this time the guard stopped her when she reached his post.

He told her to wait. Just wait.

In the hush that followed, it was almost as if the room grew hotter. She couldn't quite catch her breath. Just ahead, a man came through the elevator door. At first, she didn't recognize him. He appeared smaller than she remembered, his hair now almost completely white. He walked up to the metal detector in front of her, stopping only to shake the guard's hand . . . while all the feeling left her legs as she watched him.

Her father came right up to her. He was wearing a charcoal-gray suit, looking older, thinner, and utterly handsome. He opened his arms to her.

"I wanted to surprise you, baby," he said. Seeing that she didn't move, his smile turned bittersweet. "I hope it's a nice surprise?"

Tears came to her eyes as she rushed to him. She could hear a few feeble attempts at clapping behind her. When he hugged her, she thought she would burst. She felt as if she'd waited a lifetime for this moment.

"Surprise, baby," he whispered, holding her. "I'm coming home."

FIVE

At approximately 11:05 A.M. on Saturday morning, Russell Reck walked out of the Los Angeles Twin Tower facility, a free man. Not a bright, shining moment in the life of Sydney, a woman he most likely wanted dead.

A bad start to a bad day. Alec arguing with her for the last twenty minutes only added to the fun. *Cha, cha, cha.*

After two days in the hospital, he was waiting for his discharge papers, looking more like his old self in jeans and a gray T-shirt. The form-fitting clothes showed that a little surgery couldn't bring a good man down. Not so his complexion. Despite the five o'clock shadow, his color brought to mind the Undead. The sling he wore testified to tough times ahead.

"So I tried to put myself in your shoes." He didn't bother to look hurt but sounded it. "Tried to do the whole I'm-as-understanding-as-any-chick." He shook his head. "I still don't get it. Why you didn't tell me Russell was getting out?"

Cha, cha, cha. "Alec, what is the point of this?"

"Actually, keeping me in the dark was kinda stupid. Like I wasn't going to find out?"

"Are you finished?"

"And you are not a stupid woman, Syd."

She took a minute, figuring it wasn't getting her anywhere to keep at this. She'd known all along he wouldn't take the news of Russell's release well.

Once upon a time, Alec had dedicated himself to putting Russell Reck, "The Wrecker," behind bars. It was all he'd lived for, initiating a tangled plan that dropped him on Sydney's doorstep. Alec recruited Sydney, opening her eyes to her husband's many crimes, gambling that, once she knew the truth, she would help him destroy The Wrecker.

She didn't doubt there'd been some secret payoff for Alec—though she'd never discovered what that might be. But the last year, the dynamics between her and Alec changed. Dramatically. And it was all that drama she had to deal with now.

"All right," she said, giving an inch. "A long time ago, in a place far away, I probably would have told you about Russell's release. It would have been the right thing to do. In those days, I paid you a rather large sum of money to watch my back. But you're not my bodyguard anymore. You hung up the badge some time ago."

"And it's all about that, right? The paycheck?"

Sydney rolled her eyes heavenward.

" 'Cause hell," he continued, into it now, "you know I never did give a hoot—"

"Tell me we are *not* going to do this."

"—because, if I did . . . if you trusted me . . . you might have considered giving me a jingle when you found out the guy was getting out. Might have thought I'd care."

He looked incredibly hurt. Which managed to appear completely out of place on Alec. A lot of things didn't seem like Alec today. The pale skin, the circles underneath his eyes. The beard stubble. The fact was, Alec looking vulnerable just didn't suit.

The unkind thought came: *Careful. He's a chameleon.*

She didn't know everything about his past, just the colorful fringes. Government black operations . . . master of disguise . . . super spy. Then there was the whole she-should-never-have-fallen-in-love-with-him part . . . and the fact that he could so easily manipulate her.

Watching her, his face transformed, reading her mind like the Alec of old. "Hey. Like I give a shit, you're thinking? What's in it for me—that's more the Alec you know and love. Well, Syd, you get a gold star. So let's take this from the point of view of employment."

He was fidgeting with his hands. Alec smoked, a nasty habit he'd been trying to quit. For Sydney, he'd said. He looked like he wanted a cigarette now. Bad. "I happen to be out of work. How about my signing on? Just like before, babe." He took a short bow. "Alec 007 at your service, again."

"You know what I think? I think you cracked your head instead of your collarbone."

"What? This?" He held up the arm in the sling and just managed to hold back the wince reflected in his eyes. "Don't you worry, little lady. I'll be using more than my hands. And I know how to run interference."

"This was exactly the kind of conversation I wanted to avoid."

"So I figured. But it's too late, so give in gracefully. Just say 'uncle' and write out the check, and I'm yours."

"Alec." She waited a beat, making certain she had his complete attention. "No."

"As in Alec, mind your own business?" The bitterness came through. "You're not a part of the picture anymore?" Again his hands seemed to search for something to do. He laughed, exasperated. "Amazing. Just fucking amazing. All this Sturm und Drang because we got horizontal one night and had"—he dropped his voice dramatically—"sex."

"Imagine." She kept her expression deadpan. "That it should make a difference."

Her anger only deepened his smile. "Exactly. Lucky for you"—he stood, coming to a stop before her, making her look up as he winked—"I'm more mature about the whole thing. I can put the past where it belongs."

"And that's why, two days ago, you asked me to turn my back on Jack and give you a second chance? Sell it somewhere else, Alec."

But before she could turn away, Alec grabbed her arm. "What's the matter, Sydney? Afraid I might cloud up the picture for you and Jughead?"

"You always complicate things."

He gave a naughty smile. "Complicate? Oooh, I like the sound of that." He *tched* softly. "Like I might get the motor running again. Maybe cut little old Jughead out?"

"His name is Jack."

"Whatever." He bent down, whispering, "You listen to me. Though I would love to have your hot little body back in my bed." He reached behind her and gave her buttocks a squeeze. "I'll settle for knowing you're still alive long enough for me to convince you that you don't belong with Limp Dick."

"You can call him any name you want. It won't change a thing."

The door behind her opened. Even before she turned, Sydney could feel the heat of the nurse's embarrassment. Sure enough, the woman was staring at Alec's hand plastered on Sydney's rear.

The nurse held up a clipboard. "Your discharge papers are ready."

Alec whispered sotto voce, "To be continued," as he stepped past.

Sydney stayed exactly where she was, her heart racing as she listened to the scrape of Alec's pen on the forms. She didn't bother to turn around when the door closed, leaving them alone again. She was still puzzled by the catch in her breath, the hitch in her pulse.

When Alec had shown up on her doorstep six months ago, the idea that they could be "just friends" seemed possible, even sane. Argentina had been a long time ago. A year. Hadn't she spent that time preparing a whole new life without Alec? And Jack wasn't exactly chopped liver. Why couldn't they, as Alec suggested, put the past behind them? Say "Sorry" and move on?

Because it's Alec, crashing back into my life . . .

Alec turned her around. "Gee, baby," he said, a

familiar smile to his voice, "I didn't know you still cared. Poor Jack."

"It's not about that." Surprisingly wonderful that her voice stayed so steady.

"Bullshit." Again that smile.

"Alec. Be honest," she said, determined to put a stop to this. "The only reason you want me is because I said no."

The silence between them held, saying it all. He'd had his chance . . . he hadn't wanted her then—he shouldn't want her now.

"Ouch," he said.

"Exactly."

He kept his gaze steady, refusing to turn away from her challenge. "Okay." But his voice sounded subdued. "No more messing around. No more Jughead jokes . . . no more come-ons. I can behave."

Alec had this thing with his eyes. With just a look, he could tell you how much he felt.

"We make this about keeping you safe," he said. "Just that. Okay?"

Again the expression on his face gave away too much. It made her tell a few truths of her own.

"I don't think that's possible."

He didn't like her answer. "Then we'll have to do it the hard way. I help. Whether you want me there or not."

"Nice try—"

He gave her a shake. "He wants you dead. You ruined everything. I set it up for just that . . . so you would turn him in. Remember? I came to you and told you what kind of monster you'd married. I fed you the questions to ask him—I taught you how to pry through his computer records and dig up all the information against him. I even gave you the freaking FBI's phone number to call. I thought we could put him in jail for good. But I messed that up, because his ass is out and after yours."

Alec stepped closer, reaching up with his good hand to give her arm a stroke. "He doesn't know who I am," he said, his voice suddenly cajoling. "I made sure I was below his radar. It's you he'll want dead. Just you. How do you think that makes me feel, Syd? That when you make the six o'clock news, it will be my fault?"

She shook her head. "No, Alec. I can't live with that kind of fear. That's when Russell wins. When he makes me live every day looking over my shoulder."

"Fear is good, Syd. It's a warning. Like pain."

"It's not living. It's not life." She locked her eyes on his. "I want my life back, Alec. After everything I've been through, I won't settle for less."

It sounded good, what she'd said. Strong. That she, Sydney Shanks, could take on a man who'd defrauded the government of billions for his aerospace company, then killed his partner, to boot. A good ending note, she thought as she turned and walked for the door. Because, just then, Alec and her feelings for him might be the greater danger.

Her hand on the knob, she asked, "Are you coming?"

He watched her for a minute, then shook his head. "Nah. You go on ahead, Supergirl. Us mortals, we'll take a cab."

She almost protested, wondering if this was some sort of childish punishment. *If I can't help you, you can't help me.* But then she knew it didn't really matter. Whatever his motive, he was right. Quid pro quo.

Walking down the corridor she reminded herself of her resolve. Russell wouldn't frighten her. She wouldn't allow it. And she didn't need anyone to protect her—didn't need to put a big red target on Alec's back.

And Jack. If Russell was free to do his worst, there was no judging who he might threaten next. She needed a plan. A way to get back control.

In the elevator, she punched the ground floor. From now on she had to make certain it was only her life on the line. Three years ago, she might not have been Russell's sole motivation for putting Henry on that plane to his death, but she'd certainly been the consolation prize.

Russell, the snake, had mourned his partner's death right alongside Sydney, feigning his innocence. He'd consoled her, Henry's widow, until, in a moment of weakness, a marriage between them seemed the next logical step. His confession the day she'd called the FBI was something she would never forget. A knife in her back . . .

I did it for you, Sydney . . . you would have lost interest in me, stayed with Henry out of a sense of obligation. What was I supposed to do? You would have cut me off. I panicked . . . .

Those words still haunted her.

Well, she would never again be that weak-willed trophy Russell had so effectively taken down his path to hell. Nor did she want Alec involved . . . or anyone else, for that matter. Better that she do this alone, she told herself, walking past the hospital's information desk. Wait for Russell to make his next move and respond in kind. *Pawn to Queen's four.*

Sydney pushed through the double doors of the

hospital into the blinding light of a California summer's day. Palm trees lined the street, the golden coast's special accent. The sun somehow made her feel better. On track. *Good old California.* She could sense the courage blossom inside her with the heat, firming her resolve. *Learn from your experiences and move on.* Her new motto in life.

She saw the car out of the corner of her eye. A gray sedan like so many others.

Only, this one swerved across the street, coming straight at her.

It seemed impossible. Surreal to see that car, so strangely close. As if she were its target.

Which she was. The car was gunning right for her.

The shriek of brakes ripped through the air. She could smell burning rubber as the fender careened up and over the curb.

Instinct took over. She turned. *Jump!* The fender veered past, the grip of the metal just missing her legs. She landed safe on the concrete, only bruised as she watched the car turn, then fishtail down the street.

She kept staring, wondering what was wrong with the picture. Until she realized: *The car . . . it didn't have plates.*

People milled around, a crowd swooping in, surrounding her. A teenager with a skateboard tucked under his arm. A woman with a shopping bag filled with groceries. Sydney had the insane thought that she should warn them off. Tell them not to bother. *You can see better on the six o'clock news.*

A man looked her over for cuts and bruises, making her bend joints with professional care, asking questions. A giggle bubbled up inside her until she locked her teeth against it . . . all the while thinking, *How convenient, to have an accident in front of a hospital.*

"Are you okay?" the man asked.

Sydney covered her mouth, shaking off the hysterical laughter, the adrenaline rush. She kept looking down the now-empty street. *No plates. The car had no plates.*

Russell. He was already after her.

Grayout

SIX

There had been a time when Sydney would have given anything to be with Russell . . . a time she actually had. A time she'd sincerely believed he was a good and loving man—that his virtues outweighed his flaws.

Sitting at the posh restaurant, Crustacean, surrounded by its fish tanks and Beverly-Hills-meets-the-East decor, she wondered at her naïveté those many years. Or perhaps Russell was just a master at hiding his true nature. Certainly, he'd fooled many.

As usual today he was late.

Freshly released from the men's lock-up, Russell must have made Sydney his top priority. Without a doubt, she'd been one of his first phone calls. The incident with the car outside the hospital still fresh in her mind, she'd taken his call, wary as she listened to his reasons why they should meet. Something mysterious that needed to be discussed in person.

Listening to Russell on the phone, Sydney had one thought—*best to meet the enemy head-on.*

Russell had suggested Crustacean. He found the fish tanks soothing. Sydney had picked the hour. This time of day, Crustacean buzzed with life. Alec wanted her to be afraid, but Sydney would settle for vigilant.

During their marriage, she'd never feared Russell. It would give her too much credit to suggest that she'd acted out of anything as legitimate as fear. Shortly after their wedding in Acapulco she'd discovered Russ was having an affair. She'd hired a private investigator. Later, she'd shown up at Russell's office with the photographs.

The woman was young. A brunette. Which surprised her. She'd always thought Russell preferred blondes.

Enter Alec, stage right. He'd shown up that very night, his timing as always, impeccable. Sydney had been celebrating her fall from grace, getting quietly drunk in the privacy of her own home, wondering how on earth she had arrived at this sad and lonely place. Mascara bleeding down her cheeks—Russell's house in disarray from the "remodel from hell"— she'd been holding a bottle of champagne, swaying on her feet as she'd opened the door to find a man in uniform.

I'm from your security company. You called about a glitch in your system?

He was young, a Generation-Xer with buzz-cut hair bleached a near white, and long sideburns. He had a boyish smile and freckles. The badge he wore said his name was James and he worked for Beechwood Security Systems. Alec, wearing one of his many disguises.

And, of course, being Alec, he'd come on to her.

She remembered thinking, *So this is how it happens. The bored, neglected wife . . . the sweet boy fixing the security system.*

Only, at the time, Sydney would never have broken her marriage vows. She hadn't wanted to stoop to Russell's level. *Tit for tat.*

How she hated that woman. The trophy wife who gave up her position as assistant curator at the Norton Simon to fall asleep over fabric samples and floor plans for Russell's monstrous new house. The victim who'd cheated on Henry. The third Mrs. Russell Reck.

Now, watching Russell make his way down the restaurant's most famous feature, a fish tank built into the floor like a path, Sydney knew that at long last she'd put the silly creature to rest. Watching Russell approach, she felt nothing more than utter loathing.

Foot-long koi swam beneath his Bruno Magli loafers as he walked on water toward her. He'd chosen his Armani jacket and a silk shirt, appearing casual but nice. But how he'd aged. Apparently, jail hadn't agreed with her ex-husband.

Reaching the table, he leaned over to kiss her. "Sydney. Thank you for agreeing to meet me—"

She pulled away. "Sit down, Russell. I don't have much time."

He took her tone in stride, but the smile he gave showed he thought he had the upper hand. He ordered a drink from the hovering waiter, then sent him on his way.

His brown eyes locked on her. "The last time I saw you, someone was holding a gun at my head." He snapped his fingers, remembering. "Why, I believe that was you, Sydney. Waiting for the FBI."

She took a drink of her wine. "You're mistaken, Russ. The last time you saw me, I was on the witness stand, giving a detailed account on why the judge should keep your sorry self in jail. Not that I succeeded, I'm sorry to say."

He smiled. "And didn't you look lovely as the injured wife. I didn't know you could cry like that, Sydney. It seemed so real."

"I practiced. A lot. I wanted to get it right."

He shook his head, laughing. "I shouldn't have started this. I'm here to apologize, not antagonize you."

"Too late." She began to slide out from the booth, planning to leave.

"Sydney, please. Hear me out. That much can't hurt."

She wondered if she really had a choice. *You'll have to face him eventually.* With a sigh, she slipped back into her seat.

Russell swept up her wineglass and placed his mouth where her lipstick stained the glass. He sipped a taste of the Hess chardonnay.

"Lovely." He put the glass down. "Sydney. You're right. I have gotten away with murder."

Amazingly, she didn't flinch.

"But I plan to atone," he continued. "What I did to Henry . . . I don't even know where to begin. You were right all along about Kinnard, that spook."

Joseph Kinnard, the former undersecretary of defense for research and acquisition, had been Russell's contact at the Department of Defense . . . and the man whose black operations had defrauded the government out of sacks full of money in misappropriated funds funneled to Reck Enterprises, Russell's aerospace firm. Russell always claimed he'd been nothing more than Kinnard's puppet. His only mistake: listening to Joseph whispering instructions in his ear.

"Sydney, I let him use my fear . . . I allowed him to coerce me into putting Henry on that plane."

"You need a little more practice in front of the mirror, Russell. That wasn't even passable."

She could see he tried not to smile.

Of course, he could enjoy the show. He'd had the last laugh after all. What he and Joseph had done was murder pure and simple. They'd manufactured and tested a plane they planned to crash during a routine test flight, all part of their plan to seize more government contracts. The fact that Henry had been on board that day, mere collateral damage.

Amazingly, Russell's legal Dream Team managed to get the murder charges dismissed on an "insufficiency of evidence" argument. Afterward, Russell handed over Joseph, the bigger fish, on a silver platter to the prosecutors, negotiating a deal for himself for time served.

"I'm not that man anymore, Syd," he told her. "The Wrecker. I don't want to be that man. And so I come to you. I am trying very hard to do what Henry would want."

"Don't you dare," she told him, venom in her voice. "You are not allowed to talk about Henry like that. As if you care."

"Of course. How callous of me." She watched as he scrubbed his face with his hands, looking troubled. What a little actor he'd become. "I should have known this would hurt." He threw his hands into the air, a vision of despair. "Unfortunately, before I can make things better, I'm afraid I'm only going to make your life so much worse."

The look on his face. "What have you done now, Russell?"

"I won't mince words. My deal with the government," he said. "It wasn't just about Joseph. I had to pay reparations, you see. A fine. A rather large fine, I'm afraid. And since the money was earned during the course of our marriage ..." He looked up, meeting her gaze. "They want everything, Syd. Divorce or no divorce."

How surprising that she hadn't seen this coming. Like the car swerving toward her through traffic.

"My money came from Henry," she said when she could find the breath to speak.

He looked up from under sleepy lids, the hint of a smile hovering on his lips. "That's not how the government sees it, I'm afraid."

She grabbed her purse and signaled for the check. Then, thinking better of it, she reached for her wallet and dug out enough bills to pay for her wine.

All the while, he continued. "Your attorney is probably just receiving the government's order. I wanted to warn you first—before you heard it from anyone else. That was part of my deal, you see. That they allow me this moment to break the news to my wife. I didn't want you to think you had lost everything when they made their threats. Listen to me, Sydney. I can help you save the art center."

She sat very still at the table across from him, his words hanging in the air between them.

She heard herself ask, "What exactly are you offering?"

He leaned toward her, whispering furiously, "I've

managed, or my attorneys have, in any case, to work out a plan. Reck Enterprises, of course, was transferred into Rocky's name long before any charges were filed against me. And I have found a rather generous silent partner to keep us afloat."

The energy coming from across the table . . . incredible. *He thinks I'll do whatever he wants—he needs me on his side.*

"Through my silent partner, I have enough funding to keep Reck Enterprises," he continued, "and then some. Nothing is in my name, you understand. Technically, I'm not even allowed to conduct business in aerospace. Not for another few years, in any case. Rocky, of course, will be in charge. The gallery—it could be placed under the same umbrella. I sent Rocky over with my proposal. Your partner should be reading the papers as we speak. Hopefully, she arrived before the government subpoenaed the gallery's records."

He'd made a deal with the government that would cost Sydney everything . . . while he had planned ahead, taking precautions so that he might carry on as if nothing had happened.

"You want to help save the art center? From what you just told me," she said, "we're your sacrificial lamb."

"Don't be stubborn, Sydney. Look at my proposal. More than anything, I wish . . . I wish there was something I could do to repair what's happened. I can't bring Henry back or regret taking you from him in the first place. At the very least, let me help you save what you love."

Elbows on the table, his voice still humming, he continued. "God, Sydney. Do you remember those days? How much I wanted you, my partner's wife? How hot you made me just watching you? And the times we did it at the office, how exciting that was, having you, knowing any minute Henry could walk in and find us . . ."

She tried not to show on her face how much she hated what he was doing, reminding her of her complicity.

"Sydney," he told her. "You will always be my one true love."

"Oooh," she said with a mock pout. "I feel just so awful. What a bad girl I was, letting you manipulate me and use me."

"We had an affair, Sydney. Before Henry died." He spoke slowly and softly, for the first time, delivering a threat rather than a smile. "You know, Sydney, I wasn't the only one to profit from Henry's death. Certainly, on paper, you gained control of a billion-dollar partnership. And then, we married so soon afterward. Maybe that's why the prosecutors want your money just as much as they want mine. It's a form of justice. Don't you think?"

She stood, taking her purse. "You must think I'm stupid to have come here. To even listen to you for this long. You can't threaten me, Russell. That gullible woman is gone. You used her all up. And for the record? I told Henry about us. I confessed—I asked him for a divorce. But he wanted me to wait . . . wanted me to be certain you were what I wanted. You know how Henry was. Always thinking of everyone but himself."

She passed the white-clothed tables and looked out toward the street ahead. Her heels clicked on the same Plexiglas path with the koi swimming beneath.

In her head her fears pounded with the beat of her pulse.

How brilliantly Russell had maneuvered them. *Joseph stays in jail—I pay for Russell's freedom.*

And Russell, he would enjoy every second of his revenge.

Jack Bosse stared at the very official document in his hand. *Amazing.* Five minutes ago, the shit hit the fan in the form of a subpoena from the government asking that he hand over the gallery's financial records. Some bullshit about Sydney's money coming from Reck's fraudulent activities. The last person Jack expected to hand him a shovel to dig out of the mess was Reck's daughter.

Rocky Reck sat across his desk wearing a tank top and white leather pants that exposed her pierced navel. She'd accented the outfit with ankle-high spike-heeled boots.

"Disappearing ink?" she asked. And when he gave her a look, she added, "I mean, you're staring at it as if you're not sure it's real."

"Let's just say I'm suspicious of your father's motives."

"Really." She gave it some thought. "Gee, and here I thought I was handing over Sydney's get-out-of-jail-free card." She leaned forward and smiled. "No strings attached."

"There's always strings." But he said it under his breath, not caring if she heard him or not.

It annoyed him, this proposal from Reck. Maybe even more than the implied threat of the government's subpoena. Jack couldn't figure out the angle.

There was no way Russell Reck could delude himself into believing Sydney would take him back. So why the parachute? Men like The Wrecker never gave something away for nothing.

"Let me ask you something."

Jack looked up. Rocky had settled into the chair in front of his desk, her back molded into the upholstery. She put her spike-heeled boots up on the desk, crossing her legs at the ankles. Her smooth hair had slipped forward over one eye, and she wore a cat's smile.

"What exactly do you see in her? I mean, she's like, a century older than you? Doesn't have nearly your money. And if the government has their way . . ." She shrugged, the gesture saying it all. Sydney would be lucky to get out of this with the clothes on her back.

"It can't be the sex," she finished.

He hitched his hip up on the desk in front of her, smiling. "You know what I think? I think someone should have spanked your bottom years ago."

She grinned. "Want to give it a try?"

"Look, honey. You've been putting on quite a show for me since you came to work here." He looked her over from head to toe, trying to be as rude as possible. "It's not that I'm unappreciative, but what's really going on? What do you want from me?"

Her sexy smile . . . the sparkle in her eyes. *The girl is pure mischief,* he thought.

"Isn't it obvious?" she asked.

"Absolutely."

She bit her bottom lip, managing with the look to appear even more the naughty girl. "Are you going to tell on me?"

"To Sydney? Nah. Why give you the satisfaction?"

He stood, coming closer. "Let's get something straight. There is nothing you can say or do to get between me and Sydney."

She couldn't keep her smile in check. "I'm sorry, Jack." She stretched out her leg provocatively. "But it's not going to be that easy to get rid of me."

"Now why doesn't that surprise me."

Before she could answer, the door opened behind her. Like a fresh breeze, Sydney walked in, her steps eating up the carpet as she headed toward them. Jack felt his heart lighten at the sight of her, as if she could somehow shut off the worries brought on by the kid sitting across the desk and the interesting paperwork just shoved his way.

He stepped forward, stopping her before she reached his desk. "You won't believe what I'm holding." He had the subpoena in one hand, then grabbed up Reck's proposal with the other.

Sydney promptly took both. She glanced at the subpoena, then tossed it back on the desk. The proposal she tore in half, then in half again.

He smiled. "God, I love your style." Suddenly, it seemed as if everything was going to be all right.

Over Sydney's shoulder Jack could see Rocky Reck. He expected a scowl but saw only a mysterious expression he couldn't read. Slowly, she lowered her feet to the floor, her bravura of seconds ago evaporating in the face of Sydney's strength.

Jack forced his gaze back to Sydney, inching closer to whisper, "I can help."

"No, you can't. I just came back from my lawyer's office. I'm not sure about what he called the theory—I think something like a 'shell' corporation. Anything that you give the gallery can be construed as mine.

It won't take much for them to convince a court to freeze the gallery's assets pending litigation. Which I'm told can take years."

"How is that possible?" Jack asked, outraged.

The laughter came from Rocky. "Because she had an affair with my dad while she was married to her first husband. You know? Off the first husband, grab all his dough, and cozy up to hubby number two? Don't you watch the movies? Jeez."

Jack shook his head. Sydney had made her confessions to him long ago. He knew about her affair with Russell. "That's not how it happened—"

"That's how they'll make it sound," Sydney interrupted. "The result will be the same. Years of litigation." Sydney turned to look at her stepdaughter. "I don't want you in the middle of this, Rocky."

"You don't have to worry." Rocky stood, taking her time. As she passed Sydney, she leaned in, speaking in a stage whisper. "I'll always be on Daddy's side."

Wiggling her fingers good-bye, Rocky left, shutting the door behind her. Once they were alone, Jack shook his head. "Why do you take that from her?"

Sydney stared at the door. "She and I belong to a very exclusive club. We both survived Russell."

"You don't owe her anything."

"No. I don't."

"So why have her here, looking over our shoulders, delivering his damn proposals to put us in Reck's pocket?"

"I had drinks with Russell today," she said in an abrupt change of subject.

He took a beat. "You met with him? Without me?" *Don't get upset.* "Was that wise?"

"I don't know." She shook her head as if waking from a dream. "Jack, I had to face him."

"Look, I understand. But let me do the proper macho-chauvinist thing, show my outrage, and tell you that next time I come along."

She sighed. "All right."

"So what do we do now?" he asked.

In the papers she'd torn up, Russell Reck was handing over a whole bunch of money, the catch being that his daughter would run the gallery. Vice president in charge of community relations or some such bullshit. Like he was buying her a job . . . as if Rocky didn't deserve a position in her own right, she needed a handout from Daddy.

The effect would not only hurt Rocky, of course. It would also ruin any relationship she might have with Sydney. Which, from what Jack could figure, might be the point.

"We don't need him," he said. "We can—"

But Sydney shook her head, now pacing across the room. "Let's not do anything. Not yet. Just give me some time to sort through this. Meanwhile, maybe you can help. With that fancy law firm you keep on retainer."

He smiled. "Already made the call. We'll get our own legal team to kick the shit out of him."

She stopped before him, her eyes on his. "It's going to be rough. The government. Russell. They all want a piece of me. Don't be hasty, Jack. Maybe you should think about it before getting involved—"

He covered her mouth. "I'm not going anywhere. Don't even ask."

He could feel her smile beneath his fingers. She

lifted his hand, pressing his palm to her cheek. "Thank you."

But that was Sydney. Ever thankful.

It should make him feel good, he told himself, going over their strategy together. There was nothing he wanted more than to sit there beside her, making plans for the future. *Don't ask for more . . . bide your time.* Sydney would come around.

But when she left, a familiar feeling of emptiness washed over him. He knew it wasn't right. That he needed her physical presence there beside him. As if, once she stepped out of the room, he could disappear forever from her life.

"I love you," he said, speaking in the empty office.

Eleven months he'd known her. Five of those months, they'd been engaged. And still, neither one of them had said those words out loud.

SEVEN

Alec didn't think he looked stupid standing outside Sydney's door in the middle of the night, waiting for her to arrive home. He glanced at his watch. But boy, he was getting there.

He told himself coming here had nothing to do with the past lonely week. He didn't miss her. He just figured he'd given Syd enough time to come around—that what he'd told her at the hospital must have sunk in: She needed his help.

That's what he'd been thinking when he'd left the five damn messages she'd ignored.

Today he'd actually driven out to her mausoleum office, hunting her down. Syd was acting pigheaded—no surprise there. That's why she hadn't returned his calls, seeming to be everywhere but where she was supposed to be. Like it was nothing that The Wrecker was out of jail.

From her doorstep he could see out onto the street,

watching as she drove up and parked the Lexus. Sydney stepped out, haloed by the streetlamp. She was dressed in a suit so clingy and sweet that he had to remind himself his visit had nothing to do with the beautiful curves of her body. With that hair and that smile. He was there only to give her the elusive second chance he'd missed out on.

The way he saw it, there wasn't any need to feel light-headed as she glanced his way, almost sensing him there in the shadows. Why experience a rush of adrenaline as her gaze locked on his, or wonder how many steps it might take to meet her halfway, grab her in his arms, and shake sense into her . . . or kiss her until she did everything she was told?

Nor should he feel what followed. Tight, hot anger.

He told himself to forget that she was knuckle-headed enough to try to go it alone. *Don't take it personal.* He needed to get that much straight in his head.

So it was no surprise when Sydney stopped in front of him to give him a look and said, "I'm actually afraid to let you inside."

He smiled, trying to imagine what he must look like. He wanted her so badly.

"Ah, honey. Don't be like that." He took up a piece of her hair and twisted it around his finger. He'd gotten the all-clear from the doctor the day before. No more sling. Still, it hurt like hell to move the shoulder. He'd stopped taking the pain pills the day he left the hospital, hating that shit.

"I promise to be good," he told her.

"So many ways I could interpret that statement."

"I love a woman with an imagination."

"On the other hand . . ." She stepped around him

and opened the door. Sweeping her hand out to motion him inside, she said, "I refuse to be intimidated by you, Alec."

"Attagirl."

Once inside, he felt better. At home. Just like before, when he still had his plane and his plans. When he could come here and have something to offer . . . instead of ramming his services down her throat.

Putting his feet up, he watched her putter around, getting him coffee, fixing it just the way he liked. Lots of cream, heavy on the sugar. He was a sucker for domestic bliss—especially when that bliss was coming his way. He watched her pour herself a glass of wine, thinking he had the right of it. He wouldn't strongarm her. He would ease into it. Sweet and nice. Alec knew his women.

He took a drink of the coffee and gave her a thumbsup—while Sydney sat back in her chair, tense but trying to hide it.

"So I thought we should talk about it," he told her, putting down the coffee. "That night." And when the lightbulb didn't go on over her head. "Buenos Aires?"

She stared at him, like maybe he'd spoken a foreign language and she needed to translate the words in her head. B–u–e–n–o–s A–i–r–e–s. She took another drink before she asked, "You came here to talk about Argentina?"

"Yeah. That way we can . . . clear the air. Make things right." And when he could see she wasn't buying it, he leaned forward, saying with feeling, "I want to make it good between us, Syd."

"So that, in the end, I will do exactly what you want? Let you take care of Russell for me?"

"Don't be so suspicious."

"I am extraordinarily familiar with your style, Alec. Of course I'm suspicious."

"Do my motives really matter?" he asked, taking another tack. "In the end, it's up to you where this goes."

She thought about that. "Okay. You start."

"Fair enough." He fidgeted with the coffee cup on the table in front of him, taking his time. More for Syd than for himself. It was moments like these that he could use a cigarette. A distraction. He hadn't really intended to quit, just hadn't smoked since the accident. It felt like the start of something, so he'd gone with it, telling himself it wasn't for Sydney, who'd been begging him to quit for two years.

But the last week had been bad, nicotine patch and all. He'd been sweating out this moment. How it would go over when she heard what he had to say.

"That night," he told her, "you had a lot to drink. You thought I took advantage. But you weren't seeing things clearly."

"So why don't you clear it up for me?"

He'd been cold sober to her happy drunk. He never drank, another legacy of his childhood. When you witnessed your parents killing themselves with drugs and alcohol, you managed to fill in the blanks. Him, he'd get his thrills some other way.

"The fact was, I knew exactly what was going on," he said. "For both of us."

She put down her glass. "What a ridiculously chauvinistic thing to say."

"Yeah, but it got the job done." And because she

looked ready to bolt, he added, "We've been through a lot. We can get through this."

"And if we waited too long? Alec, I've gone on. I've made my plans—I've taken steps. Believe it or not, I'm at peace with what happened between us."

"Liar, liar, pants on fire. Shit, Syd. Tell me you can do better than that?"

"Meaning?"

He clutched his chest. "I've gone on." He added the appropriate melodrama to his voice. "I've made peace with what happened between us. Right. That's why six months later, insta-marriage with Jughead? Can anyone say *rebound*?"

"What a prince you are, Alec."

"Finally"—he had to smile, she was so easy— "something we can agree on. Now, stop grinding your teeth and listen up." He settled into his chair. "One of us was in charge that night. Maybe not the person who wanted to be . . . who should have been. That would be you. But I knew exactly what was happening. And I was careful." When he got no reaction. "I'm digging here."

"Dig deeper."

"Right. The sex. It was great. So why not do the whole marry-and-have-kids, like you wanted? Come on, Syd. We both know I'd screw it up. Of course, you would think you could make up for that. You would wave your magic wand of love and make it happen. But that's not the way this sort of thing goes."

"And you would know so much about that because . . . ?"

"I'm a diligent observer of the human experience." Again he smiled. "To illustrate, let's take Lover Boy Jack. Jack is trying to pull off the I-can-love-enough-

for-the-two-of-us . . . and it just ain't gonna work."
Alec knew by her expression that he'd hit a nerve.
For the extra point he tossed in, "Just like it didn't
work for Henry."

She looked as if he'd slapped her.

"Shit," he said. "Maybe I should have left out that
last part?"

He hated when she hurt. There was something
about Syd, a connection between them. It made it
too easy to feel her pain.

Conor once told Alec that the people who love you
hand over the power to hurt them. Because they open
up and don't hold back. Conor explained how Alec
should never use that power—another of the many
moral messages Alec tuned out.

Alec knew a hell of a lot about Sydney—some of
it, even volunteered. But most of it had been research
done long before he'd actually met her. An over-
achiever raised by a single mom. Father died when
she was nine—which was probably why she'd hooked
up with such an older man. Still looking for Pops. She'd
married old geezer number one, Henry Shanks, when
she was 29. The follow-up act hadn't been much
younger, but he'd sure been a hell of a lot more trouble.

Two years ago, Alec had needed Russell Reck gone.
It was Reck or Alec, and he had no problem making
that choice. Mrs. Russell Reck of the moment had
been a ready weapon.

But Henry . . . he should never have mentioned
Henry.

"Syd?"

She seemed to snap out of it, looking up. "Oh?
You were waiting for an answer? Well, then. Here it
is. No, Alec. You are not moving in here. You are not

playing my guardian angel. I can handle Russell."
She frowned, giving him a look. "Does that about
cover it?"

"Who said anything about moving in?" But, of
course, he had a suitcase in the car.

She stood, walking into the kitchen with her glass
of wine. Not one to be ignored, Alec followed close
behind.

"I know exactly how you operate, Alec," Sydney
said, not even bothering to look his way. "Clear the
air, make up . . . then do exactly what you wanted to
do from the first. Though abject humiliation was a
new twist." At the sink, she turned to face him. "There
is nothing for you to take care of here, Alec. Go home.
Go away."

"Well. I see a couple of nights sleeping on it hasn't
brought on any shining revelations."

"Did I disappoint you? Here's a tidbit, then. FYI.
That night in Argentina? It wasn't about marriage or
children or living happily ever after. It was about one
insane moment when I convinced myself that you
were The One. The man of my dreams. That one-in-
a-million guy I was supposed to be with. It was just
that stupid. True love."

He was glad he was leaning against the counter so
that she might not notice how her words affected
him. Like he'd taken one to the gut. He'd had women
say they loved him; that wasn't a first. So it really
didn't make sense that he couldn't move or take a
breath.

When he could talk again, he told her, "Was that
supposed to make me feel better?"

She thought about it. "No."

"Funny thing, Syd. I didn't come here to argue. I came to give a point of view."

"I think you're just worried that I dug up some home truths—"

"What worries me, Syd, is that you think I'm the problem. I am not the problem."

"No," she said, stepping up to him, taking him on. "You're just the trusty friend who comes by to tell me—so sorry, no happy ending for you. 'Cause that little wedding thing you're planning? My crystal ball says disaster ahead."

"Aww." He pouted. "I hurt your feelings." Alec grabbed her arms, squeezing hard, giving a physical pain to match the emotional one. "And here I thought you ignored everything I said."

She was breathing hard, head back and eyes on him. And that damn suit she wore puckered in all the right places, so that he could see everything he'd been missing the last year. Her face was flushed with anger; her pupils dilated with something else.

"Time's up"—she licked her lips, sexy as hell— "the door's behind you."

Alec smiled. "You wish."

He kissed her, hard, on the mouth. When that wasn't enough, he took her face in his hands and dragged her closer. She'd been drunk in Argentina— she might not remember. But for him, every second was burned into his head and ready for replay. Kissing her now, it was like she'd never left him. Never walked out of that hot hotel room smelling like a night of amazing sex. As if they were magnets and he'd finally managed to turn the anger into what they'd wanted all along. They no longer repelled . . . they attracted.

That's what he'd been thinking when Syd shoved

him back and swung, letting one rip straight across his face.

Alec ignored the pain, hearing dishes crash into the sink as he elbowed them aside, getting his balance. He reached up to catch her arm before she could slap him again. He brought her around, a waltz, trapping Sydney against the sink, cussing because his shoulder felt on fire. He held her there, trapped, one hand to either side of her waist.

He took in the sight of her, so angry . . . so excited. At the same time, he hesitated, anxious about where he was going with this. She was breathing rough. Her eyes looked impossibly dark. He brought his mouth close, teasing them both, smelling the sweetness of the wine on her breath.

"You always push me into doing this all wrong," he told her.

"Oh, certainly. *Mea culpa.*"

He smiled. "What? You don't want me to kiss you?"

She shoved both hands into the wall of his chest, catching him by surprise. He stumbled back, shoulder blades stopped by the refrigerator behind him. Before he could catch his breath, Sydney followed up. Now it was her hands that pressed him up against the refrigerator. Her fingers that reached up into his hair and pulled his face down, bringing his mouth to hers.

"You're not listening, Alec," she whispered. "I never said I didn't want you to kiss me. You never listen."

It was just like he remembered, the softness of her lips, the taste of her . . . how she could melt into him so that he wanted more.

She had such a mouth. It was the first thing he'd noticed about her. Those months they'd been tooling around in South America, Peru, Ecuador, he'd kept thinking about her mouth, imagining what it would be like to kiss her. Alec liked taking chances. He wasn't against diving in and thinking about the consequences later. But Syd did things differently. And right now, her different felt absofuckinglutely amazing.

"Be honest, Syd," he said, kissing her for all he was worth. "Can he make you forget this?"

Nah, he couldn't see Sydney with Jack . . . couldn't accept that she might belong to any other man.

"I almost believe you would seduce me just to get your way," she told him, her voice deliciously breathy.

But then, suddenly, he felt her freeze up in his arms. She opened her eyes.

"What am I saying? Of *course* you would seduce me to get your way."

"Right now, Syd, I would fucking marry you . . . if that's what it's going to take to get you to see the light."

"My knight in shining armor."

"Okay," he said, taking a breath, stepping back to give her some space. He held up his hands. *No problems here.* "Enough. For now."

Only, it wasn't. Not for Alec. Inside his head, nothing made sense. Sydney needed him. And here she was pushing him away, leaving him for Milquetoast Boy?

He shook his head, like he could get it straight somehow, standing here in her kitchen. When had the rules changed? Shit, hadn't he raced back to the States for her? Risked everything? Shouldn't that be enough? Well apparently it wasn't. Because he'd been replaced.

"Oh, yeah," he said, trying to keep the anger and hurt out of his voice. *She wants to be alone? Fine by me.* "I've had more than enough."

He turned, heading for the door. If she wanted to check into Yawnville with Jacko and settle down, that was her choice. That's what he told himself, reaching into his pocket for his car keys. Syd was a big girl. She'd walked the plank of wedded bliss before—she knew what was coming.

Only, at the door, he just couldn't leave. Like he'd hit an invisible force field. It felt too much like a repeat performance of that morning in Argentina, when he'd let her walk out all hurt and betrayed. How hard had he worked just to get a foot in the door after that?

Alec turned. He told himself he wouldn't beg . . . in the end, he told her only the truth.

"Don't marry him, Syd. It's a mistake. Right now, in that kitchen, I proved it."

He waited, watching her closely. But for once, he couldn't read that pretty face. And he wasn't prepared for her answer.

"The only thing you proved, Alec, is that I never should have let you inside."

He smiled. "Yeah. Right." He gave her a salute. "What was I thinking?"

Outside he forced his mind into a perfect blank. He didn't know when he'd lost it, but it was pretty clear he'd just blown what had been a perfectly good opportunity to reason with Syd.

And he was pissed. Why did he keep hitting his head against the wall with that woman? Why couldn't he just walk away? It's not like he wanted to marry her—he sure as hell didn't have the right. He just wanted her safe, that's all. Was that so much to ask, for God's sake? How many times had he hung his ass out on the line for her? She couldn't give just a little?

Couldn't leave her fiancé? Couldn't move in with him?

He stopped at his Chevy, shaking his head. He leaned there for a minute, getting it all straight.

"Who am I kidding?" he said under his breath.

As he gunned the engine down the street, he kept hearing her words in his head . . . *the man of my dreams.* Oh, yeah. That was him. Mr. One-in-a-million.

And then there was Henry. He couldn't believe he'd brought that up—and not just because of the pain he'd seen on Sydney's face. Henry Shanks remained Alec's secret shame. The one reason he could never marry, Syd, no matter what he'd offered her back there. *If she ever found out about Henry . . .*

You'd think he would learn. Sydney wasn't the first woman he'd disappointed. Hell, he'd made a career of it. And when the big shining light came down from on high, letting him know it was time to move on, like the commercial, he'd taken his licks and kept on ticking.

That's what he should do now. Give up that knight-in-shining-armor crap. *Move on . . .*

He rolled down the window, letting the air cool the fever inside him. When that wasn't enough, he blasted the volume on the radio, hoping for chaos. But he was thinking all too clearly: *one in a million.*

Well, he'd given Syd her chance. He knew what he had to do next. Plan B.

"Not my first choice, but hell, it's not like she's giving me any."

Alec smiled, humming along with the music. The

more he thought about what lay ahead, the more his smile stretched across his face. He started to laugh, gunning the engine.

It looked like Sydney was right. She never should have let him in the door.

Sydney collapsed against the counter, listening as Alec slammed the door behind him.

She stared at the dishes broken in the sink, then reached for the wineglass she'd left on the counter beside her. She almost threw it into the sink but, instead, placed it back gently.

"I'm not losing one more damn thing because of that man."

She hated that he could do this to her. Turn her upside down and inside out. It was like—chocolate. She knew she shouldn't eat it, but there it was. And suddenly, all that wonderful willpower she'd been building up vanished and all she could think was *but I love chocolate!*

Well, she wouldn't love Alec Porter.

"Damn you, Alec!"

Five months ago, life had been simple. The gallery. Jack. Then Alec showed up on her doorstep and wiggled his way back into her life. *No problem, Syd. We're just friends.* She'd thought, fine. *I can do this.* She could go on with Jack and realize their dream of the gallery. Alec didn't have to change a thing.

But Alec always changed things.

It just ain't gonna work, sweets . . . just like it didn't work for Henry.

She wondered if that was the part that hurt the most. That Alec was absolutely right.

Sydney sat down at the kitchen table. She buried her face in her hands. "Oh, God. What have I done?" *You're supposed to learn from your mistakes.*

Beside her on the wall, the phone rang. She looked up, knowing exactly who would be calling. It was something they did each night. Called each other to say good night.

She stared at the phone and waited for her machine to come on. She listened to Jack's voice tell her that he missed her already. *You're sure about not moving in with me? Hey, kid. You might be homeless soon. You might reconsider. Bad joke. Sorry, love. You know I won't let him beat us.*

Sydney stood, catching her breath. She told herself to get control. She mustn't allow Alec to manipulate her. *I can fix this; it's not too late.* That's what she said to herself as she cleaned the dishes and put them away. She was older now. Wiser. And she owed Jack her allegiance. Like Henry.

But at that moment, remembering Henry, she stopped her frantic cleaning, collapsing against the sink. Everything that had happened the last week flashed past.

The truth was, there was only one thing she really owed Jack.

Not to let him end up like Henry. Dead.

EIGHT

Alec Porter had always had his secrets. Secrets that had cost him his family . . . secrets that would break Sydney's heart.

Sitting across from Russell Reck at the famed offices of Reck Enterprises, he figured he wouldn't mind adding another to the list.

Even before Sydney shot down his offer, sending him on his way, Alec had prepared for the worst. Plan B. With a little help from past acquaintances, he'd created the documents that magically transformed one Alec Porter into James Flint, an Internet entrepreneur looking for a break. His new name needed a new look. Last night, he bleached his hair so that platinum spiked up from his naturally dark roots. He'd accented the style with a single gold hoop in his ear. Contacts turned both iris and pupil into the image of a miniature eight ball. A black leather jacket draped to his knees, Alec's version of the superhero cape. With his new identity, he could walk into Reck's conference room as he had today in relative safety. He could, at long last, face his demons.

"Who could have guessed the market for dotcom business would vaporize? I've lost everything," he told Russell Reck sitting across from the table. He shrugged. "But you have the resources I need." He slid the papers he'd drawn up across the table's polished surface. Alongside the proposal waited a pile of diskettes—the Collision Avoidance software he'd spent the last year perfecting.

From what Sydney had told him, as a condition of his release, Reck was out of the aerospace game. He'd wiped his name off the letterhead, agreeing to step down and let the company run without him, leaving his daughter at the helm. But he'd kept his cushy corner office with a view, presumably confining his activities to the minor role of exploring future opportunities for business . . . the lion turning into a lamb.

Only, Alec wasn't buying it—which made for some interesting possibilities. *Plan B.*

Giving The Wrecker a grin, Alec said, "I think you'll find my terms more than fair."

Alec relaxed into a no-problems-here pose, one arm across the chair beside him, ankle on knee. Beyond the floor-to-ceiling windows, sailboats bobbed in the harbor, a view only money could buy.

This wasn't his first trip to The Wrecker's lair, not that anyone here would remember him. Like he'd told Sydney, he'd been under the guy's radar.

Russell Reck flipped through the pages of Alec's proposal, giving it a look-see. Alec waited patiently. The last year hadn't been kind to The Wrecker. But Alec could still recognize the eyes of a killer.

He felt absolutely no fear. He was playing a role, closing in on the enemy. Hell, to him this was a rush.

He remembered Conor once talking about flying. *The one thing that can turn off the noise in my head,* he'd told Alec. Maneuvering into a hammerhead or a Cuban eight was pretty much oxygen for his adoptive brother.

Alec, he was just as happy to get both feet back on the ground. Those days, he and Conor flew X-planes, experimental jets they were paid to push to the limit. Not everyone walked away from the job.

No, Alec didn't get a kick out of risking his neck up in the Big Blue like Conor. But sitting in front of the man they called The Wrecker, wearing a new face and name—gambling the guy wouldn't connect the dots? Now, that got the blood flowing.

Reck tossed the contract back on the conference table. "Software to save lives," he said, repeating Alec's pitch. "You want to revolutionize air travel at a time when an aging fleet is practically dropping from the sky. You and everybody else."

"And don't I just hate being one of the crowd. Still . . ." He leaned forward, into it now. "Think about it. The software takes information from transponders carried by airplanes in the vicinity. The onboard computer determines the risk of collision and my program tells the pilots to take evasive maneuver. If he doesn't—maybe the guy's not paying attention, taking a leak or passed out—the plane does it for him."

He grinned, letting Reck take a breath before going for the jugular. "The publicity alone could turn this company around. Hey, nothing gets those day traders more excited than the six o'clock news. But then"— he frowned, like he was mulling it over—"you already know that. 'Killing the Competition: Mogul Murder Suspect to Go Free.' That had to be my favorite.''

Reck's flat brown gaze flickered up to Alec. "I'm counting on getting boring very soon."

"Maybe. But if I'm right, Reck Enterprises snags a couple of headlines on the plus side. Public relations massages it a bit, keeps it on the front page."

Reck glanced back at the diskette. "If it works."

"Like nothing you've ever seen."

"You sound so sure of yourself."

"Absofuckinglutely."

Alec knew the drill. You wear the black hat enough, you start to wonder if you'll get your chance at a wardrobe change. And here comes James Flint, offering The Wrecker a chance at the Holy Grail of aerospace. Reck Enterprises needed the public's confidence if the company's stock prices were ever going to get out of the toilet.

He told Reck, "I've been flying this software for almost a year. The current system is flawed—too many false alarms. But my system has built-in fault detection and algorithms. I call it the Golden Goose program."

"You tested it yourself? You're a pilot?"

Alec smiled, loving this part. The storytelling. "Not in this lifetime. I hired a friend of mine. I just dabble. Almost got my pilot's license on a Citabria two years ago," he added, mentioning the tail-wheel plane any enthusiast might learn on. "Not that I could afford to keep up. You hire me, maybe that will change. I hear helicopters are a kick."

"Sounds like you enjoy taking risks, Mr. Flint."

Alec stood, ready for his exit. Alec's motto: Always leave them guessing. "Pass my stuff on to your research team." He winked. "See if they think it's a risk."

But Reck wasn't finished with him. Just before Alec reached the door, he called out, "If your Golden Goose does what you say, you could have sold it to anyone. Boeing. Lockheed-Martin. I'm supposed to believe I'm your first choice? A company struggling against bankruptcy?"

Alec turned. "The way I see it? You need me. Maybe even more than I need this job." He pretended to think about it before answering, "I kinda like those odds."

Alec left, knowing Reck would be salivating over the program. He gave a salute to the receptionist as he left the office, held the door open downstairs for an old guy with a cane. Outside, he put on his aviator sunglasses, swinging around the corner for his car, his coat flapping around his knees like a cape.

Oh, yeah, he'd kept a few secrets from Sydney. Bad ones that could make her never want to see him again. But this one . . . this secret just might save them both.

Sitting in Jack's office, waiting, Sydney was thinking about dogs.

She was wondering if she should get one. Maybe a really big attack dog? The kind they put in movies that sleep at the foot of the bed like cuddle bunnies, but are ready to tear any intruder to shreds. Or a Ridgeback, like Fred and Ethel, Jack's two dogs. She should ask him about that. Get some information on the breed.

A dog could help. A dog might make it possible

for her not to wake up from her nightmares in a cold sweat. Taking pills to go back to sleep.

She should really look into it, she thought, pulling open the top drawer of Jack's desk and taking out the tin of mints he kept there. She could put it on her to-do list. Somewhere between making sure Russell landed back behind bars and breaking Jack's heart.

She stared at the mints, then dropped the one she held in her hand back into the tin. Unfortunately, that last part about Jack . . . it was coming first.

Behind her, the door opened. She swiveled Jack's chair around, watched as he smiled and headed toward her. Just that morning, they'd hashed out the newest strategy with Jack's attorneys. Lay low. See what the government comes up with once they finish their investigation. *Right now our hands are tied,* she'd been told. The ball was in the government's court.

Sydney hadn't argued much. Her head had been somewhere else. Thinking about this meeting. And the inevitable. *It just ain't going to work . . . just like Henry.* Alec's words haunted her.

Jack dropped the papers he carried on his desk, catching on to her mood. "So what's the worst that can happen?" he asked, forcing a smile. But that was Jack. Always trying to put a good face on it. "We put the art center on hold," he continued, reaching for her hand. "Get on a plane to Vegas—"

She pulled her hand back, a reflex. "Jack, we need to talk."

Watching him, the expression on his face . . . it was almost as if he knew.

"So it's like that," he said.

Oh, yes. He knew.

"Jack, I am so sorry."

"Wait." He held up his hand. "Don't go there so fast. Don't skip over everything and slide on home to the apology."

She nodded, standing, reaching to remove his engagement ring.

"Dammit, Sydney. I said wait!"

She dropped her hands to her sides, then wrapped them around her waist. She didn't know what to say or do to make this better. *Oh, Jack, count yourself lucky to be out of my nightmare life.* But she knew he would never see it that way, and she wanted desperately to make this right.

"I can't make you happy, Jack."

Even as the words came out, she knew she was starting all wrong. But the real story—Russell and his threats—Jack wouldn't understand. Big macho guy that he was, he'd just discount her fears for him.

And, of course, there was Alec's warning. *It just ain't gonna work, sweets . . . just like it didn't work for Henry.* How she'd felt when she'd heard those words.

Alec had shocked her that night, training a bright shining light on her true feelings, letting her know she was making old mistakes. She'd always thought you were supposed to learn from your mistakes.

She'd wanted so much to make Jack happy.

She walked around the desk, feeling awkward and a little dishonest. "My life this last year, Jack . . . there's just a lot of things I need to work out. You deserve more than that."

"No, Sydney." He dropped into his chair, shaking his head. "I deserve exactly what I'm getting."

Sydney turned, standing across the room from him, keeping the desk between them. It didn't help.

"Well," he said. "It's not like I didn't see this coming." He scrubbed his face with his hands. "You haven't even touched me in weeks. I thought—I thought we could make it through this. It never occurred to me I wouldn't get a chance."

She and Jack had always been in sync, almost as if they could read each other's minds, finish each other's sentences. She knew what he was going to say even before he started.

"I pushed too hard," he told her, filling in the blanks. "I rushed you. It's perfectly normal to get cold feet—"

"This isn't cold feet."

"No. I don't suppose it is. I just can't get my head around it, Sydney. That you're not going to be at the end of the rainbow. I know that's stupid—"

"Jack, please. Please don't hurt so much. Not because of me."

"Show me the happy switch so I can get there, okay?"

She walked over and took his hands in hers, sorry that she hadn't touched him in so long, that this would be the first time in too long.

"Remember when we first started talking about getting married? All the things I told you then? All my fears? I don't know how you did it. How you made it all seem irrelevant. But that was wrong. There's real stuff I have to get through before anybody can be a part of my life. Even you, Jack." And when he didn't answer, she continued, "Look, I am absolutely miserable at this marriage thing. Let's just leave it at that. But out there somewhere is a woman who can make you happy. And she doesn't come with all my baggage."

"You're giving me the you-can-do-better pep talk?"

He stood, shaking his head. "I don't think so." He jammed his hands in his pockets, as if he had to stop himself from reaching out to her. He turned, hesitating, again checking himself as if to say: *Keep it together, Bosse; don't lose it.*

He asked, "Answer me one question and do me the courtesy of being honest. Is this about Porter?"

"Of course, not." Because it was close to the truth and a lot less complicated. It had taken her most of the night to come to her conclusions—this was about her and Jack. Nothing else.

Nodding, his face impassive, he surprised her by continuing, "I guess that takes care of question number two: Are you sleeping with him?"

She shut her eyes. "Jack. Give me some credit."

"Then what the hell is going on? A month ago, everything's fine. Now—"

He stopped, taking his hands slowly out of his pockets, revelation showing on his face. He grinned, shaking his head as he walked toward her. "You're afraid for me? Because of Russell? Oh, honey. No." He reached out and wrapped her in his arms. "I'm a big boy. I can take care of myself."

She pushed him away. "That's not your choice."

"Last time I checked, it was absolutely my choice."

"I can't, Jack. I can't let anyone get hurt because of me. Not again."

"So I'm supposed to walk away? I'm supposed to just be alone for the rest of my life because your possibly homicidal ex-husband might—I repeat, *might*—come after me? No. That's unacceptable."

"Jack, you have absolutely no idea who you are dealing with."

"You're leaving me. That's what I'm dealing with.

I don't care about anything else. Look, this isn't an easy 'oh, well, guess that didn't work out. Moving on.' Not for me. If you leave, it won't be so I can find someone better. I'll be alone. Just that. So whatever baggage you bring along, that's part of the package for me. And I'm not afraid."

"Well, I am." This time, she very purposefully removed her engagement ring. "And you won't be alone. You're not that kind of man. Whether you want to admit it or not, there will be someone else."

He grabbed her wrist. There was a mean expression in his normally placid blue eyes. Even his smile didn't look right, appearing almost cunning.

"Maybe we're looking at this all wrong," he said. "How about another point of view? I mean, think about it. This whole Russell thing might be kind of convenient for you. Sydney making the big bad sacrifice. Leaving Jack for his own good." He came in close, whispering, "Come on, aren't you just a little relieved? Good old Russell gave you the excuse to walk away. Right back to Porter."

"Jack, you have every right to be angry—"

"You bet I'm pissed. I feel like an idiot. That bastard is back just a few months and everything I've worked for slips through my fingers? And here's the punch line. He doesn't even love you. Not the way I do."

"Everything you've worked for?" She nodded, agreeing with him. "Yes. You worked very hard for this, Jack. Your marriage project. I can imagine you're disappointed that the deal fell through."

"That's not what I meant—"

"It's just a point of view, Jack."

He dropped his head, getting it. "God, Sydney. I'm sorry."

"Jack," she told him, lowering her voice to match his. "You have every right to be hurt. But we never would have worked. You look at me and you see all the right components for a happy marriage—I'm educated, nice-looking, even Catholic. The right woman for the job, and you're ready for the merger of a lifetime. That's not love."

"You couldn't be more wrong."

This time, when she gave him the ring, she closed his fingers over the jewelry. "Admit it, Jack. You fell in love using your head. Not your heart."

Walking to the door, she realized everything she'd said was true. Jack was a dreamer. What he felt for her had everything to do with who he thought she was rather than any special connection between them. That wasn't love.

"Sydney, stop."

Almost to the door, she told herself to keep going. Let him be mad. Anger was good. But Jack caught up, coming up behind her.

"Don't go like this," he said, turning her around. "Can you really just walk away from me and everything we've built together?" he asked.

"Honestly, Jack. I don't see how we can keep working together."

"Then you're selling me short." Unbelievably, he smiled at her. "You know what I think? I think I should have kept my damn mouth shut just now. All this stuff, it's too much. It's making you crazy. I can understand that. But we believe in the art center. Fuck it, go back to Porter. Get him out of your system. Sleep with him. I don't give a shit. In the end, he'll leave you. And I'll still be here, waiting."

"Jack, you're talking crazy—"

"I think it's the sanest thing I've said in the last ten minutes. Let's finish what we've started with the art center, Sydney. Don't let Russell beat us without even putting up a fight. If, in the end, it still doesn't work . . . us . . . okay. But not the center. Don't take that from me too."

Everything inside her told Sydney to walk away. They'd spoken a few home truths, the perfect exit. She'd go on and fight the good fight while Jack stayed safe.

Only, watching his face, the cost seemed too high. *It's Jack.* No matter what happened, he'd come to mean the world to her. He seemed to think they had unfinished business, and he could be right. The art center, their friendship . . . these were things worth saving.

He looked incredibly relieved when she gave him a short nod. "Now," he said. "In case the guy does have a screw loose and comes after you, what's the plan?"

"I hired an agency." The company she hired hadn't been able to find out anything about the car at the hospital, but they had provided protection. "I have a bodyguard now. It's a little strange. He stays right outside my door, in the living room. But he seems nice. Very quiet. Unassuming. Almost invisible." A stranger. Brought into her life by Russell, who, once again, was taking control.

Jack seemed to realize for the first time that he still held the ring crushed in his hand. He dropped it into his pocket. But he'd been holding it so tight, the diamond left a mark in his palm.

"Good," he said, massaging the skin as if he could rub off the mark. "When this thing with Russell shakes out, we talk. All right? That's all I ask." And when she didn't answer right away, he opened his arms to her, almost begging, "Is it really too much to ask?"

She stepped into his embrace, holding him. She didn't want him to plead with her. She didn't want any part of this. "I'll do whatever you want, Jack."

They hugged each other for the longest time. But Sydney felt incredibly sad. Because at that moment she knew one thing only too well.

Despite everything she admired and respected about Jack Bosse, he wasn't the man she loved.

NINE

Rocky sat in her cubicle at Shanks and Bosse, doing some lovely impressionist work on the message pad in front of her. She was talking to her father on the phone, now a free man.

Somehow, it should feel different, she thought. Sitting here talking to him should be nothing like those days when he'd been in jail. And yet, she could be sitting on one of those benches, waiting for his name to be called, surrounded by the same pathetic crowd.

Test of faith.

She tossed the pen on the desk. "She doesn't want your money, Daddy," she told him, speaking into the phone.

Her father had spent the last twenty minutes making plans. Plotting. A week ago, Sydney turned down his proposal to join the gallery to Reck Enterprises. Now he wanted Rocky to schedule a meeting with her stepmother. Talk to her. Tell her how much Rocky wanted to be a part of this grand new venture he'd proposed between them. And if that didn't work, she might hint a little at how it made her feel, Sydney's rejection. Couldn't she swallow her pride for Rocky's sake?

Listening to him, hearing his beautifully thought-out steps, it felt just a little felonious, his intent.

"Daddy"—she lowered her voice—"if you want me to spy for you, I will."

Because she couldn't stand it anymore. She wanted the truth. What he really needed from her. To manipulate Sydney. To make her pay for what she'd done to them.

Anger, Rocky could understand. Why shouldn't he hate the woman who had put him behind bars? Who threatened to leave him old and alone. Penniless. How often had Rocky felt the same? She wanted more than anything to be a co-conspirator against the woman who had hurt him most.

But she didn't want him to lie to her. She didn't want to be used, just another weapon in his battle against his ex-wife.

Her father told her she was wrong. *How can you believe that's what I'm after, honey?* He needed to make things right between Sydney and himself, that's all. *Sydney's stubborn. Sometimes, your stepmother doesn't know what's good for her.* She was turning down a perfect opportunity to make her dream come true through Reck Enterprises, a company that wasn't even his on paper. *Just because she thinks the money is coming from me?*

And he wanted to help his daughter too. *Law school is great, sweetie, but you can do better. Here, at Reck Enterprises. It's a fabulous opportunity for you. Rocky, you practi-*

cally own the company. It's a chance I'm only too happy to give to you. Sydney was hurting herself and Rocky. Surely, Rocky could make her stepmother understand what was at stake?

In her father's scheme of things, Rocky would become vice president of public relations. The art center would be one of many projects she would oversee. As if she had any interest in writing press releases . . . as if law school were some lark? Last year, she'd scored high honors in almost every one of her classes. She was in the top ten percent of one of the most prestigious law schools in the country and she'd worked damn hard to get there.

"I'll try. That's all I can promise. Daddy, I've been thinking about Reck Enterprises. I don't really have any experience in that sort of thing, public relations. . . . Right," she answered, listening to his usual arguments. Law wasn't such an easy career choice for a woman. Why struggle through two more years of school, not to mention trying to pass the bar, when she could get started on her future right then? Worse yet, how could she turn her back on her legacy? She was all he had. His little girl. Reck Enterprises needed her.

"Yeah, I get it. Look, Daddy, I have to go. But I'll call tonight . . . no, I won't forget to mention something to Sydney. I just don't think it's going to help if I push. You're going to have to trust me on the timing, okay? By the way, I have next month's catalog."

She picked up the book featuring the center's future exhibits. Since his release a week ago, her father had wanted to know everything about the goings-on at the art center. As if he were already in charge.

"I'll bring it with me next time I see you. Love you."

She hung up the phone and tossed the catalog back on her desk. She felt dull inside. Used up. Like she was this really old person. Which was so totally weird. How she could feel this tired?

Daddy's fresh out of jail . . . and he's using me.

Test of faith.

What if this past year—the phone calls, the pleas for visits—what if it was all about Sydney? What if her newfound relationship with her father existed only because he needed a way to get to Sydney? Nothing more.

And Reck Enterprises. From what she understood, everything was in her name now. *So the government can't take it from him.* Instead, the government was suing Sydney and the art center. The last week, Sydney and Jack had barricaded themselves behind closed doors, trying to save the art center.

It's like I'm stabbing them in the back.

Rocky stood to walk around the room. She clutched her arms tight around her waist, as if she could somehow hold in all her doubts, stop them from jumping out onto the carpet and screaming at her. *He's a crook! He stole . . . he might even have killed!*

Sure, she knew a lot of times innocent people pled guilty to lesser included charges. Really, the system was totally stacked against a defendant. But all that stuff in the paper the last year, could it all be lies, like her father wanted her to believe?

What if he was guilty? Of everything. And maybe

more. Maybe even the murder charges that the government dropped . . .

Rocky shivered. She told herself she was cold. That the deep freeze inside her had nothing to do with her doubts. She grabbed a sweater from the back of her chair. They kept the air-conditioning on high in the building. Something to do with the art exhibits.

She should just get out of this freaking freezer. Maybe get something to eat. Stop thinking about what was going to happen to the art center and the kids who came here because her father had handed Sydney over on a platter to the government. After all, it really wasn't Sydney's money, right? It was Daddy's. From their marriage.

In the hall, she kept her arms crossed, still trying to get warm. She realized she had never hated Sydney more. Everything she stood for was fake. It had to be. No one was that good. No one loved unconditionally, like Sydney pretended, giving up everything— her own ambitions, her fortune—just to finance art for children. On some level, Sydney's one-woman campaign had to be self-serving.

Oh, yeah, there had to be a kickback somewhere. Sydney just wasn't being honest about it. Just like she wasn't honest with Rocky. *As if she loves me.* It was an act. You didn't bend over backward to help someone who hated you. Who made it her life's goal to get in your face, like Rocky had.

She stopped. She realized she didn't want anything to eat. She hadn't been hungry in days. She didn't want to go out either. The cold inside her had nothing to do with air-conditioning.

She just wanted things to change.

"Miss Reck?"

The guard standing at the door was smiling, already holding the door open. Max was his name. Really, he gave her the creeps, even though he was always super nice. Something about the way he looked at her. Something in his face.

Or maybe it was just because she knew he'd been in jail for something, though her father had told her it was minor. His wife accused him of something so that she could get the kids. It was done all the time. When she'd gone to visit her dad, he'd asked her to help the guy out, because Max had always watched his back. Society was always prejudiced against parolees, which she knew from law school. Really, the system was unfair. Her father asked her to put in a good word with personnel, maybe walk Max's application through. And she'd done it.

She shivered. Still, sometimes, the way he looked at her.

She backed away from the front doors. "Sorry, Max. I changed my mind," she said, turning.

At first she just walked, but suddenly she was sprinting down the hall toward the back offices. When she realized what she was doing, she forced herself to slow down, take a breath. At the entrance she saw the guy who answered the phones watching her, a confused expression on his face. She imagined what she looked like. *Going postal, anyone?* She smiled, walking toward him.

She stopped in front of Little Boy Blue's desk. Leaning forward, she let her sweater fall open to give him a view, and reached for the nearest folder.

"You don't mind if I borrow this, do you?"

He looked as if he didn't understand English. She waved the folder in front of his face, flashing her cutest smile, the one she practiced in the mirror. She knew exactly how she looked. Irresistible.

"Sure," he said, his face turning red hot. "No problem, Miss Reck."

She blew him a kiss and left with the file. She didn't have any idea what was inside, but she needed the prop.

"Miss Reck?" she heard him call out from behind her. When she turned, he asked, "You're going to bring it back, right? The folder?"

She winked. "Oh, you bet, sweetie."

She tucked the folder under her arm. Her heart was going a mile a minute. But she wasn't cold anymore.

The adrenaline hit maximum when she reached Jack's office. No one at Shanks and Bosse had secretaries. Little Boy Blue, a summer hire, mostly fielded all calls. Sydney and Jack considered a real secretary an unnecessary indulgence. Theirs was a democracy. The only thing that separated the queen bee and her prized mate from the loyal forces was a door—which they had, versus the cubicles allotted to everyone else. Sydney and Jack ran a streamlined operation. Every penny went to realizing their dream: the gallery and the studios for the kids.

The thing was, after working here a couple of months, she'd come to really like the art center, even if it was Sydney's brain child. A few weekends back, Rocky had taken her niece and nephew to one of the workshops. Just to see what the fuss was about. The kids saw a great exhibit, some mosaics shipped in from Knossos on the Greek island of Crete. That was one thing about her stepmother. In the art world, she was connected.

After the exhibit, the kids had made these tiles out

of pieces of broken pottery set in plaster. Which was the idea. First the children see the real art, then they get a chance to make their own. They'd given both tiles to Rocky as thank-you presents. Their mom's idea. Probably because the tiles clashed with the motif in Aphrodite's mausoleum house. But Rocky, she loved the tiles. She had them in her entry, one covered with dried roses, the other holding a bottle of oil with flowers floating inside.

Which was where she should be standing rather than with her hand on the doorknob to Jack's office. *This is crazy.* She closed her eyes, willing her heart to slow down.

Crazy, yeah. Exactly.

She waltzed inside without knocking.

The opponent she'd expected wasn't waiting inside. Jack sat at his desk, all right. But his powerful body was hunched over, his head in his hands. When he glanced up, she could see that his eyes were bloodshot.

She knew he'd been crying. It wasn't that Jack had a talent for communicating with a look or even that they'd developed some telepathic connection. His face. Some things were just universal.

"Go away," he told her.

It was actually weird. Here she was, feeling so much pain . . . and she'd walked in and found every bit of it on Jack's face.

She shouldn't have come, she told herself. *Leave. Leave now.* She'd just been so cold, and when she thought about coming here, barging in on Jack— razzing him—she hadn't felt cold anymore.

She closed the door behind her, leaning back

against it. "Gee." She gave her best blond look. "Is this a bad time?"

He picked up a pen and started writing on the paper in front of him. "What do you want?"

"It's kind of important. Otherwise, I wouldn't have barged in." She held up the file folder she'd taken off the front desk, then promptly hid it behind her back. She hadn't even glanced down to see what was in the damn thing. "But I can see you're not in the mood."

He closed his eyes, taking a breath. He dropped the pen and looked up. "And yet. Here you are . . ."

"Maybe I can help."

It had been a completely ridiculous thing to say. As if Jack Bosse would want her shoulder to cry on. Still, she liked it when he looked at her. It didn't matter if it was an angry look or a simple what's-up? Sometimes, she thought she would do or say just about anything to get Jack to look at her.

He was seriously older than she was. Like ten years or something. But he always watched her as if she had his complete attention. Boys her age didn't do that. They didn't open doors or pull out chairs. They took you to Taco Bell for lunch and waited as you paid for your own burrito. They looked longingly at the extra napkin you'd brought along, as if they were entitled.

But Jack, she always suspected he really *felt* things. Maybe more than other men. It made him a puzzle. Here was this self-made beefcake who looked like he'd fall apart if Sydney said "Boo."

Judging from the look on his face, maybe that's exactly what had happened.

"Hey," she said, smiling, stepping closer. "It's not like I bite."

"Not at this hour anyway."

"Ah, come on. Don't be like that." But he wasn't asking her to leave anymore. "Look, I'm just a clerk putting in time before my second year at school. What do I know? Or . . ." She pulled up a chair and sat down in front of his desk. She could feel her hands trembling. "Or I could be a willing ear."

He had these really pretty blue eyes. So clear. Fathomless. That was the word that described them best. They made him look soulful.

"Maybe I'm not Dear Abby," she told him, "but pinch me and I cry . . . cut me and I bleed—or whatever. So, has ol' Syd screwed you over? Not that I'm going to be so crass as to say I told you so." And when he didn't say a word. "Am I not being helpful?"

"Rocky, let's get something straight. My spilling my guts to you? Not if you were the last . . . willing ear on earth." He held out his hand. "What do you have?"

But she kept the folder on her lap. "Even I can see this isn't the time. You're upset."

"And you care so much?"

"You know, if you always expect the worst of people, they don't disappoint you."

He looked at her, surprised. She liked that she could do that. Shock him a little.

"I'm sorry," he said. "You're right."

"It's okay. We haven't exactly given each other a fair shot. You probably know how I feel about Sydney." She shrugged. "You're in the enemy camp. My strategy has always been to attack first and ask questions later." She bit her lip, giving him a steely look. "But maybe I was wrong. About you, Jack."

Now she had his attention. Now he didn't look sad.

He fidgeted with the pen, watching her, weighing if he should bother to answer. After a minute, he asked, "Why do you dislike Sydney so much?"

"Do you have a couple of hours?" She looked at her watch, hoping the gesture came off natural. "Or maybe I could tell you over lunch. Unless you have plans?"

Suddenly his face shut down. "You want to go out to lunch?" Pen in hand, he focused back on the documents on his desk. "Get the hell out of here, Rocky."

"Wow. Overreaction, much?" She pushed back the chair, ready to leave. "Sorry about the friendly gesture."

Jack's hand reached out and grabbed her wrist. It was like he could see straight into her heart and knew her lies.

"You know what I think? I think you're so fucking messed up that you would come on to your stepmother's fiancé"—his hand around her wrist squeezed a little harder—"Just to hurt her. If I believed it was unconscious—if I believed for one second you did it without thought or purpose—now, that I could accept. But that's not what I see going on here."

He dropped her hand, sinking back into his chair. "I feel sorry for you, Rocky. I really do. But I don't want to be a part of your grand plan against Sydney."

She had never had anyone talk to her like that. Just saying things so clearly, as if he didn't care what she thought of him. There wasn't a hidden agenda, just the plain truth. For a minute she couldn't even breathe. She couldn't talk, because if she did, she would do something stupid, like burst into tears or something. So she just stood there, hoping the tightness in her throat would ease up and let her take a breath.

Which didn't happen. She didn't say a word or make a sound, but the tears came just the same.

Jack slid a box of tissues across his desk toward her. Rocky picked up the box and threw it at him, hitting him square in the chest. The tears falling freely, she threw the file she carried at him too, papers flying everywhere.

"I guess"—the words came out all breathy, like she was going to make an idiot of herself and really lose it—"that's one way to get me to leave."

She ran out the door, racing down the hall in the stupid heels she wore. But it wasn't long before she felt herself turned around, Jack standing there, looking all contrite. She shrugged his hand away and kept going. Only Jack grabbed her again, this time dragging her past the nearest doorway, into the copy room.

He held her shoulders pinned to the wall, not letting her move. She stared right at him, chin up, daring him to say something about the fact that she'd been crying.

"I shouldn't have attacked you just now," he said instead. "All that bile and frustration wasn't meant for you. I was pretty pissed off about something else, and I took it out on you. I was way off back there, Rocky." He even managed a smile. "Truce?"

"Me too," she said, looking down. Because she didn't want him to see her smile. Didn't want him to know how happy it made her that he'd come after her. "I had a pretty lousy morning myself. I guess I went looking for trouble." She glanced up, biting her lip. "I guess I knew where I could find a good fight."

"Yeah, right." He kept staring, like he couldn't keep his eyes off her. He still had her up against the wall—he hadn't stepped away, only stepped closer. His eyes fell to her mouth in a way that just for a second, she thought he was going to kiss her. She eased forward a little.

Instead of kissing her, he jerked back. He dropped his hands to his sides, looking guilty as hell.

This time she let him see her smile.

"We are pretty good at that sparring stuff," she said, not letting him think too much about what just happened. At the same time, wondering what it might mean. "So why were you so upset anyway? What happened?"

"The job," he told her, still looking distracted, like he was stuck in his head a few minutes back, marveling at what he'd just done. "It gets frustrating."

"You were crying because you were frustrated?" And when he looked surprised. "Your eyes," she said by way of explanation. "They're all red. Like somebody died . . . or something."

"Or something," he said, leaving it at that.

"Do I still get lunch?" But she meant the kiss. She wanted the kiss she'd seen waiting for her in the look he'd given her. "I mean, I've made an absolute ass of myself. I should at least get a meal out of it."

He reached for the door behind him. "Sorry. I've got too much going on."

"Rain check?" she asked, not giving up.

He hesitated, as if he weren't sure why she was insisting. She realized that just as her father had done to her that morning, she had put doubts in Jack's head. *Maybe I was wrong about her. Maybe she isn't evil incarnate.*

She liked it somehow. That someone else could be just as confused as she was.

"It's not such a big deal, is it?" she asked. "Maybe a burger and toasting with a Coke? To seal the truce?"

"Okay," he said, stepping out into the hall. "Sure."

Rocky watched him walk down the hall. She had pretty much lost it in front of Jack. But the result had been interesting.

Humming to herself, she walked back to her cubicle. Jack didn't want to be part of her grand plan. But if she was careful—if she was smart—that's exactly what would happen.

Jack walked back into his office, feeling incredibly strange.

"What the fuck just happened?" He asked the question out loud in the empty room.

For a minute, standing there with Rocky up against the wall in the copy room, he'd had this irresistible urge to kiss her.

He told himself there were too many things going on. The situation with Sydney weighed on him most of all. The frustration—the anger, it was all spilling over.

He'd just wanted to teach Rocky a lesson. *Play with fire, little girl, and you're going to get burned.* Then she'd started crying and he'd felt like a heel. He'd been trying to comfort her. Then, suddenly . . . something else.

But come on, he'd have to be dead not to find her attractive. And didn't the kid just love to flaunt it? That stretchy blue top had been painted on, worn over this scarf thing she'd wrapped around her hips like a skirt, leaving nothing to the imagination.

He told himself she was just a kid experimenting. Trouble. But it wasn't even her age that bothered him. Rocky just wasn't right for him. No way. He wanted the responsibilities of marriage and children. Rocky Reck was still in school, for God's sake. Discovering who she was.

That's what made Sydney so perfect. She'd already made her way in life. She knew what she wanted.

But it wasn't him.

Jack rubbed his face with both hands, leaning back against his desk. He stared at the mess of papers on the floor.

Rocky was right about one thing. He had been crying.

"Like an idiot," he told himself.

You fell in love using your head, Jack. Not your heart. That's what Sydney had said to him. Like that was a bad thing?

He picked up the folder, thinking about that. He'd suspected Sydney wanted fireworks. As if she hasn't had enough already in her screwy life? Well, he didn't buy it. If you looked for fireworks, then you'd be kissing baby girls in empty copy rooms just because they were hot and you were hurt.

He shook his head, grabbing up some of the pages. Sydney was plain wrong about love . . . but Jack figured he deserved what had happened between them today. He'd known from the get-go he was pushing Sydney into marriage. He'd forced the issue, convincing her it would work out. Only, when flyboy showed up to cloud the picture, all the strings he'd been pulling simply snapped. *My fault.*

But it hurt. It still hurt.

He picked up a last sheet, then stopped. For the first time, he realized the papers Rocky had brought were part of the log-in sheets kept at the front desk. He stood up, confused. Guests were asked to sign in as a security measure.

The log-in sheet. Which made absolutely no sense.

He had a sudden vision of Rocky putting the folder behind her back.

When he'd asked her to give him the folder, she refused.

Even I can see this isn't the time. You're upset.

On the way here, she'd picked up the folder from reception with the log-in sheets?

He realized then the whole thing had been staged. The folder—the tears. It was all some sort of bizarre show to get . . . to get what?

"What the hell is she up to?"

He shoved the papers into the folder, a little shocked. Sure, Jack had been known to turn on the charm to get what he wanted. But this kid, she was something else.

Oh, yeah, he'd have lunch with Rocky. . . .

"When hell freezes over, baby girl. When it fucking snows."

TEN

Sydney stared at the books spread across her desk. Each clocked in at over a thousand pages, the print worthy of a magnifying glass. Doorstoppers, every one.

She took a sip of her coffee, grimaced. *Stone cold.* "Like my brain."

She sat back, pushing her hair out of her eyes, staring up at a framed poster of their Dali exhibit for inspiration. Who was she kidding? As if she could ever comprehend the fine points of conspiracy theory and transactional immunity?

Alongside the law books, a mountain of catalogs and multiple slides for the press called dupes completed the terrain. She'd promised Jack she'd at least read through a few of the essays written by guest curators, but that, too, waited. Her responsibilities lay piling up . . . while she tried to decipher legal tomes.

But it was the only thing she knew to do, research for a way to get Russell back behind bars. The one avenue left open to her—beat him at his own game. She needed to find a chink in his armor. And right now the only place she could think to look was buried somewhere in these books.

On the desk, the phone rang, lighting up one of the center's lines. Sydney glanced at the utilitarian clock on the wall. Almost eight, long past the hour when she might expect anyone to be hanging around.

She picked up, frowning as she listened to Charlene, the artist in charge of the Picasso workshop. Sydney had been able to get the Norton Simon to lend out a small exhibit, the paintings and sketches selected with children in mind. Apparently, the shipment of paints for the Picasso workshop that would follow hadn't arrived from their usual supplier. Now Charlie, the artist in charge, was in a state, concerned that the replacement paints wouldn't do.

"I'll be right down," she assured the woman, grabbing her jacket, at the same time wondering what possible difference it could make. As if everything weren't falling apart already, she had to convince Charlie that one shade of ocher worked as well as another?

It didn't take her long to reach the workshops. The museum itself was housed in a smallish brick building downtown, a throwback to the days before progress brought Chicago Pizza and Starbucks to the landscape. Only a central reception area separated her office from the studios and other office space. The gallery itself was made up of three viewing rooms, most of which snaked back behind the reception area, the entrance conveniently by the gift shop.

She and Jack had planned to expand. Now all of that was on hold, a victim of the government's attempts to compel Sydney to make good on Russell's debts. No more meeting with the architect or city planner's office. These days the only people Sydney spoke to had *J.D.* written after their name.

As she passed the ceramics room, a warm wave of heat chugged from the kiln housed inside. Charlene waited in their main workshop next door, pacing the length of the metal supply cabinets. An open box of tempera paints bided its time on one of the butcher-paper-lined tables.

Sydney pulled up a stool splotched with rainbow colors of dried paint and picked up a bottle from the box. "So what's the problem?" she asked.

Charlie pulled over several sheets of paper. "You see?" she said, dabbing a red streak of paint on one of the sheets. "The texture is all wrong. It's runny. And look at this." She pulled a sheet off one of the metal drying racks, showing Sydney. "I painted this just an hour ago. The paint dries flaky."

Sydney shook her head. "They're six years old. Come on, Charlie."

But obviously, Charlie did not believe that all tempera paint was created equal.

"I feel unprepared to teach a workshop I've been planning for months, Sydney. And these paints, I can't put my finger on it, but there's something wrong . . . I've never even heard of this company."

Sydney nodded. Charlene was one of her best teachers. If she had misgivings about the paints, Sydney needed to listen. The problem, of course, was the bigger headache pounding inside her head—the possibility that the Picasso exhibit might not happen altogether.

She glanced around the room, taking in the papier-mâché masks from last month's tribal exhibit, the quilts hanging on the wall, a more advanced class they'd held for older children after Sydney had put together an exhibit on the Pennsylvania Amish. Behind her loitered sculptures made of hangers and paper-towel holders decorated with leaves and sticks, part of a special Earth Day exhibit. The museum had opened in March. Now, only a few months later, would it all come to an end?

"Sydney?"

She glanced up, realizing she'd zoned out, mulling over the what-ifs of her future. "Sorry," she told Charlene. "How about this? I look into what happened with the initial shipment. In the meantime, you wing it for the first few classes. How about it? Do you think you can make do, just for a class or two?"

Charlene shook her head. "I don't know."

An hour later, with Charlie finally convinced that indeed, a six-year-old might not care which brand of tempera he used, even if it—gasp!—flaked, Sydney headed for her car. Every day she felt as if she were losing just a little more control. Her battle with Russell, her attempts to keep her head above water financially—it was all taking its toll. She couldn't seem to keep it together as acting curator, making her wonder if, in the end, *she* might be the museum's downfall.

And Jack. Today had been rough. Facing his pain, making a few realizations of her own. She'd come to think of Jack as her happy ending. Today she proposed something else entirely. *You fell in love using your head, Jack. Not your heart.*

She could say the same about herself. Just when she'd given up on love, Jack stepped into the picture, a beautiful, gentle, and brilliant man. What woman wouldn't want to be his? Only, all along, she'd been in love with someone else. . . .

She heard the car's tires long before the Chevy jumped up onto the sidewalk. Her life fell into rewind. It was just like before, the sound of brakes; a car swerving—right at her.

Only, this time, just as her heart slammed into her throat, the truck turned, tires slumping back off the curb, coming to a stop. The door opened.

"Evening, gorgeous," Alec said. "Get in."

Alec had never seen Sydney so frazzled. Funny thing, because he'd meant to scare her. Hey, what better way for her to appreciate the risks she faced?

Only, from her reaction, he'd guess someone beat him to it.

"You looked a little spooked back there." He lifted the aviator sunglasses making a show of giving her white-knuckled grasp on the armrest a look-see. "What? You thinking maybe someone might want to . . . I don't know, do you harm?"

"The only thing concerning me right now is your driving." She braced her free hand against the glove compartment. "That's a new look for you."

Alec smiled. "Like it?" He leaned over, keeping one eye on the road ahead. "What do you think? Too blond? I don't want to look cheap."

"Can you follow the speed limit? I think there's a school zone ahead. You just passed my car, by the way."

"No kidding," he said, paying absolutely no attention. "So where is the guy you hired? The bodyguard?"

Startled, she looked away, trying to hide her reaction. Of course, he'd been following her since they'd discharged him from the hospital. But Syd, she thought one little "Boo-hoo, go away, Alec," and he'd be off the case? Yeah, right.

"Hell, why even have the guy around?" he continued. "I mean, Russell let you walk away from lunch without a scratch. Gee, I have an idea. Why don't I drop you off in some dark alley and we see what happens? Just for kicks?"

She stared ahead, her jaw clenched. "I just had this horrible urge to call you all sorts of very foul names."

"Baby, don't hold back."

"I don't suppose it would do any good to tell you to stop spying on me?"

"An absolute waste of oxygen." And to answer the disgusted look she flashed him, he added, "Yeah. I know. I wish we were working together too, baby."

"Pull over, Alec. The dog and pony show is officially over."

"Which isn't the reaction I was going for. 'You're right, Alec.' Or how about 'I was a fool to meet with Russell alone.' Something like that would be more appropriate, don't you think?"

"How about this. Pull over now. Or I will open this door and get out while the car is moving."

He found a nice spot, seeing that Sydney was starting to steam a little around the ears. But before she could open the door, he grabbed her hand.

"This will only take a sec, sweetheart. I know what you're thinking. So creepy, me watching your back."

He shuddered. "Like some stalker guy. Next, I'll be calling ... sending those horrible letters asking, 'Don't you love me anymore?' "

She pressed her hand to his mouth. "I know you want to be in control of this, Alec. But I can't have you involved."

He pulled her hand away, squeezing tight. "Because you're doing such a good job of it? Right now I'm guessing your pulse is clocking at just above normal. But when I drove up?" He grinned. "Honey, that was pure terror in your eyes. So why don't we talk about that for a minute? Just to pass the time?"

Looking into those green eyes, he figured she would blow him off. But then, Sydney could always surprise him.

"As it so happens," she said, "you're not the first car to swerve my way. When you were at the hospital. He came right up onto the sidewalk. There were no plates."

It actually shocked him, how scared he could get for her. And angry. He had this urge to swing on back to Russell's office and rip out the guy's heart. Which would help about zero.

Usually, for Alec, protecting the damsel in distress went along nicely with keeping his own hide intact. Only, in Sydney's case, he'd gotten it assbackward. The fact was, the longer he hung around, the greater the risk to him. And damn, wasn't she making him work for it?

He smiled, brushing a curl from her face. "I hope that when you had lunch with your Russell Bear, you said 'pretty please' before asking him to bugger off. You know how important it is to use the magic word."

"Here's the thing, Alec. You think you're wearing

me down. And maybe I'm just a little afraid that you are. This isn't going to end well."

"He can have you," he told her. "You can be Mrs. Jackson Bosse for the rest of your life, bring up those lovely children you have all dreamed up in your head." He felt like he was choking on each and every word. "I just want this, Syd. This one tiny part. To watch your back and keep you safe. If you think this is going to end badly, more reason for me to hang around and—"

She kissed him, a lingering caress that literally stole his breath and shut him up, which he figured was the point. He reached for her, deepening the kiss, opening his mouth over hers. Even when she tried to pull away, he didn't let go, convincing her with every ounce of his being that she wanted to stay right where she was, in his arms.

But in the end, he could feel her slipping away, then fighting him. He pulled back. The way she just sat there, her hands, two little balls on her lap, he figured she already regretted their kiss.

"I wasn't talking about Russell when I mentioned a bad end," she told him, catching her breath. "It's you and me, Alec. This isn't going away, this thing between us. Only, I can't do it anymore. I can't give you a little corner of my life and listen when you tell me it will be enough. If you keep pushing, we're going to end up just like we did in Argentina, and how many times do you get to break my heart?" She touched his lips with her fingertips. "Alec, do you really want to teach me how to hate you?"

"Maybe I don't get a choice."

She shook her head. "There's always a choice."

She reached for her purse and dug through the

debris inside. She pulled out the card he'd thrown into the trash at the hospital, the business card with Travis Bentley's number.

"You call him; you meet with him . . . work through whatever it is that keeps you stuck in your past, pushing away the very thing you want most. Solve your own problems, Alec. Leave me to fix mine."

He stared at the card as if she'd just landed one right between the eyes. She actually took his hand and put the card in his palm, then wrapped his fingers around it . . . while he sat there like an idiot.

He thought over what she'd said. *Do you really want to teach me how to hate you?*

Like he'd ever expected better.

He reached across and opened the door for her. "Do me a favor? Be careful."

He watched her walk away, wishing he could be a better man for her. Give Travis a call, head on in to redemption city. Syd wouldn't be in such a hurry to push him away then. She'd hang on to her knight in shining armor, keeping him right there at her side.

But some things were like instinct. And you just couldn't shake them. That's what the past was to Alec. Stuck to him, unchanging. And he wasn't talking about his dad or Travis or any of that sorry bullshit that had Sydney so concerned. His crimes were much more recent than that.

Looking into the rearview mirror, Alec turned the car into traffic, making a U-turn. He didn't even try to hide. He puttered along behind Syd, following her, his version of the gentlemanly thing to do.

ELEVEN

Daniel thought maybe he'd painted too many clouds in the sky.

He took a step back and examined his work. *A lot of white.* But he liked white.

He thought about what Charlie, the teacher, had told him. Her real name was Charlene, but she said the kids could call her Charlie, which was great, 'cause even if the kids laughed, Daniel liked the name. It was a lot easier to remember than *Charleeeene.* Like Charlie Brown.

Charlie had told him it didn't matter what he painted because Picasso had spent his whole life trying to see things just like a kid. Well, Daniel *was* a kid. He didn't have to pretend or anything.

He squinted looking at his picture. Maybe he would make the clouds bigger!

He dipped his hands in the paint. He was supposed to use a paintbrush, but Daniel liked to feel the paint squishing between his fingers. His mom told him he "had genius," so he figured it was okay if he used his hands. Genius was a word Daniel liked a lot. He'd just turned five, so he was really young for the class. But because he "had genius," his mom made it okay with the school for him to come.

"That's really beautiful, Daniel."

He turned, looking up at Charlie. "Thank you." He thought so too. Just like some of those paintings they'd seen hanging on the walls in the gallery.

He wished his mommy were there to see his picture. He put his hands in the paint, letting it ooze through his knuckles. If he used his fingertips, he left these neat marks in the clouds. . . .

His fingers felt kind of funny. Itchy. And hot. He took his hands out of the paint. Maybe he had enough clouds for now.

They were really starting to hurt, his hands. He tried to get the paint off, first on the brown paper covering the table, then on his pants.

"Daniel, honey. Don't do that—oh my God."

He was glad the teacher was there. His fingers looked fat, like hot dogs. He wished his mommy were there too.

"My hands. They feel yucky."

Charlie's eyes got really big as she stared at his fingers. Daniel looked down. Under the white paint, he could see the skin had turned dark red.

Charlie picked him up and carried him to the sink. She stuck his hands under the running water. Daniel started to cry. Because his hands hurt and he was really scared.

"I want my mommy."

"Yes, sweetie, I know. We'll call her right away.

Just keep your hands under the water, okay? Mindy?
Mindy! Call 911!''

When Russell Reck asked his executive assistant to
set up a manicure, he'd had something very specific
in mind.

A redhead. Tall and lean. Preferably with green
eyes. Squint a little, and Sydney would be sitting across
the table in his office, massaging oil between his fingers.

Angela was a blonde. But she was good with her
hands.

She laced their fingers together, then manipulated
his wrist in slow circles. She smiled. ''Does that feel
good?''

In jail, Russell had bartered with cartons of orange
juice and chocolate milk. Now, a beautiful woman
deliciously massaged oil into the muscles of his hands.
Hell, yes, it felt good.

''You have a lovely accent,'' he told her. ''Georgia?''

She glanced up, surprised. *Oh, yes,* he thought. A
Georgia peach.

''That's very good.'' She picked up his other hand.
''I've worked hard with a speech coach over the last
year. Maybe I wasted my money, huh?''

''An actress, then?''

She dropped his hand into the crystal bowl of warm
water. She couldn't hold back her smile as she
reached for a cotton ball. ''Aren't you a surprise, Mr.
Reck.''

''I do hope so, Angela.''

The headlines about him the last year hadn't been

kind. It took a certain kind of woman not to be intimidated. Angela didn't appear the least bit.

She drenched a cotton ball in the acetone, then wiped away some of the oil she'd rubbed into his nail beds. He liked the way she watched him best. It's the way Sydney used to look at him. With hidden admiration.

It amazed Russell how quickly the days passed now. By the time he'd read the file Michaels delivered on the mysterious Mr. James Flint and his aviation software, the sun had set. Russell had thought to call Rocky, perhaps ask her out to dinner, but he'd left it too late.

These days he wanted to be considerate. It wasn't something that came naturally; he'd spent a lifetime ignoring the people who loved him. Now he wanted to make good with Rocky. Calling her so late would be inconsiderate. So he'd settled for a manicure and dreaming of Sydney.

He glanced at his desk, the file with the preliminary investigation on Flint. He smiled, thinking about the old show *Our Man Flint*. He'd notified Flint that he was hired just that morning. He certainly hoped James Flint would come through with the goods.

He hadn't found anything unexpected in the file, just a string of jobs over the last five years sliding on home into an Internet startup company, which, of course, failed for a lack of venture capital. Russell had been much more interested in the second half of the report, an evaluation of the computer program itself.

Software to save lives. He liked the drama of it. In jail, everything had been about death. Here at last was something that brought on the shining light of life.

But he had to be careful. He'd made a mistake once, relying on another's promises. Joseph, may he rot in hell. In those days Russell had been so hungry, easy pickings for Joseph Kinnard to manipulate. Russell dreamed of becoming the Bill Gates of the new millennium. Through Kinnard, he'd overreached. The shortcuts had cost him dearly.

"Do you like Picasso?"

He looked up. Angela nodded toward the museum catalog open on the antique table between them.

"My ex-wife runs the new art center downtown by the pier. She wanted a place where children could enjoy works of art, then experiment in workshops specially designed around each exhibit. My daughter works with her. She sends me the catalogs." He smiled. "I like the pictures."

"You miss her," she said, taking her own guess. "Your wife."

"I'm lonely," he corrected her. "There's a difference."

But he had wanted to patch things up with Sydney. In jail, he'd thought about nothing but their eventual reunion. As if he could somehow erase the mistakes of the last years, the losses—his fall from grace. *If I can get Sydney back . . .*

He dreamed of her constantly, remembering her extraordinary hair, her so green eyes and mischievous smile. Sometimes he could close his eyes and smell her perfume. In jail, with no one there to tell him differently, he'd concocted his fairy tale, complete with a happy ending for them.

But he could see Sydney had changed. And not

necessarily for the better. There was a hardness to her. An edge. Hate that needed a purpose. He knew he'd become that purpose.

There was a time when Sydney would have forgiven him anything.

"No, you're right," he said, giving Angela a self-deprecating smile. "I am going to miss Sydney."

Angela frowned, then shook her head as she started to pack up her case. "That sounded so final. And a little sad. Well"—she finished packing her things—"I hope that for at least a minute or two you were able to relax."

"You were wonderful," he told her.

But when she made to stand, he placed his hand on hers, keeping her seated on the leather couch in his office. "I'd like to explain my tone just a minute ago. The last year I've had a lot of time to think."

About the man he'd become, building his empire only to destroy it. Those years Henry had been alive and at his side ... how asinine of him to replace Henry with that snake Kinnard.

Russell had let himself become so extraordinarily weak those years. He'd used people, giving nothing in return. Consequently, when the chips were down, who really cared about what happened to Russell Reck?

"With my wife ... I'd hoped I could change a few things."

"But she won't give you the chance?"

He smiled. "Not in this lifetime."

Family, that's what he'd been missing. Before the government pressed charges against him, he'd been able to funnel what money Sydney couldn't get her hands on during their divorce into numbered accounts in the Caymans, money now available through a "silent partner" he'd created. Lately, he'd begun looking into the possibility of regaining his place in aerospace, his "silent partner" buying up smaller companies, using them as shells for a hostile takeover of his competition. All completely against his plea agreement, of course. But he'd learned a few things in jail. Like how to cover his tracks.

Transferring Reck Enterprises into Rocky's name was a big part of his eventual success. As long as his name stayed out of the paperwork, who could prove he was pulling the strings? Yes, indeed, a man who had family had a basis on which to build for his future.

Now Sydney wouldn't be part of that future. It was just Rocky at his side. Rocky, who loved him like no other. A woman who would forgive him anything, as Sydney once had.

"Would you let me take you to dinner, Angela?" he asked.

She waited, as if she were thinking about his proposal. But he'd known her answer before he'd asked.

"Is that what you want, Russell? Dinner? I mean, sometimes, men like you"—she glanced around his office, taking in the priceless art, the stylish furniture—"they get the wrong idea. Because I come to their offices."

He picked up her hand and kissed her fingers. She had lovely, elegant hands. "I spent a lot of time in jail waiting. I've learned patience. Dinner," he assured her. "Only that. I promise."

At that moment, with the light coming from the bank of windows behind him, she looked so much like Sydney.

"May I?" He stood, still holding her hand. "Take you to dinner?"

She hesitated only a minute. "It would be my pleasure, Russell."

He walked her to the door, something else he would never have done before. In his other life he hadn't needed to romance women. His money and reputation did that for him. Another thing he wouldn't take for granted again.

"Just tell my secretary where I can pick you up. Or, if you prefer, we can meet somewhere. Eight o'clock?"

"All right." At the door, she told him, "I just want you to know, I never do this. Date my clients. Only, you do seem lonely. It's sweet. A powerful man like you needing company."

For a moment he had a flash of another woman. Sydney, tears welling in her beautiful green eyes. *Russell, I'm so lonely.* She'd be waiting for him in that ridiculously large bed they'd shared, wearing an elegant negligee. The bed had been a Venetian antique she'd purchased, as if she were trying to make up for leaving the museum, acquiring relics for their home.

He really shouldn't have made her quit her job as curator. He shouldn't have always left her alone.

Russell, I'm so lonely.

"I am lonely," he told Angela. "And I so do appreciate your changing that."

He kissed her hand, lingering for a moment. A year ago he would have done everything differently. He wouldn't have cared so much about what this woman thought of him. He wouldn't have enjoyed her.

Now that would all change.

Twelve

Rocky knocked politely on the door to Jack's office and waited. Hearing Jack tell her to come in, she made the entrance she'd practiced the last half hour.

"I thought I would bring the food," she said. And when Jack looked up, confused, she added, "For our picnic?"

She shut the door with her foot and leaned back against it. She felt like a runaway train. No brakes. "I was thinking romantic finger food. Maybe a bottle of wine. We could eat it right here, on the floor. On one of those pretty checked blankets? Only . . ."

She held up a plastic bag with "The Magic Wok" written in script across the front. "I'm not exactly the Suzy Homemaker type. So I bought Chinese." She threw a thumb back. "There's this place right around the corner."

She stepped up to his desk, thinking, *Any second now, he'll come out of his insta-coma and tell me to leave.*

She dropped the bag of food on his desk, careful not to meet his eyes, afraid of dismissal. "It's been a week—I was starting to think maybe you forgot about me and my rain check. But then I remembered there's been a lot on your mind lately." The trouble with her father would classify as a big for instance. "So, if the mountain won't come to Mohammed . . ."

She sat down because she was shaking. She pulled little boxes of food out of the bag, put paper plates on the desk, keeping busy. "Hope you like Mu Shu pork. It's my favorite." She was talking fast, sounding giddy. "I figured you for the Mongolian-beef type." She lined the little white cartons across his desk like good soldiers. "I guess I was thinking that whole savage thing. Go figure."

Finally, he sat down. She felt a great weight lift off her chest; she could breathe again. Only, what he said next changed all that.

"The wedding is off."

She hoped the shock didn't show. She told herself to blink, act normal, say something. Instead, she watched him reach for a plate and a carton of rice.

"When you came into my office last week, we'd just hashed it out." He spoke as if it were nothing, what he was saying. "So all this trouble you're going through to steal me away? You're wasting your time."

"Ah."

She had a surreal moment in which she thought she might burst into song. Or maybe she'd start laughing, long and loud, until she couldn't catch her breath and she'd have to stop.

What he suggested, that she'd wanted to make the moves on him to piss off Sydney? *Way off, Jack.*

The guy was just so full of himself. Mr. I'm-an-

Internet-Mogul—pay attention. He was so very sure about everything and everyone around him. Jack pushed her buttons, that's all. She hadn't meant anything by it.

Still, it was weird, how she couldn't figure out what she felt about his breakup with Sydney. But it wasn't disappointment.

"My evil plans foiled again." She looked at the spread of food. "Wow. What a waste of twenty bucks."

"Not a waste." He spoke around a mouthful. "As it so happens, I love Mongolian beef."

She pulled apart a pair of chopsticks and served herself some fried rice. Just a week ago, she'd barged in and found him with his head in his hands, Sydney the reason for all the pain she'd seen on his face. Jack Bosse, love's newest roadkill. And he was probably the only one who hadn't seen it coming.

"Another happy ending courtesy of true romance," she said.

He gave her a look. "That's a hefty amount of cynicism for a kid your age."

"My mother's been married four times. My father, three. I stopped believing in fairy tales a long time ago. By the way, I'm twenty-eight," she said, automatically adding five years to her age. Because he'd been so condescending. *A kid your age.*

"We share a birthday, did you know that?" Rocky added, popping open the Snapple iced tea she'd bought. "September fifteenth, right?"

Rocky smiled. She'd turned twenty-three on February sixth.

"Your birthday is September fifteenth?" He leaned back and crossed his arms. For a minute she thought he would call her on it. It was stupid to lie. She was just showing off. Trying to get his attention. *Really dumb, Rocky.*

"Yeah," she told him, refusing to back down. "I think Sydney told me about that little coincidence."

Another lie. Rocky had looked up a lot of things about the Great Jackson Bosse on the company's computer files.

"You're exactly six years older. To the day," she said, trying to hide her smile as she poked at her rice with her chopsticks. "It's strange because to me you're . . . well, you know, so ancient. Then I think, gee, Sydney's even older. How does that work, exactly?" She frowned, playing it up. "Oops. I guess it didn't."

But Jack only smiled, shaking his head.

"What?" she asked.

"Remind me never to sit down to a cozy meal with you."

"Sorry." But she wasn't. She liked teasing him. Liked that he could take it with a smile.

"That's a really bad habit of mine," she confessed, this time allowing the smile. "My amazing attack-dog imitation. *Grrr.*" She took a drink of the iced tea. "Guess that edge will come in handy after I finish law school."

"Still going through with that?"

"Yeah. Of course. Why do you ask?"

"Your father seems to have loftier goals for you. With his company."

"Well, a law degree fits right in. I'm mean, it's going to work out great," she said, even though she'd spent the last weeks worrying about just that.

She'd never even considered the possibility that her father would want her to quit law school. Work for Reck Enterprises, sure, but as in-house counsel. This new idea of his, the deal with Sydney and the museum—making Rocky vice president of whatever? That had never been part of the picture.

"You know a law degree," she said, realizing she'd been silent for too long, "comes in handy no matter what I end up doing. It teaches you a way of thinking. Problem-solving."

"And sharpens your attack-dog skills?"

"Exactly." She grinned, getting back to her food. She took a tiny bite and waited for what she hoped was a natural pause before asking, "So, she's back with Alec?"

She tried to make it sound casual. *Just a little small talk between friends.* When he didn't comment, she added, "That must have been tough to take. I mean, pretty high on the rejection factor."

"Sorry. You're going to have to get the details from Sydney."

She nodded. "Like, if I ask, the stepmonster will tell all."

For a minute he stopped tearing into his meal. He was giving her that look, the one she hated so much. When he looked at her like that, he made her do and say all the wrong things. Because he felt sorry for her and she couldn't stand his pity.

"Yes, that's what I call her. The stepmonster," she said, answering his silence. "I've known her a lot longer than you, Jack. You're just catching on with the program."

"Is that right?" He shook his head, getting back to his food. "She's not with Alec," he said after a while.

But when he answered, his voice—Jack Bosse was still good and hooked.

"Then I guess it's okay," she said, hating his weakness, "that she freaking broke your heart. But you know what, Jack? If I were you, I wouldn't do anything hasty with that ring. You never know if she'll need it back. In fact, I predict when the center and she go up in a blaze of glory, she'll be right back at you. Lucky boy."

But she could see that for Jack, Sydney could do no wrong. The gallery wasn't shutting down; Jack's lawyers had managed that much. And though the future remained uncertain with the government's looming threat, it was obvious that he and Sydney would struggle on, trying to make their dream come true.

Amazing, she thought, staring at the rice on her plate. Old Sydney could slog through even this mess. It didn't matter that she'd ripped out his heart and served it to him for lunch. Jack would stay the faithful hound and Sydney, she'd be his golden girl forever.

"Let me ask you something."

Rocky glanced up to find Jack had put down his chopsticks, his attention completely on her.

"Now that we're all chummy—you bringing picnics and all," he said. "As I recall, you said you would tell me over lunch. Why do you hate her so much? From where I'm sitting, she's not exactly Mommie Dearest."

She made a face. "Maybe I should make you ask Sydney for the details," she said, throwing his words back at him.

"Right."

He went back to eating. The silence that followed left her empty. She could see that she'd missed an opportunity. He'd wanted an answer and she'd lost her chance to make a connection. But Sydney was someone Rocky didn't want to talk about. Not with Sir Galahad.

"It's complicated," she said, giving that much.

"I bet." But he kept his eyes on his plate. Like he wasn't interested anymore. In their conversation, or Rocky.

It made her feel a little desperate, this sudden cold shoulder. She could feel herself shaking again, like when she first came into the room wondering if he might throw her out. He'd given her such a tiny taste of camaraderie. Now, as suddenly as it had sparked, that connection vanished.

"She's nice to me," she blurted out. And when he looked up, she struggled on. "I mean, it's weird, you know?"

She felt her face flush hot. She stared at her food, stabbing the rice with the chopsticks. "It's fake. That she's nice all the time." She spoke as if it were a reasonable explanation, even though anybody who knew Sydney could see she was nothing but sincere. "I can see right through her. I mean, here I am, acting like I do, and she's letting me know she still cares? Who can be that stupid, right?"

Rocky looked at Jack. But what she saw had nothing to do with Sydney. His eyes reflected only Rocky's fears. *Nobody loves me. I'm alone.* And a disturbing truth about why she'd come here in the first place, wearing the tightest suit she owned, bringing lunch and flashing smiles.

"Wow," she said, dropping the chopsticks. "What an incredibly asinine thing to say." Everything she'd just told him sounded so much worse than the lies she'd given him about her age.

Behind her, the door opened, cutting off anything Jack might have said. Sydney barged in, concern on her face, missing everything about the tableau frozen before her. But then, why would it matter that Rocky and Jack were having a cozy lunch together? *Nothing to worry about, right?* Nothing that mattered.

Sydney focused only on Jack.

"We have an emergency," she told him. "The Picasso workshop."

He dropped everything, running out behind Sydney, shutting the door behind him. Not saying a word.

Leaving Rocky alone with her plate of fried rice.

Rocky stood, putting away the meal she'd set out so carefully on the desk. An emergency in the Picasso workshop? What? They ran out of crayons? But she couldn't even make it hurt that he'd left to doggedly follow his Guinevere. She was too numb, mulling over her new perspective as she closed the cartons, putting each box inside the bag like a puzzle piece. *If I turn it sideways, this one will fit right in the corner. . . .*

She'd had this great idea. She was going to get to know Sir Galahad, get him to like her. She could do that. She knew how to behave when it counted. Once they became friends, she could get him to lean on Sydney. Influence her to warm up to Daddy's plan.

Only, just now, talking to Jack, she realized that all along it hadn't been about Daddy or Sydney or Reck Enterprises and saving the gallery. The hours searching on the computer . . . the mean little digs . . . she'd been acting like a high school kid who wanted only one thing. To be close. To get his attention.

Fifteen minutes later she sat back at her cubicle,

the bag of food slumped at the corner of her desk like a piece of pop art. She realized now what she'd felt when Jack had told her the wedding was off. She'd been elated.

Now Galahad would report to Sydney. Tell her all about how pathetic Rocky was, her poor little step-daughter who called her a monster. *Oh, Sydney. It's too cute. She has a crush on me.* And Sydney, she wouldn't get mad—she wouldn't get even. She'd do the right thing. As always.

"Because she's nowhere near the pathetic fuckup I am," she told herself.

Without thinking, she picked up the phone and punched in the number. She waited as the secretary put her through.

"Daddy?" She tried to keep the emotion from her voice. "I have some interesting news."

Alec listened to the phone ringing. He let the machine pick up. Pretty much because he knew who was calling.

"Travis here. Again. Well, I guess I have your answer." There was an audible sigh, making Alec smile. *Gotta love the drama.* "I was hoping you'd have the courage to go through with this. But I understand. Keep the card. Maybe someday, right? I won't call again. Take care, Alec. And remember. Just remember."

Alec stood and erased the message. He'd done exactly the same with all the others.

Remember. "Nice touch. I can see why you're in journalism." Only, Alec wasn't going to give a happy ending to the fairy tale inside Travis's head. He wouldn't play the guy's long-lost family. He had a family already. Conor and Geena—the only family he'd ever wanted.

He paced around his apartment, trying to ease the pain in his shoulder. Damn thing was killing him. The apartment was on the beach, which was exactly what Alec liked about it. That cold, wet air on the sheets in the morning, the sound of the crashing surf. He stretched, grimacing at the pain shooting down his arm.

He'd been working on the laptop for hours straight, and the pain in his shoulder had revved up to feel like a red-hot poker. Two years ago he'd taken a bullet in the same shoulder, but that was nothing to the acid burn in the joint now. The bump on his collarbone where the bone healed . . . it went along nicely with the staples closing the hole where they'd dug out the debris from the crash.

"Hell, maybe if I'm lucky, I'll be able to tell the weather."

In the bathroom, he stared at the bottle of painkillers in the medicine cabinet, a kid on a dare. His hands shaking, he grabbed the bottle and tried to follow the instructions to open the damn thing. *Push down with palm while turning . . .*

He caught his face in the mirror. Under the bathroom light, the color of his skin looked like it belonged on the Pillsbury Doughboy. Sweat beaded on his forehead. He dropped the medicine bottle, watching it rim the sink and settle at the stopper, rocking there to a stop. He touched the mirror.

Alec had always been the spitting image of his old man. Right now Eddy could be staring back at him in that mirror. Strung out.

He put back the painkillers and stuffed four ibuprofen in his mouth, then leaned over to drink from the faucet. When he looked up again, Eddy's son was still in the mirror, addiction running through his veins, swimming in his DNA. But Alec didn't have a chemical dependency. He had an obsession.

He traced the scar on his cheek, the newest addition courtesy of his last brush with death. Like a flash, another face surfaced in the mirror, projected there from memories. *Conor*. Alec traced another scar, this one marking Conor's face. An angry wound splitting his left eyebrow.

He'd met Conor when he was eight, Conor, fourteen. After years of making the rounds of foster homes, Conor Mitchell and his sister Geena ended up at a state-run facility—two great kids who'd slipped through the cracks of an overworked foster care system. Alec got there straight: the home of last resort for incorrigibles.

Alec's first day, these kids were beating the crap out of him. He was scrawny but scrappy, basically because he'd never had the right stuff to eat. He'd been crying his eyes out, swinging skinny arms. He'd wet his pants.

Then, like something out of a movie, this enormous kid appeared, pulling the jerks off him. Alec remembered it like a dream. Arnold Schwarzenegger walking through the mist into the light. Conor grabbed each kid by the scruff of the neck, letting them hang there at each side, legs kicking, arms throwing punches.

One of the punks had a knife. He'd slashed Conor across the face, almost gouging out his eye. Conor had already been taking flying lessons at a local airfield. Some program to help kids like him. Project Give Kids Wings or some such crap. For a while, at the hospital the doctors had talked about how maybe Conor was going to lose the eye.

Alec remembered going to see him. He'd been so scared. Shit, he'd never done anything to Eddy, and his father considered kicking Alec's ass an art form. At least Conor had a reason to hate him. He'd heard the director at the home tell how Conor wanted to become an astronaut. He couldn't do that without perfect vision.

Alec had stepped into the room to find Geena at Conor's bedside. Standing there, watching brother and sister, he'd thought, *here it comes*. He'd waited for their hate. Just like Eddy and Daisey. Just like the foster homes that landed him here.

Only Conor had told Alec it was no big deal, the eye. He'd asked Alec if *he* was okay. Said that maybe they should start hanging out. The other kids, they wouldn't pick on Alec with Conor at his side. That's all he'd talked about at the hospital. Half his head had been wrapped in gauze, and he'd wanted to know if Alec was going to get through this.

God, Alec loved that guy.

Right then and there, for the first time ever, Alec had everything he'd ever wanted. Someone who really gave a shit. Because Conor Mitchell, he was the real deal. If he stepped up to the plate for you, Conor never let you down.

By the time Conor was seventeen, he'd impressed a judge enough to become an emancipated minor. Shortly thereafter, he passed on a scholarship to college to become a full-time parent to Geena, his kid sister—and Alec—again impressing the powers-that-be into letting him become their legal guardian. Alec had been twelve.

But Alec had learned there were limits to love. Even Conor's.

Alec turned on the faucet and sluiced water on his face. Sydney thought he needed to meet with Travis, face the past. Geena had always made the same mistake, blaming stuff on his parents. Some weird theory about Daisey taking drugs when she was pregnant so that Alec hadn't developed a conscience. The problem was, he had a conscience. A big fat pain-in-the-ass one.

Alec figured all along he'd been this big fraud— living with Geena and Conor, going to the Air Force Academy, becoming a pilot . . . following in Conor's heroic footsteps. Acting as if he could be just like Conor. The whole time knowing, *if Conor ever finds out the truth about me* . . .

There was this clock inside his head. Life became not so much *if* Conor found out what a fuckup he was, but *when*. Geena had gone on to have this great life, one of the first women to fly an F-14, finding Marc, her husband, opening the flight school with Conor. Conor had walked his own yellow brick road to success. He'd earned his doctorate, became a test pilot, gunning for the astronaut corps. While Alec kept hearing that damn clock.

That's when he'd started looking for shortcuts. He planned to get everything he could out of life before the clock went off and Conor found out what a fraud he was. And there was Russell Reck, helping him down his path to hell.

Sydney thought you faced your past and you went on. But Alec knew better. Some things you could never forget . . . you could never forgive.

Alec heard the sound of a starter pistol fired off in

the kitchen. *The computer.* Letting him know it was time to check his program. He dried his face with a towel, coming back to time present. When he'd played with the idea of redemption, he started kicking around the possibility of his aviation program. He'd been working for Sydney then as her bodyguard. But after hours he'd logged on the computer.

Software to save lives. Now that wasn't going anywhere. The way Alec saw it, there was only one thing left for him to do before getting out of Dodge. Save Sydney's ass.

He pulled the computer up to him on the table, stretched his shoulder. Any minute now, the ibuprofen should kick in. The starter pistol was an alarm he'd set to let him know the program he'd been running had finished its task. After Reck called him with the job offer, Alec had traced down any search conducted on one James Flint.

The program he'd devised was fairly ingenious. It's what Alec did best, computers. The Web server kept track of all TCP/IP numbers, the number that identified who contacted the different Web sites he'd set up to give information on Flint.

"Lazy son of a bitch," he said, seeing that the TCP/IP number indeed belonged to Reck Enterprises. They hadn't even bothered to hide their tracks, making it too easy. He doubted whoever Reck had put on the investigation would dig any deeper than the basic background information Alec had fed them.

Through the Web references Alec established, Reck would uncover James Flint's history. The guy had lost five jobs in four years. Like so many others, he tried to go it alone with an Internet company, only to fold. Too eager—no follow-through. Flint was all about attitude. The kind of personality most people couldn't harness.

Reck would love the challenge.

Alec thought about *The Time Machine,* how H. G. Wells had argued that machines would make men soft, stopping evolution in its tracks until the human race became either machines or cattle to fuel the machines. Like Reck. He'd let the machine do the work, making sure he didn't need to put in any leg-work.

Alec saw it differently. To him, the Internet was the great frontier. Like the Wild West before it, the Net was a place where anything and everything was possible.

Maybe Syd has a thing for computer jockeys, he thought bitterly, sifting through the information on the screen. Because Jack Bosse was just as hardwired for the elec-tronic age. Kinda pissed Alec off, really. Like Sydney had gone out and found her own brave new Alec. One without the flaws. Only, Sydney hadn't figured out that she'd just fallen for the improved model.

Not that any of that mattered. He and Syd weren't going to happen. Not like he'd dreamed when he'd convinced himself that even he deserved a second chance.

The thing was, Alec had pushed the limit—he'd gone beyond the point of no return. Like with Conor. *Some things you can never forgive.*

Alec stared at the computer screen. He told himself he would do this one thing, keep her safe, then, *ding!* Time to move on.

Before it all blew up in his face.

THIRTEEN

Jack stared at the walls of his office, than sank into his chair, head back, eyes on the ceiling. The plaster subtly changed, becoming a giant white screen, a backdrop for the image stuck in his head. Sydney's face.

Charlie knew. She tried to warn me. She knew not to use those paints.

That was the worst of it, seeing Sydney's pain so clearly. If only she'd listened to Charlene. Artists were very intuitive. Charlie hadn't been able to articulate the why of it, just that she knew something was wrong.

And now they had another potential lawsuit on their hands.

Thankfully, the toxic levels of lead in the white paint had only irritated the little boy's skin. They'd been able to administer an antidote before any permanent damage set in. Only the one bottle had been tainted. No one else had been hurt.

Jack stood, walking around the room. First that asshole Porter, then Sydney's ex crashes in for a landing. Now some freak accident with one of the workshops?

And as if that weren't enough to keep him in Maalox, enter Rocky Reck.

He dropped back into his chair, remembering her sitting there across from him. In all these months of antics and machinations from that kid, it had never occurred to him that she might actually have feelings for him.

Another happy ending courtesy of true love.

She'd sounded like she was a hundred years old when she'd said it.

Jack could never understand people who purposely messed up their lives. Hey, it was hard enough just making all the pieces fit so that you and yours were taken care of. For him, the day-to-day grind was the excitement. The real challenge, finding happiness. Jack's pot of gold at the end of the rainbow had always been a woman who loved him, even if he left his Jockey shorts on the bathroom floor or lost every single strand of hair on his head. A soulmate, kids . . . that was his dream.

My mother's been married four times. My father, three.

There hadn't been a lot of complications in Jack's life. Not like in Rocky's. He had perfectly normal parents who loved him. A kid brother he adored. But he'd had friends over the years, in high school and college. Friends who cheated on wives or left lucrative professions—just because they couldn't stand the thought of an ordinary life. Like it was a curse. They needed to complicate things. They thrived on the drama.

He couldn't imagine that Rocky's life had ever approached ordinary.

What surprised him most was how vulnerable she'd been. He hadn't expected it. Even her name sounded tough. And there she'd sat with her damn Chinese food, watching him, spilling all her silly truths. *Why should Sydney love me . . .*

And what she'd left unsaid—*why should anyone?*

Sydney had told him you couldn't just look at someone, add up their attributes, and determine to love them. Love wasn't a math problem. Common goals and interests didn't ignite passion. It was supposed to be like in the books. Spontaneous combustion.

Better to do something crazy and just go for it. See someone you want and damn the consequences.

Like Rocky. He could take her up on what she had offered. Even if Sydney didn't want him anymore, Rocky did.

He reached for the phone, about to call her office, then slammed the receiver back into the cradle.

"What the hell am I doing?"

Then he would be just like all those people, looking for trouble. Finding it.

He stood and grabbed his briefcase. He jammed the first files he could find inside. The damn thing was, he wasn't perfect. That day in the copy room. Yeah. He'd almost crossed the line.

He closed the briefcase, not really sure what he'd packed. Probably enough to keep him busy for another night of takeout with Ethel and Fred, his dogs, for company. He didn't need the complications Rocky offered. The comfort part—the adoration he'd seen in her eyes—it came with a big fat price tag.

And there was still Sydney to consider. She needed

him. Maybe on the sidelines, but still it was something. And when it all blew up, when the drama of her pilot crashed and burned, Jack planned to be there. He'd help her pick up the pieces, just like he did today with the Picasso workshop.

He locked the door behind him, pocketed the keys, heading out. He was just a regular guy looking to help the woman he loved. He should focus on that. Sydney. Forget Rocky and what he'd felt in that copy room.

Give me the good old ordinary, he told himself. These days, it was more than enough.

Russell Reck had been thinking a lot about his daughter lately. Rocky made it a simple thing to do, always reaching out to him, calling . . . checking up. Sometimes she would send a special e-mail or article she thought he might enjoy.

Given the chance, Sydney would stab him through the heart. But Rocky . . .

Daddy, if you want me to spy for you, I will. Oh, yes. That would come.

In so many ways, she reminded Russell of himself. Smart, good-looking . . . as well as dissatisfied with life. Rocky wanted more than she had, just like her father. He knew he could help her tame her sense of frustration. Help her to enjoy her triumphs in a way he never had.

To Russell, he had this one daughter. The others were a complete and utter waste of DNA.

That's why sitting across from her now, it concerned him, what he saw. His perfect daughter, very dissatisfied. Apparently, with him.

"I don't want you to think that I need you to spy for me, Rocky. My priority is you. But your stepmother said the wildest things to me over lunch. I'm not sure if the last year hasn't affected her. And I'm concerned."

Rocky had called him from the office and they'd agreed to meet at the Four Seasons for a drink. She sounded upset and a little strange. Things hadn't gotten any warmer with the margarita she'd ordered.

"Rocky?"

She looked up. He could see she hadn't heard a word he'd said.

"Honey? Are you all right?"

She blinked, slowly and thoughtfully, the look on her face a warning.

She said, "I was thinking about what happened at the museum with that little boy. The lead in the paint. Daddy, you didn't have anything to do with that, did you?"

He kept his smile. "What are you talking about?"

"I wouldn't ask, it's just that—you always wanted to know about the exhibits. What was coming up, the workshops to follow. You asked me for a copy of the catalog, hot off the press. You seemed so desperate to know every detail—"

"Rocky, stop. . . ." He let the words trail off, as if it were difficult to go on. "I know I went to jail. I know that I . . . accepted a plea bargain. Sometimes we do what is expedient." He leaned forward, his body language saying: *Don't lose faith in me.* "I made some mistakes. I hope to God they weren't enough to make you think I'm capable of hurting a child."

She picked up her drink. "I'm sorry. You're right. That was awful of me. It's just that things have been so crazy."

"Honey. It's all right. It's normal to have doubts."

"No. You're wrong. I never should have said those things. Especially about the fiasco with the paint. And please don't worry about asking me questions. I don't mind keeping you up-to-date. I know I'm not spying, and even if I were, I told you I didn't care."

"I just don't want you to do anything that makes you feel uncomfortable."

He stabbed at the olive in his martini. Of course he wanted to know everything that was going on. So far the information she'd provided had been invaluable. But he needed more from his daughter. Much more.

He noticed she hadn't touched her drink. "You look like you've lost weight. Are you eating?"

"I had Chinese for lunch."

"And why is that funny?"

"You had to be there. Daddy, you're worried about Sydney, right? You think she's slipped over the edge . . . gone crackers . . . a fry short of a Happy Meal. Even if you're right, what could I possibly do about it?"

"I didn't say she was crazy. . . ." He let his voice falter.

He'd had a long time to think about what he wanted. *Over a year in jail.* He'd decided to give Sydney a chance. A choice. Well, she'd made hers, throwing everything he'd offered in his face. Now it was his move.

"I just think your stepmother is making too many mistakes. Like the incident in the workshop, for which, I'm afraid, she carries the ultimate responsibility. It did happen under her watch, Rocky. Now you tell me she's broken off this impromptu marriage? It's erratic. Do you think she might have a problem?"

"Sydney's all there, trust me." She licked some of the salt off the rim of her margarita. "Why do you call her that? My stepmother." She made a face. "She's really not, you know. Not any more than Megan."

"Megan and I had children. Sydney"—he shrugged—"she always wanted children. Wanted me to reverse my vasectomy . . . and I refused. I think that's part of the reason she left me—"

"She left you because she thinks you offed her first husband."

He stared at her, nonplussed. For many months now, Rocky had been his constant champion, erasing the years of insolence he'd put up with before then. Suddenly—the look in her eyes, her tone—those years came rushing back.

But he knew not to get angry. That wouldn't help. Anger wouldn't serve his purposes.

He smiled. "I could have put it better."

"God, I'm sorry, Daddy." She pushed away her drink, shaking her head. "I shouldn't have come. I'm in a lousy mood and I'm taking it out on you."

He placed his hand on hers. "Just get some sleep. And eat. I don't want to worry about you too. What happened that has you so on edge?"

"I just screwed up on something. Badly. At work."

"And here I am, going on about Sydney. I didn't mean to ignore you—"

"You didn't. And I don't want to talk about what happened. I want to forget. So what's next? You still need me to push this contract between Reck Enterprises and the gallery? Because I'll tell you now, I think it's a lost cause."

"I can't say you're wrong." Because he could see it wasn't the right time to push. "Just be happy, okay? Take it a day at a time. Listen to me." He laughed. "I sound like one of those calendars when you rip off the page and see what wisdom the next day brings."

She laughed with him, making it better. He could see that it was going to be okay. Rocky was still his little girl.

"I guess that's what jail does to you," he said. "Too much time on my hands to read self-help books." He glanced at his watch. "I have to go. But thanks for coming. This was nice."

"But I thought we could have dinner?"

"I'm sorry. I made plans." He was standing, searching the room. He saw Angela walking toward him and smiled. "And there she is."

Rocky turned around so that she could see Angela. She looked absolutely stunning in a little black dress that managed to be both sexy and classy. After he'd asked her out, everything had fallen into place in his head. He had his plans for Sydney, yes. But that didn't mean he had to be alone.

"I just met her today. She's an actress. What do you think? Too young for the old man?"

He couldn't see Rocky's face. But he didn't need to. Angela was perfection. They had agreed to meet at the Four Seasons for a drink before dinner.

"Of course not." Rocky turned back around, but the smile didn't quite reach her eyes. "I just wonder if she's good enough for you."

He smiled, realizing she still wanted her daddy all to herself. "How about a rain check on that dinner?"

"Sure, Daddy." She stood to give him a hug. As he stepped away, she added, "I know you're concerned about Sydney, though sometimes I wonder why. The way she treated you."

That's my girl. "How about dinner tomorrow?"

"My apartment. I'll make your favorite. *Sarsuela.*"

He came in close, giving her a kiss on the cheek. "You make me happy, you know that? You're all I have now."

He smiled, making his way toward his charming date for the evening, knowing that Rocky loved him.

For now it was enough.

Rocky watched her father walk away. He met up with a tall blonde. The actress. As Rocky watched, he kissed her hand. Very romantic.

She sat down, frowning. Suddenly a margarita sounded like a great idea. She picked up her glass, drinking half in one swallow, freezing the top of her mouth.

She felt utterly alone. And confused.

Jack. Her father.

You're all I have, he'd told her.

"Yeah, right," she said, watching him leave the bar with another woman.

FOURTEEN

Sydney struggled with her keys, trying to keep a grip on her sanity as well as on the half-dozen folders tucked under her arm. She'd just come from the hospital, where she'd been told the little boy who'd been poisoned by the paint had gone home, discharged in good health. Though she hadn't been able to see him or speak to his parents, the news came as a huge relief. She and Jack had a meeting set for the weekend with the little boy's parents.

She'd given Jack her opinion. Whatever it took to make this right—even shutting down the workshops—the art center would comply. Jack's opinion: You can't make these kinds of decisions based on emotion. He'd pointed out similar instances. Crayons shipped from abroad with toxic levels of lead used at a local school. News reports of asbestos in major brands. *These things happen,* he'd said.

Not on my watch, she told herself.

The door lock clicked open. As if the sound were some sort of release, a shadow sprung toward her— a spectral jack-in-the-box zooming into her field of vision. Folders rained to the floor as she swung around, her can of pepper spray directed at her attacker's eyes.

"Don't shoot." Alec held up his hands, then nodded at the papers scattered across the floor. "All work and no play makes Sydney a dull girl."

"Alec." Sydney dropped the hand holding the pepper spray. "What are you doing here?"

He knelt beside her as she bent down to pick up the folders. He didn't offer to help. Instead, he lifted her face to his, focusing on her mouth in a near-perfect movie moment.

"You think you can just kiss me like you did the other day and walk away?"

She shook him off, snatching up the papers. "In a word? Yes." She didn't want this conversation. Not now, not when she felt so vulnerable. "And I believe *away* is the operative word."

"Well, I came by to tell you that I will not let you use me anymore, Syd. You can't have my body, then toss me like garbage, just for the hot sex." Standing with her, he seemed to think about that. "Well, okay—maybe you can use me for hot sex. If you insist. But I have a request."

Like magic, he pulled out a leopard-print thong from inside his coat. *Abracadabra.*

She recognized the underwear immediately as her own.

He smiled, all sweet innocence. "If you're going to have your way with me, will you wear these?"

She lunged for the underwear. Alec danced away, keeping them just out of reach.

"Ah-ah. You didn't say the magic word."

"I will cut out your heart and feed it to you in pieces if you don't give me those this instant!"

"That will do," he said.

She grabbed the thong and stuffed it into one of the folders. But she couldn't help a small smile. "How did you get these?"

"Actually, I wanted to talk to you about that. Where'd you find those yahoos you hired? I didn't even disturb their nap going in and taking these."

But the last thing on her mind was any threat to her. She'd spent the last week juggling work with her attempts to neutralize Russell's plans for her. The normalcy she'd struggled to find the last year vanished, missing in action courtesy of a man they once called The Wrecker. She'd been distracted, the disaster at the Picasso workshop, the result.

She mashed the underwear deeper into the folder. "I thought I'd thrown these away."

"Third drawer down, buried under an insignificant pair of gym shorts." He winked, pushing open the front door, ready to step inside after her. "I have a discerning eye. It's a talent."

She put her arm across the doorjamb, stopping him from crossing the threshold. She took a moment to evaluate Alec's magical appearance at her door, complete with disappearing underwear. "I am so not buying this. Why did you really come?"

"I miss your coffee?"

"Nescafé instant. I buy it at the grocery store. The one with the label in Spanish. It has a richer flavor. Try again."

The grin he gave her shot right through her heart. There were so many things to love about Alec, most of all his little-boy smiles. He was thirty-four years old but could pass for any age over twenty. When they'd first met, she'd made that mistake, thinking he was quite a bit younger. It wasn't so much his face as his attitude that made him such a chameleon. To Alec, life was a game—he lived it a day at a time, pedal to the metal. And he liked to have fun, preferably at someone else's expense.

"I heard about the kid," he said.

She couldn't understand her sudden embarrassment, how it flared through her in a flush of heat. As if Alec would ever judge her.

"I screwed up," she told him, chin up. "Are you here to give me a shoulder to cry on?"

"I had a little different scenario in mind." He stepped around her, telling it like a story. "Of course, I can't prove anything, but that paint. How it got there." He *tched* softly, coming to a stop directly behind her, whispering in her ear, "Just think about who might have left it on your doorstep, a tiny Trojan horse."

"Are you talking about sabotage?"

"Let me guess. The paint came from a different supplier? Out of the blue?"

Incredibly, she hadn't thought of it. The possibility that the paint was no mere accident. That Russell could be involved.

"It bears consideration," he told her.

Russell Reck was a murderer, that much she knew. It didn't matter that the prosecutor hadn't followed through on the charges—that she couldn't prove Russell had known all along that the plane would go down with Henry on board. He'd killed Henry. He as much as admitted it to her the night she'd called the FBI.

Since he'd made his plea deal, she had spent every waking hour trying to find his smoking gun, something concrete that Russell's Dream Team couldn't keep from a jury. Hard evidence that might entice the prosecutor to revisit the murder charges that were dropped.

In the meantime, Russell had her looking over her shoulder.

"It doesn't matter," she told Alec. "He couldn't have hurt me if I'd been more vigilant. I won't make that mistake again."

"Oh, yeah. You're on it."

She tried to walk around him, the idea being to put a solid door between them. Alec, of course, was way ahead of her. This time it was his arm braced across the threshold.

"Okay, I'll stop. In any case, I didn't come here to talk about Russell. Look, I was hoping for a little warm-up act before I launched into this one," he said, "but have it your way."

He leaned up against the entry and crossed his arms, pushing one foot against the wall for balance, a perfect James Dean imitation.

"As it so happens, I wanted to let you know that you're wrong," he said.

"About so many things. Which might this concern tonight?"

"Your little fairy tale. About me and my missing family. Somehow, you got in your head that I call up this Travis guy, meet my long-lost brother, and we do a scene from the movie of the week. Then I'm fixed.

Ready for marriage and the many responsibilities thereof."

He pushed away from the wall, crowding her up against the door.

"The problem is, Syd, I ain't broke. There's nothing to fix. The way I've lived my life, those were my decisions. It wasn't about some tortured past haunting me—there are no ghosts stuck in my head. So I chose not to plan for some mysterious future with a mortgage and 401k plan? So what? I don't see a goddamn thing wrong with my way."

"You came all the way here to tell me that?"

His hands traveled up her spine, a dance. She could feel her breath coming rough. When his fingers reached her neck, she tried to keep herself still, not to respond.

"Everything isn't about the happily-ever-after," he whispered. "It can be about having some fun along the way."

"You know what I think?" she said. "I think you're scared."

His face gave nothing away, granting only his familiar naughty grin. "Oh, sweetie. Right now? I'm not the one who's scared."

His mouth brushed the skin behind her ear. His hand slipped behind her back, then snapped her up close so that she was pressed against him.

"Why can't it be about one night, or one month, or one year? You turned your back on me and hooked up with Jack for some made-up shit he stuck in your head about forever. Fuck forever."

His mouth came up along her cheek. She could feel his breath on her mouth. Alec was good at this. Alec was A-number-one professional at the seduction game. Right now he was giving it one hundred and ten percent.

"You think something can last just because you sign a piece of paper?"

She closed her eyes. "You would really do this to me, Alec? Seduce me into breaking my engagement to Jack? Let me wake up tomorrow knowing that I'd betrayed a man who loves me?"

"Is that a trick question?" He kissed the corner of her mouth. "In a heartbeat."

"What a prince you are." She looked up, giving a smile of her own. "As it so happens, you're too late."

Even in the semidark she saw his eyes widen. They were standing apart, no longer touching, but she sensed how the very air pulsed around him.

"Jack and I broke it off. Last week." She waited, watching him. "Now who's scared, Alec?"

"The demise of Jerkface is supposed to worry me? And that would be how?"

"Now it's no longer a theory we're tossing around, this thing between us. I'm a free woman. Again. Free to commit. As in no longer a challenge?"

He grinned. "And you think that scares me?"

"Into the next state, I'm guessing."

He shook his head. In the light, he looked young with his dyed hair and knee-length leather coat. As if anyone else could carry off such an outfit. Alec did it with style.

But there was also something in his expression, a knowledge that told her here was a man who'd seen too much. It wasn't often that Alec became serious. Watching her now, he looked like a man who'd been born old.

He told her, "Poor Sydney. You think you want

me gone? You don't need me watching your back, because, heck—you have the amazing yellow pages to guide you, which sure as hell is where you found those idiots you hired." He came in close, talking fast. "But what if deep down inside, what you really need in your life is exactly me? Just screwed-up Alec."

He circled around, coming to a stop just on the other side, one foot on the steps that led down the walkway. "What if one day you turn around and I'm not there ready to save your butt? I wonder what you'd do then." He let the words sink in, smiling gently. "Think about that the next time you tell me to disappear."

She closed her eyes, listening to his steps on the sidewalk. She tried so hard to keep quiet.

Only she couldn't. "I'm supposed to forget everything that happened? Just walk right back into your arms? Never learn from my mistakes?"

One hand jammed into the pocket of his jacket, he said, "Oh, right. The broken-heart thing." He shook his head, as if just coming to some realization. "Fuck me, I forgot. But then, I guess I wouldn't be thinking about something like that. We all know I don't have a heart."

This time she clenched her teeth against the words to call him back. *You have to be strong, girl . . . you have to be smart.*

Let him walk away. It really didn't matter. They both knew he'd won this round.

She opened the door and forced herself to walk inside. But it made her sad, his parting jibe. It said too much. *We all know I don't have a heart.*

When he'd made love to her that night so long ago,

the only thing she could hear was his heart pounding against hers.

She sighed, feeling empty and confused. As if it weren't enough that Russell might try to kill her—that he might in fact have sabotaged the workshop—she had Alec Never-Say-Die on her case.

She looked down at the folders she carried cradled in her arms, wishing now more than ever that the only thing she needed to worry about was Russell Reck.

That's when she noticed that the underwear she'd stuffed inside the folder was missing.

Somehow, Alec must have taken it with him when he left.

FIFTEEN

Driving home, Jack Bosse knew he was way too tired for a guy who had his whole life ahead of him.

He was tired of bringing work home. Bored with his empty house and takeout food. Exhausted to his bones by the gallery and worrying about Sydney 24/7.

But most of all, he was sick of feeling so goddamn sorry for himself.

Tonight, before leaving the gallery, he'd almost called his parents, thinking he'd drop by, beg Mom to have mercy on him and cook him dinner. He could play a game of basketball with his nephew, Kyle. The kid was working on that hook shot.

Only, his parents would ask about Sydney. And he'd have to tell them the truth. That the wedding was off . . . something he didn't look forward to revealing. A week had passed since he and Sydney had reached their understanding. *You'll have to tell them the truth sometime.*

It wasn't so much their disappointment he avoided. Brian had fulfilled the obligation of a grandchild long before anybody was ready to play that role. But his parents would worry about his happiness. Because he'd wanted Sydney so badly.

Tonight he told himself to settle for his empty house. He would turn on the television for background noise, listen to the conversation and laughter of actors. He'd go over the reports he'd brought home; he'd order pizza. The new pattern to his days came like a kid's song . . . *We all fall down.*

Crossing over the main channel, the lights dancing off the black water like fireflies, he headed toward the gated entrance to the island where he lived. *Maybe I should take a cooking class.* Something interesting, like Know Thy Wok. The way things were shaking out, he was on his own for a good long time.

It was funny how he'd always thought he'd be married by now. Part of the "great plan" Sydney accused him of keeping. And maybe she had a point . . . maybe he had been a little too focused on Mrs. Right. He sure as hell thought he'd found her.

But the truth was, he and Sydney had never had the smooth going he'd imagined. All along he'd known he was holding on by a thread. And what happened in that copy room with Rocky . . . maybe that proved Sydney right. Correction. What *almost* happened.

But he had to admit the experience had been too intense. Certainly not the actions of a man in love with his fiancée.

Jack pulled up to the security gate, his mood growing worse by the minute as he mulled over the possibilities. He was about to wave to the guard inside the kiosk and drive on, when someone stepped out right in front of the headlights of his Ford Expedition.

"Shit!" He slammed on his brakes.

Unbelievably, Rocky Reck stood spotlighted in the low beams.

She was dressed in a short dress and sandals, the pink fabric clinging against her thighs in the breeze. Her fabulous hair flowed behind her, clipped in a ponytail. She looked too young for the dark red lipstick, her only makeup.

An adrenaline rush of blood pumped into his head as he watched her walk past the headlights to the side of his car. She came up to his window and tapped on the glass. He realized he hadn't moved since he'd almost run her over. Probably hadn't even taken a breath.

He rolled down the window, letting in the warm summer's night. Rocky stood on the running board and leaned both elbows on the window; the smell of bluebells deliciously followed. Jack gestured back the security guard before he could intervene.

"Can I get in?" she asked. And when he hesitated, she said, "I want to talk to you about what happened today. In your office."

He thought about how to respond. *Bad idea, kid.* For sure, he shouldn't be alone with her. Certainly, not now, with the memory of what he'd seen in her eyes at lunch. Better to ease out of a tricky situation and tell her to go home.

Only, after today, what he really felt like saying was *Why the hell not?* Tempting fate.

"I figured you wouldn't be too busy after hours," she said. Then, rubbing it in, she added, "Not since Princess Sydney moved on."

"Oh, sure. My schedule is clear."

Rocky was a beautiful woman. That fact was something he'd tried to keep in perspective by focusing on his relationship with Sydney. But tonight he felt worn down, certainly not inclined to be a gentleman. He allowed his eyes to drop to her breasts molded by the dress; her amazing blond hair.

If he took her home, she would be nothing but trouble.

We all fall down. . . .

Jack reached over and opened the passenger door. "Get in."

He must have asked himself fifty times what the hell he was doing before they reached his house. Jack Bosse took calculated risks. He didn't screw up. He researched the problem, came at it with logic. He stayed clear of trouble. *Hell, things are complicated enough.*

At the very least, he should turn around and take her someplace public, a sports bar or a café. Nothing felt right in his head; tonight, he could make a mistake.

But when he pulled up the driveway and turned off the engine, he knew he wasn't going to do any of those things. *This was a test . . . a test of character.* In thirty-four years he'd never lost one of those.

She hadn't said a word. She was dressed to kill but, he could see, nervous. He smiled. *Good.* He hoped he scared the shit out of her.

He grabbed his computer bag from the backseat. "Wait at the door until I can introduce you to the gang." He reached across her lap and pushed open her door.

The gang was his two Rhodesian Ridgebacks. He

had them lined up and somewhat calm before he let her inside.

"Meet Fred and Ethel."

She stepped closer but stayed behind him. "Are they okay?"

"Fierce-looking, aren't they? They were bred to hunt lions. They work in teams, three females and a male. The females keep the lion at bay while the male sneaks up from behind and attacks, trying to break the lion's leg, incapacitate him before the hunters arrive. They are fearless."

Actually, Fred and Ethel were a pair of hundred-pound pussycats. If Gail, his housekeeper, didn't walk them twice a day, they'd spend their lives perpetually stretched out on the sofa and love seat, snoring. Not that they couldn't serve their purpose as guard dogs. But Ridgebacks were smart. Once Jack let them know someone was okay, the only threat was getting jumped on and licked to death.

"Come here." He took her hand in his, holding her by his side, letting his dogs know this was an invited guest. Rocky's fingers tightened around his. They trembled. He waited a lot longer than necessary before he said, "Now hold out your hand, your fingers curled under, so they can smell you."

She did so, slowly. He wasn't watching the dogs.

There weren't going to be a lot of times like this with Rocky Reck—when he'd know exactly what she was thinking and feeling.

"Okay," he said softly, releasing the dogs.

The next thing he knew, they were all over her, tails wagging with enough strength to clear a coffee table. Even though Fred probably outweighed Rocky, she dropped down in front of him, fearless, laughing as she allowed the dogs to lick her face.

"I always wanted a dog," she said. "My mother hated animals. No pets allowed."

He whistled. The dogs immediately lined up on either side of him.

Rocky stayed kneeling on the floor. He told himself she was twenty-eight, not that much younger than him. She could take care of herself.

"Wow," she said, standing. "I'm impressed. You have them well trained."

"Sometimes. They're hounds. Independent thinkers. You have to earn their respect, and they test you constantly. I always take it as a compliment when they do listen. Come on."

He led her into the kitchen, letting the dogs out on the way. He opened the refrigerator as she sat down at the butcher-block island in the middle of the room.

"I have wine, beer, soda." He stood back, letting her see inside. "Pick your poison."

She actually looked shy, staring around him at the fridge. She pointed to the bottle of chardonnay. He felt his stomach clench. He'd bought the bottle for Sydney, who knew a hell of a lot more about wine than he ever would. Part of her history as the ex-society lady. He grabbed a Corona for himself and poured Rocky a glass of wine, coming up to sit beside her on the other stool.

"So what's up?" he asked, drinking from the bottle.

She was turning the glass on the butcher block. "Nice place."

"I like it."

"Kinda small though. I mean, for a bazillionaire."

"You think?"

He took another drink, not filling in the blanks. Yeah, he had money, but nowhere near the kind of cash this little princess would be used to as the daughter of Russell Reck. Bazillionaire. Right. Everybody thought dotcom guys like him had barrels of it.

The truth: Sure, Jack was well off, and he had worked damn hard for every penny. The first thing he'd done was make certain he'd never have to work another day in his life if he didn't want to. Neither would his parents, or his brother and nephew. After that, he figured whatever was left over should do some good in the world. Like the art center.

"I think," she told him, staring at the glass, "you know why I'm here. I think I made it obvious today. At lunch."

"Really?" He thought about it, then figured, no, he wouldn't make this any easier for her. "So you want to apologize for your behavior all these months?"

She smiled and took a sip of the wine. "Not even close."

She was cute when she smiled like that. If he was honest, he'd admit there were a lot of amazing things about Rocky. But that's not what he wanted this to be about.

"It could be a start," he said. "An apology."

"I'm not sorry."

He tried to hold back his grin by taking another drink from the bottle. Maybe it was time for a change of subject.

"Rocky. What kind of name is that?"

"A nickname. From school."

"And the real name is? I'm hearing a drum-roll. . . ."

"Petroula." She made a face. "Derived from the Greek word *petros*, meaning 'rock.' Hence, the nickname."

"Ouch."

"Exactly."

"All right." He put down the beer. "Putting up with Petroula made you tough. But what made you a troublemaker?"

She shrugged. "Daughter number three? I guess I wanted the attention. By the time I was born, Daddy was already cheating on Mom, and she was absolutely bored with the whole kid thing. She probably wouldn't have recognized me in a lineup."

"Well, boo-hoo."

"It's not an excuse. I don't feel sorry for myself, Jack." But the smile returned. "Maybe it's just in my genes to be bad?"

He stared at her for a good long while. She had pretty eyes and one of those mouths that looked like a cupid's bow. She was classy in a blond-bombshell sort of way. Really, you'd never expect half the trash that came out of that mouth.

"What about you? Any brothers or sisters to mar up the picture?" she asked. "Studies show most millionaires are firstborn or only children."

"Guilty as charged. I have a younger brother. He took your exalted route."

"The troublemaker to your goody-goody?"

"That's one way to put it. Luckily, he's getting his act together. He and his son live with my parents."

"You have a nephew?" Suddenly her eyes lit up. "They're the best, aren't they? Somebody else does all the work and you get only the fun parts. I'm the marvelous Aunt Rocky to my sister's kids."

Her face practically glowed with the news. It surprised him that she liked kids. They took a lot of patience, even at the best of times.

"Aunt Rocky? Now, why does that make me want to break out into"—in his best Boris Badinoff impression—"we must rid the world of Moose and Squirrel."

She gave him the sexiest look ever, her eyes sweeping up slowly with her waking smile, so that he felt that look deep in his gut. "I get that a lot."

It took him a while to catch his breath. Not a good sign, he figured. He remembered the incident in the copy room, when everything disconnected in his brain and all he could think about was her mouth, those eyes. *Don't go there, guy.*

"So now you're here." He finished his beer even though she had barely touched her wine. "And I'm supposed to know the mysterious why of it?"

"How about this, then: I am sorry I acted like a schoolgirl with her first crush," she said. "I was a jerk to you these past months. You know, I really did think it was about Sydney. Until today I hadn't realized it was about us."

"Us?" He nodded as if he understood . . . when it was all so crazy, he couldn't believe they were having the conversation. "Now it's us?"

"Like I told you. I made it obvious."

"Honey, you weren't that obvious."

"Honestly, I even tried to convince myself you were gay."

Maybe that was the best part about Rocky, he thought. Just when you thought you knew what was coming next, a surprise.

"Maybe it's the glasses," she said, reaching to take off his Armani frames and putting them on the butcher block. "Or the clothes. You realize you do have that well-tailored look."

Without his glasses the world became a nice blur. *Just a dream, guy.* "You know something, Rocky? You're a trip. And I think you get a kick out of that."

"You don't have to worry, you know. I'm not going to do anything you don't want to do."

He thought about that a minute, decided then and there to put a stop to her game. Hell, he'd had more than enough. He picked up his glasses and put them on. Or maybe he just couldn't trust himself to go any further.

"Honey, the only thing that worries me? That you're here to cause trouble. Pure and simple. Maybe you think it would be cool to sleep with the guy who was engaged to your stepmother, which is so frigging weird, I can't go there. Or maybe you think you can get me to lean on her to sign that contract with Reck Enterprises, which is more likely, and which—by the way—I would never do. What worries me, Rocky girl, is that you are so screwed up—"

"That you'll catch it, like a disease?"

"No." He looked her dead-on. "No. I won't." Meaning something altogether different.

She stood up. "What if it's not about any of those things, Jack?" She reached behind her for the zipper of her dress. "What if it's just about sex?"

No. I won't. Those words, so definite. Without nuance. But they were only words, and Jack, he stayed right where he was, watching as she pulled the zipper slowly down her back.

"That would be a very bad idea," he told her, again using only words.

Of course, she paid no attention, continuing to

unzip the dress. He realized he'd misjudged every-thing. Bringing her here, letting this happen.

Rocky held the dress up against her breasts with her hands. "She's gone, Jack. She's not coming back. So where does that leave you? Pining away, all by your lonesome?"

He and Sydney had never slept together. Oh, he'd tried, but Sydney . . . she hadn't been ready. In the end, he'd chalked it up to her bad history with men. He'd taken it slow—too slow as it turned out.

Now he wondered if all along Sydney hadn't guessed where they'd end up. She'd left herself a graceful exit.

It had been a very long time since he'd slept with a woman.

"I have been wrong about so many things." She dropped her hands, letting the dress pool to the floor. "Please, Jack. Don't let me be wrong about this."

Watching her, he kept thinking he'd never done anything like what was happening now. He wasn't this man, sitting there, tempting disaster. Begging for it.

Rocky stood in front of him wearing only her under-wear, a sexy bra with matching panties. Victoria's Secret couldn't have asked for better on their cover.

He looked away. When he'd driven her here, he'd thought he was in control. *A test of character.* He wasn't one of those guys looking to complicate his life. He believed he could handle what was going on between them.

But maybe it had been just an excuse. Maybe, all along he'd known where this was heading. That he couldn't bear another night of pizza with only Fred and Ethel for company.

"Jack?"

He pushed the beer bottle aside and stood. It took two steps to reach her. The first thing he did was pull her hair out of the ponytail and watch it slide down her back.

"It doesn't have to be more than this." Her eyes looked so desperate. "Just two lonely people comforting each other. When I go home, there's no one waiting for me either. Just tonight, okay? I'll leave you alone—"

"Shut up," he told her, grabbing her face in his hands, crushing her mouth against his.

Russell rose up from the bed, naked. He looked at the woman half covered by the sheets. She was model-thin and very pale. *Like Sydney.* He didn't like tanned women. Too many wrinkles. He'd always enjoyed the feel of smooth skin against his.

They'd had a great night together. Angela had taken him to a new place specializing in French Polynesian food, then to the Rhino Room for dancing. It was a young crowd, so he'd kept to the sidelines, letting her do the dancing. But it was nice, watching her. An appetizer for later.

Tonight reminded him of the old days, when Sydney would help him explore new experiences, always trying to surprise him with a treasured find, a well-reviewed restaurant or perhaps a gallery.

He gave Angela a last kiss and watched her smile in her sleep. *I missed this.* Before prison, sex had always been such an important part of his life.

On the way out of the bedroom, he grabbed his robe. He had it on and belted by the time he reached the kitchen. On the table lay the report on James Flint. The research guys were practically frothing at the mouth over the software he offered.

Russ picked up the phone, punching in the number from memory. There had been a time in his life when that report would have been enough. But Russell had learned a few things since then. It paid to go beyond the obvious.

He'd met Sigmund in jail. They'd kept in touch. Sigmund had a reputation. The kind of man you might need in a situation like this.

"I have a job for you," he told the voice on the other end. "And before you ask, I pay extremely well."

After he gave all the information he had on James, Russell went back to bed, carrying a bottle of champagne fresh from the refrigerator. It gave him a great deal of satisfaction to see his plans unfold so smoothly.

Angela woke up with the touch of the icy bottle on her navel. He poured her a drink as she groaned, rolling over to face him.

"Don't you ever sleep?" she asked, opening his robe and snuggling against him.

"I've done enough sleeping."

Amazing how she resembled Sydney, especially now in the dim glow of the recessed lights. He brushed back Angela's hair, wondering what would have happened if he hadn't cheated on Sydney, if perhaps she might have stayed loyal to him when it counted most. But then he thought, *no*. There would always be Henry between them. His death. And Russell knew himself well enough to understand his needs—he wanted more than one woman. Even if Sydney were in his

life, he would always be searching out that new experience, looking for the next Angela.

Kissing her ear, he whispered, "You know, baby,
you would look great as a redhead. Has anyone ever
told you that?"

SIXTEEN

Sydney lay in bed, wondering if she should invest in a new duvet cover. Certainly, French Provincial was nice . . . but those golds and greens, the ubiquitous roses, the unrestrained clumps of grapes. It suddenly appeared too calculated to match the green armoire and wine-colored carpet. Forced. When had she started to play it so safe?

She turned her head. The clock on the nightstand flashed 10:10 P.M. Fifteen minutes since she'd checked last. Only now she was analyzing bedroom decor.

Desperate times.

"Damn you, Alec."

She wasn't going to get any sleep tonight either.

She dressed in jeans and a shirt, telling herself it was still early. Maybe that's what she'd been doing wrong all along. Forcing sleep, getting into bed too early, thinking that she'd wake with the sun and start a brave new day—when in reality she'd spend most of the night tossing and turning, looking at the clock: 10:00 . . . 11:00 . . . midnight. Always remembering the good days when sleep came as she closed her eyes, without pills or clocks or worries about the personal significance of grapes cluttering bedspreads.

On the way out, she grabbed a light sweater, shaking her head when she found the bodyguard she'd hired snoring lightly.

"It's nice that someone's getting a good night's sleep." She walked past. "Maybe I should give Alec a call. Get some names."

Twenty minutes later she was sitting in her favorite late-night spot, Café Zinc in Laguna. Getting her art history degree at Harvard, she always figured that if she stayed up all night, anything she ate didn't count. The calories would melt away with the adrenaline of working her body overtime. Tonight she ordered coffee and a piece of carrot cake. The combination brought on the perfect pitch of sugar and caffeine, guaranteed to get the gallery's catalog proofed in record time.

Forty minutes later she was definitely onto something. These days, work was the best remedy for what ailed her. She wanted more than anything just to choke off this constant anxiety over what would happen next.

At least, she'd worked things out with Jack. He'd been great the last week, letting her know that their relationship was important, even if it didn't lead to marriage. Certainly now, when things were so complicated, she needed friends. Though she worried, too, that he was just telling her what she wanted to hear, sticking with his plan to wait around for the dust to clear.

Unfortunately, there wasn't any ambiguity about her feelings for Alec. That she would get over the bastard was the iffy part. But she knew it had been a mistake to get involved with Jack. She needed to wait for the I'm-*really*-over-Alec day. Alec, her own personal 12-step program.

Getting to that other business, Sydney pulled out a notebook from her bag and flipped past the notes she'd jotted there, remembering Alec's warning. His theory that Russell had somehow sabotaged the Picasso workshop managed to sound both outrageous and dead-on.

She tapped the pencil against the paper where she'd written *transactional immunity* and *breach of plea agreement*. Russell had struck a deal with the prosecutor to testify against Joseph Kinnard, his co-conspirator in the government's fraud case. In exchange, he'd pled guilty to a lesser charge. She wasn't a lawyer; it had taken her weeks to figure out the ramifications—and she was still mulling over the theories that might make it possible to revisit some of the charges against Russell.

She'd talked to a friend; read a few books at the law library. She knew she couldn't afford to jump the gun. Once she had the evidence to nail him, she needed a slam dunk: Russell behind bars, if possible for life.

Sydney packed up her notes and headed into the balmy evening. Rather than go home, she decided to check out some of the galleries. The first Thursday of every month, the sidewalks filled with locals and tourists alike for the Laguna Walk, making it possible to explore galleries even at this late hour.

Sydney felt her heart lift. Here, the bright lights

and friendly streets could bring even the dead to life. The buzz of the coffee had just begun to mellow when she walked out of her second gallery, a tiny place showing a truly gifted artist working with pencil on canvas. She'd jotted down the name, thinking she might come back, perhaps buy a piece.

Ahead of her, a crowd of young men spilled out from a neighboring gallery. Nearing midnight, only a few couples walked here and there, making the group ahead even more conspicuous. Laughing, their arms linked to hold each other up, they were obviously drunk. Sydney ducked her head, going against the current of their solid bodies, one hand on her bag slung over her shoulder, mailman style. She tried to slip past.

"Excuse me," she said, irritated when one man shoved past her, then another pushed her from behind. She felt like a pool ball bouncing off the bumpers. "Hey!"

Someone tugged her purse. She scooped the bag up against her chest, trying to push through the bodies moving in around her, making it impossible to see or to stop. She felt herded, moving almost against her will in a riptide of bodies.

She called out, then tried to elbow her way out. A hand circled around her wrist, jerking her back. She turned, her heart in her throat.

A man, his face a blur, snapped her around. Before she could scream, he grabbed her.

The alley! Dear God, he was dragging her into the dark.

He kept one hand braced around her waist, the other cupped over her mouth. The group of drunks fell back, their job done. The night closed in.

It's happening. Her fears coming true. She tried to dig her heels, kick backward. She clawed at the man's arm and face. She couldn't scream or breathe with his hand over her mouth and nose. She jabbed her elbow back, trying to connect with something—his ribs or stomach.

She felt herself being picked up, her feet leaving the asphalt. At the same time, he stuffed a rag into her mouth, choking her. A chemical smell filled her nose as her body was hurled over the fence. Her sweater snagged, wrenching her arm, a hot pain shooting up it.

She hit wet grass, the breath leaving her lungs in a loud *whoosh* of air. She lay stunned, gagging on the rag, seeing only black sky above, the fumes of some chemical burning her nose. *Move!* But her body wouldn't obey. She was falling, falling . . . Alice tumbling down the rabbit hole.

Sydney reached up, her arm too heavy, moving in slow motion. She touched her lips, feeling numb. Finding the rag still stuffed inside her mouth, she pulled it out like a magic trick, spitting it onto the grass, then, curling in a ball, she gasped for breath.

Fog crept over the ground, a surreal mist exaggerated by her semidrugged state. She groaned, the muscles of her shoulder on fire. She didn't know how long she lay there, hours or minutes, only that a low growl woke her up.

Sydney sat up, realizing she'd been dumped in someone's yard, the hair at the back of her neck rising. The mist off the grass wove in and out, playing games with the dark figure ahead. A man stepped out of the fog so that for the first time she realized a ski mask covered his face. Beside him, an enormous black dog, teeth bared, pulled against the collar he held tight.

Sydney blinked, but the figure remained. She tucked her feet under her, still moving too slow. She reached for her purse, but realized it was strapped over her shoulder.

Before she could stand, the masked man released the dog, whispering his command.

The dog broke through the mist, racing toward her. Sydney stumbled back, groping for some purchase before she fell. *Keep on your feet . . . don't look back!* Running, she could hear the dog coming up fast behind her, gaining on her. Even as she threw herself at the fence ahead, she knew she wouldn't make it.

A blow struck her in the middle of her back. She slid facefirst into the grass, breaking her fall with her elbows. She grabbed her purse as she rolled over, holding the purse in front of her face like a shield. The dog latched onto the sleeve of her sweater, pinning her there on the ground.

She searched wildly through her shoulder bag as teeth snapped for her neck. She seized the small canister inside. Aimed. Pepper spray shot straight into the dog's eyes.

The dog shrieked, rolling off her. Sydney jumped to her feet, hearing the dog's whimpers as she climbed the fence, using only one hand to pull herself up and over. She tumbled back into the alley, rolling to break her fall. Immediately, a loud *thud* hit the fence behind her, followed by feral growls.

Sydney gained her feet and stepped back, staring in almost sick fascination as the fence bowed under the dog's frustrated blows. *Oh, my God!* She turned and stumbled toward the streetlight ahead.

Running, she scrambled around the corner, aiming for the entrance of the nearest gallery. Someone had purposely led her into that dark alley, then dumped her into some yard, where she'd stayed, half drugged, for who knows how long. The man in the mist had been dressed all in black. A ski cap covered his face.

He could have killed her right then and there. Certainly, he'd had his chance. But he'd let her go . . . scaring her with the dog.

Like a game.

A young woman stood at the entrance of the gallery. Hearing Sydney, she turned. One look at Sydney's face and the woman's smile melted.

"Help me," Sydney said. "Call 911."

"I don't have a dog. And neither does anyone else in the neighborhood. Not like the one she's describing."

Half an hour later, Sydney still sitting in the same gallery while the police went over her statement. As it turned out, the young woman who owned the gallery lived in the house abutting the building. The next yard over, where Sydney's nightmare dog had almost ripped out her throat, the fenced-in yard was now conveniently empty. The dog's existence remained a mystery.

"Unless you count Moose." The girl gave Sydney a thoughtful look. "My neighbor owns him. But he's this tiny thing. A Bichon Frise. You know. White and fluffy and cute?"

"Ma'am?" The police officer stepped closer. "Could you at least describe this group of men? Maybe give a fix on one of them?"

Which is what she thought she'd been doing the last twenty minutes. Sydney picked up her purse from the antique desk at the gallery's entrance, beyond frustration. For the first time that evening, she felt anger rather than fear.

"I've made a terrible mistake," she told the officer. "The report—"

"Forget it," she said, waving him off. "Put down that I was drunk, or hallucinating. Whatever."

It took her just a few more minutes to convince the officer and his partner that she was fine. She could drive herself home. Nor did she expect anything to come of her statement. She marched down the steps of the gallery, refusing to look over her shoulder. The police had her name and number. If they wanted anything, they knew where to find her. She'd been wrong to call them in the first place. She shouldn't have given Russell and his henchmen the satisfaction.

According to the property owner, everything she'd told the police was simply impossible. There were no black, ferocious dogs in the neighborhood. No one even heard a dog barking. The group of rowdy frat wannabes turned out to be another figment of her imagination. No one had seen anything, certainly not a group of loud young men.

Whoever had planned the assault had covered his tracks. No dog . . . no man in black . . . even the rag she'd dropped on the grass had disappeared. The only thing left behind was Sydney, shaken up enough to sound like a loon.

Tires screeching, she turned her car onto the Pacific Coast Highway, earning a good long blast on the horn from the convertible she cut off. The sound barely registered.

Ten minutes later she realized she was heading straight for Alec's apartment.

She'd done it without thought. A reflex. She was in trouble and she needed help. Going to Alec had become second nature.

What if one day you turn around and I'm not there? I wonder what you'd do then, my love.

Exactly what she was doing now. Go racing to find him.

The first chance she could, she pulled over. She had absolutely no idea what to do next. But she wasn't going to Alec for help.

Sydney eased back into traffic, a bit more in control. Of course, this was Russell's doing. He wanted her scared. A frightened little mouse he could manipulate down a maze with his tactics. That he'd succeeded so well only ticked her off.

Half an hour later, she used her card key and rolled past the security gates toward Jack's house. It was the middle of the night and a great imposition. But she knew Jack. He wouldn't care. If anything, he would expect her to come to him for help. She could sleep on his couch, which was about the only place in the world she thought she might actually get some rest tonight.

She rang the doorbell, listening to Ethel and Fred bark their fool heads off. It was such a comfort to hear those darling dogs, big as ponies. If any black devil dog should come her way now, he was toast with the Ridgebacks.

Only, when Jack opened the door, a surprise. She could see she'd dragged him out of bed . . . and that he hadn't been there alone.

Lipstick, bloodred, smeared across his neck just below his ear. He smelled like perfume.

"Ethel and Fred," she said stupidly. "You left them outside."

Normally, the Ridgebacks slept at the foot of his bed. But if Jack had company, it made sense he'd want the dogs out of the way.

And Jack. Jack just stood there, staring like a deer in the headlights. "Sydney . . . I . . ."

"It's all right," she said, stepping back, feeling incredibly unprepared for this and very foolish. She and Jack had never had sex. She'd wanted to wait. Somehow, in her head, she'd even convinced herself they'd arrived at that decision together.

"I want to explain," he told her, stepping outside, shutting the door behind him. She could see he was nervous. Whoever was in the bedroom, he was afraid she would come out and add to the scene.

"No. It's all right," she told him. "I . . . it's just that . . . oh, shit. I shouldn't have come."

He grabbed her arm before she could leave.

"You're shaking," he told her.

But he didn't ask her inside.

She forced herself to look at him. She even managed a smile. "What is it, like two in the morning? And your . . . ex shows up, out of the blue? Where are my manners?"

"You're not my ex."

She could see he hurt. He didn't want to go through this anymore than Sydney. It made her want to leave twice as much. *What did you expect?* It wasn't so much that she was jealous or hurt. She felt none of those things . . . which was somehow worse.

The fact was, she only felt terribly alone.

"No matter what happens," he told her, breaking through the awkward silence, "you're important to me. Please. Tell me what you need."

"I just came by to . . . to talk. Make sure you're okay with everything that's happened this week. It was so stupid, coming here this late. I couldn't sleep and I just didn't think. Guilty conscience? I don't know. But, I can see"—she motioned toward the door, stepping back, laughing—"you're doing fine."

"That's bullshit, and you know it."

She closed her eyes. Now she was tired, exhausted by everything the two of them had faced. "Jack, you don't owe me anything. Certainly not an explanation. Look, we'll talk tomorrow. But I don't want you to worry. Really. I'm okay."

She left before he could say anything else. And he let her. It seemed surreal, the gardens, palm trees covered like Christmas trees with fairy lights. She realized she was crying, that the tears were blurring the lights.

She sat waiting in her car until the tears stopped. Everything had just caught up to her, that's all. The dog, the alley . . . Alec. And the startling realization that even Jack had moved on. While her nightmares just kept coming.

Well, she could deal. She turned on the car and moved through the residential streets, maneuvering toward the gate. The last year had forged her. Henry's death, Russell's involvement—Alec and his manipulative ways. She'd gotten through all of it. She could handle this.

Whatever happened, she wouldn't let Russell destroy another life, even if it was just hers.

SEVENTEEN

Jack came back inside and shut the door, staring like an idiot. He'd put on his jeans and a T-shirt when he'd heard Sydney knocking, calling out his name. He still couldn't believe she'd come here. She hadn't been over in weeks.

"What did you tell her?"

Hearing Rocky, he turned around. She stood in the hallway, the comforter off the bed wrapped around her shoulders and dragging on the floor. But Jack had another picture stuck in his head: Sydney, her smile slowly fading as she realized what was going on.

"Wow," Rocky said, her voice ringing with sarcasm. "Looks like you took the high road and spilled your guts to her, telling her all."

"Is that what you expected? That I would tell her you were here?"

He regretted saying it. She looked incredibly hurt

by his words. Rocky, who always had that chip on her shoulder, now appeared as if she would crumble where she stood.

She turned and ran back toward the room.

After a beat, Jack followed, knowing this wasn't going to be easy. Stupid how, in his head, he'd twisted everything around so that somehow, some way—when this whole disaster with Russell Reck and Alec blew over—he and Sydney would get back together.

Now that would never happen. Sleeping with Rocky, he'd slammed that door shut forever.

He found her back in the bedroom, trying to find her clothes. She'd already dumped the comforter and put on the lacy bra-and-pantie set. He knew he'd screwed up big-time, having sex with Rocky, letting the fact that he was lonely and hurt take over. But it was funny how those facts didn't change that she looked amazing, even scrambling on the floor for her clothes.

The more he thought about it, the more he realized he didn't regret sleeping with Rocky. For once, someone had been all there for him. Even if it was only sex, it had felt too good, falling asleep with her spooned up against him.

God, it had been years since he'd had anything like that in his life.

"What are you doing?" he asked.

She was digging out one of her sandals from under the bed. "Gee, Jack. What a stupid question."

"You don't have to go."

She sat back on her heels, holding a sandal on her lap. She didn't look at him. "But maybe I should." She said it staring at the bedpost.

Kneeling there in her underwear, she looked to

Jack suddenly so insubstantial . . . which was crazy. Rocky was your basic blond bombshell. There wasn't a damn thing insubstantial about her.

He came up behind her and knelt down. He tugged aside her hair and kissed her neck, his hands on her shoulders. She leaned back in response, rubbing her cheek against him, catlike. He turned her, giving in as she reached to grab hold of him. He realized she smelled sweet, like some kind of flower. *Bluebells.*

"She wasn't going to take you back."

She said it so fiercely, it made him smile. "I figured that out some time ago."

She stopped kissing him. "But you want her back just the same."

He sighed. What could he say? In his happily-ever-after, he and Sydney would be walking down the aisle on the way to having four or five kids. He didn't know what this night had been about—or even why he was sitting on the floor with Rocky, half naked, thinking about a second round.

Jack stood, drawing Rocky up with him. She had this face, blue eyes, blond hair. It almost hurt to look at her, she was so beautiful.

"I came here because I wanted you to make love to me," she said. "Please, don't be sorry."

"What a fucking disaster." But he was smiling.

"Do ya think?"

"I just slept with my ex-fiancée's stepdaughter."

"Ex-stepdaughter." She snuggled into his chest and wrapped her arms tightly around him, like a slow dance. "Didn't I see that on an episode of *Titans*?"

He leaned back against the bedpost, Rocky's hair brushing against his hands at her waist. Holding her, he frowned, because he liked so much the feel of her in his arms. Well, he'd have to be dead not to, right? She was a very desirable woman.

She asked, "Haven't you ever thought that someone was your destiny?"

"Yup," he answered, being honest.

Rocky glanced up. "Well, you screwed it up, Jack. Because you got the wrong girl."

He couldn't help his grin. "How's that work exactly?"

"I was thinking that, maybe . . . well"—she licked her bottom lip, a nervous gesture that also happened to look adorable—"what if Sydney was just like a conduit. The whole reason for your relationship." She traced a circle on his chest through his T-shirt. "Maybe it was to find . . . me."

"Now wouldn't that be something?"

She hit him playfully. "I mean it."

"You're full of it."

"No," she said, leaning up so that her mouth came temptingly close to his. "Not about this."

He kissed her. She could make him believe just about anything with that kiss. When Rocky kissed you, she gave everything, holding nothing back. It made him want to pull her onto the bed and start all over again.

"I've never done anything like this," he said, sounding almost confused. As if Rocky could clear it up. But it was true. Everything about this went against his nature. The "big plan," as Sydney had called it.

"Even in college," he told her, "there was this girl who drank too much at a party, and we ended up in my room, making out on the bed. And—"

She covered his mouth. "No, don't tell me. You got her dressed and walked her home."

"Yup."

"That's pathetic."

He smiled. "To save someone from themselves? I wish someone had stepped up to bat for me tonight."

She shook her head. "You are just plain pathetic."

She pushed him on the bed. He grabbed her, bringing her down with him. They wrestled, kicking the sheets aside until he held her pinned and out of breath. He stared down at her. He didn't know what he'd expected, but it wasn't this. Rocky was funny and sexy, and making love hadn't been the hot romp between the sheets that he'd anticipated. Pretty much the opposite.

She'd been so serious about the whole thing, almost shy at times. She'd let him take control. And when he'd pulled her on top, making sure she found her release . . . well, talk about an ego boost. She'd opened her eyes and looked at him as if he'd just invented the orgasm.

"I want to keep coming here," she told him. "I don't mind sneaking around. Sydney doesn't have to know anything."

He rolled over to his side and tucked her up against him, his arm draped over hers. He closed his eyes. "I'll think about it tomorrow."

"You do that, Scarlett."

She wiggled free, and when he pulled her back to him, she dug her elbow into his ribs. "I have to go pee."

He let her go, sighing loudly as he rolled onto his back. He was thinking this was a hell of his own making. How many nights had he sat up in bed with the television on, willing Sydney to ring his doorbell? But seeing her tonight, he'd felt ashamed.

Which should tell him something about where this relationship with Rocky would end up.

"Hey," he said, surprised when he saw a spot of blood staining the sheet where Rocky had lain. He looked closer, seeing that there were several specks of red.

Rocky came out of the bathroom. She followed his gaze to where the bed was stained.

"Are you bleeding?" he asked.

She picked up her dress and started to put it on. "I guess so. Maybe my period started." She grabbed her sandals, not bothering to put them on. "Listen, I just remembered I left my car parked on PCH—"

He reached out and grabbed her wrist. He could feel panic squeezing his heart in his chest. "You're not having your period."

"Stop it, Jack." She flipped her hand free and ran for the door.

He jumped out of bed and raced after her, managing to grab her just before she reached the door. He'd been sitting in bed, remembering, putting the pieces together, when she'd come out of the bathroom.

When they'd made love, he'd been just so happy to have someone in his arms. He hadn't been paying attention to the details.

"You should have told me," he said.

She put on her sandals, making a noise in her throat. "Yeah, right. Like you were going to sleep with me if you knew I was a virgin."

"No. I wouldn't."

"Which makes my point."

"Dammit. Dammit!" He just stared at her. He felt

suddenly out of breath. And scared. Oh, yeah. That most of all.

"You're not twenty-eight," he said.

She opened the door. "And my birthday isn't September 15. I lied. About a lot of things. But not about the destiny part. That was too important."

She slammed the front door behind her. For the second time that night, Jack just stood frozen in place, not knowing what to do next.

For all he knew, she might not even be legal. He'd taken some baby girl to bed. A virgin.

One who lied and manipulated him and had no qualms about throwing it in his face.

"Shit!" He punched his fist into one of the door panels.

What a disaster. What a fucking disaster.

Free Fall

EIGHTEEN

Alec had stepped inside a Norman Rockwell painting.

He was seated at a heavy farm table, the kind advertised in the magazines on newsstands. Green place mats complemented the floral plates and centerpiece of sunflowers. A girl with freckles and braids, a precocious six years of age, sat across from him, as lovely a dinner companion as he'd ever had. Beside her, her ten-year-old brother yammered about baseball, his first home run. Travis and Linda Bentley smiled as they watched their children, the proud parents.

A week after Sydney called his bluff on her doorstep, Alec phoned Travis.

Pretty much everything he'd told Sydney the night he'd ambushed her on her doorstep was bullshit—down to his reasons for breaking into her condo, which had nothing to do with the lovely panties he'd taken as a memento. They hadn't spoken since, which only added to the rift.

Alec had given it some thought, stared at the card

she'd handed him like a bomb. It hadn't taken that long to figure out he'd do whatever she asked, even come here and face this slice of Americana.

Only thing, sitting down at the table with a man who called himself his brother . . . it brought up the unexpected. All that stuff Sydney carped about dealing with the past? Until then, Alec hadn't known how much he hated it, the possibility that his old man could somehow reach from the grave and still manipulate his life.

Sure, Alec had screwed up with people he loved. Big-time. He had regrets. But he figured it was better to acknowledge he was a selfish jerk. Why blame it on Eddy, making himself out to be some sort of head case? Why give Edward and Daisey that power?

When he'd called Travis, the guy had been eager, inviting him to the standard family gathering—dinner and a get-to-know-each other talk. How could it hurt, Alec had thought? His plan had been simple enough. Give Syd what she wants, use it as an excuse to report to Commissioner Sydney, get into one of those heart-to-hearts that women love so much.

Only, the minute Travis opened the door in welcome, Alec knew he'd made a mistake.

Now, sitting there, watching Travis, shit, the guy was the image of Eddy. *Just like me.* But Alec wasn't looking in a mirror this time. He wasn't going to blink and make the picture go away.

Travis even had Eddy's voice. That soft cadence bouncing around the room, the guy's smiles, his gestures, it freaking gave Alec the willies. Made him want to shake his head and clear out the ghosts.

When he was a kid, he used to have these nightmares where he couldn't breathe. He'd wake up crying. He'd wet the bed. He'd forgotten all about that, only now remembering.

"Do you like string beans?" Travis's daughter, Katie, let him know from her tone that only an alien could eat the stuff.

Coming back to earth, Alec smiled. He pushed aside the mashed potatoes where he'd dumped a few beans. "My favorite." He winked, making Katie laugh.

Linda and Travis caught the show. They glanced at each other and smiled, the silent language of an established couple. Just looking at them made Alec break out into a sweat.

He grabbed his water glass. He'd thought he could come here, have a meal, report back to Sydney. He hadn't expected to feel anything.

What was worse, the kids had gotten a big kick about him being a pilot, asking a lot of questions. *Just like Christopher, Geena's boy.* Chris had always loved the war stories. Whenever Alec came over for dinner, he and Conor would egg each other on, each trying to outdo the other in their nephew's eyes.

Now Alec sat with string beans in his mashed potatoes, trying to catch his breath. He felt like he was suffocating, just because some guy looked like the fucked-up father he'd once had. He remembered Geena and Conor, how they'd helped him put the nightmares to rest. How much he missed them both.

"Honey, why don't you give the kids their ice cream out on the porch? Alec and I will be in the study."

"But I wanted to show him my snake." This, a protest from little Katie, the budding herpetologist. "Daddy, you promised I could take Jewel out after dinner."

Alec came out of his seat and knelt down in front

of the kid, happy for the distraction. *Catch your breath, man.* "Hey, it's not like I'm going to disappear. Let me talk to your dad here, get the business half of the evening out of the way. Then you and me are going to take Jewel through her paces. Okay?"

What he couldn't understand was the anger. It didn't seem to come from anywhere, just pumped away inside him, a mental barometer heralding bad times ahead. He didn't understand it because there was no point. *Boo-hoo, I got screwed over in the game of life?* So what?

"Lead the way," he told Travis, patting him on the back, telling himself he'd make up some excuse and get the hell out. He'd tried to please Sydney coming here. Now he wouldn't even bring it up. He just wanted to put this night behind him.

Walking into the den behind Travis, Alec could see Linda had an eye for the niceties of interior decoration. Every corner had some knickknack. Photographs covered the walls like an art gallery. Travis sat in an overstuffed chair blooming with more flowers, while Alec followed suit, dropping onto the sofa opposite him. He was counting the minutes in his head.

"Good kids," Alec said, not because it was expected, but because it was true.

"Yeah. I'm lucky." Travis shook his head. "I'm sorry I couldn't tell them who you are. I just thought it was best to wait."

In case this doesn't work out, Alec thought. *I hear you, guy.* "Probably wise."

"I'm glad you called," Travis said. "What made you change your mind?"

Alec crossed his legs, ankle on knee. *Five more min-*

utes, tops. "I thought I should face my past, what else?" Sydney's words, not his.

"Really? I thought maybe it had something to do with the lady you were with at the hospital." And when Alec stared, nonplussed, he added, "You gave each other this look." Travis shrugged. "Linda was the one who put me on the path to find Mom. She's usually the one who makes me deal with the emotional side. I thought it might be the same for you."

"That sixth sense must come in handy for a journalist."

"Sometimes." Travis laughed. "Then again, sometimes I'm just dead wrong."

Alec flashed his best smile. But inside he felt like he'd eaten one of those cartoon bombs that explode in a character's stomach, leaving a plume of smoke coming out of his ears. Just then Travis had brought it all into focus. Alec had come to please Sydney.

Bad move, he told himself. *Too late for that now, guy.* In the end, he had to remind himself that he couldn't escape his past misdeeds. They were there, waiting in the wings. *You screwed up with Syd long before you even met her.*

"Do you have any pictures of Mom?" Travis asked. "I've only seen what she looked like as a child. That's all we had around the house. I think that for our grandmother that was more comfortable. To keep her frozen in her head the way she appeared in the days before she went bad. That's what she used to call it. Going bad. Like fruit."

"No kidding?" But Alec was only half listening. *Like I give a shit.* A few more minutes, and he was out of there.

Travis shook his head. "Whenever I asked, she

would trot out Mom's pictures from elementary school. Way back when, you know? It was hard for me to make a connection. Especially when I got older."

Alec looked up. Whenever Travis talked about the woman who had raised him, he called her "our" grandmother. But Daisey, she was just "Mom" or "my" mother.

Frigging amazing, he thought. Nice normal guy like that, and he's totally screwed up.

"I don't have any photographs," Alec told him. Ed and Daisey weren't exactly into capturing the moment.

"I was afraid you were too young. Boy, I have so many questions."

"Yeah. I figured. Only"—having reached critical mass, Alec tapped his Mickey Mouse watch—"I just remembered I have to see this guy about this thing."

He didn't want to mull over the good old days with Travis. *Fucking mistake, coming here.* He'd started work at Reck Enterprises earlier that week, where he could do some good. Getting warm and cozy with Eddy's twin was a complete waste of time.

Alec stood, saying, "Man, I forgot all about it. Across town." Shit, was he hyperventilating? "I hate to eat and run . . ."

"Sure. I understand. Maybe some other time."

"Just you and me, guy. For a beer. You shoot any pool? That would be great. I'll call."

He was halfway to the door, hoping he'd never see Travis Bentley again, when the guy said, "You're lucky, you know."

Alec turned. The only luck he'd ever counted on was the one that kept his ass on this earth. Sure as hell, he'd beaten the odds. But that wasn't the kind of luck Travis was talking about.

Travis walked past and opened the door. "You knew her," he said.

Alec smiled. *You're lucky.* "Is that right?"

"I would give anything to have known her."

Alec felt his face go tight, still holding that smile. "I think I'm getting the picture now."

The idiot. The asshole. He couldn't possibly think . . .

Our grandmother—my mother.

Oh, yeah.

"Hey, what the hell." Alec shrugged, making a show of taking another look at his watch. "Maybe I can be a little late." He patted Travis on the back. "Looks like you still need to talk."

Back in the family room, he sat down in his chair, all the pieces falling into place. He could have walked out, just left things as they were, but he had to hear it for himself. That the guy could be this stupid.

"Grandma kind of hard on you, was she?" Alec prompted.

"You have no idea."

Poor Travis. He hadn't grown up knowing his mommy. He had only the big bad grandmother to take care of him.

"Like I said, I have a few minutes." Alec leaned forward, giving a look of concern. "Fill me in."

"Look, I'm not feeling sorry for myself when I tell you this—"

Nah, Alec thought. *You're not that kind of asshole. . . .*

"I just thought you should know. In case you were wondering what it might have been like. If you'd stayed, that is. Like I did."

"You read my mind."

"She was tough, Hazel. That's what she wanted me

to call her. Hazel. Her given name. Never Grandma or anything like that. Sometimes it made me wonder if she was trying to disconnect somehow. From me. Because of Mom.''

To Alec, Ed and Daisey had always been just that. First names. And not because of any disconnect.

''She took it hard that Mom was such a rebel. But honestly, I could see how someone might decide anything was better than living with Hazel. She was a hard Minnesota Lutheran. Nothing was ever good enough for her.''

Edward and Daisey lived from motel room to motel room, always skipping out when the money dried up. Food was optional and always second to their drug habit. Sometimes they ate out of trash cans at the food courts in malls. When Eddy couldn't afford his fix, he would steal, using Alec as a lookout when he became old enough.

''Wow,'' Alec said. ''That must have been tough for you.''

''I just wish . . . well, Hazel did the best she could. She was a tough woman, and she wanted to make sure I didn't turn out like Daisey, that's all. I shouldn't complain. I just wanted you to know. In case it mattered to you.''

''Shit. She didn't beat you, did she?''

''No. Nothing like that. But, boy, she had this look. She could make you feel two inches tall. And nothing was ever good enough for Hazel.'' Alec could see he was getting into it. ''Not straight A's. Not an athletic scholarship.''

''I think they call that emotional abuse,'' Alec said in his best impersonation of someone who gave a shit.

"Like I said, she did her best. And I'm not complaining. She put a roof over my head and food on the table. And she taught me the value of hard work." Travis laughed. "I wanted to get out of there so bad. College was my get-out-of-jail card. You bet I worked my tail off."

"Yeah. Dad, he really helped me make my mind up about the air force." Edward had been long dead before any of that, but Alec liked the story. "Mom was really proud. Especially when I got into flight school."

"How did they die?"

"Car accident." *Finding oblivion with their drugs.* "A real tragedy."

He could go on. Hell, he could make this stuff up without tiring, feed old Travis the make-believe family he longed for. Put that mean grandma who rapped his knuckles in her place.

"Did she talk about me?"

"Only once." Alec shook his head, looking away. "It was incredibly sad. She struggled to keep you, but like you said, Hazel had her self-esteem in the can. She always thought she'd done what was best for her boy, leaving you."

Daisey had lived her life strung-out, watching as Ed beat the shit out of Alec, too afraid for her own ass to intervene. She'd never even mentioned a family. If she had, you could bet your life Alec would have hightailed it out of that hell to find them.

Linda came in, carrying a tray with coffee. But Alec stood. He'd had more than enough.

"Sorry," he told Travis.

"No. You go ahead. I don't want to make you even

later for your . . . thing with the guy," Travis said, smiling.

"Yeah." He shook Travis's hand, already feeling the tightness ease in his chest. After this, he'd never have to look into Eddy's face again. *No more ghosts.* "Right. We'll do this some other time."

"No problem."

But at the door he felt a hand on his shoulder. He turned to find Travis watching him, his eyes dark. Maybe it was a trick of the light but—the expression on his face—Eddy had never looked at Alec like that, as if he really saw him, standing there.

"I hope there will be a next time," he told Alec. "Okay?"

For a minute, Alec thought the guy had figured him out. That everything he'd just told Travis was a bunch of bullshit and he and Alec would never see each other again. But just as Alec waited for Travis to let his sixth sense kick in, the guy smiled and gave him a slap on the back, vanquishing the moment.

"This has been great," he told Alec, letting him know that as far as Travis was concerned, all was well. "Thanks."

"Hey, no problem."

Alec said his good-byes, thanking Linda for the great dinner, flashing a smile and a salute to the kids, making sure he at least gave Jewel a look-over in her terrarium before he left. By the time he got out the door, he'd broken into a sweat.

He still couldn't believe it. Hazel had made Travis's life a living hell? Because she'd made him work hard, pushing him to make something of himself?

There was this time Eddy got so pissed, he gave Alec a bunch of cigarette burns on his chest. That was the first time they'd taken Alec away from the folks. Another time, he broke Alec's wrist in three places, slamming his hand in the door—Edward's version of tough love when Alec had mouthed off.

Daisey never did a damn thing to stop him.

"Oh, yeah. Mom was a peach."

Rage shot through Alec like nothing he'd ever experienced. Funny, he never much bothered with anger; what was the point? He had better things to do than let his emotions rule him. Only now he jammed on the brakes, sending the Chevy spinning in a doughnut that would probably have gotten him killed if there had been anyone else on the road. The wheels burning into the asphalt, he shifted gears and sped off in the opposite direction.

To Chino Hills. To Conor's house.

He reached the house half an hour later. The double lot was large enough to handle Geena and Marc's Cape Cod and still give Conor plenty of privacy in his cottage out back. *The fortress that Conor built.* Because for Conor, there was nothing in the world like family.

Alec leaned against the hood of his Chevy, breathing hard, as if he'd raced here on his legs and not in his truck. The sky was pitch black. Out in the hills there weren't half as many streetlights to block out the stars.

He could understand why Conor hadn't abandoned his compound after getting married, instead moving his bride into the cottage he kept. It was a pretty piece of land. Geena and Marc, who worked right alongside him, lived conveniently close by, for the sake of their flight school. Then there was Christopher and the twins. Why give up living next door to them?

Why turn his back on it all? Like Alec had?

He could just imagine what Geena's kids thought just over a year when Uncle Alec hit the six o'clock news, the big bad terrorist.

Amazing, these emotions. They caught him off guard. Yeah, he cared what his nephew thought of him. Which didn't make sense. If he cared—if it truly mattered—he should never have done half the shit that made him so newsworthy.

He smiled, pushing off the Chevy. Damn, even the voice inside his head was starting to sound like Sydney.

He walked up the drive, listening to the gravel crunch under his shoes. He was trying to think where he had a better shot at a welcome, Geena's or Conor's—then surprised himself by choosing neither. The fact was, he really didn't have a right to be there.

He sighed, kicking aside some gravel, wondering when he'd grown a conscience. Or maybe he was just getting older, tired of running and being alone.

The thing was, in order to have people care about you, you had to care back. Otherwise, the business just didn't work. Eventually, they got tired of doing all the work. They left you behind.

He could hear the television coming from inside Geena's, the sound making his stomach drop. Like flying. He still got that nervous when he slipped into the cockpit.

He hadn't seen the kids in over a year. . . .

Slowly, he walked over to one of the windows, drawn there despite everything he'd just told himself. The window he chose would give him a view of the family room. He looked inside, grinning when he caught sight of Christopher asleep on the sofa.

Shit, the kid was getting tall. Geena's genes at work, no doubt, because, on a good day, Marc might be able to look his wife in the eye without tipping his head. How old was Christopher now anyway? Maybe twelve? The twins were glued to the television. One of those Japanese cartoons.

Geena and Marc must have gone out for the night, leaving Christopher in charge. No way the kid would be watching cartoons with his brother and sister otherwise.

Alec figured he'd probably trade his soul to go in there right then and pretend nothing had happened. *Hi, Chris. How you doing, big guy?* But he had no way of knowing what Geena had told the kids. *If Uncle Alec ever shows up, the first thing you do is call 911 and tell them he's a very bad man and the police should come right away.*

Alec dropped down from the window and looked up the drive toward the cottage in the back. A lanai enclosed the front porch with night-blooming jasmine creeping up the side, framing the house. He could see the beginnings of an addition. Conor's growing family. He walked farther up the drive until he reached the house.

Before he could think better of it, he peered in the window. Inside the tiny front room Conor used as a living room, Alec could see Cherish, Conor's wife, holding a baby.

Conor's son. He knew all about it. These last years, he'd kept up with the goings-on of the great Mitchell clan, his adopted family. He smiled, watching Cherish's lips move as she swayed back and forth, singing to the little guy. The place was cluttered with every imaginable toy, including what looked like an airplane hanging from a giant bungee cord in a doorway.

"Attagirl," he said under his breath to Cherish.

He could just imagine how happy she'd made Conor. This was the life his adoptive brother had been meant to live, and Alec was only too happy to see him get it. Before, Conor had dedicated everything to making sure Alec and Geena reached their happy ending. It was good to see Conor get his chance.

Alec stepped back from the window. There'd been a time when he had thought he was in love with Cherish. But like everything else in his life, she'd been more about Alec's relationship with Conor.

He turned, about to leave, thinking, *they made it*. A kid. A future. *True love*.

Only, he got this prickling at the back of his neck, a familiar sensation that tuned him in. Someone was there. Watching him.

He turned around, searching the darkness.

And found him.

Conor, standing in the shadows.

He didn't know how long Conor had been there— Alec hadn't heard a thing. But then, it was Conor. Of course, he wouldn't hear the Conman.

Now he stepped toward Alec, head down. Like he couldn't stand the sight of him.

"What the hell are you doing here, Alec?"

Conor made a slight motion with his hand where he held his old revolver. He pointed the gun, bull's-eye, straight at Alec's chest.

NINETEEN

"Are you going to shoot me, Conman?"

Alec said it with a smile. But he was thinking it wasn't much of a stretch. Not with their history. Hell, it was almost fitting. The last time he'd seen Conor Mitchell, Alec had been holding the gun. *Coming full circle . . .*

"You would hesitate?" Conor asked.

"If I remember correctly, I did."

"That's right. You did. You're all heart, Alec," he said, watching with that hard stare that emphasized the scar over his eye, a scar he'd earned courtesy of Alec. "Only, in the end, your little scheme with Reck almost got me killed, just the same. But why sweat the details?"

Alec wasn't going to defend himself against Conor's accusations. Conor knew the truth, those secrets Alec had kept from Syd. Alec had used him, made him an unwilling partner in Alec's plan to save his own hide. He'd put the very people who loved him at risk—Geena and Conor. Unlike Sydney, Conor knew first-hand what kind of man Alec had become. *Just like dear old dad . . .*

"Well." Alec spread his arms, making a target. "As the song says, 'Hit me with your best shot.' "

Instead, Conor flipped open the clip and dropped the bullets to the grass, then dumped the gun. He came forward, stopping just within arm's length.

Like lightning, *whack!* He'd pivoted back, giving Alec a roundhouse to the jaw. Alec fell, slamming into the fence behind him.

"Nice," he said when he could talk past the pain. "Good to see you still have the moves, old man."

Alec came at Conor with everything, the anger and frustration that had been building inside him. He punched him, sending Conor slipping on the wet grass. He followed with another punch, this one missing its mark as Conor ducked and rammed, headfirst, into Alec's gut. Alec latched onto Conor's head, bringing him down with him.

"Why did you come here, Alec? Because Reck is out of jail? You and Reck have something going again? What have you brought to my door?"

Alec tucked his foot under Conor. Using the momentum of Conor's body, he flipped him over his head. "I just came by to pay my respects."

The door opened. Both men stood, facing off as Cherish ran out between them. Amazingly, she stepped in front of Alec.

"Conor, don't be an idiot!" she said when Conor walked around her and grabbed Alec, shoving him up against the fence. She pulled him off.

"Stop! Oh, puuleeze!" she said, pushing Conor

away with both hands. "Do I have to take you both by the ears into the house to straighten this out?"

"He's not stepping inside our house, Cher."

But Conor walked away, breathing hard, obviously upset. He bent down, picking up the bullets and the gun. Cherish followed after him. Neither looked at Alec as she took Conor's face in her hands, the gesture incredibly tender. The two touched foreheads as she whispered to him.

An emotion both painful and exhilarating struck Alec in the chest. This was what the Conman deserved. A woman who loved him. Children. People who cared about him and would watch his back.

Good for you, guy.

Conor glanced across the yard at Alec. "Get out of here. Before Christopher or the twins come outside."

"Chris is asleep on the couch," Alec said. "I looked through the window. The twins are heavy into whatever video he put on for them. And thanks, Cherish. For sticking up for me."

"No, Alec. I'm not here to help you." She shook her head. "You should have come before. You waited too long." Her expression was one of disappointment. "You never accept the consequences. It's the one thing I could never forgive. But my husband—your brother—is not going to do anything he is going to regret. I won't let you hurt him again, Alec."

Conor stepped up, taking over. "Whatever you're running from this time, I won't help you. You're going to have to deal with your garbage all by yourself. I should call the police. Give them the heads-up. Did you think I wouldn't? Because I let you off last time?"

"And if I told you I wish you would? That I just want

the damn thing over with?'' Alec asked, surprising himself.

"That's bullshit! Always your bullshit. Dammit . . . Alec, dammit.'' He looked away. "Before, I couldn't turn you in. For God's sake, don't you get it? You're my brother.'' Conor's voice cracked on the last word. "Get the fuck out of here and leave us alone.''

Shit, Alec thought. *Oh, shit.*

The look on Conor's face.

I wish he'd pulled the trigger, Alec thought. *I wish he'd shot me.*

"I gave you everything,'' Conor said. "Everything I had to give all those years. And still, I couldn't . . . I couldn't fix you. Whatever they did to you, Daisey and Edward. I couldn't . . . I couldn't make it right. And even knowing all that—after everything you messed up. Goddammit, I miss you.''

Alec didn't say anything. He couldn't even take a breath to make the words come out. Nothing prepared him for the emotion in Conor's voice.

All these images flashed in his head. The day Conor had stuck up for him with those goons at the home. The hospital, telling Alec everything was going to be okay. Swearing an oath in front of the judge to be Alec's guardian. Teaching Alec to fly . . . the first time he let Alec take the controls.

"But I won't let you hurt us again,'' Conor said, seeming to catch his breath. "I won't let you come here and say you've changed so that Cher and Geena will believe you. You slammed that door shut, Alec. Forever.''

He stepped back to Cherish. He put his arm around her, letting Alec know by his body language that in this they would stand united.

"If you don't leave now, I will call the police," he told Alec. "This time I have too much to lose."

Alec walked away. And not because of Conor's threats. Hell, he wished he had the courage to turn himself in for what he'd done. Conor would be doing him a favor. But Cherish was right. If Conor made that call, it would haunt him forever.

Reaching the Chevy, he could still hear Conor say, "Don't let him fool you, Cher. He's a self-serving SOB. And he'll never change."

He'll never change.

Alec kept hearing those words as he drove through the crowded streets of downtown. Over the last year, the thought had crept upon him that he could change. He'd actually come to like the idea that anybody deserved a second chance.

He'd held on to the fantasy that if he wanted something bad enough, he could make it happen. He wouldn't get stuck like some Greek tragedy, rolling the same rock up the same damn hill, making the same mistakes. At some point he knew he wanted to do it for Sydney. Some shit about becoming a better man.

Hard to hear those words from Conor. Even harder to see the sadness in the guy's eyes. Like he regretted every damn bit of it.

The thing was, the Conman was his hero. He'd done it all. He knew everything, right?

If Conor said he couldn't change . . .

Alec parked the truck, sitting back in the seat, taking a minute. He told himself he should go for a walk. Get some air. *The pier.* It was as good a place as any to do some thinking.

This time of night, you still had to fight the crowds on the pier. At some point Alec stopped doing battle and found a place to watch the waves rolling along the surface, disappearing under the pilings. The lights reflected through the water, making the waves glow in the dark, appearing almost unreal.

He'll never change.

Hadn't he thought the same thing about Russell Reck? Working at Reck Enterprises, wasn't he searching for evidence that The Wrecker had stayed true to form?

The fact was, Russell Reck would never allow what happened the last years to rob him of any little thing. And the only way he knew how to get ahead was to do exactly what he'd done to earn it in the first place. He'd cheat.

People didn't change. Alec was staking his life on it with Reck, looking for his shortcuts, ready to take him down.

And in the end it would only prove that Conor was right.

Alec pushed away from the rail. No matter how much he wanted to, he could never become the hero Sydney deserved. He shouldn't have shown up here, getting in her face, trying to break off things with dotcom boy. Succeeding.

You see something you want, and you take it. Damn the consequences.

That's how the bad guys did it. They screwed with people's lives.

Conor, the hero, he was all about self-sacrifice. He knew the score. He had honor. Conor had given up a college scholarship for Geena and Alec—even pushed Cherish away, thinking he couldn't do right by her. He wouldn't even give himself the satisfaction of putting Alec's ass behind bars.

Once a crook, always a crook. That's what Alec believed about Russell Reck. The problem was, now he was beginning to believe it about himself.

TWENTY

Sydney heard a scraping sound so soft she wondered if she'd heard it at all. Putting down her book, she pushed back her chair, tense. *There it is.*

The sound of someone breaking in.

Photocopied pages, notes, and law books covered the kitchen table. The week since the incident with the dog attack, she'd fired her security team. She hadn't looked for replacements, thinking that in the end she would have to bite the bullet and call Alec. Every day she told herself she would call. *Today, I'll call.* Only to wait for another day.

Now she was home alone, listening to the sounds of a break-in.

The noise continued, making her rise out of her seat and search for a weapon. She hadn't bought a gun, believing in her heart that she wouldn't be able to shoot. The anger and desperation she'd felt the night she'd held Russell at gunpoint had since healed. She wasn't a victim looking for revenge anymore.

But now she wondered if she'd just played the ostrich and stuck her head in the sand. After his little trick with the dog, she'd thought Russell would give her a few more days before he made his next move.

Again the quiet rustling.

Maybe not . . .

She crept into the main room, armed with only a hammer. Her heart in her throat, she listened as her window scraped open noisily, brazenly. A man cursed in the darkness.

She dropped the hammer. "Alec?"

She ran into the room in time to see him crawl through the window and drop to the floor, cussing vividly. She walked to stand over him as he lay sprawled on the carpet, catching his breath.

She realized he was drunk. The smell of alcohol wafted from him like cologne.

He opened his eyes, squinting despite the fact that the only light in the room was the soft glow from a table lamp.

"Syd? Shit. I didn't want to wake you. Did I, honey?" He brought his finger up to his mouth, making a soft *shhh* sound. "Go back to sleep, baby."

She couldn't believe it. "You crawled through the window?"

"I forgot my key."

"Maybe because I never gave you one?"

He snapped his fingers, remembering. "Right."

Even drunk on her floor, he was a welcome sight. A beautiful man with all his flaws. And she'd missed him despite all the complications he represented.

At least you're not wearing a ski mask, she said to herself, kneeling beside him.

Of course, something was terribly wrong. She

noticed right away the cut on his mouth, what looked like the beginnings of a nice bruise under his cheek. And the alcohol. She'd known Alec during the best and worst of times. She had never seen him so much as take a sip of beer.

"Did you get into a brawl in some bar?"

He chuckled. "Hey, you should see the other guy."

"And what was the next step?" she asked, putting his arm around her shoulder, helping him up. "After you fell through the window, I mean."

He gave her a sexy grin. "Crawl into bed with you. Make sweet love to you. In your sleep, because, God knows, you'd never let me touch you if you were conscious."

"Hmmm."

"And then I planned to confess."

She had to laugh. "This should be interesting."

But instead of laughing, he pulled her down to him, capturing her face in his hands. He seemed so serious. "The thing is. Jack. He's a good guy."

She felt her heart skip a beat, not sure this was what she wanted to hear.

"I looked up shit on him, you know? When I found out you two were an item. To make sure he was good enough for you . . . and maybe to torture myself a bit. Hell, who knows. It gets all mixed up in my head." Now, completely earnest, he said, "I messed it up for you, Syd. On purpose. Just because I wanted you. He could have made you happy."

She shook her head. "You're giving yourself way too much credit. What happened between Jack and me had nothing to do with you."

He waved off her objections. "You just don't get it. How much I want you. That I'll do anything. Some people are like that, see? Things get screwed up in their brain—maybe cause their mom took drugs and shit when she was pregnant. Geena says the neurons don't fire. It's a problem, you know?"

"That makes absolutely no sense."

"Doesn't matter. Point is, if I want something— full speed ahead and damn the consequences." His eyes, so very dark, watched her with something she could describe only as absolute adoration. "Wanted you, Syd. More than anything."

It seemed all backward. To say something so wrong with a look that felt so right. "Alec, you're messing with my head—"

"Then there's this other thing." He leaned up close again, holding his finger to his mouth. In her ear he whispered, "A secret. Terrible, terrible secret. Conor knows all about it. That's why he hates me."

She tried to laugh it off. "Alec—"

"But I can't tell you. I mean, I came over here to tell you. To confess." Her face was still in his hands. "Can't bear to see you hate me, Syd."

"Alec, you're scaring me."

"No." He covered her mouth with his fingertips, shaking his head. "It's done. Can't hurt you anymore. It's okay. Just don't want to take the consequences."

He began to stand up, slowly coming to his feet. He reached for the couch. Missed. He fell to the floor, then rolled onto his back, groaning as he stretched out.

"Shit," he said. "I think I hurt something."

She grabbed his arm and helped him up onto the couch. "I thought you never indulged in mind-altering substances?"

He landed on the couch with a thump, then surprised her with sudden agility as he pulled her onto his lap. "That's because I had no idea it was a magic elixir. A magic elixir of love." He pushed her down on the couch, following up so that his body covered hers. "And it made me horny as hell."

She had to laugh, he sounded so silly. "And you brought your horny self here?"

"To test the magic elixir." He leaned down to kiss her. Missed, kissing her cheek sloppily. "With the magic elixir, you would find me irresistible. You would cave to my every demand."

"Alec." She pushed him off, laughing. "Stop it."

But he didn't. He kept kissing her, then covered her completely with his body, pinning her on the couch with his weight.

She pushed him. "Alec. Come on. I said stop."

He had unbuttoned her jeans, then reached up inside her top and pushed up her bra.

"Alec!" She hit him on his back with her fists, tried to push him off with her knee. But he was too strong, pulling down her jeans now, reaching inside her underwear.

A sense of panic came over her. She struggled in earnest. "Alec. Not like this. Please."

He froze on top of her, seeming to realize what was happening. She watched as he closed his eyes and rolled off her. She scrambled out from under him and he curled up, almost in the fetal position, on the couch. He turned away.

His shoulders started to shake. It took her a moment to realize he was crying.

At first she didn't know what to do . . . if she should touch him or leave him alone. It was so completely alien to see Alec break down. As if suddenly gravity didn't work or the sun didn't rise in the morning. She sat down next to him, brushing the hair with her fingers, waiting as he continued to cry silently.

"Hey," she told him as he grabbed on to her, holding her tight. "It's okay."

She'd never seen Alec cry. She'd seen him take tremendous physical pain with nothing but a tight grin. Even life's biggest disappointments he'd shake off with a breezy confidence.

Now he was lying on her couch, drunk. Losing it in a way that made something in her own heart break a little. It hurt to see that much pain in someone she loved.

She'd always suspected that behind his joking and nonchalance was a heart that cared too much. That his greatest fear might be to let go and drown in those emotions he held down so tight.

The time she had been with Alec, slowly falling in love, he had never shared any emotion other than fun and thrilling adventure. He avoided serious subjects with almost religious devotion. The only tenderness he'd shown her had been in bed.

That's why she'd missed it so much. When they'd made love that night, he'd showed her something special. A connection she hadn't wanted to lose.

She didn't ask what happened to him, what devastating event had finally brought it all to the surface, where he couldn't contain the emotions. *Too painful.* It's not what he needed just then.

She crawled on the couch alongside him. Her eyes never leaving his, she reached around him and held him, making silly comforting noises that told him everything would be all right. *I'm here now. I won't leave. Don't hurt so much. I can't bear it.*

She didn't realize she'd fallen asleep until she felt his kiss. He was sitting up now, her head resting on his lap. She didn't remember moving. He must have done it so carefully, not waking her. Now he held her hand in his, looking at her as he kissed her fingers again and again.

She reached up to stroke his face. He didn't look upset or drunk. Not anymore.

"I'm sorry," he told her. "I never would have—"

She covered his mouth. "It's okay. Trust me, you've done worse."

He smiled at that. "Maybe."

She wondered how much time had passed but didn't ask. Alec never showed vulnerability. She'd always thought it had to do with his training in the military. The kind of man who would put himself in an experimental plane and happily take it through its paces . . . he had to have control. Everything, even fear, could be put away in a nice little compartment.

His breakdown wouldn't be something he wanted to talk about. It seemed too new for even Sydney to put into words.

"I want to kiss you," he said, asking permission.

She brought her face up to his, her answer. When Alec kissed her, it was always a little like drowning. He could take her breath away and slip her into a dark place where she didn't fight or care about the consequences of diving deeper. She just opened her mouth and took him in and enjoyed the hot feeling in her veins that made the crazies take over. Made the world a whole different place, where the only thing that mattered was the next touch. And the next.

This time it was Sydney who pushed at their clothes, helping Alec pull his T-shirt over his head while they kissed and kissed. He had the most incredible body. As if it were chiseled from stone. She could follow the muscles of his stomach with her fingers . . . watched as his muscles contracted when she kissed his chest, then followed the hard shape of the scar at his shoulder with her tongue. When they had nothing between them, she straddled his lap and took him deep inside her, following the rhythm he'd set inside her mouth with his kiss.

They made love on the couch, then on the floor. They continued in the bedroom, making love again on the bed. There, in each other's arms, they didn't hold back. Alec let her know with his hands and mouth that she was precious beyond the words he would probably never say to her.

When he finally fell asleep in her arms, it was her turn to watch him. He was an incredibly beautiful man. The haircuts and funky hair dyes never changed that. They never altered the shape of his mouth or the dimples. They didn't erase the freckles or his strong, elegant nose.

She suspected he'd given more of himself to her than he'd ever allowed anyone else. The problem was, she wasn't sure what that would mean to him come morning. Knowing Alec, he'd fight any changes. Particularly the big ones.

She wondered what could have happened tonight. Wondered more if he would ever trust her enough to tell her.

Terrible, terrible secret.

She shivered, holding him tighter.

An hour later she was still awake. He looked so peaceful in sleep. He even smiled in his dreams. She leaned over and kissed his forehead. She remembered the first time she'd met him. She couldn't figure out how old he was. The freckles and grin made him ageless. But his eyes. His eyes made him old. In them was a world of knowledge, earned the hard way. But with his eyes closed, he was an angel.

"It's all right. Keep your secret," she told him. "I love you."

Now, when it was still dark, it seemed safe to tell a few secrets of her own.

TWENTY-ONE

When Alec woke up, Sydney lay snuggled against him, naked as the day she was born. A sliver of light slashed past the curtains, telling him it was already late morning. With blinding clarity he remembered everything that had happened the night before.

Panic. His head pounded with it. His mouth went dry. Panic so pure, it could make you high.

I won't let you hurt us. . . . Conor's warning to him last night.

Only, Sydney didn't have Conor watching out for her.

Alec remembered making the decision to get drunk, just walking into the bar and ordering drink after drink. He'd even enjoyed it, his fall from grace. He'd toasted Eddy. *This one's for you, asshole.* He'd raised a glass or two for Travis. Whatever it took.

But he couldn't stop thinking about Conor. Images from the night flashed in his head like those old-fashioned flip books. Conor fighting tears, Cherish holding the baby . . . Christopher, now almost a man, asleep on the couch, a world away.

When the alcohol hadn't worked, Alec had driven here. To find Sydney. He'd made love to her. Drunk.

No, buddy. You were stone-cold sober.

Which only made it worse.

As if sensing something, the deliciously naked woman in his arms snuggled closer. He could feel her warm little tush press against his stomach, and he responded accordingly. He lay perfectly still, trying to catch his breath.

He had to think. Had to come up with something he could say to her when she woke up.

Look, Syd. Sorry that I let it go this far . . . again. It's just that I was feeling so shitty, like I didn't have a friend in the world. And then I remembered you, and I came here, and it just felt so good, holding you, kissing you. . . .

God. Why didn't he just get her a gun?

As gently as he could, he inched out of the bed, trying not to wake her. He looked around the room for his pants, then remembered they'd taken their clothes off in the living room before ending up here for another round.

From the vicinity of the bed, he heard a deep sigh. He turned to see Sydney roll onto her side, now facing him. The sheets tucked under her arm, a shaft of light fell on her face; the floral covers lay bunched at her feet like some Renaissance painting. Pink-cheeked, her lips slightly parted, she was an angel.

She opened her eyes and granted him a sleepy smile. "Good morning."

Any response stuck in his throat. She was so exquisitely beautiful. At the same time, he thought of

Conor. His warning. That Alec used people. Sure as he was going to hell, last night, he'd used Sydney.

She eased up on her elbows and frowned. "Alec?"

"Yeah, babe. I was just getting my stuff. . . ." He made a vague gesture toward the front room and came back after he grabbed his underwear and put them on. "I'm kind of late for this thing I have to do across town," he said, an echo of the lame excuse he'd given Travis the night before.

Sydney closed her eyes, as if she might be fighting a headache. Shaking her head, her red hair fell over one shoulder. As she sat up in bed, the sheets dropped to her waist to reveal her beautiful breasts.

"Oh, my God"—the words, just a whisper—"you rat."

She reached behind her on the bed and grabbed a pillow. She threw it at him, hitting him square in the face.

"I can't believe it! That I could be this naive . . . that you could be such a jerk! Unbelievable." She found another pillow. Threw it. "Don't cry for me Argentina, part two!"

"Come on, Syd. It's not like that—"

"Ahh!" she screamed, covering her ears. Her knees came up and she pounded the heels into the mattress. "I can't *believe* I could be this stupid!"

At the sight of Syd naked on the bed, stomping her feet and plugging her ears, the weight on his chest eased. He found himself taking a step, then another toward the bed.

"Okay, no need to panic." He could do this, he coached himself. Even a rat could have his day, right? If he focused—if he thought long and hard about what to do next—he might actually do the right thing here. It was Sydney after all. She knew all his lies and ploys. Running away only made it worse.

He sat down on the edge of the bed and patted her hand. "Maybe it's not so bad, huh? Just the same I-fucked-up Alec that we know and—"

She slapped him hard across the cheek. She told him, "You don't get to make a joke about this."

"Right. So, let's get serious. Specifically, let's address the issue of birth control. Or the lack thereof."

He should do the responsible thing, right? That's what this was about, taking responsibility. Face the consequences—just like Cherish told him to do.

"I just want you to know that"—*shit, that I could do this to Syd*—"whatever happens, I'm here for you—"

"Oh, shut up, Alec." She covered her head with the sheet. "I'm not going to get pregnant."

Inside Alec, some interesting emotions steamed to the surface. Confusing, really. Here he was, taking a stab at being the noble knight, when suddenly— something else entirely. He couldn't quite believe how quickly it boiled over, shoving off all the other noise in his head, focusing on a couple of key points.

If Sydney were pregnant, no matter what he'd done in the past, they would have a connection. Jerk that he was, he could see an up side to that.

But she wasn't. And there could be only one reason why.

"Because you're on the pill, right?" He pulled down the sheet from her face and looked at her with a smile that could cut steel. "For Jerkoff, the once-upon-a-fiancé?"

She stared at him, nonplussed. "Are we talking

about the same man you told me last night was so perfect for me?"

"I'm just wondering how this crystal-ball, I-can't-get-pregnant thing works, Syd. Because last night I don't remember taking a time-out for any kind of aids in the birth-prevention department."

If Alec and Sydney had a baby, she could hate him—but she wouldn't push him out of her life. Not Sydney. She'd always want her kid to have some connection to Daddy. Only, from what she was saying, that wasn't going to happen. And he wanted to know exactly why.

"Like I said, the pill, right? Of course, you were sleeping with the guy. I mean, you were going to marry him." He was talking himself through it. One logical step, then the next. Like a preflight workup. *Check flaps, ditto elevators . . .*

Until suddenly, logic vanished and he stood very still, even as everything inside his head kept topsy-turvy, making no sense.

He told her, "Why would the memory of unbelievable, never-going-to-happen-with-anyone-else—and don't lie, I proved it last night—sex with me just . . . make you even pause for an instant from sleeping with some other guy?"

"I'm not on any sort of birth control," she said quietly. "I'm not pregnant because it's not the right time. I'm due for my period any day now. And what in the world are you ranting on about?" Now her voice rose to match his. "That I should have a life after Alec?" She came up on her knees. "As if I'm not allowed? I'm supposed to just live on the memory?"

"Damn straight. I did."

He could see that he'd shocked her. He'd shocked himself. And he wasn't near done.

"Did you sleep with him?"

He stood perfectly still, waiting.

"You always have to win." She shook her head. A gesture of annoyance or an answer, he couldn't tell which.

Finally, she told him, "No, Alec. I didn't sleep with Jack."

He dropped down on the bed. He did a quick rewind of what just happened, taking it in, living through it. This time he detached from the whole thing, analyzing the steps that got them there. She thought he was playing a game, intent on winning. *An opinion held by many these days.*

"You know, Syd, you're going to think this is funny. Really, it's going to give you a laugh." But he knew the look on his face said anything but. "Just now, waiting for you to answer, I couldn't catch my breath. There was no oxygen in the room. And when you said no"—he looked at her—"I could breathe again."

He leaned back against the headboard. He had more to say. But he wanted to get it right. He wanted her to understand.

"In my head I always thought it was us. Sure, you were engaged to the guy, and trust me, it hurt. But until we made love last night, I kept the whole Jackson thing theoretical. Like a question on the written exam before you get your wings. If the engine cuts out, you first a) check your fuel, b) check attitude, c) grab your ass and kiss it good-bye."

He looked at her, seeing that she understood. "But until it happens, it doesn't mean anything, see? It's just an exercise getting you ready for the real thing.

Syd, just now the engine cut out. Do you understand?"

She dropped back, sitting beside him. "Oh, Alec. You're going to take everything, aren't you? Every little bit of me. This time, when you leave, I won't have anything left."

He tucked her hair behind her ear. "I'm not leaving. Just stop kicking me out, okay?"

She dropped her head on his shoulder. As her arms came around his waist, he closed his eyes and held her, starting to memorize everything about the moment. The smell of her hair, the heat coming off her skin . . . the cool sheets beneath his legs. He kissed the top of her head.

He realized he'd never been this happy. That maybe it wasn't such a bad thing, sticking around. Or maybe it was the contrast, like the heat of her body making the morning sheets that much cooler. Last night he'd been in hell. Now this.

He wished to God he could make it last.

After a while he started to laugh.

"What?" she asked, suspicious already.

He kissed her hard on the mouth. Smiling, he shook his head and swiveled off the bed, making for the door. "Nothing." Another chuckle. Then, because he couldn't help himself, he told her, "Interesting about you and Jughead. But maybe you were saving it for the wedding night, right?"

"Something like that."

He nodded. "Or maybe you figured there really wasn't—how did you put it? Life after Alec?"

"I can't kill you," she said, "but I can hurt you. Badly."

He went into the next room and grabbed his

clothes. He stepped into his pants, then pulled the T-shirt over his head. He should feel like shit. He was a heel. *Poor Syd.*

Humming, *"I've Got You Under My Skin,"* he finished dressing.

"For God's sake, Alec. Don't preen."

He turned. She was standing at the door, her arms wrapped tightly around her, wearing her robe.

But she was smiling.

He sat down on the couch to put on his shoes. "So, I'll send by a guy." When he finished, he made a show of looking around, noting each window and the different points of entry. But he already had the whole place memorized. He stood. "Set up some decent security around here. This afternoon you can fill me in on what's been going on. Put us on the same page."

She didn't say anything. What could she say? He was in. She'd as much as signed the contract. Alec 007, back on the job.

Maybe the Conman was right and Alec was this giant asshole, using everybody. But along the way he'd learned a few things. He planned to use every bit of it to make sure Sydney stayed in one piece.

At the door, he stopped. He crossed the room again. Taking her in his arms like the VE day photo in *Life* magazine, he kissed her in a way that said it wasn't nearly over for them.

"I'll call," he said. "Maybe bring over some things."

Out the door and into the street, he didn't want to examine too closely how he felt. He knew it couldn't last. That clock in his head—before Syd found out what a bastard he really was—right now it was on hold. And sure as shit, he was going to enjoy every second before it went off.

Whistling, he opened the truck and jumped in the Chevy. He fished out his cell phone, dialed from memory.

"Hey, Steve. It's Alec. You know that job I was telling you about? Well, it's on."

He went on to give Steve the address, update him on the situation with Sydney.

"Just tell her I sent you." Steve at least was someone who had a clue. "And, Steve? I have a few things in place. You'll recognize my stuff." The night he'd nabbed the panties, he'd bugged Syd's humble home, the reason he'd shown up in the first place. "And don't give me any shit about ethics, because I know you don't have any. This lady is . . . she's special. I owe you, guy. Thanks."

He hung up.

They always said it was darkest before the dawn.

Well, Alec, he was just catching his breath.

TWENTY-TWO

A week after Rocky seduced him, Rocky told herself Jack had become a real pain in the ass.

The way he watched her. Passing her in the hall or the gallery. During meetings. He'd lock on and wouldn't let go, doing his Svengali-boy act. Sometimes she'd get this overwhelming urge to jump to her feet and scream at the top of her lungs. Make a scene. Embarrass the shit out of him.

As if he had the right. As if what had happened between them meant anything to him. She'd seen the truth on his face after Sydney left. His expression, love's little antidote. *Wake up, girl. You're just a place holder.*

That night, when she'd gone to Jack's, she thought whatever happened, she'd be okay. She had her eyes wide open. *Just sex.* They were both adults; she wasn't asking anything of him.

Imagine, she'd actually convinced herself. Funny, how people could do that. Fool themselves so well.

Even after Sydney left, Rocky had been completely pathetic. *Want me; need me.* And Jack had the nerve to make a big deal about a few dumb lies? He was probably still waiting for an apology.

And it hurt so bad to think about him, she wondered why her heart didn't just stop from the pain.

Rocky stared at the contracts spread across her desk. She'd been proofing for two days and she wasn't even past the third paragraph. There were too many made-up movies running in her head, distracting her. Sydney, standing at the door, giving Jack her sexy best. Only, in Rocky's version, Jack didn't shut the door and step outside.

Sydney, I don't know how to tell you . . . I realize now it was never you I loved . . .

Rocky dropped her head into her hands and groaned. "You are a lost cause."

She pushed back her chair, getting up. Probably best to pack up and call it a day—before she began doodling *I love Jack* in the margins of the contracts. Everyone had gone for the day anyway. *Time to move on.* Put another day under her belt.

Yesterday she'd left early, and Jack had practically mugged her in the parking lot. Seeing him, Rocky had locked arms with Veronica from accounting and walked past. She knew he wouldn't confront her if anybody was around. Not, straitlaced, too-perfect Jack Bosse. He'd never admit he'd done anything as *Melrose Place* as sleep with his fiancée's stepdaughter.

Today he must have walked by her cubicle five times, making some excuse or another. Five times. That's how long it took him before he stepped past the partition and asked if she had a minute to go over a few things in his office.

"Sorry, Jack. Busy," she'd told him. She hadn't even looked up.

Very busy. Busy for the next twenty years, guy.

When he'd made love to her, it had been just like in the storybooks. Prince Charming come to life.

Jack had waited a full twenty-four hours before caving in to his guilty conscience and calling her. He actually surprised her, waiting that long. She could just imagine what he was thinking. *Oh, my God. I slept with Rocky. A virgin!* The bells going off in his head.

The messages on her machine were pretty pathetic. *Call me. . . . We need to talk. Call me . . . I know you're there. Pick up.*

Call me. Please.

Not that it made her feel any better, his persistence. Rocky had always known he'd get around to making things "right." The little Catholic boy inside him couldn't help himself. Jack was the kind of man who refused to have sex with a woman because she might be drunk, for God's sake. He hadn't even slept with Sydney, and Rocky could just imagine whose idea that had been. *Who gets engaged to a woman who won't sleep with him?* P-a-t-h-e-t-i-c.

Now, heading out to the parking lot, she thought she should probably stop coming to work. Make some excuse. Just wave the white flag and say "die." It was getting that hard to see him.

Ten minutes later she drove onto the street, steering for home. Not returning his messages was a little "in your face," but she managed. She stuck with a pattern. She came home, worked out until she was too tired to do anything other than drink a glass of wine and watch some video where, in the end, the girl gets her man.

Crying into her wine, that was the best part. She figured that was the point to half these movies. A nice long cry about love lost.

In the morning she'd down a multivitamin with a glass of milk, worried that she might be pregnant. As if that little Band-Aid might make up for a day of sugar, caffeine, and alcohol. She hadn't even thought about that possibility when she'd gone to his place . . . hadn't even kept track of her period to know it was a bad time.

The past week had been a roller-coaster existence. Her father's phone call last night only made it worse.

"Can you find out for me, sweetheart?" he'd asked, the not-so-subtle subtext being: *Will you spy for me?*

He'd called wanting to know if Sydney was taking any sort of medication. The question itself surprised Rocky. *How should I know and why do you care?* It seemed so out of the blue.

But her father claimed that Sydney had called him at the office, sounding "out of it." Given what he termed a "plague of lawsuits," and her broken engagement, he wondered if the pressure wasn't getting to her. He suggested he and Rocky might try some sort of intervention. Help her out.

"If you think she's that close to a breakdown, Daddy, then leave her the hell alone," she'd suggested. Not the best tactic with her father. Pointing out that he was the evil demon in Sydney's life.

In her father's opinion, he couldn't be faulted for the government's decision to seek restitution from Sydney. He had, in fact, made it possible for her to keep everything. It was Sydney's decision to turn down his offer after all.

"Now, of course, it's too late. I can't help the art

center. Not after the government filed its motion last week," he explained. "But I won't give up on Sydney. Rocky, I only want to help."

Who to believe—who to trust?

Rocky should have known it was just a matter of time before it all caught up to her. Certainly, she should have anticipated Jack's next move.

But no, he caught her by surprise.

Almost too late, Rocky slammed on the brakes. The car came to a abrupt halt only inches from slamming into Jack's legs.

She could feel her heart pounding in her chest. She didn't know if it was fear or exhilaration, or maybe both.

He was wearing sunglasses, so she couldn't see his eyes. He had on a European-cut suit accented by a bright blue shirt and tie. The effect would be stunning with his eyes, she knew. She didn't look forward to it.

At twenty-three, Rocky counted her greatest achievement the fact that she hadn't become a carbon copy of her mother. Sex hadn't even been a temptation when placed against the background of that albatross. Only, she'd never planned on Jack. What he made her feel every time she looked at him.

Sleeping with him had been everything she'd imagined. And, unfortunately, so much more.

She rolled down her window, allowing him to lean in.

"I almost ran your ass over," she told him with a tight smile.

"I guess you don't have my reflexes."

She sighed. He was so damn sexy. "What did you do? Stake out my route home?"

"Maybe I just got lucky."

Yeah, right. "What do you want, Jack?"

"I thought since you were being childish about the whole thing, I'd stoop to your level."

She said in a sugary voice, "I am so sorry I forced my little old self on you, Jackson. But do we really need to chew it over?"

He looked away, obviously not happy with her characterization of their night together. He told her, "Why do you have to make everything so difficult?"

She stared at the dashboard, knowing that he was right. Wishing, at the same time, he'd just leave her the hell alone. *I want to go home. Drink my wine, watch my movies. Live someone else's happy ending.*

But he wasn't leaving. Instead, he took off his sunglasses, waiting. Watching.

In the end, those beautiful blue eyes had nothing to do with her decision.

She opened the passenger door.

He'd barely shut the door before she peeled out, driving pedal to the metal. She watched him lodge his shoulders against the door and the seat, trying to keep his six feet some from careening across the cab.

"This is supposed to impress me?" he asked.

"Oh, I've stopped trying to impress you, say"—she made a mental count—"six days ago?" She turned at the corner. One wheel actually drove up onto the sidewalk before thumping down.

"I see you're acting your age."

"Wish you'd act yours, old man," she countered.

He grabbed the steering wheel and pressed his foot to the brake. She didn't fight him, letting him park the car alongside the road. He grabbed the keys out of the ignition.

"Do you really think you're the first woman to come on to me like a steamroller?" he asked. "You think I haven't had a few propositions in my day?"

"I don't know, Jack. I figured since you were chasing after rich old broads, you might be kind of hard up."

He turned her to face him. "I'm not supposed to question that suddenly you find me irresistible?"

"Great. Before, I was a mental case, ready to get under the sheets with you just to stab Sydney in the back. Now I fucked you for your money? How refreshing."

"Am I supposed to believe it's love?"

She thought about the choices she had. She could tell him then and there that she had no idea what she felt. Only, that she'd been drowning in her doubts when she'd showed up on his doorstep, fearful that she was missing the one time in her life that something special had come her way. That making love to him had made her feel, for the first time in a very long time, safe.

Like everything else, it turned out to be an illusion. *Who to trust?*

"Well," he said, "I can see by your expression that I'm scoring big-time here." He shook his head. "Rocky. I don't know what to do. This is crazy. A couple of nights ago . . . maybe there was something there. Something that despite how it came about, we need to explore. Maybe I don't want to walk away right now, and even that confuses me. Could you make this just a tiny bit easier?"

"As a matter of fact"—she kept her eyes on him; *if I don't blink, I won't cry*—"why don't we just take all these possibilities of yours and pop on over to Sydney's house? Talk it over, just the three of us? What do you think, Jack? Am I a genius, or what?''

She flashed a wide smile to take away from the possibility that he might hear the tears in her voice. She wasn't going to be anybody's runner-up. ''Does that make it any easier for you?''

Jack stared ahead, his mouth crimped in a tight frown, saying nothing.

''You talk a good game,'' she said when she thought she could speak with a steady voice, ''but I'm betting you're getting out of this car rather than facing Sydney. You haven't nearly given up your happy ending, Jack. Don't tell me you're looking for something to replace it already.''

She grabbed the keys out of his hand and started up the car. Shifting into gear, she revved the engine.

''Last chance,'' she told him.

After a minute, he opened the door and stepped out.

Rocky peeled away, hurting. Just hurting.

''You little shit,'' she told him in the rearview mirror. ''Freaking coward.''

But she'd known. She'd just known.

In life there came these moments, Sydney thought. As if the gods above decided, *It's time.* You were trapped in some psychic vortex, and suddenly everything you'd set into motion came at you all at once. You couldn't prepare or catch your breath—you didn't know if you were coming or going. Like now. With the doorbell ringing, announcing her fate. She thought it was Alec.

Last night he crept back into her life, a thief. She

had no defenses against the kind of emotion he'd shown. She could only give in, accept the inevitable— fall into the pull of the forces surrounding him like gravity. *Go with the flow.*

After he'd left, she'd sat most of the day anticipating the phone call she'd been expecting, sometimes staring at the phone, willing it to ring. After weeks of planning, her first real weapon against Russell seemed almost within reach.

Almost there . . . almost safe.

Certainly, she thought she had it all under control . . . until she opened the door to find not Alec, but Rocky on her doorstep. And she was crying.

"Hey." Sydney put her arm around her, the gesture automatic as she ushered Rocky inside. But the entire thing felt foreign. She couldn't remember the last time Rocky had allowed Sydney to comfort her.

"What happened?" she asked, because she could think of nothing else to say. She felt caught off guard. Unprepared. *Just like Alec last night.*

She guided Rocky to the couch. Rocky couldn't seem to catch her breath; she was sobbing, another woman entirely.

Sydney had known Rocky and her sisters for years. Aphrodite, the oldest, showed her emotions with ease; Carmela had elevated crying to an art form. But Rocky, she'd specialized in the cutting attack. *If I push you away hard enough, you won't be around to see me fall.*

Sydney knew instinctively that Rocky would hate this show of emotion. Stepping back, she watched her stepdaughter slowly collapse into herself on the couch. Sydney turned for the kitchen. *A glass of water.* Trying to give Rocky some time to herself.

It was Friday night. As promised, Alec had dropped

off a duffel bag of clothes before he'd mysteriously disappeared, telling her not to hold dinner. Sydney had spent the time crossing her T's and dotting her I's, waiting for the call from her contact in New York. Law books and papers covered the kitchen table. Now she shoved everything aside, placing the heap on the built-in desk in the kitchen before returning with a glass of water for Rocky.

"I'm not sure how this will help, but here," she said, handing Rocky the glass.

"Water." For the first time, Rocky laughed. But she took a sip just the same. "Not even a good stiff drink." She laughed again, catching her breath. "I'm sorry." She gave Sydney a small smile, then hiccuped. "Would you believe I was in the neighborhood?"

Sydney sat down beside Rocky on the couch. There had been a time she thought she could be a "mother" to Rocky, or, at the very least, a confidante. In those days she'd thought Rocky was her only chance to experience a family.

Of course, it hadn't worked out. Just the opposite. She'd married Russell, taking "Daddy" away. From then on, Rocky kept her distance.

She pushed back Rocky's bangs, the gesture familiar to both women. Rocky grasped her hand.

"You used to do that a lot," she said.

Sydney nodded. "I always loved your hair. I loved brushing it."

Rocky laughed. "When I let you."

She laughed along with her, remembering. "Way back when I wasn't the stepmonster."

Rocky made a face. "Jack told you?"

Sydney frowned, wondering what she could mean by that. "No. Aphrodite."

"Oh, yeah." She looked embarrassed. "You guys are friends."

Sydney had in fact kept a relationship with all three of Carla's daughters, although only Rocky had ever lived with her and Russell. One summer, during college, as Sydney recalled. Rocky had done her level best to make Sydney's life a living hell for three months, while Sydney only laughed, enjoying the younger woman's effort.

She used to think Rocky resented her for the attention Russell granted. They were just two women pining for the same man. But over the last year she'd come to see Rocky's behavior in a completely different light.

Those years with Russell, Sydney had been too weak, needy. She'd allowed him to manipulate her. She could just imagine what Rocky felt watching her— Rocky, the only other woman he belittled and abused. *Stand up to him! Please!*

No wonder she'd come to hate her.

"What happened?" Sydney asked, wondering what Russell had done now. As she'd told Jack, she and Rocky were members of an exclusive club—women who had survived Russell Reck. She could think of only one reason Rocky would seek her out, a fellow survivor.

Rocky shrugged. "A guy. What else?"

Sydney tried to hide her surprise. But when Rocky didn't clarify, she made her own offer. "Hey, how about something to eat? I was just making myself dinner. You want to join me?"

"That would be nice," Rocky said.

She followed Sydney into the kitchen, where Sydney handed her two bowls and nodded toward the table.

Rocky stared at the dishes. "Like old times," she said, ready to set the table.

They sat down to a bowl of soup and crunchy French bread. Rocky dug in with an appetite as Sydney poured them each a glass of Riesling wine.

"I forgot what a good cook you are," she said.

"Oh, yes. I'm handy with a can opener." They both laughed. But after a few minutes of silence, Sydney said, "I can give you lessons if you like. With the can opener, I mean." Then, trying to keep things light, she said, "Or maybe you haven't given up your supermodel aspirations?"

The soup seemed to stick in Rocky's throat. She looked as if she was going to take a sip of wine, but thought better of it. She said, "Sometimes it's hard to remember to stop and eat."

"We keep you that busy?"

She'd noticed the past week that Rocky appeared almost worn out. *A guy?* The way Sydney saw it, the only man who could break Rocky's heart was her father.

Rocky played with her glass. She turned to Sydney. *Here it comes,* Sydney thought.

"I know it's weird, my coming over here. I just wanted . . ."

Again that pause, as if she were searching for the courage as well as the words.

"What happened, Sydney?" she asked finally. "Between you and Jack, I mean. Why did it fall apart?"

Sydney found herself caught off guard for the second time that night.

The idea that Rocky might be genuinely curious about Sydney's relationship with Jack struck her as, well, odd. And, quite frankly, impossible. *Maybe this isn't about Russell. . . .*

"Sorry." Rocky returned to her soup, obviously put off by Sydney's silence. "I guess I shouldn't be so nosy."

"No, it's fine. You just surprised me, that's all. I mean . . . well, I can't imagine you came here to talk about me, right?" She wondered how hard to push. "Look, it's obvious you're not eating or sleeping very well. Something's wrong and I'm glad you came to me." She decided to get there straight. "But I can't help unless you tell me what's really wrong."

Rocky nodded. She had that look about her. A woman on the verge of confession. When it came, it wasn't what Sydney expected.

"I slept with someone," she told Sydney. "It was my first time."

Her words struck from left field. Sydney didn't know what to say or how to react, again wondering why Rocky would come to her about such a thing. But then she realized, *Why not?* It's not like she could give Carla, her mother, a call. And sometimes Aphrodite could get so involved with her children, there wasn't a lot left over for anyone else.

"The first time can be tough," she said.

"I know it's weird that I waited so long."

Sydney shook her head. "No. It just surprises me." *Not Russell after all.* "You were always so . . . I don't know. Let's just say you weren't shy."

"He loves somebody else." She was staring at her soup, not even pretending to eat anymore. "I knew it too. I just thought"—she frowned—"I don't know what I thought. We slept together and it was wonderful and—"

"You hoped it would change things?" Sydney finished, knowing exactly what she meant. *A lot of that going around . . .*

She watched as Rocky's face crumpled into that horrible expression of holding back tears. "I guess I did."

When she regained her composure, she looked up. Sydney could see she had more to say.

But instead, Rocky shook her head, pushing away her bowl. "I should get going."

Sydney stood with her. "Rocky, don't. You're here now. Let me help you. Please?"

The phone rang, startling them both. Sydney thought she'd let the machine get it, but her anxiety over the call must have shown on her face.

"You'd better answer that," Rocky said.

The worst possible timing. "I'll just be a minute."

She used the phone in the bedroom, picking up. As it turned out, it was a good thing she'd taken the call, which was from her contact in New York. She jotted down the information, elated, then hung up, taking a breath.

Tomorrow she would go to New York, taking the early morning flight. She picked up the slip of paper where she'd written the information. Maybe, just maybe, she'd finally have what she needed to end this.

She stopped on her way to the kitchen, staring at the paper. She told herself that what she did now wasn't just in her best interest. It couldn't be helped, how Rocky might see her plans. *She'll think you betrayed her. Again.* Certainly, after tomorrow's trip, Sydney would be the last person Rocky would confide in.

Only, when she walked back into the kitchen, she

found Rocky standing near the microwave, searching through the prescription medicines Sydney kept on the counter.

"Hey there, nosy," Sydney said, only half joking.

But if Rocky thought she was doing anything wrong, she didn't act like it. She merely held up one of the bottles.

"What's all this stuff for? Xanax? Naldecon? Paxil?"

Sydney walked over, telling herself not to be so suspicious. The worry in Rocky's voice was actually touching. "Xanax is a tranquilizer. Naldecon"—she held up the bottle, smiling—"for my allergies."

"Why all this stuff?"

"It's been a rough couple of years for me. First Henry. Then your father." She'd never been embarrassed by the medications she took. She wasn't someone averse to seeking help if she needed it.

She shrugged. "I had panic attacks. And trouble sleeping. The medicines helped."

"Are you like seeing someone?"

"You mean a therapist? I did. For a while. But not now." She took the bottle of Paxil out of Rocky's hand. "I meant to throw that out. An antidepressant I stopped taking years ago. Look, Rocky. I don't take most of these medications anymore. Things are better. Really."

"Yeah, okay." Rocky turned abruptly, a different light in her eyes. She shook her head, gesturing wildly at the medications. "I can't believe I came to you for help. You're practically a nut job yourself."

Before Sydney could recover from the verbal attack, Rocky headed for the door. Sydney ran after her.

She stopped Rocky at the door. "Rocky, what's going on?" she asked, confused. "You're upset because I took some medicines? Check those expiration dates; I'm fine." She looked closer, trying to figure out what was behind Rocky's turnaround.

"Rocky, honey. I've made a few mistakes in my life," she told her. "I'm sorry to say that your father was probably the biggest one—though I don't expect you to understand. I know you love him; I wouldn't change that. Sometimes, even if it hurts, we have to try loving someone—"

"You're talking about the other guy," Rocky said coldly, cutting her off. "The pilot."

Sydney took a step back, stunned. She'd been trying to say something to help Rocky through her own personal crises. Alec was the last person she'd expect to have thrown in her face.

It shocked her that Rocky would even bring up the subject. As if Sydney had committed some act of betrayal. Which she had. To Jack, not Rocky.

Rocky took the opportunity to shove past Sydney, closing the door in her face. *Snap, click.*

Sydney fell back against the wall, depleted. "What in the world?" She spoke the question out loud.

It seemed so strange, Rocky coming here in the first place. But the way she'd left . . .

You're practically a nut job yourself.

She'd spoken in anger, but the expression on her face . . . she'd looked so unhappy.

Sydney stepped back into the kitchen, staring at the bowls of soup, a testament to what had happened. She glanced at the research papers heaped in the corner, again experiencing that tremor of doubt.

Rocky coming here, the act itself was a cry for help—which only made Sydney feel worse about her abrupt departure.

And the phone call. Tomorrow's trip added to Sydney's unease. She should have said something. She should have warned Rocky somehow.

Prepare for the worst. . . .

Rocky started the car but didn't pull away from the curb. She could still see all those papers piled on the counter in the kitchen.

Transactional immunity—plea agreement.

Rocky pulled into the street. It was late enough that only parked cars lined the road. The windows of each house were lit up so that she could imagine the families inside sitting down for dinner. Normal folks. Normal lives.

She'd gone to Sydney because she'd been half afraid that Jack would follow her back home if she didn't make good on her threat. But when Sydney opened the door, everything Rocky had been holding inside erupted to the surface. When Sydney took her into her arms, she felt as if she was exactly where she wanted to be.

For a little while it had actually been nice. Like the old days. When Sydney touched her hair, it reminded her of so many things.

Then she'd seen those papers. *Plea agreement . . .*

Sydney was planning something.

"Something that is going to hurt Daddy."

Unless Rocky told him first.

Close Call

Twenty-three

Sydney stared at the ghost sitting on the other side of the Plexiglas barrier. She spoke into the phone.

"Russell put you here, Mr. Kinnard. Tell me you wouldn't like to save him a seat."

Joseph Kinnard hadn't changed much since his spy days. Only that nifty sense of style he'd cultivated seemed to suffer in the absence of his Milan suits. With his military bearing, he still had presence, even sporting the pajamalike prison garb.

Sydney recalled once thinking he'd played the part of spook for so many years, he'd actually begun to look like one. Tall, with white hair and colorless eyes, in prison he'd become almost bloodless, his complexion sallow under the prison lights.

"Call me, Joseph." His lips moved to the words coming through the phone, out of sync, like a badly dubbed movie. "Mrs. Reck—"

"Sydney," she corrected him. "And I go by Shanks."

"Of course." He allowed himself a small smile. "What could you possibly have to offer me?"

"I've done a little research. It appears there may be a loophole in Russell's plea deal with the government. But I need your cooperation in order to—"

He shook his head, stopping her cold. "I'm here for enough years, thank you. I won't risk adding more, even for the pleasure of having Russell here beside me. You came a long way for nothing."

"But that's the beauty of it, Joseph," she said, ready to explain the theories she'd researched so diligently. "You've been tried and convicted. Under the rule of law, any charges that might arise from your acts to defraud the government should have been brought at the time of trial. You're covered under double jeopardy. Russell's situation, however, isn't so clear."

"I'm listening."

"There's a little thing called changed circumstances, where plea agreements are involved," she said, getting into the finer points of the law. "If Russell lied about his involvement, perhaps keeping certain facts from the prosecution—facts that you might help bring to light—it's considered a breach of his agreement. The government could still prosecute."

She leaned closer toward the glass, giving him a moment to let the truth sink in. She saw it. The lightbulb coming on: *Revenge.*

"You're a resourceful man. You spent years running covert operations. Tell me there wasn't a thing or two you managed to hide?"

"Not that it helped me," he said, smiling gently, checking the eagerness she'd seen on his face.

"But perhaps," she told him, "now it can."

He leaned back, watching her. Inscrutable with his near colorless eyes. "They could prosecute him?"

"Tell me it wouldn't be sweet," she said, granting her own smile.

Overhead, the disembodied voice of the guard warned that her visit would be up in five minutes. But she'd seen what she needed. Joseph Kinnard was on board.

"You've given me something to think about," he said, allowing that much. "I'll let you know."

She watched him hang up the phone and call over the guard, waiting to be uncuffed before leaving his seat. Joseph Kinnard wasn't a young man. He was behind bars possibly for the rest of his natural life. Certainly the good years were lost, unless one of his appeals came through, which was highly unlikely. All thanks to Russell's testimony against him.

Now Sydney had dangled another possibility besides endless nights of regret. *He's going to do it,* she told herself.

Riding the elevator down, Sydney thought people like Joseph Kinnard thrived on wielding power. Today, she'd given him a taste of what he'd once had. Control over people's lives.

Shielding her eyes as she stepped into the sunlight, she felt light of heart for the first time in weeks. She donned her sunglasses, smiling as she hailed a taxi. She couldn't believe she'd done it. Boy, it felt good. *An end run around Russell.*

It wasn't until she reached the airport that she received the page.

Only her secretary knew where she'd gone for the day. Just in case. Now she heard her name called over the sound system at Kennedy.

"I'm Sydney Shanks," she told the woman behind the counter.

The representative from the airlines handed her the message slip with a tired, prefabricated smile. Sydney unfolded the sheet of paper, reading the words with dread: *Call me ASAP. J.*

She told herself it was probably nothing as she pulled out her cell phone, wincing when the symbol for a dead battery flashed on. She didn't need to worry so much, she counseled. The last few days had her on edge, that's all. She shouldn't expect the worst.

As if Jack would page her for anything less.

At the bank of phones he filled her in. She was needed back at the gallery. She'd been right to worry.

Crisis, crisis.

Jack watched Sydney throw the papers on her desk, then massage her temples. He already regretted calling her back to the office. *Hurry home, dear . . . it's all falling apart around us.* Now he watched her fight a migraine from the flight. No doubt, she'd skipped dinner. And his news for her wasn't good.

"I don't understand," she told him. "We had these things checked out. How could we have so many code violations?" she asked, pointing to the list he'd dropped on her lap.

The day she'd taken her mystery trip to New York, all hell had broken loose at the gallery in the form of a city inspector. The code violations he'd noted could probably fill a phone book.

"Even more important," Jack said, "why did they check at all? We weren't due for an inspection. Not until next year."

Waiting, Jack watched her read between the lines. From what he knew of Russell Reck, dirty tricks wouldn't be a stretch.

"So what do we do?" she asked, throwing her hands up. "It's not like we have any evidence of wrongdoing, much less that Russell is involved. Even the shipment of paints for the Picasso workshop checked out. I signed the acquisition papers myself."

But Jack wasn't listening. He was staring at the wall behind Sydney, wondering when exactly he'd begun to panic.

A sure sign that he'd lost it: hunting Sydney down in New York, having her paged at the airport. If he'd put some thought into what he was doing before making that call—like the good old days, when he actually had a working brain—he wouldn't have been so quick to sound the alarm bells. What the hell did he expect Sydney to do? Pull a rabbit out of a hat?

Maybe I'm just out of practice putting out fires. Things had just gone too smoothly for too long so that, at the first sign of turbulence—Rocky—he'd nose-dived into libido limbo, losing control. For the first time in his life, he couldn't get back on track.

"Jack?"

He looked up, realizing he'd zoned while Sydney waited for her answer. He shook his head. "I shouldn't have made you come down. Hell, this can all wait until tomorrow. What was your trip to New York about anyway?"

She seemed to hesistate before saying, "A new collection I'm considering. And don't be ridiculous. Of course you should have called. I need to be here." She pushed the code violations across the table. "If

I thought it would do any good, I'd go right over and give Russell a piece of my mind.''

"What about Rocky?"

Once he asked the question, he realized what had him in such a state. Rocky. Her involvement was something he didn't want to face.

Sydney stared at Jack, nonplussed. "What do you mean, what about Rocky?"

"You can't tell me you haven't considered it?" He circled around the desk, the blood pounding in his temples. "That she's involved?"

"Of course Rocky isn't involved."

"That sounds like blind faith talking. For God's sake, Sydney. He's her father. Look, maybe I should talk to her?"

You'd think he'd just asked if he should fly to the moon—which he pretty much had. It wouldn't make any sense, him taking on Rocky. They were oil and water. Everyone at the gallery knew they didn't get along, right? He hadn't stopped complaining about her since the day she'd stepped through the door.

And shouldn't that have been your first clue, buddy?

All his life Jack had been this even-keel guy. The fact that Rocky could get under his skin so quick, so hot . . . *Oh, yeah. Big clue.*

"Am I missing something here?" Sydney asked, her question reflecting exactly what he'd feared.

You tipped your hand . . . you practically confessed.

He circled the desk again, considering what might happen next. He should tell her. Hell, he could see the idea forming in her eyes. *Beat her to the punch. . . .*

But Sydney visibly shook it off. The possibility of Jack and Rocky together was apparently too strange even to consider. "Whatever it is, Jack," she said firmly, "we'll take care of it. Together. But don't bring Rocky into this. She has her own issues to deal with right now."

She was trying to make him feel better—which only made him feel worse. He realized he'd been walking in circles, pacing. Getting nowhere, like this conversation.

He stopped to lean over the desk, catching his breath. The thing was, he knew exactly what he had to do. He'd known from the moment he'd placed that call to Kennedy.

"Let me look into a few things," he finally told her. He tried to make it sound casual as he walked to the door. Tried not to hurry his steps. "Let's call it a day, in any case. You go home. Get some rest. The facts may look kinder in the morning. To both of us."

But just before he reached the door, she called out, "Jack."

He turned, expecting the worst. *You're not sleeping with my stepdaughter, are you?*

But she only asked, "Are you okay?"

He took a breath, even managed a smile. "Given the circumstances? I'd say I'm peachy."

Peachy. That pretty much described the last week, he thought, edging past the door. Like he had a peach pit stuck in his gut. Like he was choking on it.

He kept going down the hall, watching his feet. *One in front of the other, guy.* He felt light-headed. Hot. Like he'd broken into a sweat.

This time when he reached her cubicle, he didn't allow himself to be tentative, just barged right inside. He couldn't tiptoe around Rocky like he had the last week, trying to figure out his next step. He needed to act.

He knew she'd been staying late, so he wasn't surprised to find her daydreaming at her desk. She was trying to avoid him, that much she'd made clear. *Sorry, hon. Not tonight.*

She looked up, obviously startled to see him. Her face looked drawn. At a guess, she wasn't sleeping much. *I know the feeling, sweetheart.*

He'd been thinking about her every night. She was an enchantress in his head. Soft, smelling of flowers, her blond hair spread out on the bed, sexy as hell. He couldn't block those images, couldn't cut off his desire for her.

Of course Rocky isn't involved.

Well, Jack couldn't be so sure. He was hiding things from Sydney, information that could come back and bite him in the ass. But right now he needed to know this one thing.

"We have to talk," he told her.

Rocky stared at the *Time* magazine on her desk. She flipped back a page in that languid manner she feigned sometimes. As if she hadn't a care in the world.

"I thought we pretty much covered everything the other day," she said, flipping another page.

"Not hardly."

He closed the magazine, then grabbed her purse. He held it out for her, this silly little thing that matched her heels. He hoped the gesture fell under the "big hint" category.

She looked up with a sigh, as if thinking about it. But then she smiled, taking everything in a totally different direction. Like he was sitting on a roller coaster and that smile just signaled Big Dip Ahead.

She gave him this sly look. "Are you buying?"

"Dinner? Sure." Whatever it takes, he told himself. "Why not?"

She stood, again taking her time. As she walked past, he noticed her skirt, so tight he could see she was wearing a thong underneath.

She glanced over her shoulder, almost posing at the door. "Somewhere expensive, Jack. I don't want you to think I'm cheap."

He took her to the Twin Palms, Kevin Costner's restaurant in Newport. By the time they finished, dinner clocked in at over two hundred dollars. Not that Rocky touched more than a bite.

It wasn't so much that she was thin. Rocky had curves in all the right places, like those old-time movie stars or one of the *Baywatch* babes. But her face, yeah. You could see it there. Like suddenly she had these cheekbones. And there were dark smudges under her eyes that even makeup couldn't hide.

"Well." She smiled over her wineglass. "At least I won't feel cheap tonight."

"Why do you say shit like that?"

She sat back, draping an arm over the back of her chair. "Isn't it obvious? Because it makes you feel like the dirty old man you are."

"You think that's what this is about? Nothing clued you in that tonight might be different?"

They hadn't said two words to each other since they'd sat down, both of them buzzing like windup toys ready to snap their coil. Tonight was nothing like that evening at his house, when they'd both let down their guard.

"You think we came here because I want to sleep with you?"

Flashing an all-knowing smile, she leaned forward so that the lacy cup of her bra edged out from beneath the linen blouse. "I think you can't help yourself."

"Right."

He'd paid the bill, but neither of them made any move to stand. Rocky had been playing with her wine-glass all night. She seemed almost disinterested, the temptress biding her time. She stared out over the dining room featuring two dramatic indoor palm trees reaching for the sky.

For the umpteenth time that night, he wondered what she was thinking.

"Are you in any kind of trouble?" he asked, breaking the silence.

He'd been thinking it over since they'd sat down, putting it together. If her father was behind their current stretch of bad luck at the museum . . . if Rocky was involved . . . there had to be something pushing her, right? Something bigger than the internal demons he glimpsed every so often. She couldn't fake what he'd seen in her eyes the night they'd made love. No one was that good of an actress.

"You think I'm in trouble? Because of you?" she asked.

She was just throwing back his words, not revealing anything. He didn't know how to get into it, so he played it her way. "Okay." He gave a smile. "Let's try a different question. Your father. Why don't we discuss him a minute."

Her face changed ever so subtly, her full lips flattening into a straight line. "What about him?"

"Do you think he'd approve of me? A self-made man like himself. Do you think maybe we should meet?"

"You're not going to meet my father."

She stood and snagged her purse. She walked briskly, faster than he'd thought possible in those damn heels.

He caught up with her just outside the door.

"You listen to me," he said, squeezing her arm. "I will not let you hurt her."

"Is that how you make this okay in your head, Jack? Following me around, taking me to dinner? You're doing the Boy Scout thing? Making the big bad sacrifice to protect Sydney?"

Before he could answer, she turned completely around, facing him. She reached up, steadying his face in her hands.

She kissed him, her full lips on his in a way that pushed the panic button. Still, he couldn't help himself. He threaded his hands up into her incredible hair, pulling her against him, losing himself in that kiss.

When she broke it off, her lips bruised from his, she covered her mouth with her hands, almost tripping as she took another wobbly step back.

"Now what, Sherlock?" she asked.

The really incredible part was the look on her face. Like she could burst into tears just standing there. Like she could break.

Before he could answer, she said, "Forget it." Like maybe she'd read something in his stupefied expression and she wasn't waiting around to hear the bad news. She ran for the curb, hailing a cab.

"Just leave me the hell alone," she shouted over her shoulder, not caring who might hear.

He raced up beside her and pulled her around. Thinking action spoke louder than words, he grabbed her hand and dragged her toward the waiting valet. Everyone stared. *So much for the ordinary life.* They were making a scene.

He hustled her into his car and drove away, concentrating. *Red light coming up . . . blind curve ahead.* He told himself he would take her home and drop her off. That Sydney was right. He wasn't the man for the job. He shouldn't forget past performance. This woman could make him do things he might regret.

But when he pulled up to her driveway, she sat still in the seat beside him. She had her arms crossed beneath her chest, staring straight ahead. He waited, not bothering to turn off the motor.

"You hate me now," she whispered.

He closed his eyes. *God, I wish.* "Nothing is that simple."

She glanced at him. The light from the street slashed in from behind him, spotlighting her. There was a shine to her eyes—not from tears, he hoped. She gave him a shy smile, looking painfully young.

That was the thing about Rocky. One minute, you thought you were dealing with Attila the Hun. The next, she was reaching across the cab and taking your hand in hers, holding it so tight, like she was doing now. A little girl lost. Acting so damn sweet, it hurt.

"I've been dying to do that all night." She whispered it like a secret.

"Hold my hand?" He nodded as if that made any sense at all. "Jesus. You are so young."

"And you were born old."

She held up his hand to the light, examining it from every angle. Slowly, she matched their palms together. Liking the fit, she twined their fingers. "You have beautiful hands, Jack."

Like any of this made sense. Him sitting there, listening to this, slowly closing his hand over hers, making her hand look tiny . . . almost insubstantial.

She doesn't have anything to do with it, he told himself. *The bastard's probably using her.*

"I have these movie videos," she said. "Just dumb love stories. I watch them at night. You want to come in? Maybe watch one with me?"

She was biting her lip, everything she felt so easy to see.

"I don't think I should."

She nodded. After a minute, she released his hand and kissed his cheek. "Good night, sweet prince. Thanks for dinner."

He waited, watching her walk up her drive and open her door. She waved, as if letting him know she was okay. *All safe and tucked inside.* She shut the door behind her; she turned off the porch light.

And that was that.

A big waste of time, he told himself. He didn't know anything more than he did a few hours before. She still had all the answers . . . while he just sat there, trying to figure out what the last five minutes had been about.

He didn't know how long he stayed in the car or even when he turned off the motor, telling himself he was wasting gas. *I'll just sit here a bit longer. Catch my breath.*

He ended up at her front door, of course. He almost

even knocked before he turned away, getting cold feet. *Shit. Shit!*

Suddenly the door opened. He stood there, frozen, caught off guard. She'd changed, wearing a T-shirt and men's boxer shorts. She leaned against the door, not saying a word.

He could tell she'd been crying.

"I thought." He made some lame gesture back toward the car. "I mean, I just wondered—"

She covered his mouth with her fingers. She pulled him inside. When she shut the door, she leaned against it.

"Just don't make me feel cheap, Jack," she said before stepping into his arms.

TWENTY-FOUR

A week after he moved in with Sydney, Alec started a philosophical discussion with himself. It was like he had a freaking professor stuck in his head. Day and night, the debate went on. Even in his sleep. *Wrong vs. right.*

Sydney, for example. Like the song said: How could something that felt so right be wrong? That's what he'd tell himself making love to her in the shower, or watching her over a cup of coffee, trying to memorize just how she looked at that moment, with her hair tied back off her face and her glasses on instead of contacts, no makeup . . . and looking more beautiful than any woman had a right to.

Nothing had ever been so good in his life—and maybe that's what scared him most. Alec Porter was waiting for the other shoe to drop.

But when they came together . . . that time was perfection. The noise in his head disappeared and this quiet came over him, a gift. In those still moments, he wasn't some washed-up asshole lying to Sydney while trying to make good on some pathetic promise he'd made himself to keep her safe. Like magic, he could be anyone, do anything. For her he could be a hero.

For the first time ever, he wanted what he'd seen there in the moonlight with Conor and Cherish . . . what Travis had with his Juliet. A happy ending.

Hell, he could believe anything looking into her eyes when they made love. If he worked hard enough, if he worried, if he suffered enough . . . maybe, just maybe, he could make a go of it with Sydney.

He'd almost have himself convinced.

Then that little voice would start up: *All you have to do is lie to her for the rest of your life and make sure she never finds out the truth.* The one thing that would break her heart . . . she was sleeping with the enemy.

Which brought him back to his discussion: Wrong vs. right.

Now, standing down the hall right outside the office of the systems manager for Reck Enterprises, Alec was back at it. He'd remember how lately things were just going too right. Like now, with Donald there hightailing it down the hall in the direction opposite from where Alec was standing. He knew Donald was running for the south gate, where security would be holding a package for him. Coming out of his office, Donald looked like a kid with a spare dollar burning a hole in his pocket.

Donald, Alec found out, had a thing for radio-controlled planes. He was president of the local chapter, where guys sat around on Saturdays, playing their controls like Game boys as they piloted their planes through touch-and-go's and Cuban eights. He'd been telling Alec all about it last week over a sack lunch when Alec just happened to find a spot next to him. Donald, it seemed, had ordered this new part. A big deal. Going to revolutionize RC planes. Only, it was on back order, see?

Alec had made sure Christmas came a little early for Donald this year.

Now Donald was off, almost skipping. All packages waited at security back at the south gate. That way, the company didn't have to deal with a messy clearance for the local UPS guys. It was a bit of a jaunt; Alec had timed it. Even taking into account the fact that Donald was a fifty-two-year-old man with a hip replacement, Alec wouldn't have long.

He slipped into Donald's office, putting his coffee cup down on the table. He pulled out the cartridge he carried in his pocket and slipped it into the zip drive of the PC on the desk.

"Let's see what he's hiding," he said, typing the password into Donald's computer.

Like he'd told Syd. Russell Reck wasn't waiting around forever.

Alec had found the password written in Donald's DayTimer as a bank account number. Pretty ingenious, really. Only, to Alec, the numbers lit up like the Fourth of July when he'd flipped through. Most people had two accounts, checking and savings. Donald listed three, with the third one having a number off sequence.

As the systems manager, Donald had access to everything: system files, the mail server, even individual files. Donald ran Timbuktu, software that allowed him to call up on his screen anything backed up on any harddrive in the building.

Alec watched as a window popped up—a screen

within a screen—showing Reck's desktop. Alec had a quick look-see, not expecting to find anything. Jeez, the guy had even emptied the trash file on his e-mail. Talk about paranoid.

"What are you trying to hide, Russell?" he said to himself.

He plugged in the "awk" script program he'd brought. The program would cross-reference all e-mail accounts with a roster of Reck employees.

Like Reck had told him, his deal with the company prevented him from doing any business associated with aerospace for five years, part of the government's slap on the wrist for his being a naughty boy, defrauding our taxpayers. Reck was officially off the letterhead, sure, though he'd been allowed to keep an office. Reck's only involvement these days was research like Alec's software. The future.

But Alec figured Old Russ was still the man pulling the strings. And he planned to prove it.

So he'd done a little executive thinking. *If I were an aerospace mogul fresh out of jail and I wanted my company back on the map* . . . He figured a first step would be to set up a dummy e-mail account.

Bingo.

On the screen flashed the name Douglas Miller. Apparently, Douglas had an e-mail account here at Reck Enterprises. Only, there was no record of a Douglas Miller working for Reck.

Alec glanced at his watch. *With time to spare.* He brought up Doug's e-mail account and backed up on the zip drive. He pocketed the cartridge and picked up his coffee cup, heading for the door.

He didn't see The Wrecker until he turned the corner, practically slamming into the guy.

Alec gave him a smile, stepping aside to avoid a collision. He knew he'd slipped out before anyone had seen him coming out of Donald's office. Which didn't make him look any less suspicious to Reck. Alec was two floors from where he should be.

"James," Reck said. "What brings you to the fifth floor?"

Alec held up his coffee cup. "Coffeemaker on the third is on the fritz." Which it was. Alec had stuck a screwdriver in it himself first thing this morning.

He leaned in close, telling the secret, "And I came by to check out Mitch."

Mitch was a secretary on the fifth floor. He was also gay.

Alec winked. "Not enough good-looking men available these days, you know?"

"You're homosexual?" Reck asked.

Alec frowned, stepping back, doing his best to look insulted. "You have a problem with that?"

"No, of course not."

He gave a look as he stepped around Reck, like Alec might not believe him—like he might have to stay on guard to make sure Reck wasn't one of those homophobes. He shook his head, sipping on coffee that was stone cold. *Yum*. He figured that stuff about Mitch would throw Reck off, at least long enough for Alec to reach the elevators.

But Reck wasn't through with him.

"James. When do you think you'll have something more to show on that software? I was hoping to speed things up for a presentation next week."

"No prob," Alec said, still walking. "I'll check in with you by Wednesday."

Once inside the elevator, Alec punched his floor.

He figured he'd been right all along—it was never good when things came too easy. It meant he'd missed something . . . something that might come back to haunt him.

He had a sixth sense about stuff like that; it had kept him alive more than a few times. Right now that little voice inside him warned to speed things up, a sentiment echoed by Reck just then.

Tic-toc. Tic-toc. They were all running out of time.

Russell watched James step into the elevator. The doors slowly closed, shutting off the sight of him. Today he wore contacts that made his eyes appear like two yellow smiley faces floating where his iris and pupil should have been.

The policy at the company allowed for casual days every Friday. Bright and early Monday morning, James was wearing a T-shirt painted to give the illusion of a buxom woman popping out of her bikini top. Now he was combing the halls for a date?

Russell smiled, thinking about it. Yesterday he had met with the investigator he'd hired to look into James's background. Sigmund had some very interesting things to say about our man Flint.

"He doesn't exist," Sigmund had told Russell. "I checked it out. Everything in the file you gave me, all of it, planted on the Internet, scattered here and there to make it believable. If you'd dug a little deeper, you would have hit the more sophisticated stuff. Whoever set this up was a real pro. You got yourself a spook, Russ."

Unfortunately, Russell knew exactly what that

meant. James Flint and his magic software were both
fictitious. A hoax.

And now he'd found him skulking around the fifth
floor. The executive floor. Where Russell kept all his
secrets.

Back in his office, Russell sat down and swiveled
his chair to face the view of the bay below. His plans
for Sydney were coming together. Her trip to New
York in particular interested him. *An opportunity.* Reck
Enterprises, too, stood on the brink of regaining its
former position in the business world. He couldn't
afford James getting him off track.

On the desk behind him, the intercom sounded.
Russell turned to push the button, listening as his
secretary announced Angela. A surprise.

He smiled, remembering the night before. They'd
spent a lovely evening at her apartment, where Angela
had cooked a delicious bouillabaisse. She'd fed it to
him from a silver spoon while wearing only her apron.

"Show her in," he said.

Angela pushed the door open with the heel of her
palm. She was still wearing her beautician's coat over
a demure sheath of a dress. Her eyes blazed as she
came to a stop before him. She planted both hands
firmly on his desk.

"What the hell do you think you're doing, Russ?"

He kept his expression light. "I don't like my women
to use foul language, Angela. Did I ever tell you that?"

She smiled, stepping back. "I believe you've just
illustrated the problem. I am not one of your
women." She waited a beat. "I received an interesting
delivery today."

"I know—"

"Clothes. All designer. All beautiful . . . all worth

a fortune." She was back at the desk, hands spread apart, doing her best to look intimidating in the pose. "So tempting." She shook her head. "But not for me."

He realized the problem. *Of course.* He nodded, then rose to his feet.

A woman like Angela, self-made, hardworking. *Of course . . .*

He walked around the desk, taking her by the hand. He led her to the couch and sat down, guiding her gently to sit beside him. She made a show of reluctance before giving in, a prerequisite, he understood.

"I've insulted you," he said.

"Those clothes. The shoes. Everything. You're trying to make me over, Russ. Into some other woman. Why, I can't figure out. But, yes, I find it very insulting."

He put his arm around her because he knew what she wanted. What had brought her here in such a huff. Every woman wanted to be special. Unique. He hadn't meant to spoil that with his gifts.

"I'm sorry," he said. "I only wanted to make you happy. I don't need any other woman but you, Angela. I thought I made that perfectly clear."

He kissed her then, pushing her back onto the couch, thinking to make her feel special once again. It didn't take long before he had the coat off her shoulders, pinning her there on the couch, still kissing her, his tongue in her mouth, then gently sucking on hers. His hand slipped up her thigh, where she wore sexy thigh-high stockings under her dress. She was so wet, it didn't take long.

"Is that better?" he asked, kissing her lightly on the nose as she orgasmed against his hand.

She looked utterly beautiful, completely subdued, lying back on the couch, her white coat still off her slender shoulders. Russell only smiled. She didn't want the clothes because he was controlling her. But in the end, she would do exactly as he asked. Whether she realized it or not, Angela wanted what he'd offered. They all did.

A few minutes later, Russ walked her to the door. She stood on tiptoe to give him a last kiss. "But the clothes go back," she said, quietly now, the words, almost an apology. "Okay?"

"All but the Donna Karan dress," he whispered in her ear. "Wear that for me tonight. Please?"

She gave him a look. "You are incorrigible." But she smiled as she walked out. Over her shoulder she said, "Pick me up at eight. You'll see then what I wear."

He smiled as she blew him a kiss. People never recognize the strings that bind us. Those ties creep up on you little by little. Sydney had been a bit more difficult to convince. But Angela, she would give him no trouble at all.

Last week she'd dyed her hair. *Just for kicks,* she'd told him.

As far as Russell was concerned, Angela made a beautiful redhead.

When Sydney came home, she found Alec on her couch, channel-surfing.

"Hey," he greeted her after taking the grape Popsicle out of his mouth. He hit another button on the remote, turning on the VCR. "You made the five o'clock news. Here, I taped it for you."

Sydney stopped, keys still in hand, stunned to see her photograph from the art center's press kit fill the screen. Jack had insisted she get the head shot done. *You're one of the gallery's greatest assets, Sydney. We need to play that up.* The good old days.

Thankfully, it was a short piece, though it surprised her how much they could pack into thirty seconds. They managed not only to cover the safety violations at the gallery last week, but Sydney's sordid past—her divorce from Russell, her recent breakup with Jackson Bosse. The newscaster ended by staring into the camera, asking the rhetorical question "What are the odds of one woman marrying three millionaires?"

"That was my favorite part," Alec said, turning off the television. "They made you sound so deliciously"—he gave a shiver—"wicked."

He stood, gave a stretch, then sauntered over to grab her buttocks with both hands to press her up against him. "Hmmm. I love a woman who's after my money."

"Because you don't have any?"

"That's the thing, see. Then I know it's true love. You giving up your whole black-widow gig for me."

They kissed, slow and sweet, the kind of kiss that promised more. But Sydney pushed him away. "Hold on, cowboy. After a day like today, I need a drink."

She tossed her keys on the table at the entry. She glanced down to see that he'd brought in her mail. She didn't think she'd given him a key to the mailbox. Although, knowing Alec, that wouldn't be much of a problem.

She shook her head. He'd certainly made himself at home. Not that she minded. He was beautiful and she loved sleeping with him. And it was way too late for regrets.

Walking to the bedroom to change clothes, she thought about that, how quickly he'd become a part of her life. Just like their time together in South America, they'd fallen into this easy rhythm. As if there had never been a "before Alec," which didn't make sense. Here she was, a completely conservative creature, taking on the grand adventure of him just trying to catch her breath.

Twenty minutes later, she was still wondering as she leaned over the kitchen sink, peeling potatoes for dinner. What she'd told Jack, that love wasn't a math problem? *A true thing.* Sometimes, it was just a look across a crowded room . . . like the one Alec gave her now.

"What?" She tried to play it off even as she felt herself blush. She took a sip of wine from her glass. "Do I have potato peel stuck to my face or a milk mustache?"

"Why do you cook for me?" he asked.

The question took her by surprise. She shrugged, turning back to the sink. "I used to cook all the time." Potato in hand, she started to peel just a little faster. "For Henry. He liked my cooking."

She kept peeling, trying not to think about Henry. *Peel harder.* Trying not to remember everything they'd said on the television when she'd first come in— suddenly, trying not to cry. When she felt Alec turn her around, she kept her head down, not wanting him to see. But he just took the potato and peeler from her and put them both on the counter.

"Hey," he said, tipping her head up. He brushed

away her tears. "Baby. Tell me you're a whole lot tougher than this?"

She shook her head. "I don't know." She tried to smile, not to let her voice break. "We lost the appeal on the emergency stay. As of eleven o'clock this morning, the government has the right to examine every single piece of paper at the gallery. Eventually, they'll connect it to me and claim I've 'hidden assets.'" Assets they could take away. "Next week we're set to argue my motion to stop the government from using my money to pay off Russell's debts, and it's sure to go the same. I'll be officially broke."

"Hey now. You've got me, right?" He kissed her forehead. "Shit, how much can this little hovel of yours cost anyway?" he asked, looking around the luxurious apartment.

She couldn't even manage a laugh. Surprisingly, tears welled in her eyes. "It's been a hell of a day."

He folded her into his arms. That's all it took, that one embrace. She dropped her head and cried. She cried for Henry and Jack and the gallery ... and everything else she'd screwed up. She wished she could put on the blinders Alec offered. *Buck up!* Believe that her plan with Kinnard would work in time to save them all. But at that moment, nothing seemed possible.

"Don't let that television shit get to you," he said. "Don't let them tell you who you are, Syd. All they care about is a hot story for the top of the hour."

"No, but it's true," she said, talking through her tears. "Not that I married Henry for his money, no. But I did something just as bad. I married him because he wanted it so badly. Because I was young and stupid and had no idea about commitment."

"Now you're not making sense."

"And I didn't love him. Not the way you're supposed to love someone when you marry. Or Russell wouldn't have been able—"

He grabbed her shoulders, giving her a shake. "So you made a mistake. Maybe even a big one. But come on, Syd. You were vulnerable . . . maybe even a little lonely. You think Russell didn't notice? You think he didn't step up to the plate to become whatever you wanted right then in a man, making it so tempting? Am I right? Giving one hundred and ten percent. That's how guys like him work."

"I should have been stronger—"

"He handed you a dream, Syd. I've done it myself. Been someone's dream come true to get what I wanted. Don't be so hard on yourself because you fell for it. That dream is damn hard to resist."

"You're horrible," she said, holding him tight. "Admitting such things to me and still expecting me to love you."

But he only smiled. "As if I could pull that shit on you? You're a different woman now, Syd. God knows if you weren't, you would have succumbed to my charms long ago."

"You're that good?" she whispered against his chest.

"Irresistible, that's me."

She closed her eyes, nuzzling against his T-shirt, strangely comforted by what he'd said. She was a different woman. Though goodness knows, she couldn't judge that by her feelings for Alec. She knew only she hadn't fallen for an act, which she'd seen plenty of in the early going with Alec. It was later, when she'd met the real man, warts and all, that she'd fallen under his spell.

Tonight I'll make him stay the night, she told herself. She wouldn't let him disappear as he had most of the week, saying he had some business to attend to back at his apartment.

"I adore you, Syd," he whispered. "Never think I don't."

She smiled, nuzzling closer. It was lovely, what he'd said. But in her heart she knew he was wrong. In a relationship there was room for only one who adored, and this time she'd been cast in that role. With her eyes completely open—knowing better—she still couldn't stay away.

But she kept her theories to herself as he took her in his arms. She stayed silent, returning only his kiss. She let him carry her into the bedroom, where he would indeed adore her.

If only for a little while.

TWENTY-FIVE

Rocky slipped into her parking slot in the cement complex and popped on her sunglasses. Getting out of her car, she avoided the eyes of passersby, walking with her head down. The mood at the gallery these days was beyond morbid. Like they were piping a funeral dirge into the halls and everyone was waiting for pink slips to fall down from the ceiling or a giant taped X to appear across the doors and windows. Jack had been doing some heavy damage control, which meant they saw each other only at night.

Every day after work, Rocky came home to fret about what to wear, how to look. Sometimes, she'd rush out at lunchtime because she didn't have the right shoes or wanted a special clip for her hair. When she drove over to Jack's, she always brought some surprise. A nice bottle of wine. Thai food. Last night she'd bought him flowers, making him laugh.

She hadn't seen him do that in a while, laugh. He was pretty upset all the time now, with everything that was going on. She tried to be sympathetic. Tried to set aside her own fears. Tried to forget that her period was two days late.

Too early to panic, she told herself. But wouldn't that just take the cake? First time in the game, and she scores.

Oh, Lord. Please don't let me be pregnant.

The last two weeks with Jack had been an incredible roller coaster of highs and lows. She couldn't understand half the things Jack made her feel. One minute, she wanted to throw her arms around him. The next, she wanted to scream at him that he'd ruined her life.

She never spent the night. It frightened her a little, how wonderful that might be.

Walking up the street toward the art center, listening to her heels on the sidewalk, she thought about how complicated her life had become. Nothing made sense anymore; every day brought new questions. *Who to trust? What to do?*

Today, apparently, would be no different.

As if it were the most ordinary thing in the world, her father waited on the steps to the gallery.

Rocky froze, trying to squeeze air into her lungs. She'd been avoiding him the last week, unable to stand the emotions raging inside her. If she told her father about the notes she'd seen at Sydney's, she'd be disloyal to Jack, and he would hate her forever. But if she didn't tell her father . . .

Yes. Exactly.

She was almost afraid her father could read the truth on her face, like one of those giant messages people sometimes put on a billboard. Somehow, he would know she was hiding something. And then he'd begin to ask questions.

The last week she made excuses when he called. *Sorry, Daddy. No time today.* Instead, she'd crept back into Jack's bed, hoping to forget the choices that waited for her. Knowing that she was making her decision just by avoiding it. *Do nothing. . . .*

Now that was no longer possible.

Her father stepped down to greet her, holding his arms out to her. "Rocky, honey. It's so good to see you."

"Daddy." She returned his hug awkwardly, holding her purse in one hand, her briefcase in the other. "What are you doing here?"

He gave her a kiss on her cheek. "I can't show up to see my girl? I need an appointment? Honey, I miss you. Suddenly, you're so busy. I thought if I showed up, I might get lucky. Let me buy you a cup of coffee. That is, if you have a minute."

"Sure, Daddy."

"Here. Why don't you just drop those things off in your office? We'll walk down the block to Starbucks." He pushed at the small of her back, leading her up the steps, as always, giving her no choice.

Together, they proceeded past the reception desk toward her cubicle. She couldn't believe she was walking down the hall with her father, here at the gallery, where he was public enemy number one. She could only imagine what would happen if they ran into Jack. *Hello, Jack. I just thought I would bring Daddy by. You know, the man you think is trying to destroy your life?*

It all seemed surreal, watching her father sit down in the chair before her desk, smiling at her . . . as if one of the paintings from the gallery had come to life. *No escape.* Frowning, she put away the contracts she'd left out the day before. Like Daddy might peek over and steal company secrets.

But her father wasn't interested in the contracts. Instead, he picked up the only personal item she had on her desk. "Oh, honey," he said. "Look at us."

The photograph in his hand was of the two of them at the beach. In it, Sydney wore a red polka-dot bikini, her hair in braids. She remembered the day perfectly; she'd been ten, visiting with her sisters for the summer.

Her father always rented a cottage on the beach. One week out of each year since the divorce, he'd take Rocky and her sisters there. But even then, she saw him hardly at all.

"You were such a beautiful little girl," he told her, looking at the photograph with a dreamy expression.

Rocky shut her file drawer. "I didn't think you'd noticed."

He put down the photograph, shaking his head. "You're angry with me."

She realized at that moment that she'd been running away from just this confrontation, trying to outrun her fears. *If Jack is right and Daddy is the bad guy . . .*

They never talked about it when she and Jack were together, as if they understood the subject was off limits. A mutual vow of silence. But her father was always there, looming over them.

She couldn't just come out and ask, *Daddy, all that stuff that's been going on at the gallery, are you trying to ruin Sydney?* Just a few weeks ago she'd offered to spy for her father. At the time she'd thought Sydney was the enemy, putting an innocent man behind bars. Now she wasn't so sure.

"I'm not angry." She sat down. "I'm just confused."

He reached across the desk and held her hand. "Then we should talk."

Only, looking down at his hand holding hers—the photograph of the two of them on the desk before her—a memory rushed into her head, making her nod . . . making her ask, "Do you remember the day we took that picture?"

He kept his smile. "Of course I remember. You'd just learned how to surf. You were so proud of yourself."

"That was Aphrodite. She surfed, Daddy. Not me." Rocky hated the water, even before that day. "Remember?" she prompted him. "I was afraid of the waves."

"Yes, of course. I remember now."

Something inside her went dead, watching him lie. At that instant she knew he didn't remember. He wouldn't say it with a smile if he had.

Half an hour after Aphrodite took that photograph, Rocky had been dragged under by a wave. A lifeguard had resuscitated her, using mouth to mouth.

Her father didn't remember because he hadn't been there. He'd gone off, back to the cottage they'd rented, leaving Aphrodite in charge. It was only later, when all the drama was over, that Aphrodite even sent for him.

"Sand castles had always been my thing," she said, looking at the photo back on the desk, keeping everything she was feeling to herself.

That day she'd been angry with him even before they took the photograph. Because he hadn't wanted to help her build the castle. It was his only vacation, he'd told her. He wanted to enjoy his magazine in peace. Maybe have a drink back at the cottage.

His expression in the photograph was only a pose for the camera. An act.

She looked up, watching her father smiling across the desk at her. Just like now. And the last year. A beautiful act.

She squeezed his hand and let go. "It's the only photograph I have of the two of us." That's why she'd kept it on her desk despite the bad memories. "When I came across it earlier this year, I framed it." To commemorate their new relationship.

She pushed the frame aside and sighed, finally knowing her answer. "You're right, Daddy. I was angry. For a long time now. But I'm not anymore." And when she said it, she knew it was the truth.

She stood, suddenly understanding so many things—why she'd been so hostile to Sydney, why she knew that Jack, despite his successful career, would never make the choices her father had. Jack, who was satisfied with his lovely house and his lovely dogs, searching for his lovely wife-to-be. Those realizations had been there all along, hovering just outside her consciousness, waiting for a moment like this.

And she knew that she wanted her father to leave. Now. And not just because Jack might see him.

"Let's go get that coffee," he said with a cheerful smile.

As she watched, he took her hand and wrapped it around his waist, then draped his arm over her shoulder, orchestrating every move. *Here we are. The happy family.* Gently guiding her into the hall, walking beside her.

When she was with Jack, every touch came together naturally. Nothing seemed forced. But the last year with her father—the phone calls from prison, the emotion during her visits—it had always seemed just a little off.

Sydney tried to tell you.

Near the entrance to the gallery, her father suddenly stopped. He turned back toward the gallery behind them. "Do you mind if we have a peek? I'd really love a tour."

She frowned, surprised by his request. "It's a new artist. No one you would have heard—"

"For just a minute," he said, heading toward the entrance, again not giving her a choice.

She followed, wondering how long this would take, worried that someone would see them after all. But it was early still. The gallery wouldn't open to the public for several hours.

Stepping inside, she told herself to relax. Her father would get bored soon enough. And they had the gallery to themselves. *Don't panic.* Still, as she followed, she could hear their footsteps sounding eerily off the walls. If this were a movie, she thought, she'd be watching the scene past her fingers covering her eyes, expecting disaster.

If Jack came in now, he wouldn't know what to think. Even standing there beside her father, she felt like an accomplice.

"It's really impressive what your stepmother has done here," he said, looking around, hands behind his back as he admired one of the paintings. "I notice you didn't correct me this time."

"What?" Did she hear someone coming in behind them?

He turned, giving a smile. "You don't mind my calling her your stepmother anymore." He continued walking. "That's nice. That you're friends again. I was hoping that would happen if I sent you here to work with her."

Rocky felt a little on edge. She hadn't been paying attention. Already he was reading her, knowing something was different.

Don't be paranoid, she told herself, trying to focus on the paintings. This week's exhibit belonged to a promising young artist named Katherine Arnold. She specialized in what Rocky termed neoimpressionism. A series of crisscrossing lines covered enormous canvases, some spanning the entire length of a wall.

Her father came to a stop in front of one of the largest paintings. Rocky had met the artist and knew it depicted a garden, all done in thin, colorful lines, though the title of the work was only the number used to identify it. *Opus No. 14.*

Up close, it looked like chaos. You couldn't see the real picture unless you stepped back. Like life, Rocky thought. You had to get the right angle, try different perspectives before things came into focus and you could see the truth.

"You never told me about your stepmother," he said.

Rocky looked up. "What?"

"I asked you to look into a few things for me." He turned. "Remember?"

"The pills?" She shook her head. "There's nothing to worry about. Yeah, sure. She takes stuff to sleep and for her allergies. But it's not like she needs to. It's just Xanax. That's like Valium." She wasn't going to tell him about the papers she'd seen in Sydney's kitchen. "I mean, who doesn't take something now and then. I don't think there's anything to worry about."

"How wonderful." He kept his eyes on the painting. He looked about to say something else, but his expression suddenly changed.

"Dammit," he said. "I forgot my cell phone back on your desk. Would you be a dear and get it for me?"

She hadn't noticed a cell phone. "I'll get it for you later." Maybe she could just run in while he waited outside, out of sight. "After we have our coffee."

"I'm afraid I'm expecting an important call. That's why I had it out." He took a seat on one of the viewing benches set in the middle of the room. "It will give me a chance to enjoy this," he said, referring to the painting.

"All right," she said, still hesitating. "The best view is from over there," she said, pointing to another bench.

"Thank you, darling."

She walked out, thinking she would grab his phone and make some excuse. She didn't want to go out for coffee after all. Not today. Maybe never.

At the gallery entrance, she stopped, turning back to see her father still sitting on the bench. He'd crossed his legs, ankle on knee. Dressed in his finest suit, probably Armani, he looked absolutely regal in the pose.

It was funny, she thought. She'd been confused for so long. But suddenly, from this angle, she could see everything only too clearly.

TWENTY-SIX

Alec woke in a sweat, the sheets kicked to the foot of the bed, his head pounding. His body felt weighted down, leaden. He couldn't move. Even his lungs had to work overtime, taking short, shallow breaths.

"Hey." Sydney slipped her hand over his chest, making him think she was checking for a heartbeat. "Are you okay?"

He reached for her hand, barely registering that the gesture had become second nature. He'd been dreaming. A nightmare.

There'd been this time Eddy had passed out in Alec's bed. Alec had been four. Eddy hadn't intended any harm. Not that night. He'd just turned over, covering his four-year-old son until Alec couldn't breathe. Couldn't move; couldn't scream.

Whenever Alec had the dream, it was always the same. He was a grown man, in bed, alone. There was no one to pin him down, no one to smother him.

Still, he couldn't move from the bed . . . couldn't get up, couldn't speak or catch his breath.

Toward the end, he would stop struggling, falling into a sort of acceptance of what came next. Right before he'd wake up, he'd think: *This is what it feels like to die. . . .*

"Your heart is going a mile a minute," Sydney whispered.

He closed his eyes, willing a couple of deep breaths. When he could, he swung his legs over the edge of the bed and stood, almost shocked when his feet actually held him up. He took a few shaky steps, then headed for the kitchen for a glass of water.

He gulped down two glasses, one after the other, before leaning over the sink. He knew what had brought on the dream.

Fear . . . panic.

Yesterday he'd gone over the e-mail entries he'd backed up on the zip drive cartridge, uncovering Reck's secrets. The e-mail revealed plans to buy shares in a competitor through a third party to gain a controlling interest. A takeover from the inside. Since his release, Reck had acted as a silent partner in several of the enterprises buying shares in his nearest competitor, each and every purchase a breach of his plea agreement with the government.

The bastard was breaking the law. But Alec couldn't prove a thing. A bunch of e-mails registered under a false name wouldn't even get him a meeting with the prosecutor.

That's when his doubts began, brewing panic. *Think of something!* All along, he'd been too slow . . . ineffective.

"Don't lose it now, buddy," he told himself, shaking his head. He couldn't afford his fear. *Don't screw the pooch.*

Sydney came up behind him, her small hands sliding around his waist as she lay her cheek against his bare back. He shivered, then turned to hold her, the heat of her body now so familiar, he couldn't imagine her not being there.

He kissed her, his mouth soft against her, then open and hungry. Sydney, his new addiction.

Don't let me hurt her . . . don't let her hate me.

The conflict must have been there on his face. Sydney looked up, puzzled. She touched his cheek, her face showing her concern . . . but then, just as suddenly, her expression changed and she smiled.

"How about I make us some hot chocolate?" she asked, out of the blue.

"Sure." He brushed the hair from her face. Hot chocolate. Go figure. "That would be great."

Fifteen minutes later, they sat at the table in only candlelight, sipping the cocoa. The candles smelled like citrus mixing with the sweet from the chocolate. It was like a dream, Alec thought. This homey, wonderful make-believe.

"Well, at least you're smiling now," she said.

"It must be the sugar high."

But he was thinking something else. That he didn't deserve hot chocolate and warm smiles. Not from Sydney. And though he'd never been bothered by what he managed to steal with his charm and wiles, right now it hurt like a physical ache deep inside his chest. To sit in candlelight and think . . .

"Shit, Syd. I don't deserve you."

He hadn't meant to say the words out loud. Now her expression hovered between digging for the deeper meaning behind his words and letting him off the hook.

"Of course you don't deserve me," she answered, taking the latter course.

One of the candles on the table sputtered and went out. He took another drink of chocolate, wondering if that's what he really wanted. Another escape.

"You've had that dream before," she said, surprising him again. "And you were . . . I don't know. Sucking the air into your lungs. It frightened me. That you couldn't breathe. That's why I woke you up. I was worried."

She pushed her cup aside and crossed her arms on the table. Without looking up, she told him, "Sometimes, Alec, you truly frighten me."

He nodded, wondering how he'd sneaked into her life . . . into her heart. How selfish he must be to stay there when he knew the possible consequences to her.

You never accept the consequences. . . .

That's what Cherish had told him that night he'd gone to Conor's. The one thing she couldn't forgive. That he never accepted the consequences of his actions.

Alec pushed aside his cup of cocoa. "I used to have that dumb dream all the time when I was a kid."

He never talked details when it came to Eddy and Daisey, though he was pretty sure Syd had figured out what his life had been like. Mostly, he didn't like stories about his past because he didn't need anybody's pity. Shit, he didn't feel the least bit sorry for himself. He was in control of his life, right? Not those ghosts stuck in his head.

"Eddy passed out in bed on top of me." He surprised himself by telling her the story. "I couldn't breathe. I don't remember if later he woke up, or turned over . . . or even if maybe I just managed to squirrel out from under him." He shrugged, looking up. "When I woke up, it was another bright, shiny morning. But sometimes I have that dream, and he's still there on top of me, smothering the breath out of me."

"My God, Alec," she said, shock in her voice.

"It's just a dream," he told her. "No lasting effect. Except maybe for a while I was scared of small spaces."

"Claustrophobia?"

"Yeah. For a while. But Conor helped me get through it."

Of course, Conor. Always, Conor.

He laughed, shaking his head at the memory. "Back then Conor wanted me and Geena to be his first solo. I knew I'd never manage the cockpit of that tiny tail-wheel plane he flew. Like a freaking coffin with wings."

He got back to the cup of chocolate, remembering. He focused there, on the cup, telling it like a story. "One day, I shut myself in the hall closet, basically going for the total immersion method of therapy. I wasn't getting out until it was gone. The fear."

He could remember going nuts, screaming his fool head off because he was so afraid.

"Conor found me. He crept inside and sat there beside me. He started telling me stories. His own version of the Arabian Nights." Conor, the big brother who fixed everything.

"I fell asleep right there beside him," he finished.

"You weren't afraid after that?"

"Nah. Never."

"But you are afraid now. That you're like him."
She put her hand on his holding the cup. "Eddy, I
mean. That's why you don't drink alcohol. Why you
stopped taking your pain pills right after surgery."

He gave her a look. "I'm nothing like him."

But why lie? That's exactly what he feared most.
Sitting in the candlelight, sipping chocolate, he was
more afraid than ever.

That he'd let her down. That he'd fuck it up. Just
like Big Ed.

He told her, "Sometimes, when I look in the mirror,
I see him there, reflected in the glass."

"Oh, Alec."

"And I worry," he said. "That I won't be good
enough for the job ahead. All those things I told you
before—the secret agent shit. I made you think I was
some super spy. And now you think I'm up for this.
That I can beat that asshole Reck."

He could almost hear his heart pounding. He
wanted to tell her the truth. Like he was drunk on
hot chocolate or something. He wanted to tell her
he'd been lying all along. About everything. His
strength—his ability. And how he'd found her in the
first place . . .

"It's not all up to you," she told him.

He stood. He moved away from the table, beginning
to pace. He felt as if he were walking on a tightrope.
It wouldn't take much for him to lose his balance,
make a mistake.

"Alec." Sydney came up behind him, hugging him.
"Whatever it is. Tell me, please."

He felt as if he were choking; there was no air in
the room. *Just like in my dream.* He just wanted to get

it over with, confess everything. Tell her the whole damn sorry tale about Reck . . . and Henry. Shit, he deserved what was coming his way: Sydney's hate.

Tell her you bastard. Let her know the truth.

"I did something," he whispered, barely getting the words out. "It's bad, Syd."

"No matter what it is, Alec. I love—"

He turned and covered her mouth. "No. Don't do that." His heart was slamming against the wall of his chest. "Don't make promises you can't keep."

She looked into his eyes. And there was so much love there, it hurt. It burned.

After a while, she took his hand from her mouth. "I won't let you scare me away," she told him. "Never again."

His hand in hers, she led him back to the bedroom. She took off his pants, then dropped her robe. She kissed him everywhere, like she couldn't get enough of him. And he knew how she felt. Because Syd. She was the real deal. *True love.*

Later, he lay in bed awake, Sydney in his arms, fast asleep, looking like an angel. He kept a curl of hair in his finger, twirling it around and around, thinking.

I can't mess this up.

Only, he knew it might already be too late.

He kissed Sydney's forehead, knowing everything seemed too perfect.

Too good. Too right.

Ready to blow up.

At night there were no lights inside the museum. Certainly not in the gallery, where the paintings waited for morning.

But tonight a small red light blinked in the dark, casting a soft glow through the canvas of an enormous painting called Opus No. 14, looking as if the light itself had become part of the painting.

At a quarter past one the light stopped. A small explosion followed. Not very much sound to it. Just a slight pop and a plume of smoke.

An inch of flame crept across the canvas.

Eventually, the fire alarm sounded, chased by a downpour from the sprinklers above.

Sydney stepped around the water-soaked floor of the gallery. She hadn't had much sleep, only a few hours. She was so tired, she felt as if she were floating. *Walking on water.* Firemen wandered past, laden with equipment. Workers pushed mops and squeegees. Everything she'd worked for this last year lay in ruin.

The gallery received the worst damage, the fire having started there. She stopped in front of what had once been an enormous painting of a garden. Only parts of the wooden frame remained, the walls around it black from the smoke. She'd spoken with one of the investigators. They couldn't rule out an incendiary device.

She should have known Russell wouldn't leave her anything. She should have guessed she was running out of time.

"I'm sorry, Sydney."

She turned to find Jack standing directly behind her, his hands jammed into the pockets of his trousers. His face was a mirror of everything she felt.

"I had no idea he'd go this far," he said.

What an incredibly strange twenty-four hours, she

told herself. Alec, waking up in the middle of the night, drinking hot chocolate and telling secrets. *Like a dream.* When she'd fallen asleep in his arms, she'd been so incredibly happy. Then Jack called. *My God, Sydney, I don't know how to tell you. The gallery . . .*

She pushed her hand through her hair, turning in a complete circle. *Round and round she goes . . .*

Everything, gone. Destroyed by Russell.

"We'll fix this," Jack whispered, stepping up behind her, turning her to face him. "I promise. He won't win. He just caught us off guard, that's all. It doesn't have to mean anything. We can start over."

But she knew he was wrong. *No way out!* Knowing Russell, he was just getting started.

From the corner of her eye she caught sight of Alec stepping into the gallery. He stopped at the doorway, standing there. He'd come down with her after Jack called about the fire. Now he waited with his arms crossed over his chest.

The expression on his face . . . so cold—almost chilling.

Without a word Alec turned and left.

"Hold on," she told Jack.

She raced through the door, running after Alec. Outside, she had to press forward to catch up with his longer stride eating up the sidewalk. It was still dark, just before dawn. The streetlights had turned off long before.

"What are you doing?" she asked, keeping step with him.

"What does it look like I'm doing?" He kept walking, heading for his truck, keys in hand. "I didn't want to break up a tender moment back there with Jug Brain. I decided to get my ass out of the way."

She grabbed his arm before he could reach for the Chevy's door handle. "Alec, please. Don't do this. I need you right now."

For a moment, he just stood there. The look on his face was almost comical—as if he were confused by his own feelings. No, more like appalled. She could just imagine what he was thinking. How ridiculous, that he could feel jealous under these circumstances . . .

"If I weren't in the middle of a crisis right now," she told him, "such a show of emotion from you might give me a warm and fuzzy feeling."

He slumped back against the truck, shaking his head. "I don't get it, Syd. I used to be this perfectly normal guy."

"No," she told him, settling there alongside him. "You were never that."

He didn't respond, as if he sensed she needed a minute to take it all in. They both just waited, watching the firemen and the cleanup crew. After a moment, he reached for her hand and squeezed it.

She realized he did that a lot now. He took every opportunity to touch her. She sighed, leaning against him. It was almost strange, she thought, how such a simple gesture, his hand holding hers, could make her feel so good.

The thought came: *Russell will ruin everything . . . even this.*

Sydney held back a shudder. She'd never had a premonition—she didn't pretend to have a sixth sense. She told herself not to be ridiculous. It was natural to have feelings of doom and gloom about something that made her so happy with the gallery gone and Russell gunning for her.

"I think we should talk about another bodyguard," Alec told her.

"Russell is trying to ruin me financially," she said, as if hearing the words out loud might convince them both. "He won't hurt me. I mean, can you see the headlines? Reck Axes Ex? It's too obvious. Even for Russell."

But Alec didn't look any happier for her theories. If anything, his eyes looked bruised and worn, a tired soldier knowing the end was near . . . and worried that they might not be up for the fight.

TWENTY-SEVEN

Rocky ran for the front door, the L.A. *Times* tucked under her arm, briefcase and travel mug in hand. She didn't want to be late. Last night she'd stayed at Jack's long past midnight, getting home after one in the morning. When her alarm went off five hours later, she'd hit the snooze button four times in a row. It had taken more than her average willpower to push off the covers.

She opened the door, backing out, trying not to spill coffee as she locked the door behind her . . . and almost tripped over Jack, sitting on her doorstep.

She dropped the paper, sheets littering the stoop. Coffee splashed over the lip of the mug.

"Jack."

At a guess, she'd say he hadn't slept all night. Jack had a tendency to look a bit manicured. Not this morning. He must have rolled out of bed and slapped on the first thing he came across on the floor.

"Jack, what happened?" Clearly, she could see something was very wrong.

"I've been sitting here," he said, "trying to imagine what I would say to you when you walked out that door." He shook his head. "I still don't have the faintest idea."

She stepped down to sit next to him. His voice sounded beyond tired, scaring her. "What's going on?"

"There was a fire at the gallery."

She felt the air catch in her throat. "Oh, my God. Was anyone hurt?"

"No. But the exhibit was completely destroyed. Rocky, they determined this wasn't an accident."

Jack had these clear blue eyes. Beautiful eyes that now showed each and every accusation he hadn't dared voice.

He thinks I had something to do with it.

Even as the righteous denial rose inside, she had a vision of her father. It was like one of those trailers for the movies. He was standing at the entrance to the gallery at the museum, smiling.

Do you mind if we have a peek?

She'd thought it was strange at the time that he'd had such a yearning to see the work of a new artist. In the past, only art worthy of hanging in the Louvre had interested him.

Can you go get my cell phone?

Her father. He'd set it up to be in that gallery alone.

He did something.

"I checked the video from the security cameras," Jack said. "They didn't show much. Wrong angle. But I saw you standing with your father before the gallery opened."

"Yeah. Sure. I took him to see the exhibit." She could feel herself flush, which didn't make sense. *I'm acting guilty.* "He came over for coffee. We couldn't have been in the gallery more than ten minutes."

She couldn't imagine why she was making excuses. Why, instead, she didn't just voice her suspicions . . .

But her relationship with Jack was so tenuous. If her father was involved, of course Jack would assume the worst.

Jack stood, looking down at her. "I don't know if you're being naive, lying to yourself," he told her. "Or just lying to me."

Watching him, Rocky knew she'd made a mistake. *Now he'll think I'm an accomplice. Now he'll hate me.* He was halfway down the walkway before she stood, anger and longing tumbling one over the other inside her.

"That's right," she yelled at him, feeling desperate. "All along it's been my evil plan to destroy the man I love."

Jack turned. During their time together they'd never talked about anything but the trivial. Stories about growing up. Jack's brother. Aphrodite and Carmela. It seemed almost surreal to blurt out her feelings when before she'd been so guarded.

"Of course you don't believe me," she said. "Humiliating myself by admitting that I love you—when you've made it absolutely clear you want someone else—it's all part of my evil plan."

"Why should I believe you?" he asked. "How many times have you lied to me, Rocky?"

"Oh, yes, Jack. I lied. I lied about my age and I lied about my birthday. I can't imagine that you could trust me now."

The look of shock on his face. He hadn't expected

her to have a defense against what he'd imagined all night. It was actually quite comical, that look. She covered her mouth, realizing she was going to laugh. A release.

"Wouldn't it make it simple for you, Jack, if I were one of the bad guys?"

"What the hell is that supposed to mean?"

"It becomes so black-and-white then. You don't have to make a choice. Rocky is a bad girl. I don't date bad girls."

"Date? You keep talking about us like some kind of high school romance. Dammit, Rocky. If I didn't want you in my life, that would be it. I don't need to make up an excuse."

She sat down. It felt so good when she did start laughing. *Better than crying.*

A shadow fell over her. She looked up to see Jack standing there, his eyes searching hers.

"I swear to God, Rocky. I never know if I am coming or going with you."

She shaded her eyes to peer up at him. She'd always known this would end badly. Every night, when she'd driven away from his house, she expected it to be the last time. What they had together always felt just a tiny bit wrong.

"You're so afraid I'll ruin your perfect life," she said. "I just wonder how happy you would be. If it all came true the way you picture it."

Better to get it over with, she told herself. *Let it end now.*

But nothing between her and Jack had ever been that simple.

Rocky stood, meeting Jack face-to-face. She made certain he could read the truth in her eyes. "If my father has done anything to hurt you or Sydney or the gallery, I don't know anything about it. And I am certainly not involved.''

She picked up her newspaper and coffee mug. She walked back up the steps of her condo and opened the door, acting for all the world as if he would follow.

When he didn't, she looked over her shoulder and asked, ''Are you coming?''

She left the door open.

She didn't start breathing again until she heard the door slam shut behind him. When he turned her around and kissed her, she wrapped her arms around him, giving in as easily as Jack.

They ended up in the bedroom, making love, as if only there, linked in each other's arms, did they know they could trust. Jack always made love to her as if there were nothing else in the world that could matter as much. She'd thought it was her lack of experience that made it all seem so grand. But now, nestled up against him, she wondered.

''This is something special,'' she whispered, ''isn't it?''

His hand continued stroking her side. ''I wish I knew.''

She sat up on her elbow. ''The correct answer would be C, a simple yes. Next time use your lifeline.''

Jack sighed as he sat up, swinging his legs over the edge. He put on his chinos and grabbed his shirt. Rocky watched him dress, her heart pounding a mile a minute.

''You're leaving?''

He stopped what he was doing. ''I'm going to make you—and myself—some coffee.''

But she had barely settled back against the pillows

when he returned just a minute later. There was no coffee in sight. Instead, he stood in the doorway, an expression of incredible concentration on his face.

She held her breath, thinking: *Now what?*

He stepped into the bedroom. For the first time, he brought out his hand . . . in it he held the pregnancy test kit she'd left forgotten in a paper bag on the kitchen counter.

"When were you going to tell me?" he asked.

She glanced away. She couldn't look at him; her face would give too much away. She hadn't had the courage to take the test. *Maybe tomorrow I'll get my period.* So she told him what she'd been rehearsing the last days.

"There's nothing to tell, Jack. I'm not even that late."

He came to sit on the side of the bed. "Maybe that's what worries me. That you'll take care of everything. All alone. Look, whether we want to or not, we have an obligation here. . . . Rocky, there are worse reasons for people to get together."

"Are you proposing?" She didn't know if she was appalled or just shocked. She'd told Jack she loved him—but that kind of emotion wasn't part of the equation for him.

"How very noble of you, Jack."

After a beat he said, "I pretty much blew that, didn't I? Look, just don't do anything rash until we discuss it. Will you promise me that, at least?"

She felt herself die just a little inside. *He thinks would get an abortion.* "Don't worry so much, Jack," she said, the sarcasm dripping from her voice. "You'l get wrinkles."

She tried to scoot across the bed. Get up. Get out

But Jack grabbed her arm and pulled her back. He hugged her to him on the bed.

"Rocky, it's too important. More important than the gallery or any of this. More important than us."

She turned to look deep into his eyes. "Jack," she said, "I believe it is us."

Which perfectly illustrated the problem. Just that little difference in perspective.

He didn't say a word but lay back on the bed, tugging her down beside him. This time she didn't argue, staying there with him.

"Just give me some time," he told her.

Rocky closed her eyes, wishing it could be so simple. *Just a little time to catch on with the program.*

But she knew what it felt like to be trapped by love—that's how her father made her feel. The resentment and anger that were sure to follow. She'd seen it on Jack's face when he'd walked back into the room, no longer the avenging angel seeking justice but, rather, the meek and noble knight.

But it didn't change how he felt. Trapped. It didn't change the fact that he didn't love her.

Russell stared at the photograph on his desk. He'd had it delivered that morning by special messenger. It still shocked him to see it there. *In living color.*

Sigmund's suggestion that James Flint could be trouble had forced Russell to dig deeper. But it wasn't until this photograph arrived, procured by Sigmund and his people, that the pieces had fallen into place.

Russell had never met Alec Porter, though he had seen his photograph before. More than once, in fact. All courtesy of Joseph Kinnard, the man who found

Porter in the first place. Porter had been working for the air force then, a test pilot.

Russell hadn't paid much attention to the pilot. He hadn't seen the need. Porter was just a pawn, someone to be used and thrown away. Never in a million years would he have connected Porter to the present situation. After all, he was one of Kinnard's minions, just that.

And Russell had underestimated him.

Amazing, how he'd made himself look so different. That's why the crazy getup. The contacts, the hair— the bizarre clothes. *A disguise.*

Russell stood, walking over to the window. He stared down at the boats bobbing in the harbor below. *Thank God for Sigmund,* he told himself. He had hoped things could be different. But with Porter in the picture, he needed to speed up. Make things happen. See if in the end he couldn't salvage a little more.

He sighed, a bit depressed about the whole thing. Lately, everyone seemed to be giving him trouble. Like last night.

Angela.

They'd had a wonderful dinner. He'd never seen her look more beautiful. The dress, her hair. Everything had been perfect.

Perhaps that was the problem. He'd made her look so much like Sydney, eventually, when they'd made love, he'd forgotten who was there beneath him.

Angela hadn't minded at first that he was a little rough. She'd even whispered, *I love you, Russell.* It had been a long time since he'd heard a woman say that to him. *I love you. . . .*

Then, slowly, almost against his will, his hands had crept up to her lovely neck. *Sydney, how could you betray*

me . . . you should have loved me. Tighter . . . tighter
still.

He hadn't realized what was happening until
Angela started to scream.

In his head, it was Sydney's voice calling out to him.
Sydney telling him he was "a piece of shit." That he
should get "his dirty hands" off her. That she would
call the police.

The FBI is on the way, Russell. . . .

When he finally let Angela go, she hadn't bothered
to say a word. She'd grabbed her clothes and ran.

Early that morning he'd called the florist. He'd
paid for her to receive a dozen red roses every hour
on the hour. Not that he thought it would make any
difference.

It was always the same. Sydney, Angela . . . even his
daughter. *They always let me down.*

The last week, he'd sensed Rocky pulling away from
him, keeping secrets. After a year of acting as if there
were no one else in her world, she'd begun avoiding
him. *Not today, Daddy. I have to work late. Maybe next
week we can get together.*

It hurt to see that even Rocky would betray him.
He couldn't expect loyalty from his own flesh and
blood?

He stepped back from the window and walked
around the room, taking in the art and the furniture.
All priceless . . . everything unique. He sat down at
his desk, staring at the photograph of Alec Porter.
Focusing there.

Oh, yes. Sigmund had been worth every penny.

The report that came with the photograph
explained how Alec Porter worked for Sydney. It also
mentioned that they had become romantically

involved . . . probably the reason she'd broken off her engagement to Jackson Bosse. Apparently, Porter was quite the ladies' man.

But Sydney didn't know who she was dealing with when it came to Porter. She couldn't possibly. Because Alec Porter had committed the one crime Sydney could never forgive.

How ironic, Russell thought. She always acted so high and mighty, and all along she was sleeping with the enemy. Alec Porter. The man who killed Henry.

"It's going to just crush me to tell you the truth, dearest," he said out loud, practicing.

Russell smiled. Time to close in for the kill.

Endgame

TWENTY-EIGHT

Beard the lion in his den . . . or so the saying went. For Sydney, walking into Russell's office felt more like jumping out of a plane, only to realize she'd forgotten her parachute.

Still, she wasn't afraid. It seemed almost unnatural, her calm. Or perhaps she was just tired, believing he had done his worst. He'd put his threats inside her head, so that every day she woke up with her fears, dreamed of them each night, wondering who he might hurt next.

Taking a seat in front of his desk, she felt as if they were two warriors facing off. So what if one had a bazooka and the other a slingshot? All she needed was a well-placed pebble right between the eyes.

"I had an eventful night," she said, crossing her legs, returning his smile. "Want to hear about it?" He frowned, as if just realizing. "What am I saying? But, of course, you already know all about it."

He gave her an amused smile. "I'm afraid I did
hear the bad news. How very sad for you, Sydney."

"Not even close to sounding sincere."

He kept his smile as he took his seat. From a cigar
box on his desk he retrieved one of his favorite Opus
X cigars. Sydney had bought him that particular
humidor. The irony wasn't lost on her.

"What can I do for you, Sydney?" he asked.

"I'm just wondering what comes next. Maybe stuff
me in a cannon and shoot me to Catalina? I'm just
throwing out a couple of ideas to get your imagination
going. So far you've been rather pedantic."

"What are you accusing me of this time?"

"Or maybe we could just come to some sort of
understanding." She leaned forward in her chair.
"What do you think, Russell? Let's make a deal. You
tell me what you want, then leave off? Wouldn't that
be nice, hmmm? If we just kept it between the two
of us? No more burning down buildings or harassing
your daughter. Just you and me. I actually believe
would be more satisfying for you. It's what you've
wanted all along. To have me under your thumb."
She held her hands open, as if in surrender. "Here
I am, Russell. Take your best shot."

He watched for a moment. Using cigar clippers
he cut the end off the cigar. He'd never looked so
sure of himself. His old self. Russell was having fun.
From experience, she braced herself.

"Sydney, darling. You learned how to play the game
much too late."

He put down the cigar clippers and picked up his
lighter. He shook his head and gave a chuckle, as
bemused by some private joke.

"I have some unfortunate news," he said, his face

becoming instantly serious. "Joseph Kinnard was killed yesterday. One of those dreadful prison fights."

Sydney closed her eyes, beyond shock. *Joseph dead.* The only man who knew the truth—who could help her revoke Russell's plea agreement with new evidence. *Russell must have found out I talked to Joseph.*

All along he'd known what she was doing. And he'd taken action.

When she opened her eyes again, she felt the blood rush out of her head. She knew she was facing a killer.

"My God, Russell. You killed him."

"It's a prison, Sydney. Not a health club." He lit the cigar, holding the tip above the flame as he rolled the cigar and puffed. "Certainly a high-risk environment. And what could possibly be my motive?"

Now he was baiting her. Playing a game.

"I'm afraid there's more." He put down the lighter and lined it up with the cigar box like a chess piece. "Are you ready? It won't be nearly as nice."

He'd destroyed the museum and threatened her life. Just now he'd practically confessed to orchestrating a killing. *Get up,* a voice inside her warned. *Leave while you still can. Run!* Whatever he had in store for her, it couldn't be good. And still she couldn't move.

He rolled the smoke from the cigar in his mouth. "I can only talk in terms of hypotheticals, you understand. For both our sakes."

She hadn't slept since the fire. Sometimes, lack of sleep made life seem hazy, your surroundings cotton-coated. But she felt on the edge of a blade, everything seemed so sharp.

"You accused me of killing Henry." He put down the cigar, a prop. "As it turns out, I didn't . . . but I

know who did. And so do you. Quite well, I understand."

"I don't have the slightest idea what you're talking
about."

"You remember that day?" he said, taking them
back. "A routine flight during a press conference?
All perfectly safe."

Only, it hadn't been safe. Far from it. Russell
needed that plane to fail or there would be no more
billion-dollar contracts funnelled his way by Joseph
Kinnard. He'd sabotaged the plane, knowing
Henry—his partner and friend—was on board.

Russell leaned in, looking for the kill. "You were
right all along, Sydney. Kinnard made sure there was
a failure that day. Not to kill Henry, you understand.
But it would have looked suspicious if Reck Enterprises didn't have a representative on board when
that plane dropped out of the sky. Henry insisted on
taking the flight. A pet project of his, if you recall.
And I was still useful to Kinnard."

Sydney's fingers gripped the chair. "How nice for
you."

She couldn't show fear. She wouldn't give Russell
that satisfaction. At the same time, he held her rapt
in that chair. *I didn't kill Henry . . . but I know who did.*

"I didn't know what he was planning, Sydney, I
swear. Though I don't expect you to believe me. Henry's death, it's something that still tears me apart.
Later I confronted Kinnard. I thought the crash was
just a little too convenient, you see. One of the men
killed that day along with Henry was a great threat
to Joseph."

He granted a dramatic pause. *I know who killed
Henry. . . .*

"As it turned out, the pilot . . . I discovered he was one of Kinnard's men. Special ops, I think Joseph called it. The pilot switched out the software we were testing, causing the plane to crash. Apparently, this man was a computer whiz as well as a talented test pilot."

Sydney caught her breath. It was one of those moments. You're sitting in a chair, but the floor drops out from under you. You can't imagine you can still get oxygen in your lungs, because your insides knot up so tight, it hurts.

A computer whiz—a test pilot.

Sydney stood. "No."

He was talking about Alec.

"I'm glad you came today, Sydney. Whatever your motives. I needed to warn you. I would have told you earlier, only I just put it all together in my mind."

She took another step back, shaking her head.

"I'm afraid it's true, my love. Alec Porter is using you. After the crash, he tried to blackmail Joseph. A serious mistake. Of course Joseph wanted him dead. Porter ran scared. He went underground for over a year."

She thought of all the photographs in Alec's drawer. A jungle. A beach. Pictures of exotic places all over the world.

"He must have come to you after that. To get the evidence he needed to neutralize Kinnard and any other threat, which included me, of course. I'm assuming it was Porter who got you to call the FBI?"

She could still see the fear in Alec's eyes when he'd told her, *I did something. It's bad, Syd.*

"Porter knew if I went down, so would Joseph. Our

fates were tied together. Once Joseph was behind bars, Porter was a free man."

Sydney could imagine how she looked. The shock on her face as she stood, still shaking her head. She had to leave—she couldn't listen to this anymore. She had to find Alec. Talk to him. Let him tell her Russell was lying.

But it made a strange sort of sense, what Russell said. And she remembered. When she'd told Alec she would always love him, he warned her.

Don't make promises you can't keep.

As she left, she heard Russell call out, "Be careful, my love. He's still using you."

When the phone rang at his apartment, Alec had just walked through the door. He threw off his jacket and ignored the ringing, letting the machine pick up. He'd come here instead of Syd's to work on a program he'd written last week. The program should enable him to have a direct window into Reck's private files. Access to Reck's computer had been the bothersome little detail left in getting the evidence he needed to put the bastard away. The fire at the gallery had set off the alarm bell in his head. He needed Reck behind bars. The sooner, the better.

He was just sitting down at the table, pulling up the laptop, when he heard another alarm.

Reck's voice on his answering machine.

"If you're there, Porter, I would pick up. It's Russell Reck."

Alec dove for the phone, knowing what the call meant. *The endgame.*

"I'm listening," he said.

"Sydney just left my office." There came a pause, leaving Alec hanging. "She's very upset."

"She couldn't have been too upset if you're making this call. If it were me? I would have put one right between your eyes."

He could hear Russell laugh. "But I wasn't the one who upset her."

The air left Alec's lungs. *He told her—he told her everything.*

"You are out of your league, Porter. You always were," Reck said before hanging up.

Alec dropped the phone, frozen inside. *Panic so pure it could make you high.* He used to get a kick out of that buzz of adrenaline, facing the clear blue sky with the controls in his hands. But right now it just made him sick.

Russell Reck had told Sydney his secrets.

Some things you can never forgive.

Alec raced down the steps and out to his truck. He pulled out, the wheels screaming on the asphalt. It was a bright, beautiful day in sunny California . . . and he couldn't breathe.

His whole life, everything that mattered he'd lost or threw away. Maybe you just couldn't change that kind of luck. No matter what you did to make up for past wrongs, they were always there to come back and bite you in the ass.

He leaned into the turn, taking advantage of the empty streets. He'd thought he was so damn clever. Infiltrating Reck's organization, getting a look at company files. He'd always thought he could do this for Sydney. Be the hero. He'd convinced himself he was under the guy's radar. Now he wondered how long The Wrecker had strung him along.

She'll hate me now, he thought.

This wasn't like Argentina, when he'd been an asshole and she'd walked out. There was nothing Alec could say that could make this right. Not for Syd.

It was just like his nightmare. When he couldn't breathe, and he just lay there, accepting the inevitable.

This is what it feels like to die.

When Sydney came home, she found Alec waiting for her. She'd been trying to reach him on her cell phone, calling him both at home and at his place. She'd even tried paging him, frantic. The drive over, she'd told herself over and over that Russell had lied. He'd found out about Alec, and he wanted to upset her. It was just like that horrible dog and the car almost hitting her. One of Russell's nasty little games.

She just needed to find Alec. He would tell her the truth.

Only now, seeing him sitting on the couch, she wasn't so certain. There was something about Alec's body language. Leaning forward, his elbows balanced on his knees, he looked almost beaten.

She closed the door behind her, all her doubts rushing in.

"Russell called me," he said.

She dropped the keys at the entry. She couldn't imagine that she could walk so calmly into the room. As if it were nothing. An easy dance. As if she weren't dying just a little inside.

She stopped in front of the couch, not daring to come closer. Not yet.

"He told me you killed Henry," she said.

Alec closed his eyes, giving his answer.

"No, Alec. Oh, God, please, no."

Alec stood and wrapped his arms around her. He held her so tight, as if she might disappear . . . while Sydney's hands stayed at her sides.

"I love you, Sydney. More than anything or anyone. No matter what, there will never be anyone like you. Not for me. I love you that much. And I'll love you forever."

She stepped away and Alec made no effort to keep her there. "I wanted to hear you say those words for the longest time," she said.

She had the strangest thought. He should look different somehow. Uglier maybe. Exposed. When she discovered the real Russell Reck, everything had looked so different.

But Alec, he looked exactly the same.

"But you couldn't tell me those things before, could you? You couldn't tell me you loved me. I thought it was because you hated the idea of making a commitment. I thought you were afraid. And you were. Only, it wasn't marriage and children that scared you."

"Sydney, if I could fix this. . . ."

But he couldn't. Because, for once, Russell hadn't lied.

"Oh, Alec."

She shook her head. She covered her mouth, because she didn't want to talk or cry or even breathe. She covered her eyes. She fell to the couch, trying to figure a way out. How she could live through this?

When she settled down—When she could catch her breath—she opened her eyes again.

Alec was gone.

TWENTY-NINE

Last night Rocky got her period. She went to bed early and alone.

She'd lain there for hours, unable to sleep, trying to understand her disappointment. For sure, it was some weird hormonal flux that made her cry until her eyes were red and puffy. She was only twenty-three; she still had time for a family. Having a child with a man who didn't love her could only bring her heartache. Really, the nightmare was over.

Come morning, she realized it was only beginning.

She brought in the paper, coffee in hand, only to drop the cup, sending it crashing to the floor when she read the headline on the front page: CHILD ABUSER HIRED AT KIDDIE GALLERY . . .

She'd never dressed so quickly, never drove so fast. She was still trying to catch her breath when she stormed into her father's office, throwing the paper on his desk.

The guard. The man her father had convinced her

to hire—the man who had helped him so much in jail. *He deserves a chance.*

"You used me!"

Her father kept his face carefully devoid of any expression. "I made a mistake."

"Oh, please. I'm not that naive. Not anymore, Daddy. Now I see why you gave me the summer to decide about my position at Reck Enterprises. You needed me working at the gallery. Government subpoenas, disastrous fires, now this?" she asked, pointing at the headline. "What else do you have coming down the pike for Sydney? Where is this leading?"

He rose to his feet, for the first time showing emotion. "What exactly are you accusing me of?"

She took a moment, making certain he understood. "In law school we'd read these cases that were so screwy. Sometimes you had a hard time figuring out who was the bad guy. But the idea was to cull the pertinent facts, apply the rule of law, reach a conclusion. Maybe before, I was having a hard time doing that. But right now everything is perfectly clear."

He stepped around the desk. "This must be a terribly confusing time for you, sweetheart—"

"Don't," she said, stopping him. "Don't even try."

He watched her, evaluating. "I should have seen this coming," he said calmly. Too calmly. "I should have made your choices clearer from the beginning."

"Why does that sound like a threat?"

"You're supposed to be on my side, Rocky."

"Even I can't scrounge up that much blind faith."

She turned, moving out, the headline still imprinted in her head. *He used me!*

From the door she launched her final salvo. "The company is in my name. You needed that much from me. A safe harbor for your money. But I am putting a stop to your attack on Sydney. Right now.''

"Rocky. Don't make me your enemy."

She gave him a smile. "Oh, Daddy. I didn't know you could be so sentimental."

She could see the change come over his face. As if he hadn't realized he was vulnerable. The more he threatened—the more he put his company at risk. He came toward her then, his arms outstretched as if to embrace her. But Rocky saw only a change in tactics.

"Rocky, honey. We're family—"

She held out her hand, palm up, cutting him off. "You know what, Daddy? It's funny how long it took you to figure that out. It's a shame really. 'Cause right now the last thing I want is to be your daughter. Frankly, Daddy, you give me the creeps."

Leaving the offices of Reck Enterprises, she realized the truth. Her father was a very sick man . . . and all along she'd been helping him, protecting him.

She thought about that, driving over to the gallery. She couldn't imagine what she was going to say to Sydney when she found her. Apologize? Beg for mercy? Or just tell her the truth. That at long last she'd thought her father loved her, a fantasy that had made her vulnerable.

Pulling up in front of the gallery, she found the media three deep, surrounding the building on what must have been a slow news day. She had to fight her way up the steps. Inside, the cleanup crew still swept; every wall appeared gray from smoke. Devoid of its usual personnel, the gallery struck her as abandoned and desperate, a fair reflection of the future, she thought.

A hand locked around her upper arm, spinning her around. She found herself staring at Jack. The expression on his face—*Hang on,* she warned herself. *This is going to be bad. . . .*

He didn't say a word, just pulled her along so that she nearly tripped as he pushed her inside his office. Sydney was already there, piling boxes in a corner. She looked up and smiled . . . until she saw Jack step in behind Rocky.

"I just talked to Margie Snell. You remember Margie, don't you, Rocky? She makes most of our hiring decisions." He told Sydney, "She explained how Rocky walked in that guard's job application personally, volunteering that a man who did time for abusing his stepkids would be a swell addition to the team. Damn you, Rocky. You set us up!"

"I didn't know. Russell used me."

He grabbed her by both arms. "Not good enough!"

"What would be, Jack? You want me to prostrate myself before you, confess what a bad thing I did, believing my own father?"

"Nothing that simple, sweetheart. Tomorrow there's going to be a new guard at the front door, and your name isn't going to be on the guest list—"

Sydney pushed him back, forcing them apart. "That is entirely enough."

But Jack kept his eyes on Rocky. "You lie about everything. You don't see anything wrong with using people."

"Using people?" She choked on the words. "Who used who, Jack?"

"No way. You've been the one pulling the strings all along."

"Jack! Stop it!" Sydney yelled.

"Don't get involved," he told Sydney. "That's where I screwed up. I got involved."

All I wanted was for my father to love me. But Rocky could see that he wasn't going to give her the benefit of the doubt. He wanted Rocky to be that bad girl he could brush off and file under What Was I Thinking? How easy it was for him to play the wronged man. He didn't need to take responsibility, because all along she'd pulled the wool over his eyes.

It made her feel a little mean. Made her want to hurt him, like she hurt. "Don't worry, Jack." She couldn't keep the bitterness out of her voice. "It's not as bad as you think. At least I'm not pregnant."

Sydney's eyes widened. She turned to stare at Jack.

"Oops," Rocky said, fighting back tears as she stumbled back. "Did I let the cat out of the bag?"

She pushed past Jack, ignoring Sydney's calls to stay put. At the same time, she felt horrified by what she'd done. She'd let her anger get the best of her, hurting Jack and Sydney both.

He didn't even give me a chance.

Of course Jack chased her down, catching up with her near the entrance. She didn't stop, forcing him to navigate the sea of news crews. He didn't dare talk until they were alone in the parking structure down the street, the reporters far behind.

Rocky tried to push him aside and get into her car. He stopped her, standing between her and the door.

"It's done, Jack. We're through. My period started. I'm not pregnant. You're a free man."

"But you're not, are you?" he said. "You're still under that bastard's thumb. Is that how you plan to live your life? Leave law school, become his little mini-me?"

"And what do you care? You didn't even tell her," she said, surprised at how her voice choked up. "You didn't even think to let her know about us. I was always going to be your dirty little secret."

"How am I supposed to know what you would have been? You didn't give us a chance to find out."

"So it's my fault? I'm not buying that. Let's face it, Jack. I was never good enough for you. After all, I wasn't Sydney, was I?"

His expression changed, showing another Jack, the Internet mogul who knew how to be ruthless. "Oh, honey, let me tell you something. Your act was damn good. Especially in bed. One of the best."

She shook her head, hiding behind her smile. *That he could be so cruel.* "You know what? Up until this moment I thought I owed you something. But I think we're just about even."

He didn't try to stop her this time, guessing that it could only get uglier. Instead, he stood aside, his blue eyes watching her coldly.

From inside the car she rolled down the window. She said, "I feel sorry for you, Jack. I gave you something special. Something I can never give anyone else. And you threw it away. And I'm not talking about my virginity, you asshole."

She pulled out, practically running him over when Jack didn't move aside fast enough. But at least she hadn't burst into tears. She waited until the stoplight around the corner to let down her guard.

She shouldn't have said those things in front of Sydney just to hurt Jack. He was right; she'd acted like a child. Poor Sydney. The one person who had always cared about her, no matter what.

There was a time she'd wanted to hurt Sydney. Bad.

Maybe you can't take back those feelings. Maybe, once she put that hate out there, her pain just gained a life of its own.

And now, because of her Sydney would be ruined. Because Rocky could bail out the gallery with money, but she could never buy back its goodwill.

When the light turned green, she didn't bother to move forward. Instead, she pulled over and turned off the car.

She didn't know what to do. She didn't know how to fix this.

The apple doesn't fall far from the tree.

She didn't know how to be someone different, someone not like her father. A woman who, in the end, didn't hurt the very people she loved most.

THIRTY

Yesterday, after Alec left, Sydney didn't move from the couch. *Don't think. Don't feel.* Eventually, she crawled into bed and curled into a ball. She could still smell Alec on the sheets; his aftershave scented the pillows. The sky grew light outside with morning, but she stayed where she was. *Lie still. Don't move. Disappear . . .*

When the phone rang, she almost didn't pick up. She'd turned off her message machine to cut off the world. But as the phone continued to nag her, she considered the possibility of inching across the bed to the nightstand just to stop the noise. She counted the rings. *Ten, eleven . . .* A few more sounded before she lifted the receiver.

"Jesus, Sydney. Have you read the paper this morning?" It was Jack, the panic all too clear in his voice. She'd listened, not saying a word as Jack told her the story. *The guard at the museum, he's been convicted of child abuse. Sydney, the story broke in the paper this*

morning . . . But rather than slipping deeper under
the covers of her bed that morning with dread, an
amazing thing happened. The blood pumped back
into her head. She sat up, electrified.

Yesterday Sydney felt as if she were dying. Now,
with Jack's phone call earlier, she experienced new
life.

She'd never thought she'd be thankful to Russell
for anything. But Sydney knew she'd needed that jolt
of reality delivered by the morning headline. *Get out
of bed, Sydney! Move!* Throughout the day, she vowed
to fight the good fight. She wouldn't give up and die
for Russell. Even later, after witnessing the horrible
scene in the office between Jack and Rocky—bur-
dened by Jack's misery and Rocky's pain—she tried
to keep focused. *I can stop Russell—I must!*

By the end of the day, she clung to her resolve.
She made her way past the gauntlet of reporters
despite the doubts creeping in, whispering seduc-
tively, *give in . . . give up.* It didn't matter that the
gallery was doomed, Alec gone from her life. She
wouldn't go back to bed. She wouldn't let Russell
win.

But, for Sydney, life continued to dish up surprises—and the battle came much sooner than she
expected.

Walking into the parking structure, she felt herself
grabbed from behind. Sydney threw her elbow back.
Still fresh from her first assault in that dark alley,
she connected. Hearing a satisfying grunt from her
assailant, she pivoted, her hands locked around her
purse to swing it like a weapon. A man's arm blocked
the shot. He hooked the purse, then swept her
around. Using the purse as a lasso, he locked her

arms in place, the move that of a trained warrior. His hand covered her mouth.

"Damn, Syd," Alec whispered into her ear. "I think you broke my rib."

He turned her around, a smile on his face.

She pulled Alec's hand off her mouth. She could feel her heart pumping hard in her chest. She'd never felt more alive. "What are you doing?"

"What does it look like? I'm kidnapping you. Hold on." He picked her up, dumping her over his shoulder like a sack of potatoes. "This shouldn't hurt much."

Alec took Sydney up a mountain to the lake resort of Big Bear. He'd rented a condo at the bottom of the ski slope. It was a scenic drive up . . . if your heart wasn't in your throat as the tires squealed and the truck hugged the curves.

Sydney now sat in a chair in the middle of a rustic living room, her wrists tied to the arms of the chair. Fifteen minutes had passed and Alec hadn't said a word. He merely sat across the living room, watching her with sad eyes.

She still marveled that he should look beautiful. Impossible that she could still find him attractive. *A moth to the flame.* She remembered how different Russell had looked after she'd discovered his lies. As if all along he'd been wearing a disguise and that day the mask slipped. He'd turned into a villain before her eyes, a brute who'd tricked her with his sleight of hand.

Somehow, it hurt more that she couldn't hate Alec. That instead she might understand why he'd hidden the truth from her. She could hope in her heart that he'd changed, that by helping her against Russell, he wanted to make up for past wrongs. She could dream that what he'd wanted all along was a second chance.

Not that she could forget what he'd done. She might not even find it in her heart to forgive him. *Oh, Alec . . .*

She sighed. "What's this supposed to accomplish? Bringing me here? Tying me up?"

He stepped out of the shadows, walking toward her. She would never get used to him with that white blond hair. To her, Alec would always be dark-haired, dark-eyed. But in either guise he remained movie star handsome. A heartbreaker.

He stopped beside her chair. "I just thought, if I was going to be the bad guy"—he stroked her hand with his finger—"I should at least get something out of it."

"I very much doubt you can have your way with me, Alec." She lifted her hands as far as they would go, anchored at the wrists.

Alec knelt down before her, his eyes on hers. He had such beautiful eyes. So dark and full of mischief. Now he looked incredibly earnest. A Svengali trying to persuade.

"You think I'd have trouble seducing you in the chair?"

He pushed her skirt up her legs, baring her thigh. She could feel her skin responding to his touch. "As it happens, Syd, that's not why I brought you here."

Slowly, he lowered his head and lay his cheek on her lap. She could feel his mouth on her skin, his hands slipping up her hips to come around her waist. His breath on her exposed leg.

"I just want to hold you, Syd. This one last time."

She should feel dead inside, she told herself. Or angry. He'd lied. He'd used her. *He sabotaged that plane—he killed Henry!*

And still she wanted to be with him. She wanted to ask him to untie her; she wanted to make love, to forget this nightmare that had taken over their lives. To pretend as Alec had this past year that love between them was still possible.

As if reading her mind, he told her, "I know you, Syd. This is it for you. Once you leave here, I'll never be able to touch you again."

He tugged her blouse out from the waistband of her skirt and pushed it up her rib cage. With a sigh he leaned forward to kiss her bared skin there above her belly button. Needing more, he unbuttoned the blouse, working his way up to the collar.

He eased the shirt back over her shoulders. He reached up and cupped her breast through her bra, allowing his thumb to brush over the nipple. Once, twice. Watching as it rose to his touch.

He edged up, balancing his hands on the sides of her chair to place his mouth on hers.

"Alec . . ."

"Hush. I only want to kiss you," he whispered.

Don't, she told herself, allowing the kiss just the same, kissing him in return. When her tears slipped down her face, she tasted them in his mouth.

"I love you," he whispered. His hands came up to steady her face when she tried to pull away. "God, I've wanted to say that for the longest time." He spoke the words against her lips. "I love you, Sydney."

He deepened the kiss, making it so sweet, too tempting. She stopped trying to resist then, kissing him hard, biting his mouth, her anger coming through, taking over . . . only to kiss the very spot where she hurt him.

They kissed almost desperately, like kids too greedy to wait for a better time or place. But soon his kisses changed, becoming even more demanding, making it simple to forget that her hands were tied, making her instead grab the arms of the chair, digging her fingers into the upholstery, knowing all along that if she weren't captive in the chair, she wouldn't be free to return his kiss. Now she met each and every caress with one of her own . . . until it all felt too much . . . hurt too much.

"Stop, Alec," she cried out. "Please, stop."

He pulled away, breathing hard. It was almost as if he'd been somewhere else. A place where he had the right to make love to her. But her words brought them back to time present, so that he rested his forehead on hers, giving in, catching his breath.

"I wish. God, Syd, I wish—"

"I know," she said, because she understood only too well what he wanted. *I wish it could be different.*

He brushed the hair from her face, the gesture so familiar. It seemed almost strange to watch him untie the cords that held her, to watch them drop to the floor. She should hate him. Somehow in her heart she should find the strength to do that much.

Instead, she asked, "Tell me."

He sat back on his heels. He picked up the ropes and wrapped them around his hand, shaking his head, discarding some argument. She could imagine the dialogue. *No, not that. That's just a lame excuse. You have to do better than that, Porter.*

He walked across the room away from her to sit on

the love seat. The distance between them seemed somehow symbolic. Sydney obliged, sitting on the couch opposite, buttoning her blouse. The lamp on the stand beside Alec gave the room just enough light to see the burden he felt, coming up with the right excuse . . . or, perhaps even the truth.

"Have you ever done something really wrong?" he asked.

She thought about Russell. "A shining example comes to mind," she said.

He shook his head. "I don't mean some jerk using you." He tossed the cords on the seat beside him and leaned forward, resting his elbows on his knees. Now the shadows came up, obscuring his face.

"I mean calculated bad. Choosing, knowing the consequences . . . cheating, stealing, hurting."

It's not what she wanted to hear. "What are you saying, Alec? That you chose to kill Henry? You planned his death?"

He shook his head. "No, Syd. But maybe I did something just as bad."

"Did you kill him?"

The words seemed to echo in the room. She waited, not wanting to hear what she knew was coming.

"He died because of me, yes."

"The consequences are different—"

"The consequences are absolutely the same," he said, cutting her off. Lowering his voice, he added, "Henry is dead. There's your consequence. Don't try to finesse this, Syd."

"How did it happen?" Because she had to know. "How did you become involved?"

He nodded. "Joseph Kinnard recruited me for the job. He needed someone who could switch out the software on the prototype we were test flying that day for Reck Enterprises. Conor and I, we were the flight crew. He was the pilot in command and I was his second. But Conor, he had no idea what I was doing.''

"But he found out." Which accounted for the rift between Alec and his adoptive family.

"Oh, yeah," Alec said. "He found out. But only after he got booted out of the air force. No one knew about the software, you see. They blamed the crash on pilot error."

She closed her eyes, feeling his words like a physical blow. *You coward. You let your own brother take the fall.*

"How did you do it?" she asked, wanting to hear all the ugly details.

"I changed the software the night before the flight, talking my way on board past security. As part of the flight crew, I had clearance. No way I would tinker with a plane I was flying, they'd be thinking. So why be careful? Fifteen minutes in the air, we went down because of that software. Just as planned."

She hadn't realized she was crying. It was always difficult to think about Henry. And now she had to believe that the man she loved killed him?

"It was different with Russell," she said, explaining what she felt. "When I found out what he'd done— lying to me, cheating on me. Stealing me away from Henry, then killing him for control over the company. All so he could have more. Just that. More. I hated him. And that hate was so pure, so empowering." She took a breath, fighting for air. "I wish so much I could hate you, Alec."

He looked at her with such understanding. "Maybe you should give yourself some time. Let it sink in. You can hate me, Syd."

"Why, Alec?" she shouted at him. "Was it the money? Or was it just for the rush? Were you working your way up Kinnard's organization—"

"It was one lousy job, Syd."

He walked to the fireplace, his face turned toward the flames. She wasn't sure he was going to say anything more. And still, she couldn't understand. She wouldn't accept that she'd fallen in love with a monster.

"Alec," she said softly. "I need more than that. Please."

"Yeah, I know," he said, staring at the fire. "Only you want it to be something noble—like I had no choice or I didn't know what they were up to." He turned, letting her know by his expression that she would be disappointed.

He said, "Maybe, sometimes you're so scared of something, that fear, it gets too big in your head. It takes over. Like this cloud hanging over you, coloring everything. 'You're bad—just like your old man.' And you get so tired of waiting for it to happen, for people to discover the truth. You just want it over with, that's all."

"You're talking about Eddy? Are you trying to tell me you were afraid of becoming like your father?"

"After a while you have to put an end to that fear. You tell yourself, 'Yeah, sure. I don't deserve anything good. There. It's done. I'm bad.'" He shrugged. "After that you don't have to worry anymore."

"Because you let yourself become what you feared most?"

"You didn't know I could be weak? Come on. You didn't think I was some big, strong hero, did you?" His gaze grew hard. "Well, I'm not. I can't be that man, even for you. And I never regretted it, not for one minute. I didn't let myself. I hurt Conor and Geena and everyone I loved when I hooked up with the bad guys, and for years I said, so what?"

He looked out of breath, like he'd been running around the room rather than just standing there in front of the fire. Finally, he said, "And then I met you."

She shook her head. "Don't tell me I changed you, Alec. Don't feed me lies."

"Right." He walked around the room, pushing his hand through his hair, almost circling. "Look, Syd, I don't know what Reck told you—I mean, I can imagine. His hands are clean. And me, I'm the Big Bad Wolf."

"I didn't believe him. I came to you for the truth!"

He swung around, looking savage. "The truth is, I screwed up! Even before I got on that plane with Henry, I'd already made a nice little place for myself in hell. That day was just the high-water mark, you understand?"

He came to her, dropping down in front of her. "And I didn't stop after that either. You see, after the crash I had the goods on Kinnard—so he wanted me dead. I needed him and Reck out of the picture. And do you know how I did it?" He smiled. "Can you imagine?"

"No, Alec. Stop. I don't want to know anymore—"

"I used you, Syd. You pretty much put Kinnard behind bars for me. Remember? You had the evidence to expose him and Reck both."

"Shut up." She put her hands over her ears. "Shut up!"

But he wouldn't let her hide. He pulled her hands

away, making her listen. "Do you remember the day I showed up at your place? Pretending I was checking out the alarm on the house? I figured you for the misunderstood trophy wife, ripe for the picking. I came on to you." He grinned. "You turned me down flat."

He touched her face. She hadn't realized she was crying, that he was wiping away her tears.

"But you weren't what I expected. From that day on, Syd, things were different," he said. "You wanted me so badly to be a better man. For the first time in my life I dreamed I could step up to the plate. That's when I started working on the new software, thinking some day I could save a few lives to make up for the thing with Henry. Be that hero you wanted. What a joke, huh?"

Watching her, he looked incredibly earnest. And lost. That most of all.

"You should hate me, Syd. God, you should."

Two things happened at once. Sydney slipped off the couch, falling into Alec's embrace . . . and behind Alec, the window shattered.

Sydney followed Alec's gaze. He was staring at the sofa. On the couch where she'd been sitting, a small black hole had magically appeared.

"Shit." Alec grabbed her shoulders.

He pushed her to the floor, rolling over her so that they traveled several feet across the carpet. A spray of bullets followed their progress, seeming to bounce off the floor, slamming into the couch.

Just as suddenly as it was breached, silence returned. Sydney's heart lodged in her throat. She looked at Alec perched over her, covering her with his body. She could see what he was thinking. *This is it. We're going to die.*

But Alec only smiled. "Hang on, baby," he whispered. He grabbed her hand. "Don't give up yet."

He stood, crouching down low. Quickly, Sydney kept pace behind him as they ran, their heads down. At the kitchen they slipped behind the counter.

Alec nodded to the shattered window. "He fired from the condo next door. Second floor window, by the look of it. We have a little time." He reached up to grab the phone cradled on the wall. "Dead," he told her.

"My cell phone is out in the car. In my purse."

He shook his head. "We're not getting that chance."

She could feel herself hyperventilate. "Then what?"

"Depends on how badly he wants us dead."

She could see his eyes focus, *how to get out of this alive . . .*

"Whatever you say, Alec," she told him, letting him know it was his call.

He nodded, taking charge.

Together they ran across the living room, retracing their steps, rounding the stairs to race to the second floor. Halfway up, a series of shots peppered the wall behind them.

Legs pumping, they ran down the hall. Alec shut the door of one bedroom as he passed, then opened the next door, leaving it ajar. Quickly, silently, they mounted the steps up to the third floor loft, stopping at the landing over the bedrooms below. He pushed Sydney to the floor, waiting there beside her. He put a finger to his lips.

It didn't take long before Sydney heard the fron

door open, the creaking of the steps. *Someone walking up the stairs* . . .

Then she could hear nothing, only the blood pounding in her temples. Alec stayed still, listening until he turned to her. Incredibly, he kissed her hard on the mouth.

She thought she heard him say "piece of cake" before he stood, then vaulted over the railing of the loft and dropped down the stairwell.

Sydney jumped to her feet. She stared over the rail in disbelief as Alec leapt down a flight of stairs to land atop a black-clothed figure wearing a mask. The two men rolled down the steps, one over the other, then slipped out of view.

Sydney raced down the steps, following close behind. But when she reached the bottom floor—*too late!* In the living room she found Alec standing in front of their assailant, the man's gun trained at his chest.

"Alec!"

Like lightning, Alec pivoted. Balanced on one leg, his right foot smacked into the side of the man's head in a roundhouse kick. The gun fired, the shot going wide. His assailant turned, taking aim again, the silencer on the end of the gun making it even larger and more ominous. Alec spun back and kicked the gun out of his hand. Sydney watched as it flipped through the air, discharging on impact. Alec swung again, landing a left jab, then a right cross.

Sydney stumbled down the last steps and threw herself across the room. She reached the gun as the two men once more hit the floor. She fumbled, almost dropping the weapon before she righted the gun and rose to her knees. Her hands shaking, she aimed.

"Stop it! Now!" she screamed.

No one paid her the least attention.

She stood, the gun still gripped between her two hands. She told herself *don't close your eyes* as she pulled the trigger.

The lamp behind the two men shattered, spraying them with bits of ceramic and glass. The two men froze, both appearing shocked.

Alec rolled away first, jumping to his feet. Beside him, the masked man stayed exactly where he was, then slowly raised his hands as directed by Sydney and the gun.

In her mind it was a replay of the alley. But this time she wouldn't be Russell's victim. Alec came to stand beside her. He took the gun, keeping it aimed.

"Nice shooting," Alec said.

She told herself to breathe. *Don't pass out!* "I was aiming for his leg."

"Yeah?" He glanced at the shattered lamp. "Well, shit. I guess this is my lucky day."

"Russell killed Kinnard," she said, feeling her chest constrict but needing the words to come out. "He practically confessed to the killing. He wanted me afraid. I knew Russell was capable of murder, and still I wasn't prepared for this. I just couldn't believe . . ."

His eyes on hers, he said, "It's real, Syd. Don't ever think otherwise."

"Now what?" she asked.

Alec picked up the rope he'd left on the love seat. He tossed it to Sydney. He motioned with his gun for their assailant to take the chair where Sydney had once sat, restrained.

"Now," he told her, his gaze carefully on the man as he walked toward the chair. "You tie this guy up, then head for the car and your cell phone. You know the number," he told her. "911."

THIRTY-ONE

Alec looked up, watching Sydney dab antiseptic on the corner of his mouth.

"Like old times," he told her.

She stopped what she was doing, standing over him at the kitchen counter where she was playing Florence Nightingale as he sat patiently. He figured she was remembering all those times he'd gotten knocked around when they'd been tooling around South America.

"Did I forget to say thank-you?" she asked.

She had this way of looking at him. *Shit, Syd.* She could make him melt with that look.

"Thank me for what? Almost getting you killed?"

She put the antiseptic on the counter behind him. "That's not the way I see it, Alec."

The guy the police had taken away was obviously a professional. A hired assassin. The first thing he'd asked for was a lawyer. Alec had given the detective who showed up on the scene the details. Russell Reck would be a good starting point for their investigation.

Sydney turned his face so that, sitting on the stool before her, their eyes met. "Alec, that man, when I pulled the trigger—there aren't that many people I'd be willing to shoot to keep someone safe."

"Hearing you loud and clear, baby."

Alec returned her smile, but his thoughts weren't so cheery. Sure, with the adrenaline pumping, she'd have all these warm and fuzzy feelings. *We almost died—bygones.* Only later would she remember. *Oh, yeah. He killed Henry. . . .*

Behind Sydney, the living room window framed the detective outside. Lights blazing, the patroller's cherry top spun in flashes of red against the glass. Detective Marcus looked like he was going to give it another go with the guy handcuffed up against the patrol car. Alec hoped to God this Marcus fellow could get what they needed: A confession that included Reck's name.

"Alec, what is it?"

He frowned, knowing he was giving off the wrong vibes. Wishing he could put a smile on his face and keep it all inside.

"I'm just wondering how long this is going to take—"

"No, you weren't," she said. "Alec, I know you brought me here to say good-bye. And maybe at the time, I believed it was for the best."

Ah, Jesus, he thought. *Here it comes.*

"But I can't do that now—I don't know if I ever could. Do you understand?"

To see so much hope in her eyes . . . it actually hurt to shut it down. "Listen, Syd. Tonight your life flashed before your eyes, and now you want to grab for whatever happiness you can. Only—"

"Actually, your life flashed before my eyes. And, yes, it put a lot of things in perspective."

"For how long, Syd? How much time do I get before the past comes between us? A month? A couple of years maybe?"

She pulled back. "That is not fair."

"But it's true."

"When I saw that man holding a gun on you, I didn't care about the past."

"But you will. And that's the point. In the heat of the moment, when you're on the edge between life and death and everything gets in focus . . . yeah, that's sweet. But no one's come up with a formula to put that stuff in a bottle so we can take a hit when the doubts come creeping back. And they will, darling. The past catches up. Every time."

"So we start over. I want this to work, Alec." And there it was in her eyes, all the forgiveness a man could ever want. "I'm willing to take a chance."

"Yeah." He smiled, at last telling her what she wanted to hear. "Okay."

Let her believe the fantasy, he thought. But Alec knew what they had ahead of them.

Right then the patrol car pulled out. Alec stood, watching the detective put away his notepad. He waited for Marcus to come back inside. When he did, the look on the guy's face as he headed toward Syd . . . the news wasn't good.

"Name, rank, and serial number," Marcus said. "That's it. Nothing to link tonight to your exhusband."

Alec stopped in front of Marcus. "Except both of our statements—"

"Which won't get me an arrest warrant," he said. "I guarantee."

"This is bullshit," Alec said.

Marcus shrugged. Like maybe it was too late at night to deal with some idiot getting all hot under the collar. "Give me some time, okay? I can talk to the D.A. Maybe work out a deal with this guy to get a name. But right now I've got squat."

Alec could feel the blood pumping at his temples. By tomorrow, Reck would hire someone else to come after Sydney, if he hadn't already. Maybe next time the guy wouldn't miss.

Sydney shook her head, reading his mind. "He wouldn't dare. He's already tipped his hand, Alec. It's too risky."

"Come on, Syd. Guys like Russell, they think they are almighty. Judge proof."

But Syd was deep in denial. "I think Russell's smart enough to be on a plane on his way out of the country, and frankly, I wish him Godspeed. Let him go, Alec. I don't care anymore."

"You're dreaming." No way a guy like The Wrecker would let things end like this. Syd said it before: He'd want more.

"Alec, what are you thinking?"

She stepped in front of him, getting between him and Marcus. She put her hand on his arm. He reached up and held it like a lifeline. Because he knew what he had to do. *No more running away.*

"I have to make sure, Syd," he told her.

Maybe he'd known all along it would come to this. He just hadn't been ready—he'd been searching for some other way. Like Reck, he'd wanted more. But now he felt suddenly free to do the right thing. As if standing there, looking into the face of the woman he loved, he could find it in himself to be that better man.

Face the consequences—be the hero.

He kept squeezing her hand. Watching her, he took his time, making it last. Putting a picture of her in his head. *That sweet mouth, her beautiful eyes.*

"I have to get Reck out of the picture, you understand?"

"No, Alec." She spoke as if she could stop him.

"What the hell," he said, giving her a smile. "You know, this could be my finest hour."

Alec let her hand drop and stepped around her. "I have information on Reck," he told Marcus. "Something that will help you nail the guy. For murder."

"No, Alec. Not like this."

"I'm listening," Marcus said.

He realized as he said it, this was exactly what Sydney needed, the key to her staying safe. And maybe, just maybe, he needed it too.

"He hired me. A couple of years back. But unlike that guy you just took away, I'm willing to talk."

Now he had Marcus's attention. "You're confessing to murder?"

"Absolutely." It was weird how he felt. Like he was floating. And he wasn't scared. Not a bit. "Trust me. Reck wanted me dead tonight because I'm the loose end. I can put him away."

"Alec!" Sydney was pulling at him. "You don't have to do this."

"Like I said, two years ago. There's no statute of imitations on murder. Am I right?"

"Alec, wait for a lawyer—"

"I know my rights," he told the detective, ignoring Syd. "And I'm ready to talk. I can give you the kind of details Reck will never be able to talk his way around."

She squeezed between him and Marcus and pushed him away from the detective. "Okay. You were right." She was whispering feverishly so that Marcus couldn't hear. "I was living a fairy tale, thinking we could go on to some happy ending. You go your way; I go mine. But don't make some gallant confession that's going to accomplish absolutely nothing but put you in jail for life—or worse. Not for me." God, the anguish in her voice. "Please, Alec."

He touched her face, for the first time in his life seeing things clearly. "I'm not afraid, Syd."

"This isn't how you keep me safe, Alec. This is how you break my heart."

But he wasn't listening to that sentimental crap. This was about life and death. And Alec knew what he had to do.

"I want you to go straight to Conor. Reck won't look for you there, and Conor will know what to do."

"Alec, no!"

"It's going to be fine. Just remember that, okay? I wasn't going to work for us, Syd. And right now I don't see much working out for me without you. So I need to do this, okay?"

He pushed past her, knowing that this time he'd got it right.

This time, whatever happened to him, Alec would get the job done.

* * *

Alec spent the night in jail. Not that he got any sleep.

He spent the hours ticking off in his head all that weighed on his conscience. Conor, how much he loved the guy—how lucky he'd been all those years to have him on his side. Travis. That maybe Alec should have told him the truth about their mother. That, like Alec, he needed to face a few things. One by one, he dealt with the ghosts he'd been trying to outrace, surprised by how many he'd let pile up.

When the guard finally appeared for him bright and early in the morning, Alec told himself he was ready to face what lay ahead. He needed just to get on with it. Face the music and put Russell Reck's ass behind bars right alongside him. Make sure Sydney never needed to worry about the guy again.

Only, like everything else in his life the past year, things didn't go down the way Alec planned.

Eight o'clock that morning, Alec Porter made bail. *Surprise, surprise* . . . Life, it appeared, still had a few curves to throw his way.

Outside, in the glorious California morning, he found Conor waiting for him.

"That must have taken you all night to pull off, Conman."

He tried to sound aloof, but he knew his smile was too bright. He told himself to knock it off, make things easier for the Conman . . . avoid all that emotion he felt brewing inside him. But he'd never been so happy to see anyone in his life.

Conor just put on his aviator glasses and pointed out his Toyota 4Runner. "All night and then some he told him, walking past. "Sydney is waiting for you back at the house."

Alec followed Conor out to his car, feeling a little shaky. Somehow it didn't seem right, Conor coming to the rescue again. Like that part of his life was over, right? Conor did his best to ignore him, pulling out of the parking lot, hitting the road hard.

Finally, Alec asked, "Why did you do it, Conman? After everything I've done, why bail me out?"

Conor didn't answer for a while, easing down the road in silence. But eventually, he turned, giving Alec his first good look in years at the man he called his brother.

"They tell me you've been cooperative," Conor said. "It greased the wheels with the prosecutor. They even agreed to drop the bail. Half a million."

"You put up Dogfighters?" It was the only way Conor could come up with that kind of cash so fast. He'd put up the flight school as collateral.

"Marc and Geena. Me and Cher. Yeah, we put it up."

Alec couldn't believe it. That company meant everything to Conor. He shook his head, still not getting it. Actually, it kinda pissed him off. The guy was still taking a chance on him?

"Why the hell would you do something so stupid?" he asked.

"Yeah, well." For the first time, Conor smiled. Like it was all this great joke. "I'm still wondering myself."

Alec sat back, staring ahead. He could feel himself starting to fume. First Syd—now Conor? Didn't they get it? Alec was the asshole.

And then this little voice inside his head whispered, *Why question your good luck?*

Which only made him angrier. How many times did he get to screw with people before the lightbulb goes on over their heads, for God's sake?

An hour later, Conor pulled the car into the drive at his house. Alec just sat there thinking. Maybe he'd grab a cab back to jail. Dammit, he didn't have any right to be here. And now he'd have to deal with Syd and all that don't-do-it-for-me crap.

Conor turned in his seat. "Before we go in there I have a couple of questions."

"Yeah. Sure." But he spoke absently, still thinking about Sydney. How was Alec supposed to protect all these idiots who loved him from themselves? *Talk about being too good . . .*

"Your confession," Conor said. "You killed Henry Shanks on that plane? What bullshit is this, Alec?"

He gave Conor a look that said, *Don't screw with this.* The one thing he hadn't counted on was Conor making an appearance. Not on his behalf, in any case.

"Look, Conman. I've stepped up to the plate. I'm taking my licks. You get it? I'm the bad guy—"

"But not a murderer. No way. I don't know what Kinnard told you—maybe he needed the telemetry off, or he was testing some secret software—but you never knew switching the stuff would crash that plane. I was there, Alec, sitting right next to your ass. And I saw your life flash before your eyes. You panicked, pure and simple. No way you knew what would happen. They used you, buddy."

"Wrong. I knew exactly what I was doing. Kinnard hired me—"

But Conor held up his hand. "You know, there's this little thing called intent? Alec, no matter what shit you have done in your life—and trust me, you

have screwed up—I can't lay murder on your doorstep."

Alec frowned, not liking the way this was going.
"What does it matter what I intended—it's the consequences that count. I changed out the software; I
made that plane crash. People died."

"And if you confess to some evil plan of murder—
hired by Reck—then The Wrecker goes to prison for
good?"

"Look, Conor. You don't know shit," he said,
sounding defensive. But he didn't want to blow this.
"I knew the software was bad. I had this plan to get
out before—"

"Bullshit. When that plane failed, that was the first
time you realized what was really going down. So
don't sit there now and tell me you planned the whole
thing. Don't lie to me, Alec. Never lie to me again."

Alec looked into his brother's eyes, seeing the truth.
Sure as shit, Conor had been on that bronco ride
with him when that plane crashed. He'd struggled
right alongside Alec at the controls. Conor was probably the only man alive who had relived that flight
more times than Alec. And he knew . . . he knew the
truth.

"I almost killed you that day," Alec said softly.
"Don't you think I deserve to go to jail?"

"Yeah. Sure. For any number of things, like being
stupid enough to get involved with Kinnard and Reck
in the first place. But not for murder."

"Well I happen to think you're wrong. I happen
to think that my 'intent' doesn't fucking matter.
Conor, this isn't going to work if I say, boo hoo, that
mean, old Russell Reck used me to murder someone.
There had to be a plan—I had to be part of it. That's

how conspiracy to murder works. Sydney's husband died—your career went down the toilet, and it was my fault! And don't you ever forget that!"

He hadn't realize he was shouting. He had to catch his breath, thinking that he needed to calm down. *It's done.* No way he could change the past now.

"It's like Cherish said," he told Conor, "if I want things to change, I have to face the consequences." And then, when he could talk again, he said softly, "Just let me do this one thing, okay? I'll never ask you for anything again. I swear it."

He kept his gaze on Conor, not willing to back down. Behind him stood the little cottage of a house where Conor lived in domestic bliss with his family. In the morning light it would look like a postcard. Birds singing, flowers bursting. *Like a dream come true.* Inside waited the only woman Alec had ever considered sharing that kind of dream.

"I'm tired," he told Conor. "Just let it go, Conor. I'm very tired."

He turned, staring over the lawn. He could feel Conor's gaze on the back of his head. Alec knew how this whole gig would mess with Conor's head. The thing was, Conor had ethics, and what Alec was doing—bending the rules—it wouldn't sit right with him. On the other hand, Conor had always protected those he loved. No way he wouldn't understand Alec doing the same thing now.

After a while, he heard Conor open the car door. He listened to his steps crunching on the gravel. Conor opened the passenger door for Alec, waiting for him to step out.

When the two men stood side by side, Conor said,

"So you got the boneheaded idea that you were going to take Reck down with you?"

Alec gave his best smile. "If I confess, it's conspiracy to murder. It's the only way—you see that, right? I go to jail, and Reck comes along with me. Sydney stays safe. Forever. A damn fine plan."

Conor watched him. It was hard to know what he was thinking behind the mirrored lenses of his sunglasses. But for the first time in his life, Alec thought he'd earned a little respect.

"She'd better be worth it." It was all Conor said.

Walking up the path alongside Conor, Alec had one of those moments. Your heart just fills up, and the sky looks too blue, and you don't know why you feel good until you realize that finally, finally, you took that right fork in the road. For the first time ever, Alec knew he was doing the right thing.

Conor opened the door to the lanai. He shook his head as he took in Alec's expression. "You know, Cherish always told me love changes a man. After this, she's going to be crowing a good long while. Thanks a lot, buddy. I'm looking at a lifetime of 'I told you so.' "

But when the two brothers stepped inside the house, it wasn't good news that waited for them.

"What happened?" Alec asked, seeing the fear on Cherish's face. *Something's wrong.* "Where's Sydney?"

Cherish looked at Conor. "There was a message on her answering machine from her stepdaughter. Some sort of emergency."

"Shit." Alec was already running for the phone.

"I told her to wait," Cherish said, following close behind. "But she wouldn't. She left about an hour ago."

Alec could feel the chill rise. Even as he dialed, he asked Conor, "Reck. They've picked him up, right?"

"I don't think we can count on that," Conor said.

Syd's machine came on. He waited for the beep, his heart lodged in his throat. "Pick up! Damn it, Syd. Pick the phone up!"

No one answered.

Alec turned to Conor, seeing the truth in his eyes. "Let's go," Conor said.

They were back in the car, Alec behind the whee this time. He told himself he'd been stupid. He'c convinced himself she'd be safe here at Conor's. Bu he'd underestimated Russell Reck, the man whc would always want more. Right now, Alec could imag ine what Russell wanted most: revenge against the one person who had hurt him.

Alec couldn't think of a better way to get Sydne right where The Wrecker wanted her.

Her stepdaughter had called.

A trap.

THIRTY-TWO

When Sydney arrived at Rocky's house, the door was unlocked and Rocky was nowhere in sight.

"Hello?"

Sydney stepped inside, her heart pounding. When she checked her messages that morning, Rocky's voice had sounded strained, almost as if she'd been crying.

Sydney, you have to come. It's Daddy. I found out what he's doing. Come by the condo. It's really important.

Using her cell phone, Sydney called several times on her way over. Only once did someone pick up, and that call was disconnected, making her even more anxious.

Of course, she'd wanted to wait for Alec—wanted to be there with his family to talk him out of his "grand sacrifice." But Rocky's voice frightened her. *Come by the condo. . . .*

Now Sydney took another tentative step inside. The condo had an abandoned air. "Rocky? Are you here?"

"Sydney—"

Rocky's voice, calling her from somewhere inside.

Sydney followed the sound, turning slightly. *There, in the shadows by the hall.* She could just make out a dark shape.

"Shut the door." It wasn't Rocky speaking.

Rocky stumbled out of the dark and into the sunlight coming from the room's bay window. Russell walked up behind his daughter. He had a gun in his hand.

"Russell," Sydney said. She shut the door, doing as she'd been instructed. "What a truly unpleasant surprise."

"Hello, darling. It's nice to see you as well."

"I'm so sorry," Rocky said, almost weeping. "He tricked me into making that call."

From the bruise on her cheek and the look of pain etched on her face, Sydney imagined Russell did more than trick his daughter into picking up the phone.

"Come on now, Russ. This is between you and me, right?" Sydney tried to sound cajoling as she circled around. "I'm here now. Just like you wanted. Let Rocky go."

"Don't even try," Rocky said. "He knows the first thing I'd do is call the police and tell them to throw his crooked ass back in jail—"

Russell struck Rocky square across her face, the blow as unexpected as it was brutal. Rocky dropped into the nearest chair.

"Now, now," he said, coming to stand over her. "There's no need for profanity."

Catching her breath, Rocky pushed her hair out of her face and gave her father a look of utter contempt. For the first time, Sydney had a clear view

Blood at the corner of her mouth—another bruise at her temple.

"Look at you, Russell. What you've become," she told him.

"Like he cares. He's just a shitty—"

"She's your daughter," Sydney interjected, seeing that Russell was close to striking Rocky again—that perhaps his daughter might be egging him on to do just that, thinking to give Sydney a chance to escape.

Russell seemed to think the same, stepping back, realizing that he was being manipulated.

"It's just my fate that those nearest and dearest to me should be the ones to betray me." He brushed his hand through Rocky's blond hair. "Do you know, Sydney, she actually threatened me? She thought that now, with Reck Enterprises in her name, she could save you from my plans. It must have hurt to know that all along she'd only made everything possible."

"I swear I didn't know." Rocky sounded incredibly tired. "All that stupid stuff I did before . . . honestly, I didn't know the bad guy was my own father."

He stepped back with a mock sigh. "Now that really hurts, sweetheart. To know I have no one. My ladies have all betrayed me."

He reached into his pocket. He pulled out what appeared to be a prescription bottle. He gave his daughter a smile as her eyes grew wide at the sight. "Yes, Rocky. You had your uses."

He tossed the bottle to Sydney, who caught it in surprise. He grabbed Rocky's hair and yanked her head back, pushing the gun under her chin.

"Your unfortunate passing was going to happen a bit differently, Sydney. Distraught from a series of mishaps, you and your lover went off together. The headline would have read 'Murder—Suicide.' I knew my little phone call to Porter concerning his past wrongs would stir things up. Sometimes, when you apply the right pressure to a situation, you get lucky. That rendezvous in the mountains would have been perfect."

"How disappointing for you, Russ," she told him, trying to keep calm despite the terror she saw in Rocky's eyes.

He smiled. "Oh, well. Time for Plan B."

"Daddy, don't do this!" Rocky screamed. "I'll give you back the company—I'll cheat the government for you. I'll do anything. Please, Daddy!"

"Rocky told me you were having trouble sleeping," he continued, ignoring his daughter's pleas. "I was able to renew your prescription. Sydney," he told her. "Why don't you get yourself a glass of wine?"

"Don't do it! Not because of me. Please, Sydney."

"Be a good girl and hush now. Your stepmother will take her nice little pills. Every last one." His eyes on Sydney, he said, "Or I will shoot Rocky dead."

"I'm supposed to make things less messy for you, Russ?"

"Don't you think it's time? You should have stayed with me, Sydney. I had such wonderful plans for our future. Now, I'll have to settle for my back-up plan, which wasn't nearly as nice. When I leave here, I'm off to the Caymans, where I have a nice, little nest egg. My retirement comes a little early, true, but trust me, I'm prepared. Messy or not, it's going to happen."

"And if I take the pills? How do I know you won't shoot Rocky just the same? To tie up those loose ends?"

"No matter what you think of me, Sydney, I do no

want to kill my own daughter. You take the pills, and Rocky will go away. Young girls disappear to foreign climes all the time, never to be seen again. I understand they have quite a problem with the Russian Mafia and such things.''

"White slavery? For your own daughter?'' Sydney nodded, as if it made perfect sense. "Well, I suppose I'll get that glass of wine.''

"No!'' Rocky whipped up her forearm, slamming her hand against the gun.

Russell fired. Like a doll, Rocky crumpled to the floor.

"Dammit, Rocky!'' he shouted.

Sydney raced to her side, pushing past Russell. Rocky was breathing in short, shallow breaths. The bullet had gone into her shoulder; she was bleeding profusely.

"Don't take those pills,'' Rocky whispered. "Please.''

"Listen to me. It's going to be fine. Trust me, Rocky. Just lie still and trust me.'' To Russell she said, "I'll do it. Leave her alone, and I'll do exactly what you say.''

She stood, making certain he knew she meant every word. She walked to the kitchen, knowing she was running out of time. She made her mind go blank, erasing fear and the sight of Rocky bleeding on the floor. *You know what you have to do.*

In the kitchen she poured herself a glass of wine. She waited, holding the bottle of pills. Finally, she took the top off and dumped the pills on the counter. She heard Russell come into the kitchen.

"I'll take the pills,'' she said, her hand inching up as if to grab a handful of pills off the counter. Waiting.

"You do that, Sydney,'' he said, letting her know

from his voice exactly where he was standing. *Away from Rocky, at the entrance to the kitchen.* "You be a good girl and finish this."

Sydney turned. In her hand she held the gun she'd tucked into the waistband of her skirt, hidden beneath her blouse.

She fired.

A spot of red blossomed across Russell's chest. He dropped to his knees, shock registering in his eyes. The gun he carried fired uselessly into the wall behind Sydney. He fell forward, facefirst. Dead.

"There, Russell," she said, dropping the gun to the floor. "All finished."

Alec showed up in time to see the coroner roll onto the scene. He raced in, knowing he'd lost her. *Too late.*

He'd wasted valuable time checking Sydney's machine for messages, listening to Rocky's voice telling her to come over. He'd floored it to get to the condo as quickly as possible. *Dear God, too late!*

But instead of coming across Sydney's lifeless body as he feared, he found her sitting at the kitchen table, very much alive. The detective at her side appeared to be taking her statement.

"Sydney."

Hearing his voice, she turned. She pushed back her chair, standing. "I'm okay," she told him.

He waited there at the kitchen entrance. He couldn't seem to move even though she was right there in front of him, waiting. *I'm okay. . . .*

He'd seen the coroner's van parked outside. He'd thought she was dead.

Even when Conor came up to stand beside him, Alec couldn't do much about the distance between him and Syd. He just listened as Conor asked her what happened.

"Alec," she told him. "I'm fine. Really."

She came to him then, falling into his arms. He held her so tightly. *Almost lost her.* He couldn't hold her tight enough.

"Alec?"

"Don't ever scare me like that. Do you understand?" He pushed back her head, cupping her face in his hands, giving her a shake. "I'm dead if anything happens to you. Dead." He'd never meant anything more in his life.

"Alec. Everything you said; you were wrong. I don't want us to be apart. I'm not going to change how I feel. Cherish told me everything. You're not a murderer. Russell used you, just like he used everyone—"

He folded her into his arms again. "I'm not going anywhere, baby."

It was one of those moments—a second chance. Only, his heart was still lodged in his throat as he tried to make his body understand that she was okay. *If anything happened to her. . . .*

"Cherish was in the bedroom," she said, almost whispering. "She was feeding the baby when I called my machine to check my messages. I heard Rocky's voice, and I knew. I just knew."

"It's okay." He understood what she was telling him. That the coroner hadn't come for Sydney after all. "You did the right thing."

"I searched the house for a gun. I figured Conor would have one from his military days. I don't even know how I figured out how to load it. Before I came here, I hid it in my skirt.''

"God, Sydney. Why didn't you wait for me?''

"It's what he wanted all along. Me. Alone. I couldn't risk doing it any other way. Alec, he shot Rocky. He almost killed his own daughter. He was going to send her off to some Russian Mafia goon.'' She looked up, everything she felt clearly in her eyes. "I shot him. Straight through the heart.''

Seeing the glazed look in her eyes, he kissed her. As if by his mouth he could make her warm again, ease the numbness and the cold brought on by what had happened. He wished he could take it all away. In his mind he was already making a list of what she would need over the next months to get through this.

He sighed and gentled his kiss on her mouth. He leaned his forehead against hers. "He deserved to die, Syd. The guy was an animal.''

She shook her head, tears filling her eyes. "I killed him.''

"Hey, it's okay. Hush, now.''

He waited, trying to settle her. Making promises. She would never have to fear again. He would always be there with her, loving her. Giving her everything. Marriage, kids . . .

"The sun and the moon,'' he said, making a vow. "Anything you want, babe. Just tell me, okay?''

Finally, he turned her face up to his. He tried to picture the scene. Reck holding a gun. Sydney getting off the one shot.

"It could have gone the other way.'' It scared him just to say the words. "It could have been you.''

"He shot Rocky.'' This time when she spoke there wasn't so much fear or shock in her voice.

He smiled. "My little *La Femme Nikita*."

She looked up, surprised.

He kissed her on the top of her nose. *I shot him straight through the heart*. He couldn't imagine it, but he was thankful for the result.

"Nice shooting," he told her. "You can watch my back anytime."

The tears came again, now slipping down her face so she choked on the words as she said, "I was aiming or his leg."

"Yeah?" He hugged her, whispering under his breath, "Then thank God you're a lucky shot."

Epilogue

Alec stared up at the sky. Overhead, Conor executed a barrel roll, the wings of the plane twisting one over the other like a pinwheel.

"Perfect," he said.

Two months, and they had the thing up and running, working past the glitch in the software that had caused Alec's crash and burn. With Conor working alongside him, Alec had been able to get his program up faster than he could ever have imagined.

He turned, looking back at the group waiting out by the hangar. Geena and the kids waved and cheered, Cherish stood smiling, holding Conor's son in her arms. Sydney wore a smile so big, he could fall right into it, sharing this moment with him.

My family.

It felt too good, his heart too full. *Shit, I don't deserve this.* A second chance.

But he would take it. Oh, yeah. He would grab hold with both hands and relish every second.

Syd came running up, unable to wait. He grabbed her in his arms and swung her around, then pulled her up to give her a long, feverish kiss, telling her what he couldn't say with words. *For us, Syd. This one's for us.*

"So, how does it feel?" she asked, breathless.

"Hey, we're a long way from success here."

"But today was a big step."

He smiled, seeing Conor rip across again, this time wagging the wings in a salute. "Oh, yeah."

He put his arm around her, turning back, heading toward the hangar, where the kids still urged Conor on overhead.

"How did it go with Rocky?" he asked.

"These are such big decisions she's making. I don't feel good about it, her insisting on dismantling Reck Enterprises and using the money to save the gallery, paying off the fines. She says it's what she wants. Justice, she calls it." Sydney frowned. "But I don't know. Her own father shot her. And she was there when I killed him—"

Alec stopped, pulling Sydney around to face him. "Hey. The Wrecker as much as pulled that trigger himself. Come on, Syd. You knew the score. It was you or him, and trust me, he gets my vote."

She bent her head, leaning on him. "I still see him, again and again. Every time I close my eyes, Russell standing there, holding that gun."

"Give it time, baby." He kissed the top of her head. "Give it time."

She shook her head, managing a small smile. "Funny, that's what I told Rocky. To give herself more time. It's too early for her to decide to give up everything. She thinks she's balancing the scales, but she doesn't need to pay for her father's crimes. And now this thing with Jack has left her off balance. What if later she regrets her choices?''

"You'll be there, at her side, to make it right. Just like you always have been. She's going to be okay, Syd. She has you."

"I hope so. I only wish I could mend a broken heart."

"Did I call it, or what? I told you that guy was a jerk." He even managed a straight face as he said it.

Sydney laughed. "The funny thing is . . . Jack seems just as heartbroken. Somehow, I don't think this is the end for them."

"I thought you told me he went off to climb some hill, doing the I-wish-I-were-a-jock-but-at-least-I-have money thing to lick his wounds."

"He's off on an expedition to the Himalayas, but he'll be back," she corrected him. "For Rocky, I'm guessing. I don't know how I didn't realize what was going on between them. They put an awful lot of energy into hating each other. I should have guessed where all that emotion was headed."

He tipped her head up to his. "Sometimes, what right there in front of our eyes is hard to see."

She pushed back her sunglasses so he could read the truth in her face. "All I ever wanted is right here, Alec."

He kissed her, putting everything he felt into it.

Her eyes fluttered open, her mouth slightly parted. After a second, she licked her lips, seeming to catch her breath. "Well," she said, sounding a bit breathless. "At least you still have it, Mr. Porter."

"Attagirl."

He put his arm around her shoulders as they walked toward the hangar to watch Conor land the Marchetti. The last months had been an incredible seesaw of highs and lows. But Sydney was the pot of gold at the end of the rainbow. Incredibly, he was a free man. He'd made a deal with the prosecutor, who seemed to think that the right people had paid for Henry's death. Certainly, it hadn't hurt to have Conor and Sydney vouch for him. In the end, he'd been given probation. Now everything seemed so new. As if anything were possible.

He'd even gone to see Travis—and he'd told him the truth: Their mother wasn't the fairy tale Alec had led Travis to believe. He had to give the guy credit. He took the news well. Like he understood some of what Alec had gone through and wanted to make it up to him. Just because Travis had gotten the break, living with Grandma. Before Alec left, Travis even introduced him to his kids as their uncle, making it clear that Alec was in for the long haul.

It was pretty amazing, actually. How everything could change so much. *A second chance* . . .

"Hell, yes," he said under his breath. He grinned, looking up at the blinding blue above. He'd wanted to reinvent himself. Be one of the good guys . . . wear the white hat. In the end, he'd needed only to face his past. *Just like Syd told me* . . .

"Will you look at that," he said, for the first time noticing the pendant swinging from a gold chain around Sydney's neck. He stopped, holding it in his hands.

The jade piece he'd given to her at the hospital . . .

she'd had it set in gold so that it now hung from a necklace. He raised his brows in question. It wasn' like Syd to take museum-quality stuff for herself.

"I decided to keep it." She tucked the jade insid her shirt, so that it fell to just above her heart. Sh shrugged. "After all, you did say you would give m the stars and the moon."

He laughed, getting it. Carved into the slim piec of jade was a scene from the *Popul Vuh*, depicting th twin heroes ascending into Xibalba to become th sun and the moon, the Four Hundred Boys, slai gods themselves, the stars among them.

"So, Mr. Porter," Sydney said, walking beside hir "you've been absolved of all crimes. You've just flow a million-dollar program. What are you going to next?"

He smiled, because she'd made it sound like a co mercial for Disneyland.

But the more he thought about it, he knew wh she was asking—*what about our future?* A very go question indeed.

He stopped, looking at her. Wondering. "You ha anything interesting in mind?" Lobbing the ball ba into her court.

She shook her head. "Really, Alec. If that's a p posal, it's by far the lamest I've heard."

God knows he wanted this. Syd by his side forev Even kids. Oh, yes, he wanted to marry her somethi awful. But the whole thing scared him to death.

"Sometimes I worry that it's too easy." He brush his thumb over her mouth. "You know? Maybe I n to put in some more time at this good-guy stuff. M it stick." He shook his head. "Syd, what if I sc up? I just don't know."

"Don't worry so much." She cupped his face in er hand. "Trust me, Alec. We get to have this."

He smiled, loving her so much. "And what exactly it that we get to have?"

She stepped up on her tiptoes, whispering before ie kissed him, "A happy ending."

Complete Your Collection of
Fern Michaels